MOUNT LAUREL LIBRARY
100 Walt Whitman Avenue
Mount Laurel, NJ 08054
856/234-7319

DEMCO

Long, Lean, and Lethal

Heather Graham

Long, Lean, and Lethal

WHEELER PUBLISHING, INC.
ROCKLAND, MA

★ AN AMERICAN COMPANY ★

Published in Large Print by arrangement with New American Library, a division of Penguin Putnam, Inc. in the United States and Canada.

Wheeler Large Print Book Series.

Set in 16 pt Plantin.

Library of Congress Cataloging-in-Publication Data

Graham, Heather.
    Long, lean, and lethal / Heather Graham.
       p. (large print) cm.(Wheeler large print book series)
    ISBN 1-56895-928-1 (hardcover)
    1. Television actors and actresses—Fiction. 2. Los Angeles (Calif.)—
Fiction. 3. Large type books.
I. Title. II. Series

[PS3557.R198L66 2000]
813'.54—dc21

00-043660
CIP

To Lance Taubold and Rich Devin,
for all the extraordinary things you do, and
for being the extraordinary friends you are.
My love and thanks, always.

To Greg Marx for all the help and the
great times—thanks to you, too.

And finally, to the inimitable Janet Leigh—
a tremendous actress, talented author,
and an incredibly gracious lady.

Prologue

The shower scene…

The shower scene, oh, yes, it had been on his mind forever!

He loved films of all kinds, but most of all, he loved suspense—when the slightest look could signal fear, aggression…

Or terror.

He was a student par excellence of the genre. He knew the names of all the actors, the directors. He especially loved the "master," the one man he considered to be the best of all time: Alfred Hitchcock.

He knew how the shower scene should be done. He had learned by studying the master. Angle by angle. Each movement of the camera. He had been so close to seeing it done right again… so close. There were so many times when he had known just how a similar scene should go.

Close… never quite there.

The original shower scene, as known by the movie-going public, had been made famous by Alfred Hitchcock's cinematic triumph in the celluloid murder of beautiful, young—not entirely innocent—Janet Leigh. Yes—as known to any who studied the art—it had been in the master's classic movie *Psycho*, a film now part of popular culture, taught in every film school, shown in every history about Holly-

1

wood, further exhibited in theme parks on both coasts.

Ah, yes...the shower scene. His favorite of all time.

Such genius.

Filmed in black and white, the classic scene had elicited a gripping terror unlike any awakened before. Taking a shower had never been the same. Following the original release of the movie, hundreds of thousands of women who lived alone or traveled on their own had been driven to taking cautious sponge baths—with the doors to their bedrooms open, their eyes peeled on the point of entry.

She stood in the shower. Just like Janet Leigh in the movie, she was a vulnerable beauty. She was tall, lithe, supple, both sensually lean and curved. Her hair was darkened by the water to a dark blond, wet and clean, it gleamed down her back. Eyes closed, she tilted her face to the spray of the water, and with her head thrown back, the length of her hair waved just over the curve of her buttocks.

The water pelted her, washing away all dirt, all guilt.

The shower curtain was nearly transparent. It enhanced each movement she made. To the beauty bathing, there was no sense of imminent danger. Just the feel of a cool shower on a hot day, a delicious feel, the simple goodness of being clean.

The killer moved closer.

The audience would know. An audience would want to shout out. Warn her.

If there was an audience.

Naturally, the killer wielded a knife. A knife was necessary for a shower scene. Death was not so simple, so sudden, so clean, with a knife. It glittered, even in shadow, catching what light could be found. It drew the eye, caused the heart to stop. It gave so much pain...and yet also a hint of hope. If one could escape the blade...if the knife struck the wrong places...

Then there was the sound of a knife. Yes, the sound itself was enough to create a sense of gnawing nails-on-a-chalkboard terror.

There she was, so beautiful behind the transparent curtain. Head tilted, form perfect, lush. Like the Janet Leigh character, she wasn't at all an innocent. But an audience would care about her. Because she was just so vulnerable.

"Now!"

Was the whisper real? A director's softly spoken command. Did it hover on the air? All that could be heard was the pelting of the water. A good director knew exactly when the moment came to strike, when the knowing and the anticipation had been drawn out just long enough...

Did she know yet? Did she sense the coming danger?

The stalker moved in silence against that pounding spray of water.

Closer, closer...approaching the shower, the transparent curtain. The curtain that gave away so much of the beauty and vulnerability of the victim...

Then suddenly, forcefully, the curtain was wrenched back.

Water, dripping down her body. Sleek, sensual.

The victim...

At last...knowing.

She screamed as her eyes flew open and she spun toward the intruder. They were huge eyes, wide, the color deep and lustrous. They were purely beautiful, glorious, stunned, disbelieving, shocked.

Terrified!

Oh, yes, terrified!

She knew, of course.

Now she knew.

Because she was aware of the shower scene. She knew, she had seen, and of course, anticipation was half of fear.

Anticipation...

And she saw...

The knife...

She screamed again. What could she do against the horror of the knife? The wicked blade, long and gleaming, held high over her head...

She screamed again, and again, and again.

After all...

It was the ultimate shower scene.

Chapter 1

The tap on Jennifer's door in the morning usually meant the arrival of a script.

Except that it was Friday, and scripts didn't usually arrive on Friday—unless it was a rewrite for the scenes they were doing today. Certainly they'd had more rewrites lately than seemed humanly possible.

She opened the door to her dressing room. A thin white envelope lay there, with nothing but her name on it. She looked down the hall, but it was empty. In fact, the entire fifth floor of the building seemed to be empty at the moment. She felt a chill.

That was ridiculous, she told herself. Though she tended to be earlier than the other actors with morning calls, she knew that some crew members arrived as early as she did, and it wasn't that early at all anymore. Just a little more than an hour and they should be on the set in full costume and makeup.

Still...

She stepped back into her dressing room, closed the door—and locked it. Sinking into the chair in front of her dressing table, she slipped open the envelope, wondering why she felt so tense.

There was a brief note inside. "Jen, please

be advised we need you to stay next Friday night—filming a short scene after private rehearsals. Hush-hush set. Secret twists in plot! Love and kisses, your favorite producer, Andy Larkin."

Next Friday night. Great. Andy apparently believed she had no outside life. He was more or less right, of course. And actually, at the moment she was looking forward to more work, to avoid going home.

Deep in thought, she almost jumped at the next tapping at her door. Then she laughed.

Idiot, someone is knocking! Why on God's earth am I so nervous? I'm tired and worried, and that's that.

"Jen? Jen, you in there?" She heard her doorknob rattling along with the sound of Doug Henson's voice. She jumped up and opened the door.

"Hey, gorgeous."

"Hey, yourself, gorgeous." He was gorgeous. A tall, blue-eyed blond who worked out in the California sun. So gorgeous he should have been an actor instead of a writer. They'd tried to use him on the show a few times. He hated acting, though, and the directors had basically given up—unless it was a beach scene in which someone just had to stand there being good-looking. But though Doug hated acting, he loved writing. Not so much this kind of writing. Soap operas made him crazy—changing everything ten times at the whim of the producer, director, or even the actors on occasion, but it was a good income,

6

and allowed him to work on his great American novel in his spare time.

"What's going on, Doug? Why am I working next Friday night?"

"Plot twist," he told her.

"Obviously. What's it twisting to?"

"I don't know."

"What do you mean, you don't know?"

He walked on in, helped himself to the coffee brewing in her pot. "You know, your stuff is always so much better than the dreck on the set." He inhaled deeply. "Cinnamon, eh? Macadamia nut?"

"Hazelnut, with a touch of cinnamon," she replied briefly, getting back to the point. "Doug, pay attention here. How come you don't know?"

"There are eight writers on this show, you are aware."

"Yes, but you're all supposed to know what one another is doing. To keep the plot in order, making sense."

He sighed, sinking onto the sofa in front of the dressing table, running his fingers through his impossibly blond hair. "When, my love, has this plot ever made sense? Think about it. Last year Randy Rock was caught in an explosion and fire, killed, and buried—and he came back last week."

"Entirely possible," Jennifer defended. "He couldn't be identified, the wrong man was buried—"

"He ran around with terrible amnesia, had affairs all over the place—probably sired a half dozen children, no one has told me yet—and reappeared looking devastatingly the same after plastic surgery."

"It could have happened."

"Only on *Valentine Valley*—isn't that what our promos say?"

"What's happening next?"

"Anything!" Doug muttered. He leaned back with a dramatic sigh. "Andy Larkin's character was thrown off a cliff into the Pacific Ocean and eaten by a shark. And he came back."

"It worked in *Pinocchio*."

"That was a whale. This was a shark. What, somehow the teeth of a great white missed him?"

She laughed. "You wrote his return—"

"And did a darned good job of it!" Doug said proudly, then grimaced. "Actually, that one was simple. He came back because they just *thought* that he'd been eaten by the killer shark that had taken three lives in the Pacific, but he hadn't been touched by the shark at all. He'd swum beneath the surface, come up beneath a different boat—"

"Had an affair with the woman on board, because he had amnesia, too."

"Naturally—he had to have an affair."

"Well, but you see, it did all make sense, because he wasn't really eaten by the shark," Jennifer said. "However, now, Doug," she began, her voice warning, "tell me what's happening. And quit making fun of us."

He opened his eyes, sat up straighter, and looked at her guiltily. "Sorry, Jen. I'm not really mocking anyone. I think you guys are really

8

the best actors and actresses out there—you have to be, you make people believe all this stuff. And by God, you people get things in *one* take all the time. I was over on the set for that new studio psycho-thriller the other day, and you wouldn't believe it. Fifteen takes to get one little scene right."

"Thanks for the vote of confidence. I do appreciate it," she said, smiling and meaning it. Soap stars took some taunting as "professionals." But they did work hard, and it was nice to hear a compliment.

"It does look as if it's going to be a good movie, though. Very scary."

"Really?" she murmured. Her heart did a little flutter. She'd been offered a role in the movie. "Small but important," her agent had said. Supposedly, the offer was still on the table.

"The director is that fellow who did the low-budget teen flick last year that made all the money. He's a huge Hitchcock fan, and believes that the psychology of fear is much greater than a bucket of guts and gore."

"I'm sure that's true. The director is Hugh Tanenbaum, right?"

"Yep."

"And isn't he good friends with Jim Novac?" Jim was one of the directors on the staff of their soap, *Valentine Valley.*

"Yeah, that's why I was over there. Jim wanted me to see what they were doing."

"Why?"

"I'm assuming so that I can see how psychological terror is done."

9

"You're a soap writer."

"I assure you," he protested with smooth indignity, "I'm a writer, not a 'soap' writer. No adjectives, please!"

"I'm sorry, really sorry," she apologized quickly, hiding a smile. He was so serious about his work. "You're a writer, a wonderful one. A no-adjective, wonderful writer. But, I still don't get it. Never mind, I do get it, I'm afraid. The plot line is going to twist into a really scary suspense-type thing?"

"I don't know."

"Doug! Would you quit that and tell me the truth?"

"I can't tell you, Jen, because I really don't know."

She studied his face for a long moment and frowned. "Really?"

He nodded. "Cross my heart."

"You're not writing the scene? You must be. You do most of my scenes—"

"I am writing the scene. I just haven't been told what I'm writing. It's all hush-hush."

"Oh, come on, Doug. Even we silly actors know that there's a 'bible,' the plot structure for the year, and that all you boys and girls do the writing each week by the bible."

He shook his head firmly. "The bible says 'plot thickens, terror menaces Valentine Valley, details to be decided.' "

She stared at him, frustrated. He was telling the truth.

"Look, Jen, it's just that we're up against so much these days. They don't dare let anything get out." He sighed with tremendous patience. "I'm older than you. I admit I'm wearing rather well"—he grinned—"but that's good clean living for you. You're too young to remember the old days, I'm not. Once upon a time there was no cable, soaps did darn well. Now the folks at home can turn to us, or the cooking channel, or they can learn how to repair their house, garden—or how to speak French. Or they can turn to a prime-time movie in the afternoon. We have to protect our plot lines like Dobermans—it's survival of the fittest!"

"You're ticked because they won't tell you what you're writing," Jen observed with a smile.

He grinned back. "You bet your ass. Can you believe that? They won't trust me."

"Maybe they're afraid your actress friends on the set will torture it out of you."

He shrugged. "Yeah, maybe." He brightened suddenly. "I can tell you some of next week's general plot—until the end, of course."

"I can probably tell you about next week's plot," she murmured.

"Ah, dear and alas," he teased, his voice going very deep. "Do I detect a note of bitterness there?"

"No. Of course not," she lied. Turning, she pretended to fix the makeup on her counter.

"So..." His voice trailed tauntingly. "You're just thrilled to pieces that we're bringing in Conar Markham? For a small fortune, I might add."

"It's none of my business, is it?"

"Actually, I'd imagine it is."

"Not really—"

"He's coming to Granger House—your home."

"It isn't my home—it's my mother's house."

"A minor detail," he said, and through the mirror she could see him waving a hand in the air. He leaned forward in a conspiratorial manner, meeting her eyes in the mirror. "Let's get down and dirty here. Tell me that you're not just sick to death of hearing how wonderful Mr. Markham is."

Jen spun back to look at him. There was such a bright, teasing light in his eyes that she had to laugh. She put her finger in her mouth in a pretend gagging motion. "I shall throw up the minute I see him if I get any sicker!" she admitted, which caused Doug to burst into rich gales of laughter.

Then his laughter faded, and the amusement left his eyes. "All of us are joking about it, of course, but Jen, don't be upset. I know that Abby invited him, but..."

His voice trailed off.

"I'm not upset at all," Jennifer lied. Her life had always been somewhat strange, but that was what happened if you were born the child of a living legend. Her mother had garnered two Oscars, three more nominations, and was still considered to be one of the most beautiful women alive. Jennifer had spent half her life trying not to live in California, and when she had graduated from school, the last thing in the world she had wanted to do was

12

become an actress. Next to her mother, she had felt like an ugly duckling, and certainly an underachiever. She had tried so hard to be different. Yet no matter what her fame, fortune, or obligations, Abby had always been there for her daughter. Jennifer had been her mother's priority all the time that she had been growing up. Not long after she had realized how much her rebellion and resentment had hurt her mother, Abby had gotten sick with Parkinson's. She'd hidden it for a long time. Too long, Jennifer thought. They might have gotten help earlier. And now...

"You really don't feel, well, resentful at all?" Doug asked.

Jennifer shook her head firmly. "He was Abby's stepchild for a long time. They always had a relationship."

"And you don't mind that."

She actually grinned. "I was kind of a brat as a child, I'm afraid." She grinned and lifted her hands out. "I had a chip on my shoulder about this big. I was kind of cold to my mother on a frequent basis in those years, and I'm very sorry now—"

"She adores you."

"I know it," Jennifer said softly.

There was a soft tapping on the door that startled them both. "Jennifer, makeup!" Thorne McKay called to her.

"Whoa, look at the time, will you? You're on call." He rolled his eyes. "And I've got a meeting with the big boys. But hey, I forgot the real reason why I came."

"Oh?"

"How about an invite?"

"What?"

"To Granger House for the holiday weekend."

She hesitated. She was disturbed by the fact that Conar Markham was coming. Abby had been acting...*strange* lately.

It was true, in her heart, Jennifer was upset. Why did her mother suddenly *need* Conar? She was her mother's biological child, she had moved back to be with her—*why wasn't she enough?*

"Hey, kid, I'm talking to you," Doug reminded her.

"Doug, you know, I do have my own apartment, and if I were living there right now, you'd be welcome anytime, you know that. But now...you know, I don't own Granger House. I'm just a guest myself. It's my *mom's* home, and she isn't doing very well—"

"You'll need moral support. Trust me. You need me."

"I'm a big girl, Doug—"

"You still need me."

"Look, I'm all grown up and mature—"

"Nobody's that mature. I know you have to resent this guy. *I* resent him coming in here, and I'm not even an actor, and Abby isn't my mother! See what a good friend I am—I even emote for you."

"Doug, I emote just fine for myself."

"And if all that is not enough," he said, coming closer to her, "there's a rumor going

14

about that you're having a cocktail party tomorrow night to welcome home the conquering hero."

She sighed. Her mother had mentioned a party. Small. Impromptu. Just good old friends and a few folks from the soap. But Granger House was almost as legendary as her mother, at least in these parts of the world, and she wondered if her mother would really be up for a party. They never really knew when a bad spell would set in, even with her medications.

"Jennifer!" Thorne pounded on her door again. "You may be a beauty, my darling, but I'm a makeup man, not a magician!"

"I'll be here when the day's shooting is over. Luckily, I've packed a bag," Doug said.

She had to laugh. Maybe she did need the moral support. And Doug loved her mother, and her mother loved Doug. He would be helpful and understanding if they had guests and the stress did prove to be too much for Abby.

"Okay. Let's head out the moment my scenes are shot."

"You got it," Doug said.

He opened the door. Thorne almost fell in. He looked at them both. "Did I interrupt something?"

"Yes," Doug said.

Thorne pointed a finger at him. "But you're gay."

"Ah, but my arm can be twisted. There's always room in life for experimentation,"

Doug said wickedly. He walked on out, leaving Thorne to stare at Jennifer. She tried to keep a straight face, but his eyes were so big, nearly bulging out of his bald head. She had to laugh, and she saw in his return gaze that he knew he'd been taken.

Back to L.A.

La-la land, they called it, Conar Markham thought. He hadn't thought that he'd come back here—certainly not yet. But though he thought that Abby Sawyer was completely off her rocker, he owed her.

And he loved her.

And so he was back.

Arriving at LAX, he was surprised by the reporters waiting as he exited the plane. Not that he didn't have his share of self-confidence; he did. But he was a realist. There were a lot of big fish to fry out here. For the past two years he had been working the theater circuit, and that was far different from the land of movies, where millions of people saw your face in one shot, and even the worst flick was better known than the best play.

"There he is!" someone shouted, and the next thing he knew, he was surrounded; flashbulbs were sizzling, he was half-blinded, and a brazen young reporter had one hand wound around his arm, while the other popped a microphone in front of his face.

"Conar! Conar Markham! Back in L.A.! We're so excited out here."

Always, always, be good to the press, Conar. You never know when they'll turn on you. Abby had taught him that. So he forced a casual smile to his face. He couldn't help but look at the perfectly manicured hand on his arm, though, and ask politely, "Do I know you?"

The girl with the deep brown eyes, reporter's sleek dark haircut, and perfect nails had the grace to blush—moving the microphone as she did so. "No, um, we've never met. I'm Vickie Warren from Flick TV, a new cable channel that focuses on popular and commercial entertainment."

His smile deepened. "Well, nice to meet you, Vickie," he said. "It's good to be home," he said, fingers closing over the microphone she held, bringing it back toward his mouth. "I love New York, and God, I love Broadway, but I am a California boy, and it's good to be home."

She had been afraid, he realized. This was one of her first big jobs, and she had been petrified but brazening it out—and so now she was grateful to him.

Abby would have been proud. He smiled, lowering his head as he walked through the crowded airport.

They stayed with him.

Reporters were scrambling with their tape recorders and notepads; cameramen were aiming and walking at the same time.

"Mr. Markham!" His name was called by a man in a wilting business suit, camera crew at his side. "Is it true that you're going to be receiving an unprecedented amount for accepting your role in *Valentine Valley*?"

He should have expected that one.

"So they say," he replied cheerfully.

"How much?" someone else called out. The anorexic blonde to the rear of the crowd who had the pinched look of a nervous terrier?

"Come on now, folks, I'm not at liberty to say," he stated firmly, still smiling. And walking. He had to keep walking. It was almost comical, the way they all seemed to be sticking right with him.

"Are you afraid the other actors on the show are going to resent you?" Vickie asked him the question, her dark eyes grave.

"I certainly hope not," he replied.

"What about your *stepsister*?" someone else demanded.

He hesitated, wondering if he should simply say that he'd only met his "stepsister" a few times, and he surely didn't know what she was thinking—other than that her mother was very ill, and she was very worried about her. "If you all will excuse me, it's been a really long flight and I've got to get home."

"Home—how is Abby Sawyer, Conar? Will you be staying with her?" Vickie asked.

"Is she as sick as they say?" the other woman asked.

"Will she be returning to films?" someone else asked.

"Is she dying?" Vickie asked softly.

"I heard it's Alzheimer's!" one of the cameramen commented.

"She isn't dying, and it isn't Alzheimer's. Abby's doing just fine!" he heard himself say. His smile was starting to crack. "In fact, I'm sure she sends her love. You know how good she has always been with the media. Now, please, if you will all be so kind..."

"Do you think that living at Granger House is affecting her mind?" Vickie asked.

"There's a story out that Abby is crazy, losing her mind, and that it all started when she bought Granger House," a young man with bleached hair and a nose ring said. "That she really got sick when she moved into the house."

Abby had moved into the house for good when she had realized her illness, Conar knew. But he didn't say that.

"You're looking too hard for a story," he said softly. "Abby isn't crazy, she's one of the most intelligent women I've ever had the pleasure to know. And as to the house, come on, people! A lot of places around here come with rumors and stories. This is Hollywood, a land of hopes—and of shattered dreams. Bad things have happened, as they have happened everywhere. Granger House is just a house, a very beautiful house," he said.

"You're not afraid of staying there, are you?" a male reporter asked.

"Personally—no! I love it. It's a really fine, handsome place, modernized, incredibly comfortable. I'm not afraid in the least."

"Abby stays there, Jennifer Connolly stays there—" Vickie observed.

19

"Yes, but still—" the young man with the nose ring interrupted.

"There are so many stories!" the older woman finished.

He hadn't expected to get into this.

"Half of L.A. County is haunted, as is the White House, if you want to listen to stories," he said impatiently. "If you don't mind, I really am worn."

He got past them and fled. Like a pack of hounds following a meat truck, they hurried after him, the sound of the women's heels staccato against the flooring. Luckily, he saw Edgar Thornby, Abby's very proper British butler walking toward him now, a worried look on his face. "Mr. Markham, sir, forgive me." Edgar was white-haired, lean-faced, just a hair short of his own six-two in height. His suit looked as if it had been ironed while on his body. "Your flight came in earlier than expected."

"A full twenty minutes," he agreed. "It's fine, Edgar."

"Oh, sir, I should have been there to get you through the wolves."

"Edgar, I'm a grown man, and like Abby says, without the wolves, we wouldn't have jobs."

"But you must be tired."

"Jet lag is worse going the other way, Edgar. I'm fine. Now, tell me about Abby."

Edgar's lean face went, if possible, leaner. "Ah, Abby," he said sadly.

"The disease is progressing?"

"It's degenerative, sir. You know that."

"Of course, but she's still relatively young. People have it for years, and there are medications and…" His voice trailed off. "Edgar, it's not supposed to affect her mind, is it?"

Edgar didn't answer right away. "Let's collect your luggage, sir, and get on out to the car. The 'wolves' are still behind us. I wouldn't want them listening in, if you don't mind, sir."

"I don't mind at all, Edgar. If you'll just stop calling me 'sir' every other sentence."

"Yes, sir, of course, sir."

Conar sighed. "There are my bags, Edgar, right there. Grab the small one; I'll get the larger."

"But, sir—"

"Edgar, I'm twenty years younger than you. Do as I say."

"Yes, sir."

"And stop—"

"Calling you sir. Yes, sir."

He glanced sidewise at Edgar. Edgar didn't notice. He shook his head, picked up his bag, and they headed out of the airport and for the car.

They were on the freeway when Edgar suddenly answered him. "It's the drugs, sir."

"I'm sorry, what?"

"The drugs she takes. Her medicine. The prescriptions. She doesn't think clearly on them; she doesn't see clearly. She talks to people who aren't there."

"But other than the drugs, is her mind clear?"

Edgar seemed to hesitate. "I think so."

"You think?"

"Well, I think that sometimes, when she's drugged, she thinks that she sees or hears things...and then they follow into her rational mind. Do you understand?"

"I'm not certain."

Edgar looked at him through the rearview mirror. "Like this thing with...with someone trying to murder Jennifer."

Conar was quiet for a moment. "So she's told you that she believes someone is trying to kill her daughter."

"It's why you're here, isn't it?"

"I had a great job offer. That's why I'm here."

"Oh, yes, right. Is that what Jennifer believes?"

"I haven't the faintest idea what she believes," Conar said, staring straight ahead at the road. "I hardly know her."

"I wonder if she'd be angry if she knew the truth," Edgar mused, more to himself than to Conar.

Conar replied anyway, almost repeating his original answer. "I don't know. Like I said, I hardly know her. But tell me, what do you think? Is Abby—" He hesitated, then asked bluntly, "Edgar, is Abby losing her mind?"

Edgar slowly went crimson. "Most of the time she's fine."

"But is she imagining things? She sounded...different."

"It's not for me to judge—"

"Oh, come on, Edgar. You've been with Abby for years. Since she bought that house, before she ever lived in it. You've been more loyal than any husband. What do you think?"

The butler's carefully shielded expression was suddenly haggard. There was deep sorrow in it. "I seldom leave her anymore. She insists that I take my days off, but frequently I just pretend to leave. When I do, I try to make sure that one of the day maids is with her. What do I think? I think that she didn't deserve this. I think that the disease is horrible and cruel, dehumanizing, and she didn't deserve it."

"But is she losing her mind?"

"I don't know," Edgar said, and it sounded like a groan. "I don't know what to tell you. You're going to have to see her for yourself."

Conar was thoughtful. "Well, she has always been a bright woman. Medications affect people, but she seemed pretty good when you came to New York last year."

"She's changed in the last year," Edgar said quietly.

"Is it the house, do you think?"

"The house?" Edgar said, startled.

"Well, it has a reputation."

"Abby loves the house," Edgar said flatly.

"I know."

"Houses aren't evil," Edgar said.

"Edgar, I didn't suggest that the house was evil. I think it's a wonderful, handsome house, with a bit of sad history."

"It's a good house!" Edgar said, showing more passion than he had in all of their conversation to this point. "I've lived there, working for Abby, for years now."

"Edgar, I'm very fond of the place myself," Conar assured him.

Edgar wasn't assured. "Strange things happen, and bad things happen to people, but houses aren't evil."

"Of course not," Conar agreed.

Edgar turned to him suddenly, a strange tension about him. "But people can be evil, Mr. Markham. People can be very evil, indeed."

Chapter 2

"So, am I invited?"

Since Jennifer, dressed in nothing but flesh-covered body strips, had just crawled into bed with Andy Larkin, both producer and actor on the show, in the role of hunk and general trouble causer Dale Donovan, she couldn't avoid him—or the question. They were just about ready for the take.

She sighed, shaking her head.

"Hey, watch that world-weary and distasteful look you're giving me," Andy teased. "We're in the middle of high passion here."

"Andy, this whole thing is getting out of hand—and damn you, Andy, watch your hands, will you?"

"Jen, you moved, not me. And quit trying to get out of this. I'm invited, right? Hey,

I'm not just an incredibly good-looking man who acts with you on the show—I'm one of your two producers as well. A man you need, a man you want to impress."

"Well, hell, Andy, if you put it that way, of course, you're invited."

"Thanks. That was so gracious."

"Andy, I'm very good at my role. If you're not impressed with me by now, you're not going to be."

"Are you going to give me a speech about being a great actress and tell me that you get dozens of jobs and you don't need me?"

"No, I like working on the soap. I really enjoy it."

"Glad to hear it." He grinned, then told her, "And, of course, this is part of the plot here—not a casting couch."

"Thank God. I didn't think you wanted sex, just an invitation."

He laughed. They were surrounded by people. The director, makeup man, set designer, two of the prop staff, three camera operators, one caterer, and a few of the other actors, chatting off set, waiting for their cues.

In fact, others could probably hear their conversation. Andy didn't seem to mind. Not much bothered Andy, and he wasn't at all after her, she knew. If he was interested in sex with anyone on the show, it was his real-life ex-wife, Serena McCormack—and her *Valentine Valley* sister character—who would be breaking in on them at any minute.

"If you hadn't invited me, I'd have gotten

Conar to have me over," Andy told her. "He'll be living there as well, you know. Abby insisted. It will be his home, too."

"Really, I had thought that he'd be a guest in my mother's house, the same as I am myself," she murmured.

"Oooh, I think some cat claws are showing there, Jen."

She didn't get a chance to reply.

"And we're on in five, four, three..." Jim said, mouthing and denoting the two and the one with his fingers. Jim was a good guy, easy to work with. In his mid-to-late thirties, he was laid-back but very good at what he did. He wore jeans and cotton tailored shirts to work and his sandy hair was usually falling over his forehead as he checked out a camera angle. The soap usually had a second director, but Harry Osterly, an older man who had worked with them previously, had suddenly retired, and as yet Andy Larkin and Joe Penny hadn't found anyone they liked enough to replace him.

"Action, baby," Andy whispered against her ear, then grinned, leaned over, acted out a passionate kiss.

The set door burst open.

Serena McCormack, playing Verona Valentine, the oldest of the three sisters on *Valentine Valley,* entered the caretaker's cottage dramatically, with the shadow of a man behind her.

"Oh, my God!" she cried out.

Andy broke away. Jennifer sat up, grasping the covers to her chest.

26

"Oh, my God!" Serena repeated. "Look, they're together!" she said, outraged. Serena was beautiful. In her mid-thirties, she was the epitome of elegance with wickedly long legs, classical features, auburn hair, and eyes that were almost a true aqua. The shadow-man behind her moved slightly—he was Jay Braden in real life and Randy Rock in the soap—Jennifer's character's current *Valentine Valley* husband, a tall, lean, dark-eyed man with ash-blond hair.

Serena was a wonderful actress, her performances so real in situations so absurd, she had garnered ten Emmy nominations and two awards. She spun to Jay Braden. "Don't come in, you'll only be hurt."

Jay, stricken by his wife's infidelity, tightened his facial muscles. A pulse at his throat ticked dramatically. It was one of Jay's special talents.

"Let me go, Verona!" he said, pulling away from her and accosting the two in bed.

"I'll kill you!" he told Jennifer furiously. "I'll kill you—"

"As if you haven't been cheating on your wife with her own *sister*," Andy protested, trying to protect Jennifer's character.

"I'll kill you, too," Jay said, spinning on Andy. "If I carried a gun, you'd both be dead now!" He reached for Jennifer as he had been directed. "But you, dear wife, you're coming home with me—now!"

"Stop it, stop it!" she cried, shrinking into the bed.

"Leave her alone!" Andy said, going for Jay's throat.

"Stop it, both of you stop it!" Serena cried, throwing herself between the men.

"As if this isn't what you wanted, Serena," Jennifer told her soap sister. "Randy, leave me be. It's over between us, I have nothing—"

He swept her up, covers and all, and she struggled against him. "Not tonight!" he told her. "It isn't over by far!" he exclaimed, and striding away with her, he exited the set.

"You bitch," Andy accused Serena. "You did this on purpose."

"Maybe," Serena said softly.

"He'll kill her. He will kill her," Andy cried. Camera angles automatically shifted as he rose in the bed, reaching for his pants. He stumbled into them, staring at Serena.

"Maybe," Serena repeated.

"And maybe he'll wise up and kill you," Andy told Serena.

She turned to leave.

"Oh, no," he told her, catching her before she could exit the set. "Oh, no, sweetie. You want to interrupt my night? Then you can just remember that you're my wife."

He pulled Serena into his arms.

"Cut!" Jim Novac called. "A perfect take. I could kiss you all—one take, the camera angles were great. Have a great holiday weekend. Hey, Jennifer! I'm invited to that party you're having, aren't I?"

Jay Braden had set Jennifer upright. She self-consciously adjusted her flesh-colored and far too brief strips of set "clothing."

Everyone was staring at her.

Serena had a look of sympathy on her face. She was a good friend.

Jennifer grimaced and lifted her hands. "Of course, you're all invited. What would a party be without you all?"

Abby was seated in a wicker chair by the pool. The afternoon wasn't that cool, but she had a blanket drawn up on her lap.

She was as beautiful as ever, and simply seeing her there, he felt a wave of emotion sear through him. She was no blood relation, but she was still the best parent he'd ever had.

She was sixty-something, and though she looked frail, and the disease had certainly worn some ravages with her, neither time nor illness could ever dull the beauty of her perfect features, her enormous blue eyes, her generous, full-lipped smile. Abby *radiated*. The magic that she had given to stage and film alike was not an act, but a warmth from within her, and a love for the world around her. She had lived her life with passion; she had made mistakes. But she had never lied, and she had never paused for regrets, and she had saved his life when he might have gone in a far different direction. She had taught him to take responsibility for himself; to realize that he couldn't blame his own life on other people, but must take charge of it himself. She had been far more loving and nurturing to him than those who should have cared for him the most.

"Abby!"

She smiled, seeing him. She reached out her hands.

They shook—but only slightly.

He hurried to her, taking her hands. His grip was firm, and he was glad to see that there was strength in the hold that returned his own. He bent to kiss her cheek. "My God, darling, you look wonderful."

She smiled ruefully, a slightly wistful look in her eyes. "Drugs and makeup do wonders, don't they?"

"Abby—"

"Now, now, dear boy, don't say a word. I'm not feeling sorry for myself. I'm simply being a realist. Come here, closer, let me kiss your cheek. It's so long between times when I see you!"

Conar bent down by the chair, kissing her cheek, allowing her to kiss his. She smelled of Shalimar; she always did. She smiled at him, her eyes touched with a mist of emotion. "Ah, Conar. Your father was not the best husband, but you've been the very best stepson."

"Well, you know, Abby, you've been awfully good yourself," he reminded her, trying to speak lightly.

"How does it feel to be back?"

He grinned, taking the handsome wicker lawn chair across from her. "I haven't been back that long. So far, so good."

"I hope you don't regret this decision. I heard you had a great offer over in Europe."

"Well, now that's true, but the sci-fi flick could be a major bomb—it's another one about a flight crew fighting bugs from outer space," he said, making a face. "You know, with something like that, you could have a classic, like *Alien*. You could also have a cheap-looking cheesy disaster as well." Should he have taken the job? Maybe. The director was a Hollywood powerhouse at the moment.

He shrugged, looking at Abby, who was staring back intently. "I like soaps. I like the work ethic. And I like the money Joe Penny offered me. Did you have anything to do with that?"

Abby smiled, shaking her head. "Not really. I just suggested that you might be available—if the price was right."

"What does your daughter think about all this?"

Abby's brow lifted slightly as she considered her answer.

Conar felt strange knowing so little about Jennifer Connolly, Abby's daughter from her marriage to writer Tom Connolly, and that, in all these years, they had spent so little time together. Connolly had supposedly been the love of Abby Sawyer's life. She'd been young when she'd met him; he'd been ten years her senior. He'd been breaking fiction and literary charts while she'd been a skyrocketing young starlet. Tom Connolly had died in a plane crash ten years after their marriage. The Hollywood rags had claimed that the marriage had been on the rocks. But years later, knowing Abby, Conar had begun to realize that the papers had been woefully wrong. She had lost the one man she had really loved.

His father had been husband number three for Abby. Conar had been seventeen at the time of their marriage. His mother—bless her now deceased soul—had been a product of her times, a beautiful, liberal folk singer with an addiction to musicians and cocaine. His father had been a semi-famous ballplayer, divorced several years from his mother at the time of his marriage to Abby. Jules Markham had been a traditionalist with a habit of falling for passionate, opinionated women. He'd wanted to love Abby, just as he had wanted to love his son. But his work was on the road; he never really knew either.

When his father met Abby, Conar felt himself to be on the bottom of the barrel. He played ball—because it was expected of him. Football, baseball, basketball. He didn't really have a feel for any of them—or maybe it was just that he was his father's son. He should have been great. Instead, he'd liked the partying with the team. He started with drinking and doing drugs when his father failed to remember little events such as his birthday, the anniversary of his mother's death—even the concept that his son might want to spend Christmas with him. In fact, Abby came into his life on the Christmas Eve of his senior year in high school.

That year he'd taken refuge in his flashy car, the fastest girls in school, and in booze. He'd spent Christmas Eve day out—with friends, until all his friends had gone home to be with their families.

Then Conar had gotten sick.

Abby found him half-dead before the tree at the Malibu beach house. His only excuse for the way he had behaved toward her was the fact that he had blamed her for his father's absences. He'd been wrong.

Abby had picked him up, thrown him in the shower, poured coffee down his throat—and yelled when he'd started to whine about his father's absence. "He's left us both, it seems. And you know what? I'm hurt, but I'll deal with it. But you! You should be ashamed of yourself. A handsome young man like you. The world is out there! If someone isn't standing right here to hand it to you, go out and grab it. You're old enough now to get out there and be responsible for yourself."

He found out later that night that Abby had been on the lonely side herself—her daughter was spending the holidays in Georgia with her father's family. "It's you and me, kid, and we're going to make this a happy holiday, you got it?"

The next day, he'd found that she was forthright and fascinating, and he loved talking to her. He admitted things to her he'd never said to another human being. He'd admitted that he'd royally screwed up his chances to attend college.

"What do you want to do? What do you like, what makes you happy?" she asked him.

"Travel...I think. Exotic places. Discovery. People—what makes people tick, why they do what they do."

She grinned. "You could certainly do travel spots for television. You're articulate, well spoken, and handsome, you know. Like your dad."

"Yeah, I've broken my nose like him, too. He got smacked in a World Series game. I got knocked out in a barroom fight."

"You know what you should do?" she said softly.

"What?"

"The service."

"Like the Army?"

"Or the Navy. You're a California boy at heart—stick with the water. Maybe the Marines. You'll learn a good sense of responsibility, get some on-the-job training—and you'll quit worrying about what Daddy is doing."

At first, he thought she was full of it, but two weeks later he enlisted in the service. It was the best move he ever made. The service gave him the opportunity to see the world—parts of the Middle East and Western Asia he had never imagined existed—and the chance to pick up a liberal arts degree. His last two years he spent as a commissioned officer in a special diving investigation unit.

But by that time Abby and his father had divorced. And a year after the divorce, his father suffered a severe heart attack. He entered the hospital and survived several weeks, clinging to life, but dying slowly and irrevocably. Conar was surprised to discover that he could stay at his father's bedside offering comfort and support. Somehow he was at peace with his father, and himself. Abby had given him that serenity as well.

And Abby came back to be with them both at the end.

When it was over, Conar and Abby stayed friends. She wrote to him. When he could, he visited her. No matter how on top of the world she was—and Abby flew, for sure—she had time for him.

Conar spent some time working for a dive shop. He did piecework as a free agent for local law enforcement agencies, looking for missing persons who might have drowned. He worked on some pleasure craft as an instructor. He usually had better ideas about how to do certain things, and so he toyed with the idea of opening his own dive shop, but the capital he needed for what he wanted to do was fairly steep. His father, the semi-famous ballplayer, had gambled away his considerable income—which was fine. Conar had wanted no part of it. Abby had taught him that it was important to make your own way in life.

Because of that, he wouldn't allow her to finance him. He meant to earn the money himself.

Abby suggested acting. He thought she was crazy then, too. But he needed the money.

He started with clothing commercials,

mainly because the financial rewards were so great. In those days Jennifer Connolly had been attending her last year at a boarding school in Massachusetts. Then he had his own stint on a daytime soap—nearly missing Jennifer completely when she returned for her summer of graduation, because he was heading out on location to do a P.I. movie.

He hadn't been terribly impressed by her. At eighteen, she'd been striking, but cold and distant, and she had resented him, no matter how courteous she had kept her insults.

He returned to the soap come the fall— but by then Jennifer had left to attend a fine arts college in New York. Then, almost by pure accident, he garnered a small, but Emmy Award-nominated role as a ballplayer dying of cancer in a made-for-cable movie. He'd fallen in love with Betty Lou Rodriguez, his co-star. Betty Lou played the poor Mexican girl the ballplayer loved and who returned his love—too late. In real life she was a bundle of energy, always laughing, and always seeing the best in everyone. They became passionately entangled and agreed to marry. He was certain it would be forever.

Would it have been forever? He didn't know. The passions that had driven them together might well have torn them apart as well. Betty was fond of certain drugs; he had a well-learned aversion to them. Life had made him cynical, and in their last days together, he feared that much about her that he had loved was a facade she carefully maintained. They argued, threatened to walk out— and made up. Eternal love? Maybe. They might have split in anger. They might have worked it out.

But he would never know.

Soon after the movie wrapped, Betty Lou had been killed by a stray bullet in a shoot-out in downtown L.A. Ironically, she'd been attending a benefit for a new hospital in the ethnic neighborhood where she'd grown up.

It had been a bitter time for him, but as usual Abby was there to help him. He had seen Jennifer then—she had deigned to come to the funeral. She even expressed real sympathy. He had almost liked her. But he'd been in too much pain, guilt, and confusion to care too much then about anyone other than the wife he had lost.

He'd been a hot property, and now he was a tragic romantic hero. He was loved by L.A., but he wanted nothing more than to escape the city that had so wronged the woman he had loved. He'd been offered work on Broadway, thanks to Abby. The concept of live theater appealed to him, and he left for New York. Jennifer Connolly began working on the soap.

She had made one trip to New York with Abby. She visited him backstage there, but she was distant again—not just to him, but to Abby. And when Abby was briefly swept away by old friends, he'd still been grief-ridden enough not to give a damn about what anyone thought of him—even Abby's daughter. So he'd had a few choice words about her behavior.

She'd walked out.

And he hadn't seen her since then, though he knew that she'd moved into Granger House with Abby, and there hadn't been a tabloid able to claim anything other than that Jennifer had been a completely devoted daughter.

"Abby, what does Jennifer think about all this?" he repeated. She still hadn't answered.

Abby smiled at last. "She thinks I've asked my stepson to spend time with us since he's coming back to California to work."

She was lying, of course. He couldn't help but grin.

"What does she really think?"

"She thinks I'm crazy as a loon—and that you're an obnoxious egotist with nothing better to do than steal some other poor actor's bread-and-butter job when you could probably have any role out there."

His smile quickly faded. "If she knows that you brought me in—at double everyone's salary—it's natural that she should resent me. Especially when she finds out you want me here to look after her."

Abby looked down at her lap. "Well, it's true, I don't think she understands all the experience you've had in the past with situations other than acting...but don't worry. Jennifer will come around."

He doubted it, though he really didn't know. Besides those few hostile occasions they had met, he'd seen her only on talk shows. Strangely, she appealed to him as a talk show guest—she was strong, articulate, and passionate when

she cared about a subject. She had a beautiful smile—Abby's smile. On talk shows, she
seemed to be entirely grounded. She almost
seemed to have a vulnerable side. But he knew
as well that appearances could be deceptive.

This wasn't going to be an easy relationship,
especially because, in her illness, Abby seemed
to think that Jennifer was being stalked by a
killer. And that he could somehow help.

"Abby, I still don't understand. Why are you
so convinced that Jennifer is in danger? No
matter what is happening on the soap, none
of it is real."

"Someone does want to kill Jennifer. You
must protect her," Abby said, distressed.

She had been doing so well. Now he saw that
her hands were shaking more and more visibly, one with greater spasms than the other.
Her head was shaking as well. He hadn't
noticed it before. He had upset her.

He touched her hands again, feeling awkward. "Abby, is it time for your medication?"

"No, no, I don't want any pills right now.
Every time I take pills, everyone thinks that I'm
seeing things, hearing things…that I'm crazy."

"But, Abby, the medication does—"

"Have an effect on me, I know it. Oh, God,
do I know it, Conar!" she said, and the distress in her voice cut right to his heart. "I know
it—I see people in the walls when I'm on
enough pills, Conar. But don't go feeling
sorry for me. The people in the walls can be
nice; they're my friends, we have great conversations."

"Not real, Abby—"

"I know they're not real!"

"So—"

"The threat to Jennifer is real. There is a killer out there, stalking her."

"Abby, I'm trying to understand just what has convinced you that Jennifer is in so much danger. Was it Joe Penny choosing her character to be threatened by so many people in the show? Abby, are you afraid they're trying to kill off her *character* in the soap?"

"Good God, Conar, do you really think I'm so foolish?"

"Then, what has you so worried?"

"The whisperer, the one who called me."

"A man called you?"

"I don't know if it was a man or a woman—it was a whisperer." Her lips were pursed, and he felt horrible. She was shaking violently.

"Abby, I've got to call Edgar. We've got to get you some medication—"

"I shake, Conar, it's part of the disease. I shake a lot, and I shake wildly. Why do you think I've hidden myself away like this?"

"But, Abby, you don't need to hide from me. I love you as if you were my mother, you know that."

"Then...believe in me, Conar," she pleaded.

"But you've just told me that the people in the walls talk to you when you're on medication. Maybe, just maybe, the people in the walls whisper things that you heard during the day, they play on your subconscious—"

"Conar Markham!" she interrupted furiously.

He fell silent, staring at her. "Abby?"

"Are you going to help me or not?"

"I'm here, aren't I?" he cross-queried softly.

"Maybe, the people in the walls do whisper," she said tartly. Then she leaned toward him. "But they don't write notes!"

"Notes?"

"Yes, notes, letters, actually! Postmarked from downtown L.A. The people in the walls do not write letters, Conar Markham."

"Letters that say...," he prodded.

Then he was startled, for she was very still for a moment.

Her voice was an even whisper: " 'Jennifer Connolly is going to die.' "

"Abby! Did you call the police? If you received a letter, you need to show it to the police."

"No!"

She lowered her eyes. Her head was bobbing more severely now. Conar knotted his hands into fists, wanting to help her somehow, but also needing to understand her fear. Was any of this real?

"Abby, the letter can—"

She looked up at him. "The letter is gone."

"Oh, I see."

"No, no, you don't see at all! You're patronizing me, which is what Joe Penny did, and Edgar, and even that wretched policeman when I did call him. I...I..."

She broke off suddenly, trying to moisten her lips.

He leapt up. "Edgar!" he shouted.

41

Abby reached out; clenched his hand. "No—"

"Abby! You're choking, you have to have some medication."

"Then the people...the people in the walls will talk. You won't believe me."

"Abby, we can talk more later. When you've rested, when you're feeling a bit better."

Edgar was coming. Abby nodded and lowered her head.

"It was stolen, you see," she managed to whisper softly. She looked up at him again. "It was stolen right out of my purse before I could do anything about it."

Chapter 3

Friday was supposed to have been his day off. He'd been looking forward to the long weekend, earned after a brutal year of endless workweeks with no such thing as overtime. Well, it went with the territory.

Still, he knew as the phone rang, somehow, that he was in trouble.

He looked out to his driveway. His Jeep was there—already loaded. Fishing poles, ice chest, camping gear. One of the things he'd always loved about L.A. It was possible to go from the city to the wilderness in a couple of hours.

He answered the phone.

"Liam!"

"Yeah. Cap?" he acknowledged.

"Thank God I caught you."

"What's up?"

"We've got a murder."

They had lots of murders. It was L.A. County. They also had lots of homicide cops, though he was well aware that Captain Rigger liked to put him on the high-profile cases.

And too often witnesses walked over footprints; even the uniformed officer who was often first on the scene sometimes destroyed more evidence than he preserved.

Liam Murphy had been a cop for ten years. Straight out of college, against the wishes of his parents, who had expected him to go on to law school, he had joined the force. When he'd done enough years, he applied for detective, and he'd been working in homicide ever since.

He stared at the Jeep longingly for a moment, then turned away. He was good at what he did. So good that his personal relationships had fallen by the wayside for most of his adult life. His dates tended to be irritated when he was drawn from bed to the morgue.

"Liam, I know you had the long weekend, but—"

"Who was it?"

"Brenda Lopez."

Liam grimaced at the receiver. Brenda Lopez was one of the hottest young stars on the Hollywood scene. This would be front-page news across the country. It was a case that would make LAPD look bad if it wasn't solved.

"She was found nude, tossed down Laurel Canyon."

"She wasn't killed there?"

"No, according to the preliminary from the M.E. She's pretty badly cut up, and there's not enough blood in the area for it to have happened there."

"Who gave the I.D.?"

"Her face was barely bruised. Every cop there knew who she was, instantly." He was quiet for a moment. "Anyway, get on down to the scene, would you? Rick Taylor is already down there."

"All right. Is the information out to the media yet?"

"The vultures showed up almost before we did," said the captain. "This is an ugly one, Liam. You can just imagine the media pressure we're going to face. We have to find this killer, and quickly."

"Yeah." There was a slightly bitter twist to his voice. Lopez had been rich and famous, so they had to find her killer fast. What about the rest of the poor bastards killed in L.A.? Many of them would return to ashes and dust without justice ever being done.

"I'll head right down there," he said.

He quickly changed his clothing.

He didn't bother to remove his fishing gear from his vehicle.

It was a beautiful day. The sun was up, but it wasn't too hot. California could be so beautiful, the hills, the mountain, and the valleys.

Brenda Lopez's body hadn't been the first to be discovered in Laurel Canyon.

It wouldn't be the last.

"Cut!" Jim Novac called at last. At long last. Friday afternoon, not so late, but it felt like midnight.

With a huge smile across his friendly, broad features, Jim strode across the room toward his actors, applauding.

"Perfect children, you were wonderful."

"Hey, how about my camera angles?" Roger Crypton, head cameraman, asked Jim.

"Oh, yeah, brilliant, you were brilliant."

"And I slipped in and out of that room like a real shadow!" Niall Myers, a young prop man, said with a wry grin.

"Yeah, yeah, yeah, kid. Give a prop guy a job as a stand-in and suddenly he wants an Emmy," Jim moaned.

Niall grimaced to Jennifer. "He forgets I had a life and career before I came here."

"A life? A career? Kid, you're twenty-two years old, barely out of diapers," Jim said. "And while we're at it, pick up your props, get busy, it's a holiday weekend, let's all get the hell out of here! Oh, by the way, Jennifer, I guess we'll all see each other at your party tomorrow night?"

"Maybe she should just announce it in *Variety*," Serena murmured dryly.

Jim didn't seem to notice. "It's going to be a really big shindig, huh?"

"Not so big," Jennifer said. "It's really just us. And whoever my mother decides to invite. It is her house."

"Is she up to a party?" Jim asked.

She hadn't shared much about her mother's illness with anyone, but they all knew she was sick. The entire world knew that Abby Sawyer was sick.

"I guess. If she isn't, we'll just have to cancel," Jennifer said innocently. She caught Serena's gaze. Serena winked.

"Oh," Jim said lamely.

And he seemed so dejected she that she found herself saying, "I'm sure that my mother is going to be all right."

"I've never been in the Granger place," Jim said, awed.

She hadn't heard her director sound awed very often. It was just a house. They were all being ridiculous.

"Well, you'll be there tomorrow night," Jennifer said lightly. "Jim, will you excuse me? I'm freezing in the air-conditioning here." She indicated her almost-clothing.

"Oh, sure, of course, of course!" Jim said.

And she smiled, and turned, and walked away from them all. And she did manage to walk, even though she felt like running.

Conar was deeply concerned about Abby.

By the time Edgar had taken her in for her medicine, she had been shaking with a vengeance. There had to be something that

46

could be done. Abby was relatively young. Despite her discomfort, she had fought the idea of taking her medicine. She "saw things" once she took it. And she knew that she lost her credibility.

He thought about Abby the entire time he drove her Mercedes XL down to Sunset Boulevard. He was due to meet with Joe Penny, *Valentine Valley*'s executive producer, at Mirabella—away from the soap set.

Abby was much, much worse than she'd been last time he'd seen her.

He knew there were treatments that might help her. They involved surgery. Scary surgery. He didn't know exactly where Abby stood on that subject, but it was worth looking into. He made a mental note to discuss it with Jennifer—whether Jennifer wanted to discuss it or not.

On Sunset Boulevard, he miraculously found street parking and walked into the restaurant. The hostess recognized him, but the hostess saw lots of actors and actresses. Her eyes widened, then she composed herself. "Mr. Markham, Mr. Penny is here. He said to watch out for you."

As he neared the table, he saw Joe Penny. At fifty, Joe had a dignified look that somewhat contrasted with his occasionally—what Abby called—*smarmy* manner. Joe had power, and he liked to use it. His hair was forever perfectly colored—an ash blond that defied gray. He paid a lot for the color. He worked out daily, and he'd invested in a bit of surgery. He

47

looked mature but far younger than his years. His eyes were large and dark, his chin was aggressively squared, and he had an aura of confidence and power about him. Conar liked him—he tended to be completely honest about his manipulations and his many vices.

Joe gave Conar a quick embrace, then drew back. "Don't want to draw too much attention to my star of the hour when he's trying to lay low," Joe said.

Bullshit.

Joe thought it a major coup that he had lured Conar back for a soap opera. And he wanted all the attention he could get.

"Sure," Conar said dryly. He took his seat; Joe did the same. Joe lifted his hands in a would-you-believe-it gesture, then dropped them. He shook his head. "Would you believe it? I've really got you. You're here, you're in Hollywood, you're going to do my soap."

"Joe, for what you've paid me, you could have had any actor out there."

"Did I pay you too much?"

"Frankly...maybe." Joe looked entirely deflated. "Well, hell, no," Conar lied.

"I paid what Abby said I'd have to pay."

"Are you all right with it?" Conar asked.

"Sure. It's what Abby said would lure you back."

Abby had lured him back.

"Well, good. I'm glad you're fine with what you're paying me—I'm not giving it back."

"You mean, I could have gotten you for less?"

48

"Hell, yes!" Conar grinned.

Their waitress came by. She was about twenty-one, slim with big breasts, blond with huge blue eyes. "Were you ready for the Dom Perignon, Mr. Penny?" she asked sweetly.

Conar stared at Joe. Joe shrugged sheepishly. "Conar, meet Dawn. Dawn, Conar."

"Oh, I know who Mr. Markham is," Dawn cooed.

He nodded in acknowledgment.

"Isn't she beautiful?" Joe asked him.

He nodded again. Sure. Most women in Hollywood were beautiful. If they weren't, they bought beauty. Even a certain amount of youth was for sale.

"She's an actress," Joe said.

"An actress. Imagine that." How was it possible that neither of them seemed to notice his sarcasm?

"She could play a waitress in the show."

"I'm sure she could."

Dawn smiled brilliantly, showing pearly white teeth.

"Sure, honey, get the champagne now," Joe said.

She walked away. "Isn't she something?" Joe asked.

"Sure." He wondered suddenly what got into him. "You fucking her?"

"Hell, Markham—" Joe began. He shrugged. "Yeah. But what does that matter? She would make a good waitress on the show."

"Hey," Conar said with a shrug, "what do I care?"

"Yeah, well...you know, Conar, you are going to be so glad that you agreed to come on board. We are going in such different directions. I mean, we are really getting mainstream. I have the plot twisting and turning so much your head will spin."

"My head will spin. Are we doing a repeat of *The Exorcist*?" he queried lightly.

Joe took him seriously. He shook his head. "No, no, but we are going after the old masters. Some of them so old that the new generation doesn't really remember just how great things once were."

"What are you trying to say, Joe?"

Joe leaned closer. "The best. The very best."

He sat straight again. Dawn was returning with the champagne. "And I special ordered this, too. A really exceptional bottle, even for Dom Perignon."

"You could have just bought me a beer," Conar said.

"Hell, no—you're my brightest and my best."

Dawn opened the champagne and Joe tasted. She poured. With her pearly white smile ever in place, she set the bottle on ice and left them.

Joe leaned forward again. His eyes were bright. "Hitchcock!" he said with a flourish.

Conar stared at him. "Hitchcock?"

"Suspense. We're going for the master of suspense."

"I thought we wanted good old daytime smut."

"Really, Conar."

"No slur intended—I'm here, aren't I? But we reflect life, right—maybe in an exaggerated sort of way."

"And life is full of suspense."

"Sure, but—"

"The shower scene."

"I'm sorry?"

"Hitchcock's most famous. We're going to re-create it."

"For a soap?"

"Hitchcock is an issue? Conar, we do marriage, and marital breakups. We do sex."

"Daily."

"Most people have sex—"

"Maybe most people wish to hell that they did have sex daily."

"Right. And we feed the fantasy."

"Joe—"

"But life is scary these days."

"Life has always been scary."

"I grant you that. But our audience wanted affairs; we gave them affairs. They wanted travel; we gave them travel. They wanted divorce, mixed families, unwed mothers—we gave them what they wanted. Now they're even more sophisticated. They want more and more."

"They want..."

"Suspense!"

"Joe, it's not like that would be new."

"There are no new stories, just new ways to tell them," Joe said by rote.

"All right, I'll give you that, but—"

"No one knows. We've kept the plot a deep dark secret."

"So—"

"You've got to promise to keep a secret as well."

"Joe, you know if you've asked me not to say anything—"

"Right. So..."

"So?"

"The shower scene!"

"The—"

Conar started to repeat Joe's words. He never got a chance. The young hostess suddenly rushed over to them, visibly upset.

"Oh, my God! Have you heard?"

"Heard what?" Joe asked quickly.

"She's dead!" the hostess said.

"What?" Joe said.

"Who?" Conar demanded with a deepening frown. *Abby!* he thought, his heart trembling.

"Brenda Lopez! Brenda Lopez!" the young girl said. "Murdered!" she cried. She stared at them both. "She was found in Laurel Canyon...dead."

"Dead—how?" Joe persisted, wanting more detail, his voice gravelly.

"Slashed to death, and thrown from a cliff!" the hostess told them. "Oh, my God!" Then, wide-eyed, she walked away.

"Hell," Joe Penny said, shaking his head. "Brenda Lopez."

"What a shame. She was a smart, beautiful young woman," Conar said.

"Smart?" Joe shook his head. "Smart, hell.

She went and got herself killed. She was a bitch who didn't care where she made enemies."

"She was aggressive," Conar agreed. "Ambitious, but—"

Joe wasn't listening. He was still shaking his head. "Shit! Slit to ribbons, and thrown into the canyon." He shook his head again, gritting his teeth this time, then stared at Conar. "I will not let this ruin my plot line. I will not!"

Conar lifted his drink. "Well, of course not. Life—and death—have to have their priorities, don't they?"

Joe stared at him.

"You're mocking me, Conar."

He swallowed his champagne. "Why would I mock you, Joe?"

Fifteen minutes after the last take, Jennifer was out of makeup. Standing and putting the last of her personal makeup back in her purse, she cringed at the sound of a tap at her door. Shaking her head, she reminded herself that she had already invited everyone here to her mother's house tomorrow night—or rather, they had invited themselves, and she had agreed.

"Jennifer, you still in there?"

It was Serena. Jennifer felt her tension ease. "I'm here, come on in."

Serena swept in, smiling ruefully. "You know, if you really don't want people at Granger House tomorrow night, I can put a stop to this now," she said. She slid into the makeup chair in front of Jennifer's mirror,

53

shaking her head as she gazed at her reflection. "Isn't it pathetic? I could feel that pimple growing when we were standing under the lights. Seriously, I could just feel it taking root and shape and substance as we finished the last take. The indignity of it. I always thought that my skin would be clear when it became a wrinkle exchange. I don't know whether to buy acne medicine or age-defying moisturizer."

"You're absolutely gorgeous, and you know it," Jennifer assured her.

"You're a doll, but the truth is, I'm thirty-six and have nothing to show for it," Serena murmured, still staring critically at her reflection. Then she suddenly jumped and spun around in the chair, laughing. "Oh, my God! Don't ever let me sit in front of a mirror like that. I'm starting to remind myself of my ex-husband."

Jennifer had to laugh, despite the fact that her friend was dead serious. Serena had spent a year married to Andy Larkin. She had opted out of the marriage as gracefully as she could. She never said an ill word about him to anyone; she had even taken interviews with any magazine that had asked, and stated leisure-time conflicts as the reason for the breakup. "He's mountains, I'm water!" she told them all. The truth, she had admitted to Jennifer, was that they could never make any appointment on time. Andy Larkin—definitely smooth, charming, and very good looking—was his own biggest fan. He could never tear himself away from the mirror. He obsessed over losing his hair, though he had a rich head of it. He spent hours in tanning beds, days at salons. It had been too much for Serena.

"I promise," Jennifer said, "I'll knock you in the head anytime I see you go near a mirror."

"I think I'm beginning to age-obsess."

"You're thirty-six. They won't let you have Medicare yet."

"No, but..." Serena shrugged. "It's just that I have my work...and some great friendships. But other than that...one marriage, a disaster ended in divorce."

"You do have a great career. You're adored," Jennifer told her, studying her. "Ah," she said softly, "I see. You're afraid that you've gained the world, and lost your soul."

Serena shrugged again, a light in her eyes. "Well, I'm not so sure that working in *Valentine Valley* is like gaining the world, but yes, it's a good job."

"Hey, I was told this morning that we're the hardest-working and the best—we learn our lines, and we get them right, all in one take."

"Sounds good to me," Serena laughed. "I just...It's the biological clock thing. I want a family."

"You're only thirty-six. Women are having children later and later—"

"Yes, but I'd really just like to have my children the old-fashioned way. Making love with a man with whom I'm *in* love. I'm hoping not to wind up on fertility pills, desperately planning the right day and the right hour,

God knows, going for in-vitro or something that's even less certain. Not that I think that people shouldn't—people should follow any path they need to take for a dream—but I'd just *like* it all to be the usual way."

"Serena, you're giving yourself a whole list of problems that probably don't exist."

"Maybe not, and I hand it to women who do go through all kinds of pain and heart-breaking determination to have their children. It's just that every year I get older now, I'm putting myself in for a greater possibility of problems."

"I don't think you're that old yet. And actually, I'm getting up there, too."

"Twenty-eight? Sweetie, you're just a babe. Not even thirty yet."

"Serena, if you want a child so badly, lots of women are opting for single parenthood."

Serena smiled. "I don't know what my problem is. I want the whole package. The guy, the love, the forever after, the works."

"Well, the guy must be out there some-where. Go find him, take a few chances."

"The last time I took a chance," Serena said woefully, "I married Andy." She shud-dered. "Oh, my God, could you imagine chil-dren with him? A little baby with a mirror attached to his bottle?"

"I see your point on that one."

"Oh, well, I didn't come to talk to you about my own midlife crisis."

"Midlife crisis!"

"Life expectancy is in the seventies somewhere. I'll be thirty-seven soon. Double it and you've got mid-seventies. But that's not the point. You know that I can be really pushy and mean and brazen when I choose."

"Just like a cobra," Jennifer lied politely.

Serena made a face. "Well, I can handle the hairy monsters around this place, and you know it. If you want this party called off, tell me, and it will be done."

Jennifer hesitated. She hadn't wanted the party; didn't want it. But her mother had been the one who mentioned it. Because of Conar Markham. Abby was probably telling him right now to make her house his house, to bring in anyone he wanted, anyone at all.

"No...," Jennifer said slowly. "I think it's going to take place one way or the other. I'd like to feel that I have a little control over the situation."

Serena was watching her, as if she were about to warn her not to obsess over Conar Markham being her mother's stepson. She seemed to reconsider.

"All right. Do you need me to come over tonight?

"No, I'm really fine, but if I weren't, Doug has already invited himself for the weekend."

"Doug invited himself over?"

"As my moral support. To be honest, I don't need any moral support. But you know, Abby has always loved Doug, so I thought he'd be a good...unrelated-in-any-way type person to have around."

"Ah," Serena murmured.

Another tap sounded at Jennifer's door. They both swung toward the door. "Surely, it's Kelly," Serena said.

"Jen?" It was Kelly.

Kelly Trent played Marla, the third sister in the great Valentine family of the California wine country. Like Serena, she had become a close friend of Jennifer's. Somehow, on the show and off, the three women managed to complement one another very well. Each had a touch of red in her hair. Jennifer's was the lightest, Serena's the darkest, and Kelly's was in between, almost a light auburn. Serena was the tallest; Jennifer was a half an inch shorter, and Kelly, playing the middle sister, was just an inch below Jennifer's own five feet, eight inches. They had all been with the show since its inception four years ago—as had most of the cast, including the part-timers with recurring roles such as the waiters at the Valentines' favorite restaurant, the fictional Prima Piatti.

In the soap, the family was known to band against the outside world while bickering continually among one another. As friends, the three were one another's constant support.

Kelly came in with grave concern written in her wide hazel eyes. "Serena, you're here, oh, good! Jen, are you doing all right?"

The depth of Kelly's concern caused Jennifer a twinge of guilt. Nothing terrible or traumatic had happened. The "Prodigal Son" was returning, that was all. The rich, famous, almost relative whose arrival was thrilling everyone else.

"I'm fine. Except that I'm beginning to feel more and more like a fool—and a weakling."

"It's certainly not as if you need to be afraid of him, or anything," Kelly said. She moved comfortably into the room, perching on the dressing table near Serena's seat in front of it.

"It never occurred to me to be afraid of him, really," Jennifer said. "In any way."

"Of course not. He's not out to do any harm to you," Kelly said.

"And you do know him," Serena said.

"Not very well. We've crossed paths a few times through the years, but..."

"To be honest," Serena said, "I hate to admit it, but I'm dying to meet him."

"Well, there you have it," Jennifer said, "it's the simple truth. Everyone is dying to meet him."

"Well, I imagine that he's already at your mother's house," Kelly said, powdering her nose, and meeting Jennifer's eyes in the mirror. "There were huge write-ups about him in today's paper. Did you read any of them?"

"No," Jennifer murmured.

"You should. In self-defense, if nothing else," Serena mused.

"Self-defense?"

"Face it, no matter what you say, you've been seething ever since you heard that he was coming."

Jennifer was quiet for a moment. She really

wanted so badly to meet this situation with nothing more than calm, casual maturity. But there was just something about him. From the first time she'd met him, he'd...

Irritated her! That was it. He was straight from damned Central Casting, rugged, dignified, a frigging morph of Conan the Barbarian and James Bond. Every time she was in a room with him, her temper just burned.

Even when his wife had died, she'd wanted to show some sympathy. But he'd suddenly blown it, lost his reserve, his cool aura of forced courtesy. He'd lashed out at her like a scorpion.

"Like I said, I really don't know him very well," Jennifer murmured. "I'm seething like everyone else—he's getting our pay raises."

"We've all been curious, dying to meet him—*and* seething on the inside. Have you heard what they're paying him?" Kelly asked.

"The rumor, of course," Jennifer said.

"Kell, whoever said this business was fair?" Serena queried in stern warning.

"I wasn't actually complaining," Kelly said, casting another glance toward Jennifer. "Just commenting."

They both stared at her.

"All right, all right. So I'm whining. But remember how happy Joe Penny was about his coming. Ecstatic. He said that we should all be dying to have him in the show. So even if I am whining, I really do like my job here, and the freedom we have with asking for breaks and all. And think about it, even if we resent his paycheck, Conar Markham is sure to be a

60

tremendous addition to the cast. He's so very popular...and dynamite. A really handsome, ruggedly good-looking, man's-man-type man."

"But Jennifer still has a very valid reason to resent him," Serena said softly, watching Jennifer.

Jennifer laughed. "Well, I do. He's staying at the house where I'm living with my mother. Who is ill. And he's staying there because my mother invited him."

"That's not really such a horrible thing," Kelly said.

Jennifer lifted her hands. "That's true—it's not. I'm mad at myself because I'm upset. It's even a little bit ridiculous. I'm upset because I think my mother asked him here because..."

"Because...?" Kelly said.

"Because what?" Serena asked.

"Oh, my God," Kelly breathed. "Oh, dear, you're upset because you think that your mother has some kind of a *thing* for him, and that he has a thing for her—"

"No! Oh, no!" Jennifer protested in horror. "Oh, God, no, nothing so horribly Oedipal. I'm upset for a number of reasons. It's terrible to see my mother suffer, for one."

Serena watched her for a long moment before speaking very softly. "Then if Conar makes her happy, why does it bother you?"

"Naturally, I want her to be happy," Jennifer said.

"Then...," Kelly persisted.

Jennifer found herself forced to grin. "I can't help it. The fact that he makes her happy pisses me off."

Kelly grinned. Jennifer's smile faded.

"Seriously, this is what makes me more upset than anything else. I just think that my mother manipulated his arriving here because she's worried about me—and I'm afraid that the medications are beginning to make her lose her mind."

Kelly and Serena looked at each other.

Kelly carefully formed the next question. "Okay, why, exactly, do you think that she invited him here?"

Jennifer hesitated for a minute. "Because she's afraid for me. She thinks she's gotten threats regarding me."

"But that's crazy," Kelly said.

Jennifer didn't have time to answer. The door suddenly swung open. Doug burst into the room without knocking.

"Doug—" they began to protest in unison.

"Have you heard?" he demanded.

"Heard what?" Jennifer asked sharply.

"Turn on the television. Evening news." He didn't wait for them to follow his command. He squeezed past them in the small space and turned on the television in the corner of the room.

Puzzled, the three women shrugged to one another, and turned to watch the news.

"Oh, my Lord," Kelly breathed.

A deep, masculine newscaster's voice was coming over an eight-by-ten picture of a beautiful and well-known actress.

Brenda Lopez.

She had been found dead.

Her nude body had been tossed into Laurel Canyon.

She had been brutally murdered before she was thrown into the canyon—more than sixty stab wounds had crisscrossed her neck, chest, and abdomen.

Nothing further could be divulged until the L.A. Medical Examiner's office had completed the autopsy.

The news continued. They all stared blankly at the television.

Then they all turned and stared at Jennifer, and chills swept through her body.

Her mother was going mad. It was the medicine. It had to be...

But she was suddenly very afraid.

Murder happened in L.A. There was absolutely no reason the death of Brenda Lopez should have anything to do with her mother's wild fears for her.

But still...

She couldn't help but feel a strange hot shivering inside.

She didn't want to be found like Brenda Lopez.

Chapter 4

Doug followed her home since they both had a car, so thankfully, she didn't have to keep a conversation going. And by the time she had driven to Granger House, she had the world—and her own mind—back to rational.

L.A. County could be a fierce place. Once, when she'd gotten into some trouble with a group of fast-driving, drug-taking friends, she had been brought to see the county morgue. It had been enough to make everything else in life seem trivial for a very long time. So many traffic fatalities, drug overdoses, shootings, stabbings, deaths from domestic violence, the infamous and the not so well known, children beaten to death by their own parents—parents killed by their children, suicides, homicides, fratricides, bodies mangled beyond recognition due to automobile accidents. Any time she remembered that experience, she usually put her own life into grateful perspective. Today, she used it to calm her sudden and irrational fear. She had met Brenda Lopez a few times. She had been a talented and beautiful woman. She had wanted to make it big in the movie industry—not on stage, and not on television. She wanted feature films, and she wanted to be in the multi-million-dollar category for any deal she made. She was aggressive and determined—which she needed to be in Hollywood. Rumor had it that she was willing to make a few enemies along the way. Rumor, as she knew, could be false. But she knew Brenda, who had flatly told her that she was willing to do one hell of a lot— including stepping on a few toes—to get where she wanted to be.

Was that why she had been murdered?

Whatever the cause, it could surely have nothing to do with her mother's strange fears for her. L.A. wasn't just a place that had seen violence before, it was a *big* place, a very big place, and terrible things did happen.

She pulled her car into the sweeping portico of old Granger House. It was a brick structure, set high on a cliff, which added to its reputation as a haunted house. When fog came in, it shrouded the base, and the house seemed to rise right out of the mist. Jennifer had always loved the house. The views from the third-floor tower were magnificent.

Doug exited his little Mazda with a whistle. "It's even better up close," he told her.

"It's just a house," she said.

"Um. Just your run-of-the-mill ranch, sure."

"I didn't mean that. It's a beautiful house, a great house. But that's all."

She started for the front door. It opened before she reached it. Edgar, in his perfect duck-tailed uniform, had known she'd arrived.

"Good evening, Miss Jennifer."

She had tried to tell him time and time again that "Miss" was not really part of her first name.

"Hello, Edgar. How is everything?"

Everything meant her mother, and Edgar knew it.

"Very well. Mr. Markham arrived safely—"

"His flight was good and he survived the raptors at the airport, eh?" Doug asked, coming up behind Jennifer.

"Well, hello, there, sir," Edgar told Doug. "Yes, he evaded them very well. He's in the den now, reading, before dinner. Your mother, Miss Jennifer, is quite well, but resting before dinner herself."

"Thank you, Edgar. Doug is going to stay the weekend. Have we a good place to put him?"

"Something like a presidential suite?" Doug suggested.

"I'd been thinking of the basement myself," Jennifer murmured.

Doug wrinkled his nose at her.

"I think we have a pleasant guest room free upstairs," Edgar said evenly. "Do come in. Why don't you adjourn to the den for a cocktail? I'll take Mr. Henson's belongings to his room."

"Thank you, Edgar."

Edgar took Doug's bag. "Shall we proceed to the den?" Doug asked softly at Jennifer's ear.

"Didn't you want a tour?"

"Later. I want to meet Boy Wonder."

"All right, fine. Actually, good. I can introduce you, then see to my mother."

"Ah, you mean you can introduce me to Mr. Markham—and run away."

"I certainly don't need to run away. And I

66

am concerned about my mother. This is a lot of excitement for her."

"Maybe you're overprotective."

"Are you really suggesting that I'm overbearing?" she asked worriedly.

"No," Doug said seriously, taking her hands. "I know how concerned you are."

She kissed his cheek. "Thanks."

"Let's go meet the dragon."

"This way."

She led him through the foyer and the grand hall. Both were handsomely decorated in carved wood cornices and designs. The light-colored walls were decorated with swords, coats of arms, and works of art. Much of the art was Abby's; the design pieces had been set in the days of David Granger, a very rich English actor and amateur magician. Not long after building his magnificent mansion on the cliff, he had, like the great illusionist Harry Houdini, become more and more obsessed with the occult. His parties, arranged so that the living could contact the dead, were successful in a bizarre way— several of his guests met their own deaths while attending. Thus had Granger House achieved its reputation for being haunted. But it was a beautiful home, and after Granger's death, his wife, and then his daughter, had remained in the house for many years before giving up the property to return to England. The house had happy memories as well as the grim ones, and Abby had never been daunted by a ghost story. The dead were the safest people she'd ever known, she'd sometimes told Jennifer.

Jennifer had never felt anything in the least negative about the house herself. It had been dark in what she considered an Old English sense when her mother first bought the place. But though they hadn't touched a bit of the woodwork, there had been lots of soft beige put on the walls to highlight the art, old tapestries had been given a number of good cleanings, floors had been scrubbed and polished, and the grand old place truly had a majesty about it again. The cliffs, and the fences—not to mention her dog, Lady—kept people away. An Irish wolfhound, Lady wasn't among the breeds usually considered good as a guard dog, such as a Doberman, German shepherd, rottweiler, or pit bull, but her size alone was impressive, and since she was known to howl at the moon occasionally, she kept up the lively speculation regarding Granger House.

"Jennifer!"

Her name was said in a strange, low whisper, and for a moment she froze. Then she felt like a fool. It was only Doug behind her.

"Is that the den door?" he said in his best Bela Lugosi voice.

She spun around. "Practicing for an audition at Disney? You'd be absolutely wonderful at the Haunted House."

"Jennifer, that's the den door, is it not? Feel free to enter the den."

"Very funny, Doug."

"I'm dying of curiosity."

"It did kill the cat."

"I refuse to die until I've met Mr. Markham."

Jennifer pushed open the den door.

He was there, all right. Reading, just as Edgar had said. Hearing the door open, he looked up, closed his book, and stood.

Stood? *Towered*. Tall, dark, arresting. Yes, instantly his presence filled the room. She could feel her hackles rising. *Be nice,* she warned herself. *He hasn't really done anything to you. Smile. Greet him warmly.*

Doug let out a very soft whistling sound behind her. "Well, we are talking true stud here. He's better in person than he is on the screen."

She elbowed him, hard.

"Conar!" Warm—was that warm?

"Jennifer, it's great to see you."

He said the words with his dusky, deep voice, then walked across the room toward her. Naturally, she walked toward him as well.

"And it's just...great to see you, too!" If this were an audition, they would be saying "Next!" already. No, she sounded warm enough. "Great! Yes, it's just great to see you."

Conar Markham was six foot three, his hair was rich and dark, eyes silver-gray, sharp as tacks. His face was handsomely molded in a classical cast, but it wasn't his features that gave him his appeal. He was rugged, yet seemed to possess a casual carelessness— take him or leave him, he didn't give a damn.

He wrapped her into his arms with a brotherly hug. For an alarming moment, she found the heat of his touch pleasant. He smelled of a very nice aftershave, and his arms were powerful. The kind that would be easy to rest within. She was tense and tired, and suddenly, ridiculously tempted to bury her face against his broad chest and tell him, "Go ahead, take over, see if you can do any better than I can, cure my mother."

He drew away from her, studying her. His hands still touched her. She was tempted to shake him off. Too much lightning cracking. Better to get away from him.

"You look wonderful," he told her.

"Thank you. So do you." She eased from his hold with all the grace she could manage. He still must have noticed. What else that was totally banal could they say?

"Jennifer—" he began, his tone serious, a frown creasing his brow. He was about to get to the nitty-gritty of why he was here, and how they had to get along.

But he didn't get a chance.

Doug, still behind Jennifer, cleared his throat.

"Oh! I'm so sorry. Conar, this is Doug Henson. Doug is a writer on the set at *Valentine Valley*. I'm sure you'll be working together in the future."

"Hi, Doug," Conar said, shaking Doug's hand.

"Hi. It's great to meet you. You're pure legend around here, you know."

"Well, it's hard to live up to being a legend," Conar said casually. "Don't put too much pressure on me. I hope I do well for the show."

Doug grinned. "You will. Our ratings increased significantly when it was announced that you were joining the cast."

"Ah, the curious," Conar said. "Well, let's hope I can keep them happy. May I get you a drink?"

Jennifer had been about to say the same thing. She suddenly felt displaced. Irritated.

Yes, Conar Markham was already at home here. He was walking toward the handsome old English bar even as he spoke.

"Scotch on the rocks, thanks," Doug said, following him. "So are you all set to start working with us on Tuesday?"

"Yeah. Met with Joe today; I'm ready to come in." He fixed Doug's drink, looked up. "Jennifer?"

"I'm not sure what I want yet. I'll make my own, thanks."

"Stoli, soda, and lime?" he suggested.

He had a memory, all right. How many times had they actually had drinks together? Once, twice?

"Sure. Thanks."

He made the drinks and turned around. Silver-gray eyes pierced into hers. "Did you hear the news about Brenda Lopez?" he queried.

"Yes, it's horrible, isn't it?" Jennifer replied.

"You knew her?"

"Yes, I met her a few times. You?"

He nodded grimly. "I did. She was a strong woman."

"Not strong enough, evidently," Doug commented, taking his drink. "And the word 'strong' is rather kind, I think. Brenda was pushy, aggressive, and upon occasion, mean as a cobra." He nodded his head as if he did so with deep understanding. "She went after the Hollywood bigwigs with teeth bared."

"Doug!" Jennifer said.

"Well, it's true," he said defensively.

"Oh, really. Because it's Brenda, she was pushy and mean as a cobra. When one of our male counterparts goes after the bigwigs in such a manner, it's all hail the fellow with the courage."

"Jen," Doug protested, hurt, "I just meant that she wasn't like any little Miss Innocence and Virginity. She might have walked into something..."

"Asked for it?" Jennifer demanded indignantly.

"No, no, of course not." Doug looked at Conar. "Help me out here."

Conar was studying Jennifer. "I think he means that Brenda made enemies, that's all."

"Right—exactly. And you're turning this entire discussion into a protest for suffragette city," Doug said, shaking his head at her unreasonable treatment.

"But—" Jennifer began.

Edgar entered the room. "Mr. Henson, excuse me, but I think that something leaked in your bag, and I thought that you might want to know right away. May I escort you to your room so you might assess the situation?"

"Of course, of course, excuse me, will you?"

"Doug, it's probably nothing," she protested.

"I'll just check."

In a second, he was gone with Edgar.

And she was alone in the room with Conar.

The sudden silence between them seemed staggering. The tension between them was palpable.

He spoke first. "I'm sorry that you're upset that I'm here."

"Why should I be upset?"

She was terribly afraid that she sounded like a child.

He raised his hands in a shrug. "You must feel I'm stepping on your toes."

"You're an actor who has accepted a job. What does that have to do with me?"

"It's your soap."

"It most certainly isn't. I act on it. It's a job."

"A drone rather than a queen bee?" he inquired lightly.

"The point is that you're more than welcome to work anywhere you choose."

"Really?"

"Of course."

"I'm so glad to hear that. Your soap—and your house. And you don't mind a bit."

"It isn't my house. It's my mother's."

"She has always told me that any home she has belongs to you," he told her, lifting his glass to her. It was a nice thing to say. So nice that she felt a slight thawing. But then he went and ruined it all. "Always, even when you were acting like a true horse's ass to her."

Her fingers tightened around her cocktail glass. "Thanks so much. And that from the original bad boy himself."

"Um," he murmured dryly. "Yeah, the bad boy invited here by your mother, and making a mint, and pissing off everyone in the place. Well, I don't know if I'm worth it or not, but it's what they've offered, and I'm not giving it back. And I owe your mother."

"You don't owe my mother. She does what she chooses to do for people because she wants to. She doesn't want anyone in debt to her, or feeling as if they're in debt to her—ever."

"All right, then. I love your mother."

"Do you really?" She hoped the question was casual, voiced with no more than polite interest.

"Yes, I do. Really. Do you love her, really?"

Jennifer could hear the phone ringing, but she didn't really notice. Edgar would answer it. She felt as if she were engaged in a very strange battle. His eyes on hers, hers on his—and the room crackling and sizzling with tension. What was she hoping to win? It was like a staring contest.

"She is my mother, not a woman who was once my *step*mother. And, as I said, it's Abby's house, and it's not my personal soap opera. I'm glad that my mother considers her home my home, and naturally..." Just then she realized she hadn't seen Abby yet this evening. She threw up her hands. "I'm sitting here arguing with you—about what, I don't even know." She needed to get away from him. "Excuse me," she said. "I have to—"

74

"No, I won't excuse you. Not for a moment, Jennifer. Let's get this out. Now."

"I haven't seen my mother yet, Markham. You can wait."

"No, you can wait just one more minute, Miss Connolly, until I've had my say."

"It had better be quick."

"Fine, then, understand this. Abby has asked me here."

"Yes, she has."

"And I'm here for her."

"Good for you."

"Whether you like it or not. And I'm here to stay."

She lifted her hands, staring at him, feeling as if she were hot enough to explode. Somehow, she remained still. "Like I said, hey, good for you."

"I plan to be cordial and polite while I'm here," he told her, taking a step closer. She was about to step away, but she refused to be intimidated. Even if she was furious—and her knees felt like water at the same time. *Why does he always have this effect on me?*

"Well," she said smoothly, "I'll try my best for courtesy as well."

"Good. You try."

"Now, excuse me, I do have to see my mother."

"Go on, then. I'm glad to hear that my being here isn't a problem to you at all."

"Not at all. I will certainly try to be civil."

"Oh, yeah. You're civil."

She turned, setting her Stoli and soda on an

end table. But then she walked fast out the doorway, and before she knew it, she was running down the hall.

Really, it was totally legitimate. The first thing she always did when she returned home was check on Abby. Of course, she didn't usually have to escape unwelcome visitors.

Sometimes when she came home, her mother was sleeping, having been heavily medicated. If so, she tiptoed away. Sometimes Abby had done well during the day, and was awake and wanting to talk. And sometimes her medication had affected her so that she was convinced that they were joined in the room by a group of strange people who lived in the walls. It was difficult to be with Abby then. They had to include the wall people in their conversations.

Abby's room was down the full length of the hallway, far from the den, but it was purposely on the first floor. The room had once belonged to Granger himself. He'd suffered with arthritis later in life and had found stairways difficult. Abby hadn't always been in this room, but it was difficult for her sometimes to maneuver, and she abhorred the idea of a moving chair. She had easy access to the rest of the house, and to the pool area. There were French doors with wide beautiful windows that led out to the pool area from her room. They were carefully locked once the evening had come and she'd been given her medication. Jennifer had experienced nightmares about her mother drifting into a fantasy world, wandering out to the pool—and diving in.

Edgar had seen to the locks.

She stepped into her mother's room. Abby was lying on her bed. Jennifer tiptoed silently over to the bed. Music played softly from a central system. Abby often watched television, but the set was off. Jennifer was glad to find her mother sound asleep. Or maybe worn out, Jennifer thought resentfully. She had probably spent the day trying to assure the wonderful Mr. Conar Markham that Jennifer wouldn't be too miserable to him.

There was nothing to do here. She never woke her mother when she was in a peaceful sleep. Tears stung her eyes. She really did love her. Maybe she had rebelled, as Conar had pointed out, but that had been long ago. She and Abby had been a team for years now.

And where had Conar been all that time?

With a new rise of anger spurring her on, Jennifer headed back to the den. He was reading again, as if he'd never been interrupted. Maybe she hadn't been an interruption before. Just an annoyance. Now she meant to interrupt, big time.

"Let's have a few ground rules. I will be civil, totally civil. And honest. My mother wants you here. Fine. I will try."

He looked up politely. "Jennifer, of course you will try. You really have no other choice."

He was laughing, she thought. Speaking in a deep, level tone, but there was laughter beneath it.

"I have no choice?"

"None whatsoever. But I'm glad you're out-and-out hostile. I do like honesty."

She hesitated, trying to control her temper. She didn't seem able to win. She was furious, he was amused. He was so casual. Sorry, but hell, this was just the way things were.

And he was right.

She smiled, walking toward him, picking up the drink she had left behind, her fingers tightly vised around the glass. "All right. You like honesty. Let me give you deep-down truth. Do people mind that you're here? Hell, yes! The rest of us have worked our asses off for years—and they bring you in at double our salaries. As to my mother...well, I've been struggling with a massive downhill slide in the degeneration of her disease here for almost a year. It would have been longer, but she hid her illness from everyone, including me, for so very long. You—"

"Jennifer, wait—" he interrupted.

But she wasn't waiting. He'd pushed it. She was going to have her say. "No, you wanted this discussion—*you* listen, then I'll wait. You insisted on knowing if I was upset. Upset isn't the word. You see, I've watched her suffer, I've been to the doctors, we've tried one medication and then another, and different doses. We've dealt with tremors, choking, violent shaking, the medications, the delusions caused by the medications—and so on. Now, pay attention here. You've been...away from Abby. I've—"

"Jennifer," he interrupted again. His voice had a warning tone she had no intention of heeding. They were going to have this all in the open.

"Conar! I've not finished. Through all this I've protected her, I've talked for her, I've done everything I can possibly imagine. Because I do love her. There have been times when I've thought she was dying, times when I've thought that she's totally lost her mind. Times when I've just held her hand because she's been shaking so badly that she's called my name just for a safe anchor to cling to! But here you are...riding in like the Lone Ranger. Yes, quite frankly, I wish you'd taken a wrong turn somewhere and fallen right into the La Brea tar pits. There, you've got it. I don't think I can be any more honest. Are you happy now?"

He had arched a brow to her, looking not in the least dismayed by her tirade. A slight nod of his head indicated the doorway behind her. She spun around.

Edgar was there, as was Doug, as was a tall, well-built man of about forty in a polo shirt and Dockers.

She felt a flame of crimson burn through to her cheeks. She realized that he'd tried to stop her. It didn't help. She felt ashamed and humiliated—and all the more furious with him. That it wasn't his fault didn't help. It just made him all the more the golden child.

The dead silence seemed to stretch and

stretch. She wanted to talk. Sound didn't come to her lips. Thank God. If it had, it wouldn't have created intelligible words.

Golden boy saved the day.

"Liam," he said with sincere pleasure. He walked past her to greet the stranger standing in the doorway—witness to her tirade—along with Edgar and Doug. "Hey, how'd you know I was here? I would have called you—"

"I know you would have. And naturally, I damned well knew you were here. It's all over the media, every rag in the state of California is carrying your picture."

The stranger had a voice nearly as deep as Conar's. There was a slight twang to it, as if he might have originally hailed from Texas or Oklahoma. His eyes were dark, his skin was bronzed, and his hair was nearly black. Jennifer wondered if he was an actor. She didn't recognize him if he was, but he had the rugged type of good looks that would have served him well if he was.

He and Conar shook hands and embraced like old friends.

Conar turned to Jennifer. "Jennifer, Liam Murphy. Liam, my stepsister, Jennifer Connolly."

"How do you do? Naturally, Miss Connolly, I'd have recognized you anywhere."

"Oh? It's a pleasure to meet you, Mr. Murphy, but I'm afraid I don't recognize you, though you are obviously great friends with...with my stepbrother." She arched a brow, trying to sound as natural as Conar. But then, he hadn't been the one in the middle of a tirade when company came. It was so hard to sound casual and courteous when she knew that her cheeks were a thousand shades of crimson.

"I knew Conar way back when, Miss Connolly."

"Jennifer, please," she said ruefully, glancing at Conar. "After all, any friend of my step-brother's...well, you know the saying."

"Oh, yeah. I'm sure he can just imagine," Conar murmured.

"I had meant to do proper introductions," Edgar said dolefully. He remained where he had been, in the doorway to the room.

"It's all right, Edgar," Conar said.

"Yes, of course, Edgar, it's fine," Jennifer said.

Edgar remained red-faced.

So, she was certain, did she.

Liam Murphy was nonplussed. He grinned, accepting the hand she offered him, shaking it politely. Then his grin faded, and he seemed to be studying her. She stared back, feeling that the situation was going from bad to worse.

"Liam, why do I get the feeling you didn't just come to welcome me back to town?" Conar asked, breaking the awkward freeze.

"I'm sorry I didn't come just to welcome you back to town," he said, glancing at Conar. "You've heard about the Brenda Lopez murder?"

"We heard, of course," Jennifer said. "It's horrible. Absolutely horrible."

"You knew her?" the newcomer said.

"I didn't know her really well, but I certainly knew her," Jennifer said, frowning and wondering why this man was asking questions about Brenda Lopez and why she was answering him.

"She wasn't a close friend?"

"No, but, of course, it's still horrible, and I'm so sorry for her."

"And you knew her, too, of course?" he said, looking at Conar.

"Of course," Conar said.

"Excuse me, but what's going on? Why are you asking all these questions?" Jennifer demanded. He and Conar were obviously old friends. So why was Conar's friend giving them the third degree about Brenda?

Doug, who'd been standing in the doorway with Edgar, strode into the room to give her the answer, his eyes alight with curiosity. "He's a cop," Doug supplied, and he took up a defensive stance behind her.

"A cop?" she repeated blankly, staring at him. She frowned. "I thought you were an old friend of Conar's."

"Well, I am. A very old friend."

"She assumed you were an actor," Conar provided.

"We met doing dive and rescue work," Liam said. She still continued to stare at him blankly. "Scuba. We both subbed as police divers out of the military; the police force hires outside divers frequently for big jobs. I went on to become a detective, and..." He paused, flashing Conar a smile. "Conar there went on to become…a heartthrob." He said the word teasingly, as only a real friend would do.

"Heartthrob, hm," Conar retorted. He turned to Jennifer and Doug. "He's trying to tell you he has a real job and we're all making a disgusting living playacting."

"I didn't mean to offend anyone," Liam assured Jennifer.

"The truth in this case isn't offensive," Conar said. "We do make a disgusting living at what we do."

"Some of us make a more disgusting living at it than others," Jennifer said sweetly.

"She thinks *I'm* overpaid, but naturally, *she* isn't."

"You are paid much more," Doug murmured. "From what we've heard, of course."

"They're giving you more money?" Liam said incredulously. He winked at Jennifer, still taunting Conar. "You? She's much better looking."

"But Conar is kind of like the prodigal son," Doug exclaimed.

"You worked for the soap before?" Liam asked.

"He left Hollywood for New York," Doug explained.

"And so they're giving him more money?" Liam said, shaking his head as if there were no justice in the world. "Aha! Sibling rivalry here?" he asked Jennifer.

"Oh, no, not really. We're just thrilled to

have Conar," she said, offering a brittle smile to Conar. "After all," she added softly, "a good heartthrob is hard to come by."

As Liam laughed, Conar arched a brow. Doug suddenly decided to defend Conar.

"Conar will be great to write for," he said cheerfully.

Jennifer inadvertently turned on him.

"Fresh blood, you know," Doug said.

Liam cleared his throat. "And speaking of fresh blood..."

"Yeah. You mentioned Brenda's murder," Conar said, frowning. "Are we involved somehow?"

"Is someone here a...suspect?" Jennifer asked incredulously.

From the corner of her eye, she saw Doug turning toward Conar. She looked at him herself, feeling a strange chill. She wasn't happy that he was here, but she'd never thought that badly of him.

Just how well had he known Brenda...?

"Good God!" Edgar said from the doorway, startling them all.

"No, no, I haven't come here to accuse anyone of anything," Liam said. "I don't have a good grasp on time of death yet, because the medical examiner hasn't finished with his report. But I think Conar would have had to move darned quickly to have flown in, gotten to Brenda, and back here and all cleaned up."

Of course he would immediately clear

Conar, Jennifer couldn't help but think. Conar was his very good friend.

Don't be an ass! she warned herself. She didn't want him here, but she certainly had never suspected him of anything horrible.

"Was she raped?" Doug asked suddenly.

"Again, I've not seen the complete autopsy report," Liam told them.

"Liam," Conar asked, shaking his head, "just why did you come, then? Not that we're not glad to have you, but..."

"It's where the body was found."

"What?" Conar said, startled.

"Here?" Jennifer protested. "What on earth do you mean?" Suddenly, chills were snaking down her spine. She felt forced to make a strong denial. "The body wasn't found *here.*"

"Very near, I'm afraid."

"Brenda's body was found down in the canyon," Jennifer said.

Liam nodded. "Yes, that's true. But you see, I can tell you this. Most of the information about her death is already in the news reports—or it will be. She was found in the canyon, but she wasn't killed there. She was dumped there. And according to the forensic experts, she might well have been thrown down into the canyon."

"Thrown down?" Jennifer asked.

"From this very property," Liam finished.

Chapter 5

Her mother's room was never totally dark. Far down the hallway from the den, parlor, dining room, and other entertainment areas, it was quiet and large. And grand. The furniture was antique mahogany, handsomely carved. The headboard was magnificent. The sheets were Laura Ashley, and Abby always went to bed in a beautiful gown, her makeup removed, her hair brushed. Keeping up morale was very important. Jennifer had never liked affectations, but now, even when Abby was feeling worn and careless, Jennifer was insistent. Abby had an innate beauty, but keeping up a certain regimen made her feel better. Jennifer even insisted they get pedicures now and then. She teased her mother, telling her she had great toes, they had to keep them in shape.

When Jennifer tiptoed in that night, she thought that her mother was sleeping. Her head was on the pillow and her eyes were closed. She didn't seem to move. As she always did when she came into her mother's room, she approached the bed and touched Abby's cheek softly. She couldn't help but feel a certain panic every time she came near. She had to assure herself that Abby was alive.

"Hi, sweetheart." Abby's eyes were open.

"Mom! I didn't mean to wake you."

"You didn't. I wasn't sleeping. I was just lying here."

Jennifer sat by her mother on her the bed, taking her hand, squeezing it. "Edgar said you'd had a long day."

"No longer than any other."

"Yes, but you had the excitement of Conar arriving."

Abby laughed softly, squeezing Jennifer's hand, then releasing it to push herself up in the bed. "Don't sound so reproving. You'd think you were the parent."

"I'm not reproving."

"You hate that I asked him here. I really am sorry that you feel that way. You've seen him, I assume?"

"Yes."

"You weren't too unpleasant, were you?"

"Mother, I was completely charming."

"Yelled at him, did you?"

"I didn't mean to—he was just so condescending."

"I think he's really trying to be nice."

"Of course. And I'll try, too."

Abby stared at her, beautiful eyes luminous in the shadowy room. "Now, that scares me. I'm not so fragile, you know."

Jennifer hesitated. "I'm not so fragile either, Mom, you know."

She was sorry she spoke. Abby's fingers began plucking at the bedcovers. Stress and worry made the tremors much worse.

"Look, Mom, things are going to fine, honest. So we're both a little tense. We'll get past it, okay?"

"Is Liam still here?" Abby asked.

Jennifer started, wondering how her mother could be aware the cop was in the house—or even how she knew him.

"Liam?"

"Yes, dear, Liam Murphy, Conar's friend."

Jennifer frowned. "How did you know—"

"My hearing is excellent."

"But...you heard us from the den?"

"The doors to the pool must be open, and my sliding door is open, I believe. I didn't hear everything, but...voices carry, you know."

"Yes, he's still here."

"And Doug?"

"You knew that Doug was here, too? I wouldn't let him come see you tonight—I thought you were sleeping."

"Honey, I heard Doug, too."

Had her mother heard her ripping into Conar? Of course, that had been the loudest monologue of the night.

She was glad of the darkness; she felt her cheeks reddening. For an actress, she had pathetically little control over her blushing.

"I hope you don't mind. He kind of insisted that he come for the weekend."

"I don't mind. Moral support against your evil, money grubbing stepbrother, right?"

"Mom!"

Abby laughed. Jennifer was glad of the sound. But then she sobered. "Jennifer, please..."

"Mom, I'm going to get along just fine with Conar."

"Honey, please, let him...let him watch over you."

"I don't need anyone to watch over me."

"I wonder if Brenda Lopez felt the same way."

Again, Jennifer started, angry that Abby had heard about the latest sensational L.A. murder. "Who told you about Brenda?" Had Conar done so? She gritted her teeth. He should know better than to play into her mother's fantasies. "Who told you about Brenda? Really, Mother, he shouldn't have—"

"He didn't. I'm not blind, deaf, or dumb. I spend hours watching television. Her death was in the news immediately."

Jennifer inhaled slowly, nodding. "Of course. Mom, I'm very sorry about Brenda."

"I'm sure you are. I know that you thought well of her." Abby suddenly wound her fingers around Jennifer's wrist. Her grip was surprisingly powerful. "Please, baby, just let Conar hang around you."

"Mother, I've got a life to lead, you know."

"Not really. You've been doting on me too long."

Abby broke off.

Her disease often made her feel as if she were choking. As if she couldn't breathe, and couldn't swallow. She always kept a handkerchief at hand, ready to discreetly soak up any saliva she couldn't manage.

"Mom, Mom, please!" This time Jennifer took her mother's hand, and her grip was tight. "I'm going to be okay. You know I've never been anything like Brenda Lopez."

"And what does that mean? That she was

killed for being a 'bad' girl or something of the like?"

"No! Of course not! But she was known for throwing her weight around, for being demanding—and ruthlessly ambitious. She had enemies. To the best of my knowledge, I haven't stepped on any toes. I'm very happy where I am."

"A job structured so that you can stay with me," Abby gasped out.

Jennifer shook her head. "I love the soap. Honestly. And you are the priority of my life right now, and that's that."

"I'm glad, then. But you're still in danger."

"Mom, you know that the people in the walls talk to you, so why can't you believe that threats against me might have been...a dream?"

"I'm not crazy," Abby whispered. "I do know reality from fantasy. I'm trying to keep you safe, Jennifer."

"Oh, Mother, I know that. But I can't have Conar following me around. I'm careful— I'm street smart. When I go out, if it's late, if I need protection, I never head out alone. I have my dog. Lady. My very big dog."

"She's a lamb."

"But no would-be attacker knows that."

"Unless the would-be attacker knows Lady."

"Mom, no would-be attacker would know my dog. And what if I'm out on a date?"

"Jennifer, you have no love life. You've been looking after me."

"But you never know when I just might get a love life."

"Jennifer…"

Abby was starting to gasp again.

"Do you need your pills?"

"It's almost time."

"I'll get them."

"Edgar will come. He'll be here any minute. Edgar is always looking after me. The poor man, he really has no life of his own."

"Edgar Thornby is indeed a gem. But—"

"I don't want to take any more medication than I have to!" Abby said firmly.

"All right."

"Help me."

"Mother, you know that I would do any-thing—"

"Then tolerate Conar."

Jennifer opened her mouth, then fell silent. She was more or less trapped.

She had trapped herself.

"Mom," she said suddenly, thinking of a way to change the conversation. "You know how you said you wanted to have a little welcome party? Well, word got out. We're having a party. Maybe more than a 'little' party. The cast and crew started inviting themselves today; I hope that's all right. I keep trying to explain that it's not my house."

"What's mine is yours; you know that," Abby said. Her voice was raspy, as if she didn't have quite enough breath.

How was she going to manage a party?

"We'll be warm and inviting and welcome them in—and get them out fast," Jennifer said, laughing. "Serena was great, of course.

She said she could end it all in two seconds if I wanted, but of course, I know that you did intend to have something for Conar—"

She broke off at the sound of a light tap at the door. Turning, she saw Edgar coming in. He brought her mother's medications on a silver tray. She stood.

"Miss Jennifer," Edgar said. "I didn't mean to interrupt."

"You didn't, Edgar. Mother needs her medicine. And you know what? I'm bushed myself. I'm going up to bed. Good night, Mother." She kissed Abby's forehead.

Abby found strength and hugged her back.

"Mr. Markham is in the Granger Room, Miss Jennifer. Mr. Henson is down the hall in the Blue Room."

Conar was in the Granger Room. The "master's room" in the house. It had once been her mother's room. Before that, it had belonged to Granger, the master magician, the creator of the mansion himself. Naturally, they had put Conar there. It was the nicest room in the house.

She could have taken it anytime she wanted. She hadn't wanted it, so it was ridiculous to resent Conar being there now.

She smiled. Hard. "That's wonderful. Great. Thank you," Jennifer said sweetly.

She glanced at the tray that held a carafe of water and her mother's medications. So many pills. Dopamine, cinamin. Parkinson's was a neurological disease. It tormented the brain. Naturally, the medications messed with the mind.

She kissed Abby again. "Sorry," she whispered. "Love you, Jenny."

"Love you, too, Mom. Good night, Edgar," Jennifer added, and left her mother to her privacy, her pills.

And her delusions.

"So why did you come back?" Liam asked.

Conar was seated on the leather chesterfield. Liam had taken the huge wing-backed sofa and was slowly sipping a Scotch. He wasn't on duty. He might be a cop and he might have come with a few questions, but he was here as a friend.

"A good job offer," Conar said with a shrug.

"That's bullshit," Liam said flatly. "You said you'd never come back. After your wife was killed, you said you hated California."

"I did hate it…and I didn't. I hated what happened. It was horrible. But…" He paused, lifting his hands. "A violent man with a chip on his shoulder killed the beautiful woman who was my wife. She was killed by a man, not a place."

Liam lifted a brow. "Still," he said, "the last time I talked to you, you were living in New York, and you said you liked it a hell of a lot better than L.A. You were thinking of doing an 'on location' movie somewhere in the Caribbean."

Liam knew him too well.

"All right. I came back only because Abby asked me."

"She's that sick, huh?" Liam asked softly. "Is she dying?"

"It's not a kind disease, but she could live for years and years—in total misery. There is a surgery..." His words trailed off, and he shrugged. "I don't know. I just got here."

"She called the cops not long ago, you know," Liam said.

Conar nodded. "I know. She told me."

Liam leaned forward, rolling his ice in the glass. "She said she was getting phone calls; whispered threats against her daughter. And she said that she'd gotten a note, but that it had disappeared."

Conar nodded.

"It wasn't that the police don't take all threats seriously, but we couldn't trace any unusual calls, and the note couldn't be found. I'm afraid I didn't get out to talk to her. I would have, but—"

"It's all right."

"She imagines things?" Liam said.

"She admits to some delusions, but insists she knows the truth about this."

"Suppose there were threats. I mean, Jennifer is a well-known actress. There's a lot of jealousy out there."

"That there is," Conar agreed.

"Abby asked you here specifically because of Jennifer?"

"Yeah." Conar had been staring at his glass, but he looked up suddenly, not sure why he was suddenly aware that Jennifer was standing in the doorway.

Elegantly slim, perfectly shaped, she hugged the door frame, eyes wide in her beautiful face. Her eyes were like her mother's, large, expressive, luminous. Her features were more slender, her lips were more generous. She had her own distinctive look—and personality.

She had probably heard her name and paused to eavesdrop.

"Jen, you can hear better in here," he suggested. Then he gritted his teeth. So much for getting along. She resented the hell out of him, and he wasn't helping matters. He rose, indicating that she should take a seat with him.

She walked into the room, ignoring his silent invitation to sit. Liam rose, and she offered him an apologetic smile. "Sorry. I really didn't mean to eavesdrop, but the whole thing just makes me a little crazy. My mother is feeling...well, she's overanxious. It's because of the disease."

"Maybe she has good reason," Liam said, staring at Jennifer.

Conar frowned. "What makes you think these threats might be real?"

"Nothing," Liam admitted. "It's just that—"

"What?" Conar asked sharply.

Liam shook his head, standing setting his drink glass down. "You should have seen the body, that's all," he said softly. "Brenda's body. Violence can...well, it can happen anywhere. It won't hurt to take care."

"I'm always careful," Jennifer told him.

"Well, don't resent a bodyguard, eh?" Liam asked her, indicating Conar.

"Hey," Jennifer said with a shrug. Her eyes touched his. Blue fire, steel—and hostility.

"He's living here, isn't he?" she added sweetly. "And God knows, he's such a hunk. Nothing like a good *heartthrob* to keep his eyes on you. I couldn't feel safer."

Liam laughed. "Yeah. Good. Well, I'll get going then. I'll see you tomorrow night?"

"Tomorrow night?" she said.

"Conar invited me to your party. You don't mind?"

"No. No, of course not," she said too quickly. Her eyes fell on him. "He is living here, Mom's house is my house—and his house as well. Our resident heartthrob-slash-body-guard is more than welcome to invite guests into *his* home."

Conar smiled with little humor, walked to her side, and put an arm around her shoulder. He'd had enough. "Let's see our guest out, shall we, sis?"

Her eyes narrowed. She would have escaped him, but he didn't allow it.

He propelled her hard behind Liam as they walked him from the den down the hallway and through the foyer to the front door. They bid Liam good night. He felt the stiffness in her shoulders; the fury in her form. But she didn't wrench free from him until the door was closed.

"What the hell was that?"

"That was nothing—except that I never really got to give you a good answer earlier. So here it is. There was just a nasty murder in L.A. Your mother is afraid for you. In my opinion, you're still a spoiled little bitch, but let's lay it on the line. Abby wants you protected. I'm going to protect you. So don't fuck with me. Sorry, that's the way it is. I'm a guest in her house—the same as you. She loves you, I love her, that's why I'm here. Got it?"

She was staring at him as if she might explode. Her eyes were blue daggers. If looks could kill, he'd have been bleeding all over the floor.

But she didn't touch him. She didn't have much of a rejoinder.

"Asshole!" she hissed.

Then she turned around and headed for the stairs.

Jennifer lay in bed, staring at the ceiling. She was exhausted, but her mind wouldn't seem to turn off.

Abby seemed worse than ever today. So fragile. Trembling, unable to talk, choking. When she was in bed. When she should have been a bit more peaceful.

It was Conar's arrival.

She tossed, turned, and closed her eyes. She wanted to sleep so badly.

Closing her eyes wasn't such a great idea. She saw with her mind's eye instead. Saw Brenda Lopez. Her striking face and features, sweeping long hair, beautiful dark eyes. Saw them flash, heard her laughter.

Saw her as the news had described her...

Stabbed.

Again and again.

Tossed down Laurel Canyon. Just below them. She could have been thrown from this property...

She tossed again, lay on her back. So tired. Don't think about Brenda. Doug was here, funny, sweet. Which way was the soap going, what was the rehearsal, what was the new plot? The house was quiet, so quiet. Then it creaked and groaned. She knew the creaks and groans. It was an old house, settling all the time. She loved the house...

She must have dozed at last, because her sleep turned to a nightmare. She saw Brenda again...rolling down the hills and cliffs, naked, her beautiful body covered in dust and dirt, grime encrusted in the multitude of mortal wounds. She landed at the foot of the cliffs, deep in the canyon, surrounded by brush and dust and dirt.

Jennifer came to her, wanting to see her. Repelled, wanting to run, she stared at Brenda.

Brenda's eyes opened.

"You have to be careful, so careful out here!"

Flies buzzed around her head. She laughed, and bugs began to crawl from her lips...

Jennifer nearly screamed. She caught herself; her throat was raw and sound didn't come. Her eyes flew open.

She nearly screamed again. Someone was standing over her. A shape in the pitch darkness of her room.

She gasped—trying for sound. Blinked. The shape was gone. Panicked, not knowing if she had dreamed it or seen it, she leapt from her bed and flew for the light switch.

The room burst into light and color.

Still gasping for breath, shaking like a leaf, she spun around.

Nothing. She was alone in her room. The door was closed. She walked to it. Locked. She had pressed the lock when she had gone to bed.

Something she didn't usually do.

She had never been afraid in Granger House before.

Still shaking, she sat at the foot of her bed. She had dreamed it. She had dreamed about Brenda, then dreamed that someone was in her room. What a dream. Her throat was dry. Her heart was pounding.

Lie down, go back to sleep, it's going to get worse tomorrow, she tried to tell herself.

But she wasn't going to be able to slip right back into bed. So she had imagined the figure above her in the night. She still couldn't sleep.

She decided she was going to go down for a drink. That might help steady her nerves. Maybe she'd go down and bring up a whole bottle of brandy. If she couldn't steady her nerves, she'd just knock herself out.

So thinking, she slipped into her soft terry robe, opened her door, and slipped out into the hallway. There were always night-lights left on in the house. Right now they seemed to create shadowy images. Creatures, dragons, monsters.

"Goose!" she whispered aloud. Tying the

belt of her robe, she took long strides down the hallway. She paused, looking back. The Granger Room was behind the large door at the far end of the hall. She narrowed her eyes. Was the door to it just closing?

She thought she heard a little clicking sound.

Had Conar been awake? Why would he sneak around the house—and stare at her while she slept?

She looked down the hallway. The door to the Blue Room, the guest room where Doug was sleeping, was closed. She glanced at her watch. Three in the morning. Naturally, he would be sleeping.

And Edgar would be sleeping as well. He had a small suite in what had been the attic, complete with his own little kitchen and sitting room. Privacy for an old and trusted servant.

She took a breath and hurried for the stairs. She hadn't bothered with slippers, but the polished wood was carpeted with a crimson runner and her feet weren't too cold.

She headed into the den. Opening the door, she headed straight toward the bar.

Then she saw Conar.

He was standing by the rear French doors to the pool and patio area, staring out. Wearing nothing but a pair of trouser-style pajama bottoms. He turned and watched her as she reached for the brandy bottle.

So he was up.

By all appearances, he, too, had gone to bed and awakened. And wandered the house. And he might well have been standing over her bed, staring at her. Scaring her half out of her wits.

She set the brandy bottle on the bar and walked over to him, shaking. "You stupid bastard," she hissed. And to her horror, she raised a shaking hand and slapped him.

He hadn't expected the assault and hadn't made a move to stop her. But then his fingers wrapped around her wrist with a powerful grip that threatened to crack bone. His cheek reddened with the imprint of her hand, and a pulse ticked a staccato beat at the base of her throat.

"What the hell is the matter with you?" he demanded furiously.

"You...you scared me to death."

"By standing here?" he said incredulously.

"By coming in my room."

"I wasn't in your room."

"You...you were. Standing over me, staring at me."

"Don't flatter yourself. You overestimate your appeal."

She blushed with a vengeance, working to free her wrist. He was holding her too near. She felt acutely uncomfortable, almost touching his naked chest. The crisp, dark hairs brushed the terry of her robe, and almost touched her flesh beneath the fabric she wore. His shoulders glistened in the eerie half light; muscle and power delineated by the play of shadows.

"I wasn't flattering myself. I assume you were trying to frighten me."

"Why would I want to do that?"

"So that I would be appropriately grateful that you were here." He still held her wrist, and she still fought to free herself.

"Someone was in your room?"

"Will you let me go? Look, as far as I can tell, you're the only one awake in this house. Maybe I imagined it. I was having a nightmare."

"About what?"

She paused, staring at him. His eyes were on her so intently. She swallowed, shaking her head. *What the hell is it to you?* she might have shouted. But she didn't. She still felt shaky.

"I...It was about Brenda."

"Let's go to your room."

"What?"

"Let's go check out your room."

Him? In her room. Half-dressed?

"No, I must have imagined it. I just told you, I was dreaming. I probably kept dreaming. I woke up afraid..."

"We'll go see."

He was turning. His grip on her sure and strong, dragging her along. They reached the hallway, then the stairs, then the door to her room.

"Conar!" she whispered with vehemence.

She stopped dead, jerking back hard, causing him to turn. She spoke softly but with determination. "I...I must have imagined it. The house is all locked up. There are gates. The dog is out at night. She wouldn't let anyone near. And..."

She broke off herself, frowning, feeling like an idiot.

"And what?" he demanded tersely. His voice was louder than hers.

"Shush!"

"Keep talking."

He wasn't going to shush.

She moistened her lips. "My door was locked. I...I don't usually lock it, but I had done so tonight. I don't know why. I woke in a panic...but I noticed it was still locked."

"Because you thought I would come into your room and stare at you while you slept?" he demanded.

She prayed that they weren't waking anyone else up with their conversation. He still had her wrist in an absolute vise.

"No, don't be ridiculous," she said, and she hoped she sounded equally contemptuous. "I guess I locked it...because of what happened to Brenda."

"But you feel so safe. You don't need protection."

"Conar, you'll wake everyone up."

Wrong comment. He opened the door to her room, pulled her on in, and shut it. And through it all, he never eased his hold on her.

"Conar, really, I swear. You can't imagine the power of the medications she's taking. She talks to friends in the walls, for God's sake. Truly, I think that my mother is imagining any danger to me."

"So why were you so afraid? Why lock your door—why slug me?"

"I didn't slug you, I slapped you."

"Pardon me, I'll grant you the difference."

"Look, what we both need is some sleep. I'm sorry I slapped you, I'm really sorry. Please, if you would just…" She tugged at her wrist. He seemed very tall in her room. As usual, his presence seemed to fill all space.

And he also seemed very…

Naked. Heat seemed to radiate from his bronzed chest and shoulders.

"Conar…please."

She lowered her eyes, stunned by the pleading in her voice.

He dropped her wrist. "When I leave, lock your door again."

"Look, honestly, I don't think that—"

"Lock your door!" he snapped.

He turned and left, closing the door behind him.

She stared after him, annoyed to realize that she was trembling.

"Lock it!"

She jumped at the sound of his voice coming through the wood. She quickly stepped forward and locked the door. Apparently, he heard the click and was satisfied. She heard him walking away.

She stood for a long time, then walked back to her bed. She sat down. Her mind was still spinning. Now she was really never going to sleep.

And she hadn't even gotten the brandy. Lord, she would really love a drink.

She didn't get up. She kept sitting on the side of her bed, embarrassed to realize that she wasn't about to leave her room and go down the stairs again.

She might run into *him* once more.

Swearing to herself, she rose, pulled back the covers, doffed her robe, and crawled into her bed.

She loved her bed, she reminded herself. The mattress was perfect. Her pillows were plump and soft. The sheets were always clean and fresh smelling.

She stared at the ceiling, wide awake.

Later, hours later, when she finally began to doze, she wondered once again just what had happened.

Had there been a shadow? The door had been locked...

But what had Conar been doing downstairs, wide awake, staring out at the moonlight?

Out at the moonlight...

Toward Laurel Canyon.

Chapter 6

Saturday dawned like the day from hell. Jennifer awoke after a night of almost no sleep to find out that the police were crawling all over the yard, trying to find any traces of Brenda Lopez. They questioned her, Edgar, Conar, the two maids—Mary and

Lupe—who worked daytime shifts, and her mother. Lady, who spent a lot of her time in an elaborate kennel due to Abby's allergy to dogs, was even inspected. She didn't impress the police as being much of a guard dog, since she lavished wet kisses over most of them, wagging her tail at every intrusion into the yard.

Liam, with the police, apologized but said they had to track down every lead they had. Abby understood completely. She was glad of the police.

Conar was in complete control, creating a liaison between the police in the yard and Abby in the house. He stood with Liam watching as they inspected the cliffs and the manicured lawn area of the house.

Gloved men and women went over the grounds inch by inch.

Around two in the afternoon, Abby came out by the pool. She looked beautiful. More slender than ever, she had a pale, ethereal quality. She didn't have a tremendous amount of strength, but on Conar's arm she walked to a chair by the pool.

She might have been holding court. One by one, the officers came to her and payed homage. She encouraged them, telling them she was more than willing to do anything she could to help them find the murderer.

Jennifer sat beside her mother at the pool, Lady curled by her side. Abby didn't sneeze at the dog's fur as long as she wasn't confined inside with it. She loved Lady as well, but had to wash her hands soon after if she offered the dog a show of affection. It was difficult, because Lady adored Abby. She was a huge dog, too, not so much in bulk, but in height and size, and beautiful with brown-and-tan fur.

"They have found nothing in the yard?" Abby asked Liam.

He hunkered down to pet the dog.

"It rained early this morning," Liam said. "But...," he added, sweeping his arm out in an encompassing gesture, "it's equally true that she might have been thrown from the vacant land to your left, or from the back of the house immediately to your right."

"They think she was murdered at her own house, then thrown down into the canyon?" Jennifer asked, a hand on Lady's soft head.

Lady whimpered, as if she understood the seriousness of the conversation.

Liam's dark eyes met Jennifer's. "They know she was murdered in her home," he said simply.

"I understand that you're joining us tonight, Detective Murphy."

"If you'll have me."

"Of course, Liam, you know that. I'm very glad you're coming. An old friend of mine is coming who might interest you."

Jennifer looked sharply at her mother.

"Drew Parker. He was my real estate agent when I bought the house, and he knew the old magician who had the place built. If there is anything missing in your inspection back here, he might be able to help you."

"I look forward to meeting him. He must be a fascinating person."

"He is."

"Thank you for allowing me to come. Excuse me for the moment, will you?"

Abby followed his departure with her eyes as he left to converse with one of his men.

"Mom..." Jennifer reached a hand out to her mother.

Abby squeezed her fingers. "I'm fine."

"I think we should cancel the party."

"Not on your life, dear. You just heard— I've done some inviting here myself. We can't cancel, Jennifer. The cast and crew of *Valentine Valley* are expecting a welcome for Conar."

Conar looked as if he could be one of the cops. In jeans and a tailored shirt, tall, stalwart, brows knitted in a frown, he was listening to one of the forensics men as he explained something to Liam, drawing patterns in the air with his hands.

"Of course."

"You two are getting on all right?"

"Just peachy," Jennifer murmured. She bent down to scratch her dog's neck. "Get him, Lady, eat him up, devour him."

Lady whimpered and wagged her tail.

"Mom, you need to rest."

"Soon."

"It's time for some of your medications."

"Edgar will have them directly on time, you know that."

Of course. She looked up. Edgar was standing a few feet behind her mother, a bit to the

108

side. He was like a good old guard dog himself.

Abby sighed suddenly. She lifted a hand toward her mouth; her fingers were shaking. "I guess it's time to go in. I do need some rest."

Jennifer jumped up, taking her mother's arm.

Both Edgar and Conar instantly turned, as if they had special radar for Abby's distress. The two men nodded at each other. Edgar held his ground—protector of the property. Conar came forward to take Abby's other arm.

"I can probably manage just fine," Jennifer murmured, trying to sound friendly and cheerful.

"I'm sure you can," Conar said, smiling at Abby. His eyes touched Jennifer. "But I'd like to be here with you. May I?"

Abby laughed. "Conar, you may be with me anywhere."

"Well," Jennifer said, "if you're going to help Mom in, I just may keep my eyes on Lady and the guys out here."

"If you think it's necessary, dear."

"Can't hurt," Conar supplied. He had slipped on a pair of sunglasses.

She wondered if she could blink her eyes and make him disappear forever.

"I'll check on you in a bit, Mom," she said.

"Thanks, dear."

They left, Abby leaning heavily on Conar, but Conar making it look as if she were not having any difficulty.

Jennifer turned away from the pair, wondering

why her eyes suddenly stung so much. This illness had been going on a long time now. And she knew people who suffered greater tragedies—sick children, cancer, severe accidents, murder...

The breeze suddenly seemed to turn cool. She jumped when she realized that Liam Murphy was standing behind her.

"She does very well, you know," he said softly.

"She suffers so much. It's so debilitating..."

"She's bright and smart. And you have help now."

"Pardon?"

"Conar," Liam said.

"Oh, yes, of course."

As he grinned, she flushed, remembering that he had been witness to her tirade against her mother's stepson last night.

"He does love her. Very, very much, you know," Liam said.

She lifted her hands. "Maybe."

He watched her steadily. "I spent some time talking with your mother this morning, in the house."

"I know."

"And you disapprove."

"I don't think she's up to your questioning about Brenda Lopez."

"We didn't talk about Brenda."

"Oh?"

"We talked about you."

Jennifer sighed. "There's no reason to associate this with me. Brenda was someone I worked with a few times, nothing more."

"She died horribly."

"I know that. And I'm very sorry."

"You didn't see the body, Jennifer. Maybe you should. Then maybe you wouldn't mind people wanting to protect you so much.

"I can take care of myself, Detective Murphy. I don't go into dark alleys. I know the trouble spots of L.A. I carry pepper spray, I have a very loud alarm on my key chain. I think I'll go in and lie down for a while. Excuse me."

She walked away.

She felt him staring at her.

Abby took a good long nap from the afternoon into the early evening. Jennifer had thought to help her get ready for the party, but Abby wanted a really festive occasion and she told Jennifer she wanted to look her best. She'd called Thorne McKay, Jennifer's makeup man from the show, to come help with her hair and face. That left Jennifer to her own devices. She found herself dressed and ready way ahead of time, and downstairs in the den staring at the bottles on the bar.

Extra help had been brought in for the kitchen, and young men and women, dressed in tux-like uniforms, had been hired to do the serving. Saying hello to a few of them, she saw fresh, eager faces—young hopefuls. Like thousands before them, they had come to L.A. to become stars—and like thousands before them, they would do stints as waiters and waitresses.

She shouldn't drink, she told herself. It was going to be a long night. She needed to be on the lookout for Abby, ready to sweep her away if she looked the least bit uncomfortable. She prowled the room. She paced in front of the bar, wondering why she was quite so tense.

It was a tense situation.

"Cat on a Hot Tin Roof?"

She spun around. Conar had come into the room. He was in a black sports jacket, tieless tailored shirt, and black pants. His hair was freshly washed, sleek as a raven's wing.

She hadn't expected to see him so soon. The police had only wrapped up in the backyard at about four o'clock, and after that, he had left with Liam Murphy.

She exhaled slowly, holding his gaze, determined to be civil. "I'm hoping this isn't going to be too much for her."

Conar moved behind the bar. He poured himself a soda, squeezed a lime in it.

"May I have one of those?"

He looked up, arching a brow slowly. "Um. I think something a bit different." He lifted the glass to her. "You look as if you need a real drink."

"And you don't?"

"No, I don't. Not at the moment. God knows, I may soon enough. But right now...yes, you definitely need something with a bit of a bite."

She didn't reply, keeping her eyes fixed on his. He smiled grimly, then fixed her a drink.

With bite.

She sipped it. Strong. Very strong.

"*A* drink, maybe. Not *ten* in one," she murmured.

"It's already been a long day," he said.

He seemed strange. Casual with her, ready to get on with the party.

She grimaced suddenly, leaning on the bar. "I feel as if I've hit a brick wall today."

"You look it."

"Thanks."

His lip curled just slightly. "Miss Connolly. You know that you are a striking young woman, and I am referring to the fact that you appear frazzled rather than anything less than entirely beautiful."

She arched a brow to him. "How kind. I think."

"It's not a compliment. Just a comment."

She started to move away from the bar, but he set a hand on hers. "She's so worried about you, and you're so worried about her."

She stared at his hand on hers. He didn't release her. She could jerk away, but she had a strange feeling that his mood was irascible at the moment, that no matter how pleasant he was—no matter that he was drinking plain soda—he was far more tense than she.

"Naturally I worry about her. And this party. She is so uncomfortable when she starts to shake in front of people."

"Yes, she is. She hides. She shouldn't. She's still a beautiful and gifted woman. I'm glad she's having company tonight. Even if the circumstances today have been more than a bit grim.”

“Mother has handled herself admirably.”

She managed to extract her hand from beneath his.

“Yes, she has.”

“I wonder how long she’ll stay down here tonight,” she murmured.

“There’s the surgery.”

She felt her breath catch in her throat.

“What if her heart isn’t strong enough? What if it kills her?”

“She’s young enough now. Let it go, and she gets older every year. The disease progresses every year.”

“She could die from the surgery.”

“Is she really living now?”

“How can you be so ready to take a chance with her life? You see…”

“You see—what?”

“Nothing.”

“You were about to tell me that I don’t care as much as you do, that you’re really her daughter, I’m just the son of a man she married once.”

“No—”

“Why not? It’s the truth. You are her child.”

“Look, I’m not ready to argue this—”

“I’m not arguing. I’m agreeing.”

“Fine, you’re agreeing, but making me feel like…like you know more.”

“Maybe I can just see more clearly because you are closer. But I do know Abby. And I know how much really living means to her. I think she’s more than willing to try the surgery.”

"And I'm holding her back!"

"Aren't you? I know I'd take that chance if it were me."

"That's easy for you to say—because it isn't you!"

"It's not easy at all. I do love Abby."

She wound her fingers around her glass. The doorbell suddenly rang. She nearly crushed the glass. She started when his fingers curled lightly around hers.

"You may need ten more drinks," he said in a tone that both teased and warned. "The stage is set—the players have arrived. It's all happening, so breathe deeply and enjoy it the best you can. Trust me in this—Abby will do well."

"And if she doesn't?"

"She has us."

Escaping his hold, Jennifer started out of the den and by the huge great room to the foyer. Joe Penny had just arrived with Vera Houseman, the actress who played Marina Valentine, the matriarch of the Valentine family, mother of the ever-straying girls, and wife to the ever-philandering Angelo Valentine, patriarch of their daytime dynasty.

Vera hadn't been on call all week. She had been vacationing in the Caribbean.

"Jennifer, dear, thanks so much for having us!"

Vera, with silver-blue hair and brilliant eyes to match, as lean and put together as a refurbished supermodel, swept into the foyer, doffing her fur stole, spinning to survey the house. "It's magnificent! Thanks so much for having us!"

"Thanks for coming. It is my mom's house, though. She gave out the invitations."

"Well, we couldn't be invited if it weren't for you. And Conar."

So Conar was standing behind her. She should have known it. Here a day, and he was master of the house.

"Dear, dear Conar," Vera said.

"Vera, how are you?"

He took the hands she had offered, and took a hint as well, kissing her on the cheek she inclined his way.

"Thrilled that you're here, darling, just thrilled."

"Well, thank you," Conar said.

"It is a thrill, isn't it?" Joe said smugly.

"Joe, Vera, what can I get you to drink?" she asked.

"Something strong, darling, very strong," Vera said. "Joe was just telling me that Brenda Lopez was found dead in Laurel Canyon."

"Can you imagine?" Joe said.

"You hadn't heard?" Jennifer asked Vera.

"No...I was truly on vacation, at a spa."

"Drinks are in the den," Jennifer announced, turning to head back. They followed behind her.

"The poor girl," Vera said. "Oh, but she was a hardhead. I never worked with her, but I met her at a charity event last year. She refused—absolutely refused—to be in the dunk tank, and the whole thing was for such a good cause. She wore a bathing suit without blinking, of course, but she wasn't about to have her makeup jeopardized. Still...such a little daredevil, too."

Jennifer slipped behind the bar. Something strong for Vera. Hm...

"Wild Turkey on the rocks, dear, that will do nicely," Vera said. She swung around, facing the men. "Tell me the whole story, I still don't understand. Maybe they have it all wrong. Maybe it was an accidental death."

"An accidental death!" the exclamation came from the den doorway—Andy Larkin had arrived. Solo, it appeared. He had paused dramatically in the doorway. "Accidental?" he repeated, shaking his head. "Vera, my good woman, I do not think so!"

"Vera, she was stabbed over sixty times," Joe said.

"Oh, dear Lord! Make that a double, dear, will you?" Vera said. "Over sixty times..."

Jennifer was startled to find Conar standing beside her behind the bar, his manner suddenly tense, controlled, and impatient. "Joe, Andy, what can we get you?"

"Scotch and soda," Andy said.

"Skip the soda," Joe told him.

Jennifer, still plopping ice cubes into Vera's Wild Turkey, was surprised that Conar's fingers brushed hers in his haste, and that he barely seemed to notice. In fact, he seemed oblivious to her being beside him.

"Jennifer!"

Serena had arrived. Prodding Andy gently

through the doorway, she approached the bar. "The place is magnificent! Conar, hello, how are you?"

Serena was gorgeous and gracious, leaning over the bar to kiss Conar's cheek. He welcomed her warmly in return.

Jennifer gave Serena a look. *Traitor.*

Serena shrugged with a helpless grimace. "Can I help you back there? I'll just run a few glasses out, how's that?"

"I'll help you."

Andy was suddenly right beside Jennifer.

Serena was never, ever getting back with Andy. Andy, however, didn't seem to realize that. He had hurried over the moment Serena had gotten close to Conar.

Interesting, Jennifer registered.

"Fine, we'll both help. Kelly just got here— I know she'll have white wine; she never has anything but. Who's that handsome old fellow who just arrived?"

"It's Drew!" Jennifer said with pleasure.

She came around the bar, hurrying to the slim, steely old man with the iron gray hair who had just entered the room, chatting with Edgar, who had led him here. He saw Jennifer, and his bright hazel eyes widened and sparkled.

"Jen, Jen! You're a sight for sore old eyes," he exclaimed.

She came forward, grasped his hands, kissed his cheek, then let go and hugged him.

Drew Parker was seventy years old and still built like a bull. He was handsome and sweet, shy and retiring; an amateur magician, now taking an occasional role as the grandfather in a movie, an actor who hid from the limelight. People always recognized him, though they never knew exactly why, or what it was they had seen him in. Years ago, wary that sustaining roles might not come along as he got older, he had gotten his real estate license. It was a perfect job for him—people might not always recognize him, but he knew everyone in Hollywood. He knew who wanted secluded property and who wanted to be in the limelight. He knew who was suddenly floating in money, and who was spiraling on a downward trend, who had invested, and who had blown it. He could keep his own counsel like no one else, and so he was always entirely discreet. He had, in his youth, known David Granger, and knew the truth behind some of the legends regarding the house. He was the agent who'd made the deal when Abby bought the house fifteen years ago from Granger's daughter. He'd helped her see to the restoration and refurbishing of the place, and he had remained a good friend through it all.

"Drew, it's so good to see you. Mother is going to be so glad you were able to come."

"I would never refuse an opportunity to see your mother," he told her. "Or you. Jen, you're looking magnificent."

"And you're..." She broke off laughing. "You're gorgeous."

"Old as Rip Van Winkle," he said.

"Ageless," she told him.

"Where is your mother?"

"I'll go down to her room for her soon," Jennifer said. She hesitated. "She only lasts so long. I think she wants the party to be in full swing before she makes her grand appearance."

"Jennifer!" Serena called.

She turned. Serena still stood by the bar. She motioned to the door. Thorne McKay, bald head glistening, was standing there. He motioned to her.

"Excuse me, will you? I think Mom is about ready."

"Go ahead, Jennifer, please. I'm just fine here."

"It's the soap crowd here tonight, you know."

"Mostly. I see Hugh Tanenbaum over there."

She hadn't realized the movie director, close friends with Joe Penny and Andy Larkin, had arrived. He was chatting with Kelly Trent and Jay Braden. There were a few strangers in the room now, and a lot more of her soap associates from props, camera, lighting, and sets.

"I'm all right—just fine to mingle," Drew insisted. "You go on."

She started toward Drew, but moving away, he smiled.

A second later, before Jennifer could reach the doorway, Abby made her grand entrance.

She was exquisite. Her hair was swept up, soft and natural, into a loose knot at her neck. Her makeup was perfect—her skin appeared flawless, her eyes large and luminous.

She was wearing a sweeping red silk caftan with large gold jewelry.

If you're going to make an appearance, she had once told Jennifer, make it a real statement.

Abby could not be accused of being shy. Her entry was remarkable, a very bold statement. There was a hush in the room, and all eyes turned to Abby.

"Hello! Welcome, everyone. Thanks so much for coming."

"Abby!" The name was whispered by at least a dozen pairs of lips. And the company began to flock to her.

She looked frail in the encompassing caftan, Jennifer thought. Too frail. She had taken too much medicine; she wasn't shaking. Not now...

Ah, yes, there were the telltale signs. That movement of her chin; the trembling in her fingers as they fluttered. Yet she ignored the symptoms that plagued her, turning graciously, talking, chatting, smiling, laughing, putting on a performance.

"Drew, Jennifer."

She glided across the room and kissed her daughter, smiling slightly. *See, my darling, see how well I can do? You mustn't worry about me so much. You don't need to lock me away just yet.*

"Drew!"

She did tremble more evidently in greeting her old friend. The emotion in her voice was deep and sincere. "I'm so glad you're here."

121

"I'm glad to be here as well. I miss the old place. Haven't been here in ages now, Abby."

"You've got great stories, I imagine," Serena said.

"I do. In fact...come along, anyone who is interested. I'll tell you the truth behind the legend of the stained glass in the foyer above the stairway."

As the company began to file out, Abby leaned on Drew.

Jennifer hung back.

Conar remained behind the bar. He was straightening up. She walked over to him and sat on one of the bar stools before him. She ate an olive. He mechanically washed glasses in the whirling-brush machine.

"What's the matter?" she asked him.

He didn't look up. He shrugged. "David Granger bought the Tiffany piece for his wife after he'd been accused by Genevieve Borthny of fathering her child. I've heard the story," he said briefly.

"I don't mean that. Why did you suddenly get so strange?" she asked him.

His steely gray eyes shot up to hers. He was still moody and tense, she thought.

"Why are you suddenly so concerned?"

He wasn't hostile. In fact, he was insultingly indifferent.

She smiled. "Because you were almost human just a few minutes ago, and now you're nastier than ever."

He hesitated. She thought she might have drawn a smile at that, even a mocking smile.

But the sharp gray eyes continued to assess her without humor.

Disturbed, she said, "All right, look, I'm sorry, whatever I said, whatever I did."

He turned the water off. "It wasn't you."

"Oh."

He wiped his hands, then leaned them on the bar. "I went with Liam today when he left here."

"I know," she said, then realized he was halfway answering her. "All right, where did you go with him?"

"To the police station," he said flatly, then added, "On his desk were a slew of pictures. You should have seen her. Really; in fact, you should see her. You wouldn't mind my being here so much."

"Brenda Lopez?"

"Yes, Brenda Lopez, except that you'd hardly know her. You can't imagine what that kind of violence does to a human being."

She felt a sickness at the pit of her stomach. "I didn't realize...I mean your mood seemed to be fairly decent before...I don't think that Vera meant to be flippant. She's just a bit of an airhead."

"I know that she didn't mean anything."

"Then..."

"I saw those pictures. That's all. I pushed it all back in my mind, knowing how important tonight was to Abby. But when Vera said that, well...I guess my mood changed."

Vera Houseman burst back into the room in a blur of motion. "There you are, you two."

"Vera," Conar murmured. He tried for pleasant; his voice was stiff. *Cat on a Hot Tin Roof.* He seemed as tense and hostile as a caged beast suddenly.

"Séance!" she said.

"Séance?" Jennifer inquired warily.

"Yes, my dears, a séance. How fun! Come along, children, we're heading into the great room. With the double doors open, we can sit in a group, hands touching, see the magnificent window...and try to contact the spirits of those who haunt this house."

"Oh, Vera, really—" Jennifer began.

"Drew Parker knows all the low-down dirt! He's a fascinating man. Come, come. Your mother has given her approval, and we're all in on it."

Vera disappeared. Jennifer and Conar looked at each other for a moment, then followed her, nearly colliding at the door.

They both paused, caught together in the old and slender space. She *smelled* him. Felt him. He smelled very good. His body radiated greater heat than a furnace.

"After you," he said politely.

She nodded and hurried on through.

The long, dark oak medieval table had been taken from the side wall and set in the center of the great room. Chairs from all about had been dragged in, and the guests were gathering around the table.

Drew Parker, smiling a bit ruefully since he had accidentally started it all, was seated at the head of the long table. Abby was across from

124

him. Vera, charming and flirtatious, was next to Drew. Joe Penny was next to Abby, and Hugh Tanenbaum was to her right. With their backs toward the open doors to the patio, between the two "head" seats, sat Kelly, Serena, Doug, Andy Larkin, Jim Novac, and Hank Newton— the silver-haired, impossibly straight, baritone-voiced patriarch of *Valentine Valley*. On the other side were the various "techies."

"Hey, kids," Hank called deeply, indicating the empty seats on his side of the table. "Hey, Conar!" He rose, shaking Conar's hand. "Welcome! And thanks—you're going to raise all our ratings."

"Well, we'll see," Conar said. The scene was interrupted as others in the gathering, who hadn't seen Conar as yet, rose to greet him.

"Hey!" Andy protested then. "Conar knows we're all glad to have him. Hell, we paid him a fortune. Let's get back to this. The spirits are waiting."

With the commotion going on around her, Jennifer had lost sight of Abby. As people sat again, she looked at her mother. "Mom...," she began, feeling uneasy about the proceedings.

"It's fine, darling, do sit down."

"Such a scene was filmed here once, you know," Drew told them. "David Granger was a good fellow, but a wannabe in the worst way. He wanted to be a great director or an actor. He mostly wanted to be Houdini—the greatest magician ever. He rented out the house. That great séance scene from *Death in the Dark* was filmed with a company around this very table, just as we are now."

"How exciting," Vera said.

"Exciting," Drew said flatly. "Except that Celia Marston, the star of the film, died soon after visiting Granger and his wife."

"That's the allure," Vera said.

"That's the tragedy," Conar murmured.

Jennifer was surprised to realize he had his hand at the small of her back, the bulk of his body behind her. She was more surprised to feel a certain comfort in the fact as he courteously pulled out her chair. She didn't know if he was actually paying any attention to her at all. He didn't like the séance. He was still, in his mind's eye, looking at those pictures on Liam's desk.

"This is Hollywood," Drew said, "land of dreams—and the death of dreams."

"Technically," Doug said, "we're not in Hollywood."

"Oh, close enough," Vera said with exasperation.

"We're going for mood here, people," Jim Novac told them, grinning.

"Yes, Drew, what do we do now?" Hugh Tanenbaum asked. He winked across the table at Jennifer. The director was in his late forties and had been around as long as she could remember. He had worked with her mother years ago, and they had remained friends since. He was known as a money-maker because he did films on reasonable budgets that drew crowds at the box office.

126

It didn't matter what the decade—people liked to be scared.

"Really, let's do this. I'm starving," Jay Braden announced.

"All right, all join hands," Drew said. His hazel eyes sparkled. He lowered his silver head—after winking at Abby.

Jennifer joined hands with Conar and Hank. She looked down the table. Her mother was now watching her. She smiled in assurance as she joined hands with Joe Penny and Hugh Tanenbaum.

"Shall I turn out the lights, Mr. Parker?" Edgar asked from the doorway.

"Yes, please, Edgar, and see that the French doors are open to the pool area."

All of them fell silent as the lights went out. The French doors opened, seemingly on their own, since the darkness had hidden Edgar's trek across the room.

Jennifer didn't realize that she had tensed up until she felt both Conar and Hank ease their fingers from her death grips. They held her hands then rather than allow her to choke their bones once again.

"Celia Marston," Kelly said, "what happened to her? I know you can visit her grave. In fact, I think she's right near Marilyn."

"Marilyn?" Doug asked.

"Monroe," Thorne McKay supplied with exasperation.

"Hey, all of you," Andy Larkin said with aggravation, "this is a séance, not a coffee klatch."

"Yes, but how did she die?" Jim Novac asked.

"She fell, they say, down the cliffs at the back of the house," Hugh Tanenbaum provided.

"She did fall," Jennifer said, aggravated. "According to all the reports about the incident."

"Ah, but did she fall—or was she pushed?" Andy demanded with deep, husky dramatics.

"We'll never really know, will we? None of us was here," Conar said.

"Oh, but I was here," Drew announced.

"If we're going to chat all night, can I get a drink to bring to the table?" Jay Braden asked.

"Come, come, children, let's play nice or not at all," Jim Novac directed.

"So was she pushed, or did she fall?" Andy demanded.

"May I get a drink?" Jay asked again.

"Jay, we're supposed to keep holding hands," Serena reminded him.

"Celia Marston—did she fall, or was she pushed?" Jim Novac asked, repeating Andy's question.

"I don't know. I heard her scream, but nothing more," Drew said, his tone provocative. "And then there she was...at the bottom of the canyon."

"It had been a wild night, and everyone had been drinking, and God knows what else, and she certainly just fell," Conar said. His tone was curt. Silence fell around the table.

He was still seeing that other body at the base of the canyon.

"Well, we're having a séance, right?" Abby asked lightly, looking at Conar. She smiled, as if they shared a secret. "Drew will just summon Celia to the table, and we'll ask her."

"All right, concentrate now. Listen to the air, the world, feel the night around you," Drew directed. The room was no longer completely dark. The lights from the pool area spilled in, causing a deep cavern of shadows and forms. Outside, the moon rose high over the pool, where palms dipped and waved, the foliage whispered...

"Hold hands," Drew instructed.

"We're already holding hands," Serena reminded him.

"Close your eyes and concentrate. Celia...Celia Marston...," Drew intoned. "Years ago you left this very table where we are joined now. You were young, you were beautiful, you held the world in the palm of your hand. You left this house that night. And wandered...and plunged to your death. We've come to help you, Celia, to solve the mystery. Talk to us, Celia, let us know that you're with us..."

A wind suddenly ripped through the room. Something fell over with a thud; the curtains flew and fluttered.

A scream was heard from the other side of the table.

"What is it?" Jennifer cried, jumping up.

"Andy Larkin, get your hand off my thigh," Serena sputtered.

"Serena, I wasn't—"

"Oh, bull!" Serena announced.

"Hey!" Joe Penny protested. "This was going pretty well. What a great breeze! We should have had a camera going. Serena, hell, the two of you were married. What difference does it make if he slipped a little?"

Serena let out an aggravated groan. "Joe, you really don't understand what a wretched chauvinist you can be."

"Serena, sweetheart, darling—"

"I rest my point."

Conar stood, ready to turn on the lights.

Suddenly, there was another scream. They all froze. There was a figure in the center of the open French doors, a silhouette created in the light and shadow. Standing there, staring at them. As if on cue, lightning rent the sky.

A shadow, a form that didn't disappear.

So still, standing, staring, watching them, as if summoned from the depths of hell.

"The Grim Reaper!" Jay Braden whispered.

"My God!" Kelly breathed.

Lightning split the sky, but the shadow remained, dark and ominous, staring, watching, waiting...

There, dark and haunting, against the night sky.

"She's come back!" Vera whispered. "She's come back!"

"Who...who...?" Kelly began.

"Who has come back?" Serena whispered.

"Oh, my God!" Vera cried out, rising, her

hand flying to her throat. "Oh, God, oh, God! You have summoned the dead!"

"What the hell's going on?" a deep voice demanded.

The silhouette stepped forward.

Chapter 7

Drew Parker quickly rose to reach Vera as she slumped in her chair.

Conar swore—and reached for the lights. Brightness flooded the room.

"Is everyone all right? Just what the hell is going on here?"

The "ghost" was Liam Murphy, standing between the double doors that led to the patio. He was wearing a trench coat, Jennifer realized, which had given him the appearance of a floating, spectral visitor.

"Liam," Abby breathed.

She had remained calm and rational, not panicking like Vera, who was now back in a chair, flushed, her eyes opening, enjoying the attention of those who hovered around her. Kelly had gone for water, Drew was fanning her.

"I knocked at the front door, but no one seemed to hear me. So I came around and the gate was open...What the hell is going on?" he demanded.

"A séance," Serena explained, studying the newcomer.

"And who are you?" Jay asked.

Abby laughed softly. "Don't worry, he's not another actor."

"A cop," Andy suggested.

"This is Detective Murphy," Jennifer agreed.

"Lord," Hugh Tanenbaum exclaimed, "you haven't found another body, have you?"

Liam smiled. "No," he said softly.

Andy Larkin rose and walked over to him. "Well, how do you do, Detective? Andy Larkin, producer, actor, *Valentine Valley*. You sure do look the part. If you ever need extra work, we can always use a good cop on the show. Anyone want a drink?"

"Hell, yes!" Joe Penny announced.

En masse the company rose from the table, heading for the bar.

The food was delicious. Abby had done the menu, Edgar had done the ordering and the hiring of the help. There were elaborate vegetable plates for the vegans among them, sushi, delicate egg rolls, spiced chicken wings, turnovers, patties and pastries and fruit.

Jennifer freshened drinks for the company, hovering near her mother, who was holding court in one of the large leather wing-backed chairs in the den.

Hugh Tanenbaum was trying to get her to accept a role in his movie. "Just a cameo, Abby. You're so beautiful, so sensational."

"And so not up to it at the moment," Abby told him politely.

"You're as stubborn as your daughter," Hugh said.

Abby's eyes touched Jennifer's. "Hugh offered you a role?"

"Um," she murmured.

"The two of you in the same movie...You've never appeared together, have you?" Hugh asked.

"Hey," Joe Penny protested, "if Abby does any more acting, she does it for me."

"You're a soap, I'm a movie."

"You mean you're legitimate and I'm not?" Joe said sharply.

"I didn't say that at all. Movies are just easier. I can work around Abby far more easily if she isn't feeling well," Hugh said.

Andy Larkin sniffed in protest. "We'd do anything for Abby."

"You know, I have scriptwriters who can do anything," Hugh said.

Doug lifted his glass, clearing his throat. "Excuse me. They have a scriptwriter who can bring bodies back to life out of the bellies of sharks!"

The laughter that followed his statement eased the tension that had begun to grow.

"You know I admire your work," Joe told Hugh. "I sent my writer to study your moviemaking."

Hugh lifted a glass to Joe. "You all are the best soap out there."

"Hear, hear," Drew said and applauded.

"We're quite an admiration society," Jennifer murmured, filling Hugh's glass with ice. He wanted another Stoli on the rocks with double lime.

She looked up. Conar was across the room leaning against the mantel of the fireplace. He had been watching her, she realized.

Her...

And Abby.

"You make a fortune with your films," Joe Penny commented to Hugh. "You must be pleased."

Hugh shrugged, smiling at Abby. "Well, I pay the rent. But things just aren't the same anymore. Abby and I can remember when filmmakers were great, when actors *acted* rather than relying on special effects. The greatest filmmakers...created excitement, fear, suspense...from thin air."

"Special effects can create amazing films," Jennifer heard herself argue.

Joe nodded. "Yes, and there are great special-effect films out there. But look at the old *Haunting* with Julie Harris and Claire Bloom. Nothing happened. Nothing really. A few doors rattled. It was all atmosphere and psychological suspense. Spectacular. It's still a scary movie, a very scary movie."

"Fear is all in the mind," Conar said. "And there's nothing as frightening as what the mind can do, is that what you're saying?"

"Exactly," Joe agreed.

Across the room, Liam Murphy made something like a strangling sound. "There's real fear, too, ladies and gents," he said flatly.

"Of course," Conar said, walking across

the room. He set his glass down on the bar, barely noticing Jennifer there. "Real...and psychological. You, Hugh, and you, Joe. You're both obsessed with the films of Hitchcock."

"Obsessed is a rather strong word," Hugh protested.

"We admire him," Joe said, looking defensively to Hugh for agreement, as if the two, who had argued just minutes earlier, were now the best of friends.

"Hm. Well, the 'psychological' with, say, Hitchcock's famous shower scene," Conar continued, "is that the knife never touched Janet Leigh. We saw the knife, saw her face, saw the flashing blade, saw the shadow of the killer. But the result was the 'real.' She was stabbed to death."

"The point, of course, is that we don't really need all the gore."

"I agree. Hitchcock was a great filmmaker," Conar said. He stared at Joe Penny. "So why do we try to imitate him? We should move on to something new. Especially in a soap."

"Soaps should have suspense," Joe protested.

"Thank God I do movies," Hugh muttered. "And Abby, you've a part anytime. We'll rewrite anything for you. And Jennifer. And hell, maybe we could talk Conar into a role. Wouldn't that be the feat of the century?"

"Conar would never agree," Andy Larkin said.

Conar shrugged suddenly. "Who knows? If Abby and Jennifer were to agree..."

"A whole damned family affair," Drew Parker muttered.

"If you all will excuse me...," Abby announced. "I'm so delighted that you've all come, and I've had a wonderful time. But..."

Conar was instantly at her side.

"Let me help you, Mom," Jennifer said quickly, setting down her glass and walking around the bar. Conar already had her arm, Jennifer could see that her tremors were beginning to set in. Abby had waited a bit too long.

"Jennifer, stay with our guests. Conar will see me to my room."

She kissed Jennifer's cheek. Jennifer was loath to let her mother go.

"Good night, Mom."

"Good night, everyone. Once again, thank you all for coming."

Conar escorted her, and Abby swept out. She kept her chin high. She might have been walking down the aisle after the Academy Awards.

"Jennifer?" Hugh Tanenbaum said.

"What?"

"Your mother looks wonderful."

"Absolutely wonderful," Andy agreed ruefully.

"She doesn't want to work," Jennifer said firmly.

"She didn't say that," Joe told her.

"Hey, lay off," Serena butted in.

"Serena!" Andy said sternly.

"Abby is ill, and you are all fools if you don't see it," Serena persisted.

"Jennifer is here with her all the time; she's her daughter, and she knows what Abby is really thinking and feeling," Kelly said.

Andy started toward Jennifer, stopping right in front of her.

He smiled, crossing his arms over his chest. He was a solid man, tall and broad in the shoulders, and imposing when he chose to be.

"Maybe Jennifer is just a little jealous."

"What?" she demanded sharply.

"You are like a pit bull, keeping everyone away from Abby. Abby looked great tonight. Abby was really famous. Maybe you're just a little jealous, wanting to keep Abby out of the spotlight."

Jennifer felt her face flood with color. She didn't think that she had ever been so furious. She wanted to hit him. "Andy, you're an a—"

She didn't say the words that might have gotten her fired. Help came this time from an unlikely source.

"Andy, you can be an idiot," Conar said, striding casually back into the room. He had obviously heard the comment. To Jennifer's surprise, he came to her side. Smiling, he said, "My stepsister is surely one of the loveliest creatures to ever grace the earth. She adores Abby and wants to keep her from being tormented by money-hungry mongrels like you, Joe, and Hugh." His eyes remained on her for a second. "She has an assistant pit bull, now, you know."

Andy turned and walked away. "Maybe, just maybe, Abby wants to work," he said.

137

"I'd never keep Abby from working," Jennifer flared.

"Hey, we're keeping that horror movie in mind, right, Jen?" Conar said dryly.

"Oh, certainly. Right."

"Enough!" Vera announced suddenly. "This is Abby's house, Jennifer was kind enough to invite us. Mr. Parker, do tell us more about the legends regarding the house."

"Vera," Jennifer protested, "you passed out when you saw Liam in the window."

"I didn't exactly pass out," Vera protested.

"No," Hank said teasingly. "You *swooned.* Far more ladylike."

"Very Southern." Jay Braden laughed.

"Are we supposed to be Southern?" Kelly asked.

"Southern Italian, if anything," Hank assured her.

"I think my character was originally from the South," Vera said, fluffing up her hair. She winked at Jennifer and smiled. Jennifer smiled back. Vera could act like an airhead, but mostly it was an act. Vera had been drawing the fire away from her.

"What else happened in the house?" Vera persisted.

"There was the magician in the box," Doug said.

"I even heard that story," Thorne announced. "He was supposed to escape—like Houdini. He wasn't in the box when they opened it the first time, certain that he couldn't make

138

it out on his own and that he'd suffocate if they didn't bring him out."

"Well, what happened?" Kelly asked.

"This is a great story," Hugh commented, sipping from his drink.

"A day later, the magician still hadn't shown up. It was as if he disappeared into thin air," Drew said.

"Where was he?" Serena asked. She grimaced to Jennifer—drawn into the story although she hadn't wanted to be.

"Where he was when they couldn't find him, no one knows," Drew said. "Where he was when the police finally arrived was back in the box. Dead."

"Of asphyxiation?" Kelly breathed.

"Heart attack," Jennifer provided.

"But how—"

"No one knows," Drew said, his voice throaty and suggestive again. He was the perfect storyteller. "He disappeared, and reappeared, dead. That's all anyone knows."

"Oh, my God, no wonder the house is said to be haunted," Vera breathed.

"The house is not haunted," Jennifer protested. She was back behind the bar again. This time she put ice into her drink and squeezed a lime into it. Her head was spinning. Dumb. She was going to have one hell of a hangover. She prayed her words weren't slurring. Maybe the house was haunted. It seemed to be swaying and spinning a bit. Special effects in the wall, maybe. And the floor. It was dipping and weaving.

A few minutes later, Serena said she had to go. Jennifer walked out to the car with her and Kelly. "Well, life is interesting," Serena mused as she paused by her bright blue Mazda. "Conar Markham is...compelling."

"A hunk," Kelly supplied dryly at her side.

"Of course. Why else hire him?" Jennifer asked, trying to sound blithe.

"Why else?" Serena asked, smiling. "Well, I am glad he's joined the cast. He will improve our ratings. He has...a chemistry that kind of jumps out at you."

"Animal magnetism," Kelly supplied.

"He's just a charmer," Jennifer agreed, clenching her teeth.

Serena, studying her, laughed. "Okay, fine, don't like him. But I do. You don't mind that, do you, Jen? I mean, I understand about your mom and all, even if those assholes working around us don't begin to get it."

"Go right ahead. You should like him," Jennifer said. "He, well, he doesn't spend a lot of time in front of a mirror. Not that I know of, at any rate."

"Too much raw animal in him," Kelly teased.

"And you were telling me you're afraid of that biological clock ticking," Jennifer murmured. "He's perfect, you're perfect...It would all be..."

"Just perfect," Kelly said, supplying an ending once again.

"Hey, guys, I just meant that I'd like Jennifer's permission to be friends with the fellow, that's all," Serena said.

"Serena," Jennifer said uncomfortably, "you don't need my permission to be friends with him. You're making me feel awful."

"I didn't mean to do that. I'm sorry—I just phrased it all badly," Serena protested. "It's just that...well, I am *your* friend first."

"We're just like the three Musketeers, 'all for one, and one for all'!" Kelly said, her eyes alight, laughing. "But, Jen, it would be kind of sad to waste a studly hunk like that."

"Oh, God, don't waste the hunk," Jennifer said, shaking her head.

"But if you feel—" Serena began.

"I'm serious. He's trying to be decent—I think," Jennifer murmured. "Get in your cars, go home, you all have my blessing to fraternize with the enemy."

'That's the point. I don't want to fraternize with your enemy," Serena said.

"Tick-tock, tick-tock, tick-tock, go away, biological clock!"

At the sound of Doug's voice, all three of them spun around. He grinned, walking in among them, taking a seat on Serena's car. "No, don't panic. I'm the only one who happened in on this girl talk. Wonder Boy hasn't heard a word. The studly hunk is inside, talking in a studly manner, with the studly cop."

"Doug, it's really rude to join in uninvited on the conversations of others," Jennifer informed him.

"I'm just trying to save a few friendships here, so I'm going to insist on honesty. Jennifer, you don't care if Serena makes a play for the new

141

hero, even though he has come to usurp your position in life and the world, and you're doing your best to be dignified and civil."

"Doug, you're being overdramatic. You'll never write the great American novel that way."

"Ouch, that hurts."

"I never asked anyone to be rude or nasty to Conar."

"Serena, feel free to sleep with him."

"Hey, I didn't say I wanted to make a play for him, or sleep with him, or—"

"Jennifer, you said that someone should sleep with him, didn't you?"

"Doug, go home."

"I'm staying here."

"Not if you don't behave."

"I'm wounded. I came to protect her from the evil machinations of the stud muffin, and she stabs me in the heart."

Jennifer gave him a sniff and waved a hand in the air, "Johnny Walker, I think."

He sniffed back. "Vodka."

"Don't go sniffing me. I had one drink hours ago, and went to soda and lime and coffee. Go to bed, both of you," Serena said.

"Good night," Kelly said.

Motors seemed to be humming all over the grounds. Others were leaving. Jennifer said and waved good night in all directions.

Doug gave her a kiss on the cheek as they neared the house. "Good night, Jen. And hey, thanks so much for having me. I'm really enjoying the weekend."

"You're going to bed?"

"Before I pass out."

"But..."

He didn't seem to hear her. He started up the stairs. Then he paused, turning back. "Hey, Jen."

"Yes?"

"You know, we have some pretty special friendships on that set. You and Serena and Kelly and me...and a few more, of course."

"Of course."

"So make sure you mean what you say."

"Look, I'm really trying to be nice and knock the chip off my shoulder and—"

"I believe you. I just think there's more. Chemistry, you know."

"I don't know what you're talking about."

"You drank too much tonight."

"*You* drank too much tonight."

Doug grinned. "Night, sweetie."

She shook her head, starting back toward the den, then hesitating. She should just follow Doug upstairs, go to bed. Leave Conar to say good night to Liam and close the house down for the night.

She hesitated too long.

"Jennifer?"

Run up the stairs? Why? She wasn't afraid of the enemy within. She squared her shoulders and walked on into the den.

They'd been sitting in the wing-back chairs by the mantel, but both men had risen, knowing that she was coming. She didn't head toward them, but found herself veering for the bar. This wasn't going to do. She was only a social drinker, one or two at a party. Tonight, she had probably changed her blood levels.

She could just imagine the conversation she'd eventually have with him. *Could you leave, please? I really do love my mother, I'm trying to get through this, and you're turning me into an alcoholic.*

Ah, yes, he was already looking at her disapprovingly. *I didn't make you drink too much. Only you could make you drink too much,* he would say. Mr. Perfect. Always right.

She poured herself a drink, ignoring them both for a moment. Then she smiled radiantly at Liam. "I'm so glad you came to the party tonight. Did you enjoy yourself? We're an eccentric crowd, certainly."

Conar approached the bar and took the glass from her hands after her first sip. She stared at him indignantly. "Don't patronize Liam. He's been around lots of movie and TV types before."

Her eyes widened. "I wasn't patronizing anyone, Conar, and I'd greatly appreciate it if you'd let me say what I like."

She was startled to see Liam had come to the bar, too, that they were both looking far too serious. "Detective Murphy, I meant no offense."

"I know you didn't." His smile was charming. He had a great, broad chest. She wished that she could throw herself against it. She'd definitely had a few too many because she was suddenly wondering if that would work. Telling

Conar that he could go away, she was going to start sleeping with a big brave cop and she'd be fine.

Color rushed her cheeks with the thought. She didn't know if the cop was married, engaged, or what. She gave herself a shake. She'd been taking care of Abby too long.

"I feel a little edgy here, like a cornered rat," she murmured.

"We were just talking," Liam told her.

She reached for her glass, feeling their scrutiny. Was there a large dirt smudge on her face? Spinach in her teeth—no, they'd had no spinach. And she hadn't eaten.

Conar's hands were firm on her glass. "Jen, enough."

"Detective Murphy, could you inform Mr. Markham for me that it's a free society, I'm in my home, I'm over twenty-one—"

"Liam was just telling me something I thought you should know," Conar said.

"What?" she asked uneasily.

"You know what Luminal is?" Liam asked.

She frowned. "Yes, I think so. The police spray it to show traces of blood that can't be seen with the naked eye."

"That's it," Conar told her.

"We sprayed around Brenda's home this evening, trying to trace the exact movements of the killer. The house had appeared to be in perfect order, but..."

"She was definitely killed in the shower, Jen. Stabbed to death in her own shower," Conar supplied.

She suddenly wanted to escape them both. "I'm so, so very sorry about Brenda!" she whispered. "But what does it have to do with—"

"Shades of Hitchcock, Jennifer," Conar persisted, staring at her. "Who are the sort of people who would try to imitate Hitchcock?"

She felt a strange shivering of fear again, deep down inside. She recoiled from it, and she was furious with both of them.

"Just let us watch over you, huh?" Liam asked softly, meeting her eyes. "I've got to go; early morning," he said. "Good night, Jennifer. Thank you. It was a great party."

"I'll walk you out," Conar said.

They left the den and went outside. Jennifer hesitated, then hurried out herself. She wanted to get up the stairs and into bed before Conar returned.

Almost to the top of the stairs, she missed her step. She didn't exactly tumble down the stairs. She slid. She landed at his feet. Her cheeks turned the shade of a cardinal's robe. He reached down, helping her up, and managing to somehow pin her to the wall as he did so. He was tall. Whipcord hard. Chemistry. She didn't want to feel it, she had denied it for years...

"You're drunk. I'll help you."

"I'm not drunk. Anyone can tell you that I barely drink at all."

"You've been making up for it tonight."

"Well, you and a cop keep trying to tell me that someone is going to kill me."

"I never said that."

His face was close to hers, his eyes... The color was like steel, sharp, probing. His body was hot, nearly touching hers. He had a handsome face, well formed, and yet rugged. She found herself fascinated with the texture of his cheeks. His scent, at this close range, was intoxicating.

Chemistry...

He did have it. Yes, definitely...

"You and Liam are badgering me."

"Because you don't listen."

"What am I not—"

"Let me look after you."

"I'm not stopping you."

"You've quite bluntly told me you resent my being here."

"Look, I..." All she could picture was Kelly, laughing, telling her and Serena that he was a *studly* hunk. She started to smile.

"What?"

"Nothing."

"Jennifer, you've got to quit arguing with me all the time just for the sake of argument."

She was suddenly certain that she could *feel* the alcohol running around in her veins. It was as if she were on fire. Was it the alcohol, or was it...

Him. She could feel it in places she didn't even remember.

She kept smiling.

"Jennifer—"

"I'm not fighting with you," she said, trying to sound very sober.

"But when the holiday weekend is over, you're going to try to run off to work without me. Leave the building before me..." He looked at her more closely. "What is the matter with you?"

"I...I really need to go to bed."

He stared at her a moment longer, then swept her up into his arms. She issued a short protest, then closed her eyes.

The world was spinning.

She opened her eyes again, realizing that she had clutched him. He smelled wonderfully of aftershave and masculinity. She closed her eyes again, letting her head fall to his chest.

"Please, Jennifer, for real, don't fight me on this."

She looked up at him, knowing that she was smiling ridiculously, but unable to stop herself. "Fight a studly hunk like you, Conar? I wouldn't dream of it."

"A studly hunk?"

"I didn't make up the phrase. The other girls did."

"The other girls?"

"Kelly, I think. Maybe Serena."

"At least someone appreciates me."

"They don't know you."

"Oh? And you do?"

"They don't live with you."

"Neither do you. Not really. I mean, not enough to know if I leave the toilet seat up, run around the house scratching my groin, or insist on total possession of the remote control."

Her smile deepened. He was moving along

up the stairs, nearing her room. Her head was spinning very badly, and she groaned. "I couldn't fight you if I wanted to. I don't think that I could walk up the stairs."

"Don't you dare be sick on me."

"I'm not going to be sick."

"Such an exquisite beauty would never be sick."

"Are you making fun of me?"

"Never. The words are Liam's, not mine."

"Oh," she murmured, silent for a minute. "Conar?"

"What?"

"I am going to be sick."

He swore and moved faster, pushing her door open with a foot, propelling her toward the bathroom. She wavered on her feet, then steadied. He meant to hold her, but that would be far too much humiliation.

"Let me help you. You'll crack your head wide open."

"No."

She managed to push him back out of the bathroom. Her stomach rumbled, and she made it neatly to the toilet.

Amazingly, she felt better. Much, much better. She drenched her face in cold water again and again. Rinsed out her mouth, brushed her teeth.

"Jennifer!"

He was tapping on the door.

She leaned against it. "I'm all right, Conar. I...thank you," she said primly. "Thank you very much. I'm going to take a shower now."

She leaned against the door another moment, humiliated, breathing deeply. She felt better— but still horrible. Maybe a shower would help.

She stripped down, stepped beneath the water. She needed to take something for her headache. Maybe that would help the hangover she was bound to suffer in the morning. She shook her head beneath the spray. She hadn't done anything so wretched since she'd been eighteen.

Finally, she turned off the water and stepped carefully from the shower stall—very precise with her every movement. Hair and body wrapped in two towels, she leaned against the door again to steady herself, then stepped out.

She stopped short.

Conar was standing by the window, looking out on the patio and the cliffs to the canyon below.

"Conar, is there something..."

"No," he said, turning toward her.

"Then, um, why are you still here?"

He lowered his dark head for a moment, and she saw the small smile that curved his lips. He looked at her again. "If I heard you fall in the shower, I intended to rush in before you could drown."

"I'm all right."

He nodded, still watching her. Then he walked over to her. She was surprised by the way her heart started to thud as he did so. Blood seemed to curl and boil within her. She hated herself. She was aroused, just watching him walk, wanting to feel his hands...everywhere. She was tempted to drop the towel, curl against him. Chemistry. Too much to drink. Too much time alone, no life except the working and the worrying...

He put his hands on her bare shoulders. Her flesh burned. Great hands. Very large. Long fingers. Her eyes dropped to them. He lifted her chin. His eyes were steady and serious. "Let me be in on this, all right? I don't want to take anything away. I just want to help."

She couldn't breathe. Her heart was pounding way too hard. Could he hear it? How embarrassing.

"Is your head clear enough? Can you understand me?"

"I need an aspirin."

He left her standing there, and walked into the bathroom. She was simply too undressed. She raced to her bed, wrenched her nightshirt from beneath the pillows. It wasn't what she'd had in mind for such an occasion. It was soft cotton with a little Tweety Bird on the right shoulder. With the speed of light, she slipped it over her head anyway, shimmying from the towel that had been wrapped around her body. The towel fell from her hair as well. She reached for it—cracking her head on the nightstand.

"Shit!" she swore softly.

Conar was instantly back, helping her stand, eyes anxious. "You all right?"

She nodded. No, she wasn't. Now her head really hurt.

He lifted her again anyway, set her on the bed, against the pillows she'd cast into disarray to get the nightshirt. He sat by her side on the bed. "Hang on; I dropped the aspirin."

"I'm all right; really."

"You're getting there."

"Conar, this is just too...I mean, Abby is worried, the police are worried, I think Abby is...seeing things. So you become my bodyguard, work with me, follow me, haunt me, live with me, sleep with me—"

She broke off. Where the hell had those words come from?

"Sleep with you?" His brow arched, the curl about his lips deepened. "Was that an invitation?"

"No...I...I..."

He leaned forward, kissed her forehead. He seemed all chest and shoulders and masculine scent. "I never said anything about sleeping with you."

He straightened, laughing, and walked to the door.

The door opened and closed.

She felt like an idiot.

Jennifer leapt up and raced to her door, threw it open. "It was *not* an invitation!"

She heard his amused laughter echo softly from down the hall, but then he turned back to her.

"Lock your door, Jennifer. Get in, and lock your door."

"Against you?"

"Against anyone walking in the night."

He turned toward his own room again.

And strangely, standing in the hall in her Tweety nightshirt, she suddenly felt a deep chill.

As if...

She were being watched.

As if there were eyes in the shadows of Granger House.

As he had suggested, she turned quickly, slipped into her room, closed the door, and locked it.

She leaned against it. The chills faded.

A sense of humiliation swept in again.

She swore quietly and ran across the room, burying herself into the soft safety of her bed.

Chapter 8

He had seen dead bodies before. In diving on search and rescue missions he had seen his share of death.

But he had never seen anything like the corpse of Brenda Lopez.

Slash marks marred nearly every part of her body. Blood had pooled beneath the skin. Dirt had found its way into the cuts. And yet her face had not been touched by the knife. Being thrown down to the canyon had done some damage to her once perfect features. But the knife had never touched her face.

She invaded his dreams. She haunted him in a nightmare realm of his sleep. He wanted to waken, but couldn't. He just kept seeing her, picture after picture after picture.

"Her eyes were open when she was found," Liam had told him when he realized Conar was looking at the photos. "She fought him," he went on. "See the slashes on the hand, on the arm? She saw him. She tried to fight him off."

She had seen him, her eyes had been open...

In the night, as he slept, Conar saw it all, too. A figure of darkness stalking, approaching the plastic curtain. And Brenda, seeing her attacker.

Yet it wasn't Brenda.

It was Jennifer. Reddish hair falling wet against her neck and shoulders. He could hear the almost incredible hum of water. Jennifer's eyes were on his.

Huge, blue...

Conar...

She whispered his name, pleading...

Help me...

He awoke with a start, shaking.

The room was pitch dark.

He had never been afraid of the dark, even as a child. The drapes in David Granger's old room were thick and heavy, and they blocked out all light. He lifted his wrist to his face and stared at the dial of his luminous wristwatch.

Five a.m. Not quite morning. Still, he rose, restless, ill at ease. He took the terry robe from the foot of his bed and slipped into it, walked over to draw back the drapes to the windows

154

that looked out on the rear of the house, the pool and patio, and the cliff.

The morning was still dark outside, but pink streaks were beginning to break through. Staring out the window, he experienced the strangest feeling. Hackles rising. Something teasing his spine.

He spun around.

Nothing. No flurry of movement, nothing.

Just the *feeling*...

He walked across the room and turned on the large overhead light. Nothing.

It was a great room. David Granger's vision and imagination were evident in the decor. There was a huge, carved four-poster bed with Viking motifs and symbols. A large desk with clawed feet, a bureau, and even a swivel mirror with handsome carving on the legs had the same design. Chairs and a love seat were arranged before a fireplace with a stone mantel, and there were doors to the closet and dressing room and bath.

Feeling a bit foolish, he walked to the closet, opened it, walked in. His clothing was neatly arranged on the hangers, shoes on the floor. He closed the closet door and opened the door to the bath and dressing room. The latter was a long mirrored hallway with a chair and a stool and extra towel or clothing racks. The bathroom was elaborate, with marble and a huge whirlpool bath in the center, his-and-her johns in separate closed rooms, separate shower stalls, and a massive double sink. It was a very masculine room in all, yet one that invited feminine companionship. Granger had been married, so his wife must have been a tolerant soul.

The bath was empty, as the closet had been.

He turned off the lights, closed the doors, and returned to the bedroom.

He sat at the desk, looking at the journal that was open there. He had taken to keeping a journal years ago, after he had first started diving. Marking down dive sites, times, and conditions for underwater and counting time had been a curiously rewarding activity. He had written experiences during his time in the military, and taken to jotting down thoughts or notes that might be used at a later date.

He thumbed through the last year.

"Abby called today. She isn't at all well. Wants me to take a job on her daughter's soap. Thinks there's a plot. A plot? In a soap. Is Abby mad? She doesn't seem to realize her daughter is a porcupine, a snotty little brat, no, an out-and-out little anorexic bitch. Too tall, too thin, too much red in her hair. And a forked tongue."

He flipped forward.

"Abby sounding panicky. Is she losing her mind? I hate California, but sure do love Abby. But dragon-child is there."

Was Abby losing her mind? She had no real evidence for the things she said. She admitted she had delusions, but stuck to this story.

He flipped through more pages of his journal.

A few days later.

"Going to California. Will get muzzle for dragon-child."

He flipped to that day's date. "Okay so dragon-child is pretty good-looking. I've always known she was beautiful. And now that I've actually seen her up close and personal in a towel, she isn't at all anorexic. Actually, it's a hell of a shape..."

He laid the pencil down.

Picked it back up.

"Testosterone raging. She is still a dragon. As prickly as a porcupine. But hell, I'd like to get past those quills..."

Lust. What a pathetic male instinct.

He set the pencil down again. "Ass!" he told himself out loud. "She got sick. How sexy!" Yeah, right, like that did anything to dampen the way she looked wet, and in a towel...

He started writing again. "She's still a dragon-child. We're going to fight over the operation; Abby is desperate to have it. She wants quality in her life, not this nightmare of not being able to breathe, to swallow, fearing that she'll drool in front of people, that she'll shake in pain and humiliation forever and ever. Jennifer must see this. She does love her mother. Her eyes are very beautiful when they touch Abby. Her voice is soft and tender. She can be exquisite. And then flippant, and rude and..."

He dropped the pencil, swore, then picked up the pencil again.

"On other matters—Molly should be arriving any day now with Ripper. Abby says we can

157

try keeping him in the house, I told her we didn't have to, Ripper can just get used to the kennel the same as Lady. I don't want Jennifer having more fuel against me. Don't want to aggravate her when I don't have to, though honestly, sometimes I want to knock the chip off her shoulder. Then there are those moments when I'd like to reach out and feel the lines of her face..."

He threw the pencil down this time, as if it were suddenly in flames. He gritted his teeth. He slammed the book back into the top drawer of the desk. He rose, flicked off the overhead light, and lay back down. No good.

He swore again, headed into the shower, and turned the spray on cold.

The shock of it had pretty much the desired effect. He closed his eyes, stood under the spray, and let it cascade over him. At length, he turned it to warm and lifted his face.

He turned off the water, toweled dry.

It was still five-thirty. He was exhausted, and he was going to be a bear himself if he didn't get some sleep. He lay down on the bed.

There was light in the room. He had forgotten the drapes. Pink illumination seeped in.

Close the drapes...

He'd have to get up to do that. If he got up again, he wasn't getting back down.

He dozed, and had the nightmare again; he knew it, he struggled to free himself from it, knowing worse was coming.

He awoke with a start, bolting up. He looked at his watch. After six.

158

Might as well get some coffee. Hell, coffee had to be an improvement over the way he felt right now.

Aspirin might have helped. Sure, her headache might have been worse. She could have felt as if her head were actually going to explode rather than just pound out a merciless jungle beat all day.

Abby liked to go to church. She liked to attend the ten o'clock mass, and Jennifer always made sure that she took her. Edgar usually drove them; she usually sat in the back with Abby, watching her anxiously. Theirs was a neighborhood church where the parishioners were accustomed to the rich and famous, and the infamous, and their privacy was maintained.

That morning Doug attended with them. He was cheerful, as was Abby. The two kept up a pleasant conversation. Conar drove. He was as adept and assured with Abby's Lexus as Edgar had ever been.

He looked exceptionally good as well. Clean, lean, sleek in black slacks, black knit shirt, and beige jacket. His dark hair was freshly washed, combed back. He had a great tan. How had he achieved that in New York?

He was wearing dark glasses, so she couldn't read his eyes. But looking at him, at least he didn't seem as if he were laughing at her. Which he might have been after last night. Actually, he seemed far too grave.

159

Church was uneventful. Abby seemed to be having a good day. She was shaking but almost imperceptibly. When they left, she suggested donuts. Delighted to hear her mother excited about the prospect of food, Jennifer quickly agreed.

They talked about the party, and Doug told them earnestly, "The house is haunted. I can feel it."

"Doug Henson!" Abby protested. "Don't you go spreading rumors about my beautiful house."

"Oh, Abby, I love your house. You know that. And I'm so grateful to be a guest in it." Doug squeezed Abby's hand. "And thank the good Lord for holiday weekends. I have another night in the house. That is, if you're not shipping me out?"

"Not if you promise not to start rumors," Abby said.

"I won't start any rumors. But it creaks at night. And you can hear things…"

"Things?" Jennifer said, a little too sharply.

"Ghostly footsteps, moving along the hallways." He waved a hand. "Movement in the air. I locked my door, I can tell you."

Conar set down his coffee, staring at Doug through the dark lenses of his glasses.

"If ghosts are tramping the hallways, why would they pause for a locked door?"

"I don't know," Doug said with a shrug. He grinned. "Hey, any little hindrance."

"Oh, Conar," Abby said suddenly, "your friend Molly called this morning. She expects to be in by this afternoon. Lovely girl. We chatted, and she was vague about her plans, so I insisted she stay for the night, at the least."

Molly? Who the hell was Molly? Her mother's house was becoming Grand Central Station.

"Well, that's great," Conar said. He rose. "Shall we head on back?"

Jennifer glanced quickly at her mother. Her physical condition had deteriorated as they sat there. The donut shop was filling up. It was time to go.

In the car, Doug sat by Abby, holding her hand, telling her jokes, making her laugh. In front with Conar, Jennifer felt a swell of resentment growing within her. She tried to be rational. She loved her mother. Conar made Abby happy. And if this Molly person made Conar happy, then it should all just be fine.

When they reached the house, Edgar told Jennifer there had been a call for her from Serena. She quickly called back. "What's up with you for the day?" Serena asked. "I'm feeling like a large, lumpy couch potato."

"I feel as if my entire body is a headache. I'm going to lie out by the pool. Keep Lady company. I feel so guilty that she has to live outside."

"She has an air-conditioned sun porch and a huge piece of property," Serena reminded her. "Edgar cooks choice meat for the dog. She is not suffering."

"Oh, I know. But some days, when we have long hours, I barely see her."

161

"Abby was saying that she goes out with her frequently. That as long as she's outside with the dog, the hair doesn't bother her."

"That's true. But still..."

"Want company to sit around with your dog?"

Jennifer was surprised to realize that she hesitated—just a second. Serena in a bathing suit. She was just a shade jealous. She'd never been jealous before. Serena and Kelly were her best friends. What was the matter with her? Her face was burning. She hated herself.

"Jennifer—"

"Sure," she said quickly, "it would be great if you wanted to come over."

"Think that cop will come hang around?"

"Liam?"

"Um."

"I...I don't know. I'll suggest to Conar that he invite him."

"Maybe I can get Kelly to come, too. Oh, do you think it will all be okay, with your mom and all?"

"I think so. The company last night seemed to make her very happy." The company *had* made Abby very happy. Had she been overprotective? No, she hadn't wanted her mother's picture on every rag in Hollywood, with the reporters talking about the terrible decline of such a stupendous actress.

"We'll see you soon."

She had called on the extension in her room. She hung up, changed into a swimsuit and cover-up, and headed back to the den.

Abby was there, with Edgar at her side, helping her with the pills from the silver tray he carried. "There you are, sweetheart. I'm going down for a nap," Abby told her.

"Okay, Mother. Serena and Kelly are coming by to swim. Is that all right?"

"That's lovely. If I can sleep, I can actually spend some time with you all later."

"I'll walk you on down."

"No, no, I'm fine. You go see to that big, beautiful monster of yours."

Abby looked very frail suddenly. She was shaking as she rose, kissed her daughter's cheek, and started down the hall. Jennifer longed to go after her, but she refrained. Abby needed some independence, and some dignity.

"Edgar," she said at last, realizing they were both staring after Abby. "I was thinking maybe we could barbecue by the pool."

"I'll get right on it, Miss Jennifer."

"Thank you, Edgar."

"How many people are you expecting?"

"Just two."

"I'll plan for at least ten," Edgar said, and left her.

She exited to the pool through the French doors. Walking out to one of the lawn chairs, she saw that the pool was already occupied. Conar was swimming laps, cutting sleekly across the forty-foot length of the pool. Lady was nearby, paws crossed, as she lay by his lawn chair, waiting.

There were books on the patio table by his

chair. Sitting on the next lounge, she picked up the top book, the one he had been reading. *Hollywood Murders*. She began flipping through it. It started with the murder trial of the famed comedian Fatty Arbuckle. It included suicides, bizarre deaths, and more. She frowned, studying the case of a man name Albert Frecky. Turned down for one role too many, he began murdering young actors who were selected for the work he had coveted. Each murder had been different—the actor chosen for a Houdini movie had been sawed in half in a box; the man chosen to star in a sea movie had been drowned. In all, he had killed five of his competitors before being discovered by police.

Water dripped on her arm. She looked up, startled. Conar towered above her.

He wore boxer trunks to swim, but the bared part of his body was muscled, lean, and sensual. She felt a fluttering that caused her to grit her teeth.

"Cheery reading material."

"Interesting," he returned, reaching for his towel and stretching in his chair.

Lady made a whimpering sound and headed up toward them. Jennifer went to reach for her dog. The huge creature set her face on Conar's knee. He absently scratched her head.

"Why are you reading this? It's grisly."

"I found it in Abby's library. It looked interesting."

"Conar, Brenda's murder was an isolated incident. Maybe—"

164

"I thought that this case was interesting. This jealous fellow who killed his competition."

"You think Brenda was murdered because she was competition for someone? My God, Hollywood is all competition."

"I don't know. It just interested me."

"I wish you would find something more pleasant to read." She turned away from him, adjusting her sunglasses.

Out of the corner of her eye she saw Lady nudge Conar's knee, wanting more attention. He patted and stroked her long head, then looked up.

"Oh, that reminds me. Molly is bringing Ripper."

"Ripper?" she queried.

"She's a good friend."

"From New York, I take it."

He nodded gravely. "She was driving out the week before I left. She's a dancer and an actress, a good one. God, you should see her dance! And her voice. She's a nightingale. Anyway, she's doing a show in L.A., and she was driving, and I was tying up loose ends...so she has Ripper."

"You have a dog. *Ripper*. And you're bringing it here."

"Him." He slid his glasses back on and leaned back.

"My mother is allergic to dogs."

"She manages with Lady. We'll work it out with Ripper. She knows all about it."

"I don't see how you can do this! Bring another *dog* to my mother's. That's so presumptuous. And what kind of name is *Ripper*? What is he, a rottweiler? A German shepherd? If your Ripper so much as pulls a hair out of Lady's body—"

He pulled his glasses off, staring at her. For a moment she felt a chill. "Ripper belonged to my wife, Jennifer. She loved him. I will never get rid of him, got that? Your mother understands. In fact, she's anxious to meet him."

She felt the steamy heat of resentment rising in her again. How could she feel so angry and so...attracted—

Aroused! All in one.

Oh, God.

She strode quickly to the pool, shaking, yet managed to execute a perfect dive into the eight-foot deep end. She swam the length beneath the surface and rose at the far end of the pool. The water was cool; the days were growing cooler. She swam to the other end, swam again. This time she swam right into Conar. "Sorry, I thought you were done with your laps."

She had touched him. The fluttering was going on again. Hot, acutely uncomfortable, deep inside her...

"You are jealous, you know."

"Over your dog? I just think it's rude, presumptuous, and discourteous."

"You're jealous over me."

"You have a movie star mentality, Mr. Markham. You think you have to beat would-be lovers off with a stick. Well, you're mistaken.

We're not all ready to throw ourselves naked at your feet."

"No?"

He grinned. She turned and used the wall to shoot away from him. She was a fast swimmer.

He passed her in an instant. He was waiting at the far wall when she arrived.

"Do you know what I think?" Keen gray eyes surveyed her pointedly. Reflections from the water made his eyes glitter.

"Do I care what you think?" she countered.

"Yeah, I think you do."

She turned, kicking away from the wall again.

Once more he was at the other end, waiting. She plowed into him, fingers scraping his chest and belly, feeling the ripple of muscle, the heat of flesh.

He grinned, catching her hands, drawing her to him before she could shoot away again. His grip was strong, his breath was hot, his whisper husky. "I think you're just about desperate. I don't think it's my ego—hell, I don't think it's even me. I'm male and heterosexual and suddenly in your life."

"Oh, fuck you, asshole," she told him, trying to free her hands, her face on fire. He didn't let her go. He caught her chin. She went still suddenly as he studied her eyes.

"I dare you," he teased. Then his mouth ground down on hers, his tongue parted her lips and filled her. She felt a shot of fire streak directly between her legs. From a kiss, she thought with panic. He was right; she was desperate...

She pushed against his chest, but somehow her hands lodged there. He was touching her as well. Fingers over her shoulders, teasing over the bra of her bathing suit, just slipping into the waist band of the pants. She could have crawled all over him. She didn't feel the sun or the water; she forgot where she was, time and place. His hand, his fingers, crept farther. Some sound mewled in her throat. She wanted to impale herself against him...

"Hey, there!"

She drew back like a bolt of lightning, horrified by the sound of Serena's voice. His fingers were tangled in her top, and it came away. She had to swim back for it, stand perfectly still against him as he laughed and tried to retrieve the situation. Her back was drawn to his front. She gritted her teeth, ready to cry with both outrage and frustration at the feel of his arousal against her.

"Oh, jeez," Serena began, halting in midstride. "I'm sorry if I interrupted something."

"No! You didn't!" Jennifer said quickly.

"We just got snagged here," Conar said. "There you go, Miss Connolly. You should probably double-knot that thing if you don't want accidents in the future."

Accidents?

She swam to the far end of the pool, leapt out, and gave Serena a quick hug. "Wow, you got here fast."

"Hey, you're getting me all wet," she said,

168

stepping back and slipping off the caftan she was wearing over a teal blue suit. "Kelly's right inside. She was ready to go, just waiting for someone to call with a plan for the day." She lowered her voice. "And the cop is inside, talking to Doug and Edgar. Thanks!"

Jennifer felt a twinge of guilt. She hadn't even thought to ask Conar about giving his friend a call. Fortuitously, he had arrived on his own.

"How's the water?" Serena called to Conar.

"Cool—but great. It's better in than out. And the sun is warm when it gets through the breeze," he called.

Serena dived in. A picture of grace and beauty as she swam toward Conar. Jennifer headed off to greet Kelly and Liam. She was not turning back.

She heard their laughter. She didn't turn. *Molly* was coming anyway.

Doug, Kelly, and Liam were talking in the den, near the doors.

"Hey, Kell," Jennifer said, greeting her friend with a quick hug. She walked quickly to Liam, offering him a hand and smiling when he pulled her closer, giving her a hug.

"Are you here on business?" she asked him quickly.

"He just came to hang out," Kelly offered.

Liam had been smiling, but he sobered. "I'm still on the Brenda Lopez case. We've already formed a task force. Six guys."

"No clue as to her killer?" Jennifer asked.

"Well, we've all kinds of information—but no real *clues*. Is Conar here?"

"Out back."

"We were just waiting for a tray of special purple margaritas Edgar is whipping up," Doug said.

"Oh," Jennifer murmured. She noticed Edgar behind the bar, getting ready to pour the drinks. She walked to the bar and realized that she was still dripping slightly from the pool. She had probably soaked Kelly and Liam. "I'll take the drinks. Thank you very much, Edgar."

She carried the tray out. The others followed her to the pool. Liam hadn't brought trunks, but he could borrow from Conar.

Joe Penny slept late. Hours past noon. He was awakened by the phone call. As he reached for it, he noticed the body lying next to him, dead asleep. It was that "starlet" who was trying to get a role on the soap, and slept with him to help cement the deal.

"Hello?"

"Hey, Joe, it's Hugh Tanenbaum."

"Oh, hi. You woke me up out of a deep sleep."

"Joe, what the hell are you doing sleeping?"

"What the hell are you doing bugging me?" Tanenbaum fell silent.

"I need help."

"With what?"

"I need a name. A draw."

"You've got money. Hire a name."

"I need a name that can act."

"So?"

"I want Jennifer."

Joe was so startled he didn't answer for a moment. "Connolly?"

"She's the only one you've got that I know of."

"Why Jen? She's a soap name."

"And she's done big-name television specials, movies, more."

"Call her agent."

"You can influence her."

"Hey, she's got a busy schedule, working for me, remember?"

"I'll film around your schedule. I...I'd met someone else I might have used, but..."

"But what?"

"I can't find her."

"Who?"

"Oh, just a bit player, but a pretty girl, bright...Jennifer would still be better."

"I'll talk to her, Hugh, but I can't make her do anything."

"Hey, I have a good reputation."

"Yeah, yeah, I know, you can make her a star."

"Well, hell, yeah, maybe I can. Talk to her for me, will you? I'm not having a great day. I need to get this movie wrapped up fast. And I need a long vacation."

"What's the matter with you?"

"Nothing. Maybe I'm drinking too much. I can't remember..."

"What? You can't remember what?"

"Nothing, nothing. Just help out if you

can, huh? Come on, remember how I gave a job to that girl when you asked?"

"Yeah, yeah, I remember."

"And she was damned good, right?"

"In your show?"

"No, buddy, in your bed. Don't you remember telling me she was the hottest piece of a—"

"Yeah, yeah, yeah."

"See what you can do. While I've got an ounce of sanity left, okay?"

"Sure."

Joe winced, and hung up. As he turned back to lie down, he saw the sleeping beauty beside him. Shit, all he wanted in the morning was to be left alone. He'd promised her he'd see about getting a part for her, hadn't he? Young women were always throwing themselves at him. He eyed the smooth curve of the starlet's shoulder. She'd been good, very good. But now, on the morning after, stuck with her in his bed, he only wished he could wake her up and throw her out the door.

That would be treating her like the trash she really was.

A while later, Hugh Tanenbaum "just happened" to stop by Granger House. He sat by the pool, sipping a purple margarita, trying to convince Jennifer once again that she should do his movie. Brenda had been scheduled to do a small but important cameo role, maybe Jennifer would be interested.

Hugh seemed so blasé. Damn. He had lost an actress. It was almost as if he had misplaced her. She felt a chill.

Edgar had steaks, chicken, lobster tails, and vegetables for the grill. Everyone seemed to be having a wonderful time. They ate. They drank, except for Jennifer. She kept sipping a soda rather than touch anything remotely alcoholic.

Drew Parker arrived—he also just happened to be in the neighborhood.

Abby came out in the later part of the afternoon, sat with Jennifer, Drew, and Hugh, and argued pleasantly about the amount of gore in the movies these days. Yet after a while Abby grew tired. As she spoke, Jennifer noticed her mother making an effort to swallow. The tremors were becoming more pronounced.

Jennifer rose anxiously.

"You see, I'm tiring right now, and thank God that I'm blessed with my daughter who knows my every move." She smiled at Jennifer.

"I'll come in with you, Mom," she said.

"Walk me down the hall, dear. That will be nice."

Jennifer walked her in. They went down the hall and into her mother's room.

"Mother, you know, I'm so sorry, all this seems to be so much for you. I tried to keep people away for the longest time, and I seemed to do so well, and now—"

"Jennifer, I'm enjoying the company. My darling, I'm uncomfortable at times, but I'm not dead yet."

"Mother!"

"And I want you to have a social life."

"I have a social life."

"Okay, a love life."

"I'm young. I have plenty of time for a love life."

"Well, sex, at the least. God knows, I'm much older than you and I miss it like crazy. And it would improve your disposition. You wouldn't be so cranky."

"I'm not cranky."

"Frustrated."

"Mother, really, I don't want to have sex just to have sex. It should have meaning,"

"Well, in most cases I would agree," Abby told her, smiling. "But not for you. You just need some good sex."

"Mother!"

"I would dearly love grandchildren."

"Well, maybe we can hire a few from Central Casting, Mom," Jennifer said, aggravated. "Mom, I'm not in love, I'm not dating, and you'll have your grandchildren. You were several years older than I am now when I was born, so please, give me a few years here, eh?"

"Doug is so handsome and so charming and just a sweetheart. I love him dearly."

"Mother, Doug..."

"Yes, dear, I know. He's of a different persuasion. It's a pity, though, you do like each other so much, and I'd have gorgeous grandchildren if the two of you got together."

"Maybe he'd sell me some 'good-looking

grandchildren sperm,' Mother," Jennifer said, embarrassed, unable to believe she was having this conversation with her mother.

"Not a bad idea," Abby said, lying down and grinning up at Jennifer. "Except you'd still be frustrated and cranky."

"Mom, please."

Abby laughed. "How on earth did I raise such a straight-laced young woman? No matter, I'm very proud of you."

"Thanks," Jennifer said.

Her mother caught her hand. "I waited, yes, and had just one child. But what a child I had. I don't want anything, Jen, except for you to be happy."

Jennifer leaned over and kissed her mother's forehead. "I love you."

"If I can get better, though, I do intend to have sex again. Lots of it. With that nice Mr. Vic Tyler."

"Mother, Vic Tyler is in worse shape than you are."

"He would not appreciate you making such an observation. But he's going to be better. He is going to have that surgery."

"That will kill him," Jennifer said softly, a lump in her throat.

Abby closed her eyes. "Go back to the party, dear."

"Mother—"

"I can't talk any more right now, please."

Was that the truth? Or did she just want to avoid the argument? Jennifer hesitated, gnawing her lip. Her mother's eyes remained closed. She kissed her forehead again, then tip-toed out of the room. As she returned to poolside, she realized she hadn't had a chance to talk with her mother about the fact that *Molly* was coming.

With *Ripper.*

Ripper. The dog was probably a man-eating mastiff. A macho dog, for sure.

Liam was in the pool with Kelly and Serena. Conar was sitting with Hugh, and Jennifer took a chaise lounge near them. Near enough to over-hear their conversation. They were talking about Brenda Lopez.

"She slept with a lot of people," Hugh was saying. "In fact, Conar, I heard you had a rela-tionship with her yourself."

"I knew her. She'd been friends with my wife. We were friends."

"It's my understanding that you had an affair with her about a year ago."

"An affair? No, not really." Conar sounded uncomfortable. "She came to New York about a year ago, yes. We spent an evening together, we slept together. Then she came back to California. It wasn't an affair—" He glanced over, and saw that Jennifer had heard him.

"So it was a one-night stand," Hugh said.

"Look, it was just something that hap-pened. I don't really want to talk about it."

Jennifer was so disturbed, she almost jumped when she heard a voice in her ear.

"It's getting cold," Serena murmured. She'd gotten out and wrapped up in a towel.

A breeze had suddenly picked up, Jennifer noticed. Kelly grimaced as she came out, too. She turned toward the canyon and shivered. "I'm going in," she said softly.

"I'm right behind you," Serena told her.

"Well, I guess I'd best go in and entertain as the live-in house guest," Doug said.

One by one, the others began to follow. Jennifer followed, still upset by learning that Conar and Brenda Lopez had been intimate.

Inside, Edgar had made coffee, and she ran upstairs, slipped out of her suit and into a short knit dress. When she came back downstairs, it looked like grade school—Serena and Kelly were hunched together in chairs by the mantel, and the men had taken coffee cups or brandy snifters to the sofa and wingback chairs in the center of the room. That was just fine with her. She didn't want to have to talk to Conar right now.

They chatted awhile, and then Kelly said:

"Serena, we should get going. It's getting dark, and your night vision isn't great."

"Excuse me?"

"You told me yourself. You're getting older, your eyes aren't as good as they used to be."

"Kelly, I hope I get a face-lift so good I look a decade younger," Serena moaned.

All three of them watched as Liam went out into the hall, heading toward the kitchen with Conar.

"That man has a great walk," Kelly said.

"Oh, bull," Serena told her. "You mean that he has a great butt."

Kelly sighed. "Serena, I'm really sorry about mentioning the eye thing."

"And I'm not mad. You mean that he has a great, sexy backside and that it wiggles well when he moves."

Kelly laughed. "I'm not afraid of the word 'butt.' He has a fine backside. And so does...the man upstairs."

Serena glanced at Jennifer frowning, then said to Kelly, "The man upstairs...Kelly, what are you talking about? *God* has a great butt?"

"No! That's blasphemous, Serena. Conar has a great butt." She grinned. "Tightest cheeks I've ever seen."

"You two are horrible," Jennifer protested.

"No, we just live in Hollywood, where there is far too much tinsel, and not much that's real. And I'm aging more rapidly every second I spend with Kelly. We should get going."

They walked outside. Serena gave Jennifer a quick kiss before she slid into her car. "We may be back tomorrow," she said gaily. "We still have another day off."

Serena gunned her motor, and shot down the driveway.

Lady appeared out of nowhere, tail wagging, inspecting one of the front bushes. "Here, girl," Jennifer called.

For a moment, Lady ignored her. She watched as Serena's car left the drive.

"Lady, come on, pup."

At last her dog turned and trotted to her. She grabbed the wolfhound's collar. "Come on, stay with me. We'll walk through the house. It will be all right this one time. After all, *Ripper* is coming soon."

As she walked into the house, Edgar met her in the hallway. "Miss Jennifer...?"

She knew that in his totally unreproachful way, he was asking about the dog.

"Edgar, would you mind taking her out to her kennel for me?"

"Not at all, Miss Jennifer. Not at all. Come, girl."

Lady knew who had been feeding her lately. She obediently trotted right to Edgar. He smiled. "Such a great dog, Miss Jennifer."

"Umm, well, did you know that Mr. Markham's dog—*Ripper*—is coming tomorrow?"

"Yes, miss." He hesitated.

"Ripper?"

"Yes, miss. Well, he belonged to Mr. Markham's poor deceased wife..."

"I know," Jennifer murmured, wondering how Edgar had managed to make her feel like such a heel. "But still, if this Ripper makes one move against Lady—"

"Miss, Lady can manage quite well on her own," Edgar said, his tone a touch indignant. Jennifer had to smile. "Don't you worry any. I'll take good care of Lady."

"I know."

She went on into the living room, but it was empty. Then she realized voices were coming from upstairs. Going up, she heard conversation coming from the Granger Room.

Doug, Conar, Drew, Liam, and Hugh were in the room. Drew was tapping at the paneling on the wall to the left of the bed. Doug was sitting at the laptop computer Conar had set up at the desk, and the others were watching with skeptical interest as Drew continued tapping. "Well, it's here, I'm certain it's here."

"What's there?" Jennifer asked.

They all turned to her.

Drew grinned at her sheepishly. "There's a stairway that leads down to the first floor, to the garage."

"A stairway?"

"A stairway, yes, secret stairway. Old Granger liked to disappear and reappear at his parties. He could also sneak women into his room when he chose without his wife having any idea of what he was up to."

"She didn't notice another woman in the room?"

"They didn't share quarters," Drew said. "I know that the staircase exists. I've seen it in the plans. I know it's there. Oh, here!"

He tapped a place in the wall. There was no doorway revealed; instead, Drew's tapping had produced a revolving shelf. It suddenly spun out. There were three black-eyed heads upon it, which caused Jennifer to gasp in horror.

"Masks!" Conar said. "They're just masks. Old theatrical masks, worth a fortune by now, I would imagine. Look, there's a wolfman."

"And I imagine that's a mummy," Doug pointed out.

180

"And the third is a pale, chilling Count Dracula," Drew said.

Jennifer walked up to them, shivering. The eyes looked black and void and evil because there was really nothing there—they were eye holes.

"Strange," she murmured. "These have been behind that panel all the time."

"Well, I give up. I can't find the stairway. Let me try over there, other side of the bed. There should be a secret hold," Drew said.

"A hold?" Jennifer asked.

Conar, following Drew, paused at her side. "A hold—a secret hiding place."

"Voilà!" Drew said with pleasure. Amazingly, without a sound, a large piece of paneling spun around. It would easily accommodate a man, or some personal treasure to be hidden.

"You could hide a body in there," Doug murmured grimly.

"Well, the man wanted to be a magician, what can I say?" Drew told them with a shrug. "Ah, well, no stairway, I'm sorry. I give up."

"It's all right. Maybe we can find the plans some other time," Jennifer said, lightly.

Yet all the time she was thinking about the feeling she'd had of being watched. If there were secret compartments, what other secrets did the house have?

After everyone was gone, she took a long hot shower. In a long silk nightgown, she crawled into her bed. She still didn't feel the least tired.

She stared at her ceiling. She tossed and turned.

He'd slept with Brenda. Just once, he'd said. And, admittedly, half the men she knew had slept with Brenda, or so it seemed. If they hadn't slept with her, they wanted to claim that they had anyway.

Still...

It haunted her. That meant Conar was a suspect. And he was living in her mother's house.

She didn't believe for a minute that he had done it. Conar? Never. He could be infuriating, imperious, a bit condescending...

But slash a woman to death?

She was angry and restless, and at a loss as to why she was having those feelings. Her anger suddenly grew. She shouldn't have been so surprised.

She rose, slipping into her robe. It wasn't the worn terry cloth she usually wore around the house. It was a silk creation from Victoria's Secret that matched the gown. She tentatively opened her door. The hall was quiet. She marched down the hall to his room, and tapped on his door.

"Yeah?"

She hesitated, then opened the door. He was in the massive carved bed, hands laced behind his head, very bronze against the light sheets. He had apparently lain there in thought, lights on. Now he stared at her without moving.

"What?"

His tone of voice put her annoyingly on the defensive.

"You never told me that you'd slept with Brenda Lopez," she said.

He stared at her, eyes glittering sharp as knives.

"I've slept with a number of people. Do you want me to list them?"

"I don't know. Would we be talking something as thick as the Yellow Pages?" she retorted.

He sat up in the bed, jaw locking for a moment. "No, Jennifer. Since you're asking so nicely, I've slept with a *moderate* number of people. As to Brenda...you never asked. So if you want a list, tell me now. I'll do my best to deliver."

"You had a relationship with a murdered woman. And we've been talking about little else since you've arrived. You might have mentioned that you'd been intimate."

"You heard what I told Hugh. I didn't know Brenda that well. I hadn't seen her in a year or so. She came to a show in New York. She had been good friends with my wife, Betty Lou. They'd been very supportive of one another. You should remember, Brenda said a few words at Betty Lou's funeral. What I said is what happened. We had dinner, a few drinks, talked about old times. She stayed at my place and left the next morning."

She needed to say something. She didn't.

"Is that all?" he asked brusquely.

"What?"

"Is that all? Was there something else you wanted? If so, please enter. Any more in the vein of a third degree? Or are you standing there for another reason? Take off those sexy things and crawl right in if you're looking for companionship. If not, would you mind? Would you please leave me the hell alone?"

She felt as if an iceberg had settled over her.

She narrowed her eyes. "I just thought I should mention once more that if your *Ripper* gives Lady any trouble in the least, I'll be ripping him right into little pieces."

"I'm sure Lady can take care of herself against my dog."

"Your dog's name is Ripper, Conar."

He stared at her, not deigning to reply.

She tried to turn and exit with dignity, but her dignified spin was a little too close to the door frame. She bumped right into the wall and had to back up.

So much for a regal exit.

She was shaking more than her mother ever did.

Back in her own room, she slammed and locked the door, and crawled into bed. And lay awake.

Damning him for coming here, for being her mother's stepson, for sleeping with Brenda Lopez.

For keeping her awake. Making her feel as if she wanted something so badly...

It was deeply disturbing to realize she knew exactly what she wanted.

Hugh Tanenbaum found himself driving, and driving, and suddenly on Sunset, where lots of places were still in full swing.

He didn't feel like full swing. He wanted a quiet bar, a place to think.

He got a parking place on the street. Hands in his pockets, he whistled as he walked along. He loved L.A., Hollywood, all the glamour and all the tinsel. He'd never changed his name, but he'd changed everything else about himself. He'd been born in the garment district of New York; he'd been expected to become a tailor like his father, and grow up to help take over the family tailoring/dry-cleaning business. His entire family had thought that he was weird, reading all the time, hanging around Broadway, eager to do anything that had to do with theater or film. Finally, his father managed to get him a job. One of his repeat clients was an assistant director for an independent film company. He managed to get Hugh a position as a production assistant for a film.

He'd headed to Hollywood.

He hadn't become a Kubrick, a Lucas, or a Spielberg, but he'd done darned well in the B movie world. He had a feel for the cliffhanger. The nicest comment he'd read on his directing had to do with his ability to "scare, really scare" an audience. He might not go down as a Hitchcock, but he had a rock-solid reputation, and a sterling record at the box office. That was good enough for him.

And aging as he was, with good-looking, Hollywood dignity, he liked to think—okay, slightly repaired dignity—he was still doing damned well with life.

He felt shaky tonight, though. He hadn't mentioned to Conar his own recent relationship with Brenda. Not actually a great passion there, either, though she did say that he was really magnificent. Brenda had been like that. Those who knew her understood. Sex was like a handshake to her. She'd agreed to a small but important part in his movie.

"Hugh!"

He heard his name called and turned.

The woman summoning him had been sitting at the end of the bar. She'd just noticed him, he realized.

She was beautiful. Blond. A natural blond? What difference did it make?

Young. How young? Sometimes not so easy to tell out here. She approached him. No...she wasn't quite so young anymore. She was at that age where perfection began to slip. Some might say it was a great age, when character began to slip in. But this was Hollywood. Yesterday's beauty was today's discard. There were so many actresses. What was her name?

"Hugh, you do remember me, right? We met at one of Rob's parties a few years ago. How nice to see you. I hear your new movie is going to be spectacular. I'm so pleased for you. I just wrapped a project, and if..."

He shrugged, smiling. She was almost on top of him. She was still stunning. Put together like an hourglass. She was leaning against him. He could feel the heaviness of her breasts. His grin deepened. Silicone. What the hell. He didn't have anything against silicone, and he was feeling very lonely tonight. Besides, being a director could kind of be God-like. He could help her career, a real value.

"There are a few places I could probably use you before we wrap. You understand, however, that my real leads are taken...We could discuss what's left."

Her eyes, like enormous blue cornflowers, widened. She set delicate, perfectly manicured fingers upon his shoulder.

"I'd love to discuss what's left."

"Want a drink?"

"I don't live far from here. Walk me home, and we'll get a drink at my place while we discuss what's left."

"How do you feel about being a victim?" he inquired.

Her blue eyes rolled. She slipped her arm into his, squeezed closer.

"I'd just love to be one of your victims," she purred. She let her hand trail discreetly down to his lap. "Oh, yeah, honey, I would just love to be one of your *victims*. Anytime."

Her fingers moved delicately. Touched.

Stroked.

He stood, gravel in his throat as he called for his check.

Hell, yes.

She could be his victim.

Anytime.

Sometime, late in the night, Jennifer actually slept.

Even later, she awoke, bathed in sweat, jerking up. In panic, she leapt from the bed and began turning on lights. Her door remained locked. And yet...

Yet what? She had awakened from a nightmare. With the awful feeling that...

There were eyes in the night.

"Jennifer!"

She almost screamed at the sound of her name. Then she exhaled instead. She should have felt anger—or fear. She heard a tapping at her door after the soft call of her name. Conar was in the hallway.

She walked over to her door, but didn't open it.

"What?"

"Are you all right?"

"Yes, of course." She hesitated a moment, leaned against the door. Then she opened it.

She was minus her robe. The Victoria's Secret gown was scant on its own, revealing, and form-hugging.

He was wearing boxers, as if he had hastily grabbed them and run down the hall.

For a moment her breath caught. She forgot being scared. Her eyes started to slip downward. She jerked them back to his. "I'm fine. Why?"

"I thought I heard you scream."

"Nightmare," she said.

"I'm sorry."

"You can't help it that I have a nightmare."

"No, I'm sorry for being an ass."

She had to smile. "That's all right. I'm not sure you can help that either."

Her eyes were slipping downward again. Great shoulders, great chest, muscles...

He'd kissed her in the pool with such sudden determination she'd nearly swallowed his tongue. Touched her and she'd nearly...

She backed away, moistening her lips. "I'm fine now, really."

"And I'm sorry, really. It wasn't a big thing between Brenda and me. I did know her, and it just sort of happened."

"I really do understand," she said.

Did she? Was she even thinking about what he was saying? He was intense, serious. His pulse ticked at his throat. The air around him seemed full of sparks and heat. She took another step back. "You'd best get some sleep. After all, Molly is coming. With Ripper."

"Right. Well, good night."

"Good night."

He turned away.

She closed her door. Leaned against it.

What if she turned again? Threw caution to the wind. Was she desperate, or was he just that appealing, or both? What would it really hurt if...

Molly was coming. And who exactly was Molly?

No.

Yes.

She spun around and threw open her door.

His was just closing.

She bit into her lower lip. It would have felt good just to be in his arms. It would have felt better to swallow his tongue again, feel his hands...

She closed and locked her door, and forced herself back to bed.

She dreamed through the night.

Strange. She always knew that she was dreaming. She couldn't awaken, though she was restless. She didn't want to awaken, actually. She needed to listen, to pay attention. Because Brenda was in her dreams.

Yes, it was Brenda, haunting the halls of Granger House. Wafting about in a flowing, floating white robe, the way ghosts appeared in old movies. She was trying to tell Jennifer something, trying to warn her. Jennifer strained to hear her, tried to listen. Brenda kept floating, floating away. She followed, followed, followed...

Brenda was leading her off the cliffs.

No...

She awoke with a start, shaking. She'd awakened just in time. How? Why?

Then she heard barking. It was just Lady. And another dog.

Ah, Molly was here. With *Ripper*.

Jennifer leapt out of bed as if she had been catapulted. Old Ripper was here. Conar's killer dog.

A sense of guilt suddenly plagued her. *The dog had been Betty Lou's.* How could she be such a nasty pissant about it all? She didn't mean to be. She had barely known the woman to whom Conar had been so briefly married, but she had seemed sweet and certainly admirable, and the actress's death to random violence had been a true tragedy. She was very sorry. She closed her eyes, wincing, thinking, *I'm sorry, honest to God, I'm sorry, but...*

The barking had started up again. A baying. Lady, outside, and upset, joined by another deep, harsh barking sound. They had the dogs together. Ripper could rip Lady to mincemeat.

She threw on her terry robe and came flying down the stairs to the foyer. Edgar was there, along with Doug, showered and dressed, an unknown petite blonde, and Conar.

Conar was hugging the blonde.

Jennifer skidded to a stop. She felt like a fool. Her hair was a wild tangle, her robe was tied at an off-center angle, her feet were bare. She looked like hell.

The petite blonde stepped away from Conar. She was in her mid-thirties, buxom and cute, with a heart-shaped gamine's face. Her smile was deep and earnest and sincere. She had been excited to greet Conar; now she was anxious to meet Jennifer.

"Hi!" she said softly.

Conar turned. He'd been up to greet their guest. He was showered, dark hair combed back, casual knit shirt open at the chest, wearing denim cut-offs and sneakers.

"Molly Talmadge, Jennifer Connolly. Jennifer, Molly..." He hesitated a meaningful moment. "A very, very good friend."

She smoothed back her hair, trying for some dignity. "Welcome, Miss Talmadge, although—"

"Molly, please."

"Molly. Excuse me, I'm worried about Lady."

"Lady?" Molly said, looking at Conar, puzzled.

"She's afraid Ripper will tear Lady to pieces."

"Oh, but I don't think that's possible," Molly protested. She was a real blonde, nearly platinum, eyes a powder-puff blue. Cute as a damned button.

Jennifer heard the sound of ferocious barking once again.

"Excuse me."

She tore through the hallway to the den and out to the patio. She came to a stop as she saw her mother sitting at one of the patio tables, Lady by her side.

"Mother, Mother! That's dangerous! Get away from Lady if that killer dog is out here."

"My dear, whatever are you talking about?" Abby began, but Jennifer was already on her way over, grabbing Lady's collar.

Her wolfhound instantly gave her a face bath with her huge sloppy tongue.

"Mother, where is Ripper? If they fight—"

"Sweetheart, they're not going to fight."

"I have to get you in—" She broke off, turning back. The rest of the household and their new guests were staring at her, all lined up by the den doors to the patio. Edgar, Conar, Doug, and Molly Talmadge.

"Conar, this could be dangerous. My mother is out here. Where is this Ripper of yours?" she demanded angrily.

"Jennifer, dear, Ripper is right here," Abby said.

"Where?" she demanded.

Her mother lifted her hand from her lap. Jennifer didn't see anything at first. Then she did. A little fur ball or something.

"Jennifer, he's just adorable," Abby crooned. She looked at Conar. "I don't think the little thing is three pounds. He fits in the palm of my hand," she marveled.

The fur ball suddenly barked. The bark was deep, as if it belonged to a mastiff.

"They call him a teacup Yorkie, Abby. And he's small, even for that. I think he's about three pounds," Conar said.

Jennifer was glad her back was to him. She felt like a fool, and she was furious. Yeah, well, Lady should be able to hold her own against a hairball like that.

The creature had eyes as well. Jennifer saw them at last. A tiny, delicate face, black and tan, all surrounded by well-cut hair. Its tail was wagging away.

Lady bayed again, wagging her tail in return.

Jennifer turned around at last and faced

Conar, ready to kill. He had made an ass out of her, and he knew it.

She stared at him, hoping that she showed her utter contempt for him, Molly—and their hairball creature. She swung back to her mother. "Mom, your allergies—"

"They aren't bothered by him, Jen, can you imagine. They have a different kind of fur. Well, it's not fur, really, is it, Conar? It's hair. Hair that gets cut, just like people hair. I haven't been inside with the beautiful little bugger yet, but, oh...Conar, he is sweet."

"Lady is sweet," she heard herself say defensively. She could have kicked herself.

Abby looked at her, the way she might have if she had accidentally hurt the feelings of a small child. "Of course, dear, Lady is sweet. She's a beautiful dog, a marvelous dog. She's just...she's just a big dog."

Jennifer realized suddenly that Doug was standing by her. He cleared his throat. "You're, uh, exposing things there," he whispered.

She looked down. Her robe was open, and she'd pulled the corner of her nightgown down when she'd reached for Lady's collar.

Her own mother hadn't noticed. She'd been too preoccupied with the barking, wagging ball of hair in her lap.

Jennifer wrenched her robe closed, lobster red and humiliated, and irrationally furious. Edgar was watching her mother; Molly, too, seemed preoccupied with Abby and the dog.

But Conar was watching her. And laughing.

"Excuse me, I'll get dressed," she said

194

politely. She strode from the patio to the house, passing Conar.

He caught her arm. He was still smiling, suppressing an outright laugh. "I told you it would be all right."

"Jerk!" she hissed, wrenched free, and walked on by him.

She was startled to realize that he had followed her. He caught her arm again before she could start up the stairs.

"Look, damn you, if you'd just leave me alone—"

"Are you angry because my dog didn't eat yours?"

"I'm angry because you didn't tell me your dog was a three-pound hairball."

He shrugged, eyes narrowed, releasing his grip on her. "You never asked, Jennifer. You just assumed. Sometimes when you make assumptions, people just feel obliged to correct you."

"Is that all?" she asked, staring back at him. "Is there anything else? If not, I'd like you to leave me the hell alone."

"Yeah, that's all," he said, starting back for the den. But then he paused, turning back to her. And to her annoyance, of course, she was still standing there. Just waiting. Watching him.

"One more thing," he said seriously.

"What?"

A smile curved his lips. "Nice breasts," he told her. "You show them often?"

She didn't dignify the taunt with a reply. She

managed to turn with grace and start fleeing up the stairs.

Too bad she tripped on the fifth step.

She didn't look back, but she knew he was still watching her. Silently laughing, she was certain.

Chapter 9

Hugh Tanenbaum woke in his own bed. He dimly remembered driving home.

Whoa. His head was pounding. When he tried to sit up, it felt like his head weighed more than a bowling ball. His tongue seemed to be the size of a foot. A nasty, hairy foot at that.

He closed his eyes again, praying the pounding would cease. It did not. Water. Water and aspirin. A touch of the hair of the dog that bit him.

A shower. That had to improve things. He could smell a really foul odor, and that odor seemed to be him.

He made it to the shower. He stayed under the spray forever and ever. Finally, he stepped out and brushed his teeth. He almost drank a bottle of Scope, squishing it through his teeth over and over again. On the third try, some of the hair on his tongue seemed to have gone away at last.

He stared at himself in the mirror. Pathetic. The bags under his eyes were like giant suit cases, carrying an extra little set of overnight bags themselves. There was little white in his eyes; they were pathetically red-rimmed.

"I am too old for this shit," he told his reflection seriously.

"Work tomorrow," he murmured. "Thank God you've an afternoon and night to get yourself together. You're off the booze, old man. Off, off, off!"

He shook his head. His towel slipped. His midriff was pouching. Come to think of it, everything was pouching.

With a disgusted shake of his head, he headed into his dressing room, found boxers, jeans, and and a T-shirt, then sat down on the chair there to put on his shoes and socks.

He was a neat man, always organized. His shirts and suits were hung by color and style. His trousers were well pleated.

He stared at his clothing without really seeing it. His head was still pounding like thunder. Time was passing, and he was too old and too smart to tie it on as he had last night. To forget everything. Know nothing.

He stood, exiting his dressing room and heading for the kitchen. Suddenly, halfway there, he paused. Something was wrong about the bed. Frowning, he headed back.

He stood in the door to his bedroom, staring at the bedclothes.

The sheets were covered with a large dark patch. It looked like...

He went to feel it. It was cold and sticky to the touch. He jerked back. He looked at his bed, and felt tremors of dread shoot through his body.

He remembered a blond actress in a bar. What was it? Blood? Wine? Stage blood?

And...

What the hell had he done?

Liam Murphy's precinct station was a zoo.

Still, it wasn't that difficult to find him. He was sitting at a desk burdened down by paperwork. Seeing Conar, though, he rose, pleased but surprised.

"Hey, what are you doing here?" He pointed across the table where a slim Eurasian man was sitting. "Joe Hong, Conar, my partner. Joe, Conar..."

"Markham. Hi. I know the face."

Liam said, "Let's go have coffee."

Down the hall there were machines. "That one actually makes pretty good cappuccino," Liam advised.

"Aren't hard-boiled cops supposed to drink black coffee?"

"Yeah, when I have to, I do," Liam said, putting quarters in the cappuccino machine. "Actor sorts...hmm. Want some herbal tea?"

"Coffee, black," Conar told him, shrugging.

"Got to keep up that macho image, eh?"

"No, just a little lactose intolerant," Conar admitted.

They walked down to the end of the hallway. "So, what's up?" Liam asked.

"Brenda's case. It's been bothering me."

"You and all of L.A. We've sent samples off to the FBI behavioral analysis lab, we've combed her place, the Sawyer property, and half the canyon. So what else is interesting you?"

"The particulars. She was found in the canyon, but murdered in the shower."

"Right. So..."

"Shades of *Psycho*."

"We're not stupid. We're aware of that."

"Have there been other such murders here recently—or in the not too distant past? Not just knife murders, but *staged* murders?"

"Hey, I'm a detective. Don't you think I went through the computer right away, looking for similar situations?"

Conar stared at his old friend. "Yeah," he said sheepishly. "Yeah, of course. Except that I still don't think..."

"What?"

"What happened to Brenda was so violent. Passionate, frenzied. I'm not any kind of an expert on psychotic behavior, but I read, and...I don't know. Wouldn't a killer like that have committed other crimes?"

Liam hesitated a moment. "Who knows? Yes, a lot of the time." He hesitated again, then said, "I accessed the computer to cross-reference open cases, but I haven't had any real hits."

"I'm sure you're working your tail off. It's just that Abby thinks there is a killer after Jennifer."

"Tell me, do you think that there is going to be another attempt?"

Liam hesitated.

"Maybe it was a vengeance thing. Brenda did have enemies."

"I wish I thought so—but I don't. This is a strange one."

Liam studied him a moment. "Is this about Abby and Jennifer?"

"Yeah. Yeah, I guess so."

"I wish I could tell you that we've made some progress, but we really haven't. That's not just cop speak. Right now this is a cold case going nowhere."

There was nothing to be said to that. "Well, thanks, anyway. I'll give you a call. We'll get together."

Conar left the station, feeling a deeper and deeper unease. He sped most of the way back to the house. He burst into the foyer, and through the hall to the den.

He heard voices from the patio. Abby, Jennifer, Molly.

A sense of relief filled him, and he wondered why he had felt such an awful panic. The situation was simply playing on his nerves. *Get a grip,* he warned himself. *Hell of a lot of help you are.*

At the sound of water splashing, he walked toward the rear and looked out on the back. He saw Jennifer leap from the pool, slim arms strong and tanned. She was laughing at something someone had said. She strode to the diving board in her bikini. She posed in perfect form. Tall, lithe, graceful...

Um. She was alive. And *very* well.

But that didn't mean anything unless Liam could get a break in the case.

Dinner was a pleasant enough affair.

Doug was in high spirits after a morning spent planning the week's episodes. He was excited about the way the show was going, refusing to give out any information about the Friday shoot, but providing Conar and Jennifer with their scripts for the next day's rehearsal, which they would have gotten at their nine o'clock calls.

Abby left the table after the main course, feeling tired but not ill, she assured Jennifer. No reaction to Ripper's fur at all.

But she was shaking a lot. The shaking had increased over the weekend. Also, Edgar informed Jennifer discreetly, Abby had been experiencing more difficulty swallowing, and was asking for her pills before she should be taking them.

Tomorrow afternoon was her mother's appointment with the neurologist, an appointment Jennifer dreaded. Her mother would press for the surgery. Now that Conar was here, he would press for it as well.

After Abby had gone to her room, Jim Novac came by. Doug had told him that he was coming for dinner, and Jim thought that they might not mind if he showed up later.

So over coffee they glanced at the scripts for the next day's shooting. Jennifer's first scene was with Kelly at the breakfast room in the Valentine mansion. Jennifer was home, having left her husband after his abduction of her from the caretaker's cottage. Kelly was sorry for the disaster of her sister's marriage, but excited, mentioning the return of the son of the family scion from the next vineyard down. He'd been studying in France ways to improve their chardonnay. She'd seen him at Prima Piatti the night before, and he'd asked her out.

Instantly protective of her own family's interests and their unique, award-winning chardonnay, Jennifer's character—newly estranged from her husband, with the family lawyer already drawing up divorce papers—plotted to waylay the newly returned heir to the DeVille Vineyards, and find out if he was after her sister or the family wine.

In truth, she'd had an affair with David DeVille the previous summer in France, never letting on to any of the Valentines. The families had long been at odds.

The next scene was a flashback to the affair, putting her with David DeVille in a garret in France. She had not known his real identity, despite being in his bed. David had been careful to keep that information from her.

"Great," Jennifer murmured, setting the script on the table and looking from Doug to Jim. "Is there any day in the next two weeks where I get to wear a complete set of clothing?"

Jim hesitated, picking up his cup. "Friday," he said, then he frowned. "No, never mind. A day with all your clothing on..." He smiled and said cheerfully, "Nope, sorry, not this week."

She groaned softly.

"Oh, but your character is so loved," Molly advised her. "She's so deliciously sleazy, so cruel, and yet with that little streak of vulnerability."

"We seem to love things evil," Conar agreed.

"What's happening Friday?" Jennifer demanded of Jim and Doug.

They looked at each other, shook their heads.

"But you will be happy," Doug promised her.

They left shortly thereafter, and Jennifer went to check on her mother. In the hall to her mother's room, she saw Edgar just leaving. He shook his head unhappily. "She had such a wonderful day. And now..."

"I'll go in with her."

"She's had her pills. She should drift to sleep soon."

Jennifer nodded, entered her mother's room, and closed the door behind her. Abby was on the bed, staring into space. Her medication was working; she was trembling at a constant speed, but not jerking, nor did she seem uncomfortable.

"Jennifer, Jen!" she said softly, reaching out a hand for her daughter.

"Mom." She took her mother's hand and curled up beside her on the bed. She smoothed back a lock of her mother's hair, kissed her forehead. "Mom, I'm so sorry you're having such a bad time."

"No, I'm not, darling. I've been chatting with Mr. Peacock there."

Mr. Peacock was a figure in the walls. Abby often chatted with him while under her medication.

"He's so pleased that you're not alone here anymore," Abby said.

"Mom, I've never been alone here. It's your house, you live here."

"Mr. Peacock says that it's easy to be surrounded by people, but still be alone. We all put up walls, but walls have gates and doors. You have to open a few gates, dear." Abby's hand tightened on Jennifer's. "He's still very worried about you. Mr. Peacock can hear the house, and the house is distressed.... The house loves you, but it can't help the danger, it...well, you're not alone anymore. He's here."

"He—Conar?"

"He'll watch over you, dear," Abby said, and her eyes closed.

"I don't need to be watched over, Mom. That isn't fair to him, to me..."

Her voice trailed off, for her mother had gone still. The shaking had stopped. Worried, Jennifer rested her ear against her mother's heart. There was a steady beat. She breathed a sigh of relief.

For a while she lay there with Abby. She dozed off, then awoke with a start.

Coming down the dark and silent hallway, she nearly screamed when she ran into Edgar. "Miss Jennifer, it's very late. I didn't want to

204

disturb you, not when you were with Miss Abby."

"I fell asleep on Mom's bed, Edgar."

"So I figured. Well, you have an early call tomorrow."

"That's right. I'm going on up."

"Good night, miss."

She walked upstairs. The whole house was darkened, but beyond the night-lights, there was a glow from down the hallway, coming from the Granger Room.

Conar was still up, and not alone.

He was entertaining Molly in his bedroom. Great. She heard whispers and soft laughter. Intimate voices in the night. She was surprised by the wave of emotion that washed over her as she stood there in the hallway. It was longing, she realized. Longing to laugh, to have a good time.

If only! she found herself thinking.

She was standing at her door, shaking. She was looking forward to filming, to doing an intimate scene with Conar. She'd done dozens of scenes. Talia Valentine got around. But she hadn't felt this way before. Anxious. Wanting to touch...to feel. She was certain he was hot. Like flames. His hands were powerful. He knew how to kiss, to devour a whole mouth. She wondered what his lips would feel like on her breasts...

"Sweet Jesus," she breathed aloud, pushing open her door. What the hell was the matter with her? She closed the door behind her, leaned against it. "Get over this," she commanded herself.

I have no real life, and so I'm having pathetic fantasies about sex with the enemy. It seems so strange that I've always disliked him so much, and that now he walks into a room and I feel as if I'm as liquid as warm rain, as if, should he do more than touch me, I'd...

No! She wouldn't even think such thoughts.

This was not just a normal, healthy appreciation for a good-looking male suddenly cast into the fold. No, this was different.

And humiliating, under the circumstances. *I never said anything about sleeping with you,* he had told her. Still, he had kissed her in the pool. That had triggered it.

And he had suggested she could crawl in with him last night.

Because he'd known that she wouldn't.

Yet, standing against her door, she could still hear the laughter coming from his room. Adorable, charming little Molly. Molly, who was stunning—yes, definitely—the little platinum blonde with her huge chest and tiny waist.

She was, no denying it, jealous. How could she be jealous? She had disliked Conar for years, years...

Or was it just that she didn't really have anything of her own? Or maybe her mother was right, and she was just desperate for sex...because she really had nothing of her own, just a life on film, in the American living rooms, in *Soap Digest*—and that was all? She hadn't even had a touch to give her so much as a little thrill until...

206

Until he had come along.

She heard again the sound of laughter. Hers—soft, light on the air. His—deep, husky.

Maybe she'd go sleep on the sofa in the den. Maybe she should take a shower. Drown out the sounds.

That was it. Determinedly walking to her bathroom, she shed her clothing as she went, tossing her shoes, shirt, jeans, and under-garments in the air, leaving them where they fell. She turned the shower on hot, then cold, scrubbing strenuously—and having evil thoughts all the while. He really was getting to her. Nothing like a wild—noisy!—fling in her mother's house.

Her flesh began to wrinkle, she'd been in for so long. She twisted off the water with such vigor that the old pipes groaned.

But when she stepped from the shower, even in her room, she could still hear the sounds of muffled laughter. She marched out to her closet and found one of her better robes, a long red velvet one that belted around the waist. Knotting it firmly, she tossed her hair back, gritting her teeth. Would they ever stop?

She could ask them to at least quiet it down. That, or...

Escape the sounds.

Not certain if she meant to interrupt the love fest or run from it, she started out of her room. She managed to march out into the hallway just in time to see Conar's door opening. Molly, in a knit nightshirt that molded to her perfect compact form, was slipping out.

"Jennifer, hi, did we wake you?" she asked, concerned.

"No, of course not," Conar commented, smiling.

She ignored him. "You didn't wake me. I've been down with my mother."

"She's wonderful. So beautiful, and gracious," Molly said.

"Thank you," Jennifer said.

"Good night. And thank you, too, so much."

"For?"

"For having me here."

"You're quite welcome, but it is my mother's house. And as for having you...well, you're Conar's guest as well."

He heard the snideness in her tone, she was certain, even if Molly didn't. She could have kicked herself. She hesitated. *Having you.* It was amazing that Molly hadn't heard the insinuation. What the hell was the matter with her? She didn't used to be like this.

"You're leaving?" she asked, trying to sound more polite.

"Tomorrow morning. I'm meeting friends in San Francisco."

"Well...," she murmured, looking at Conar. "Thanks so much for bringing Ripper."

"Sure thing. Well...good night, thanks again."

"You're welcome. Come back anytime."

Did she still sound so false? She must, the way Conar was looking at her.

"Thanks. I've loved it."

Molly stood on tiptoe, her hands against his chest, to kiss Conar good night. She waved at Jennifer and disappeared into the guest room next to the one Doug had just vacated.

Conar, in a velour robe, folded his arms over his chest and leaned against his open door. "Were you coming to see me?"

"Of course not. You were...occupied."

He arched a brow. "I thought maybe that you were ready to join the party."

"Don't be ridiculous. I was just..."

"Yes?"

"Quite frankly, I was going downstairs. Away from the..." She let her voice trail off suggestively, and with a definite hint of contempt. "Away from the noise."

"Oh?" he inquired. But he was grinning, she thought. Laughing at her.

He left his bedroom doorway, walking toward her. *Swaggering* toward her was more like it.

"Conar, I don't really care to chat at the moment." She instinctively started to back into her room; then realized she was being an idiot. Why panic? His robe was partially open, displaying a bronzed V section of his chest. Silly. She'd seen all of his chest before. His legs were bare beneath the robe.

"I wasn't planning on *chatting*," he informed her.

"Well, good. So go to sleep. I'm going downstairs."

"Why?"

"For a drink, for milk and cookies. It's none of your business. I'm just going downstairs because I want to go downstairs."

She meant to walk away with such dignity. But he was too close. Smiling with a strange light in his eyes. An almost tender look. And one that still had that mocking light of laughter. She felt the urge to kick herself again. She was really losing all sense. He'd spent the night laughing and God knew what else with Molly.

She needed to *move*.

She did walk at first—with all the dignity she had intended. Then she was walking fast, and when she reached the stairway, she was almost running.

Soundlessly, he moved faster. At the foot of the stairway, she felt his hand on her shoulder. Felt him catch her arm. Spin her around.

A powerful hand.

She swore.

And found herself swept up into his arms.

Chapter 10

Anger coursed through her. Damn, he was built like a Mack truck, hard chiseled face, piercing gray eyes. Yes, he'd made his mark, he ruled his world. Not hers! Not hers, she couldn't fall for him...She struggled, pressing against his chest, her fists balling. "What are you doing?" she demanded.

He grinned down at her, a strand of clean dark hair over his forehead. "What I should have done a long time ago. Taking matters into my own hands."

"Conar, put me down. I'll scream. My mother will—"

"You're going to call Mom for help?" He was so amused, so mocking.

"Conar, damn you, I mean it!"

"Do you? I don't believe you."

"You're being ridiculously dramatic," she informed him, trying for a tone of impatient annoyance.

"Dramatic? All life is drama, and once an actor..." he murmured, and she realized that he was staring ahead at the mirror at the base of the stairs. "Ah, here we are. High drama. Echoes of *Gone With the Wind*. Great scene, that at the foot of the stairway. So intensely sensual. Both characters so furious, in such a tempest, and the sweeping rise up the great stairway...and then all left to the imagination. Of course, I think he was in a white shirt, black breeches, something like that. But that robe of yours...it's bright. Some real shades of *Gone With the Wind* there. Red is such a telling color. Provocative. Are you trying to be provocative, Jennifer?"

"Conar, you ridiculous bastard, you don't even like me."

"You're wrong. I do."

"I don't believe you."

"That's ridiculous. I've been lusting after you for years."

"You are really a sorry liar." She swung her fists suddely against his chest.

"A sorry liar? No, not really."

"You thought I was a bitch."

"Oh, I still think you're capable of being a bitch. But put together right. I didn't say I was secretly in *love* with you—just in lust."

"Put me down."

"I was probably always harboring fantasies about suddenly seeing you take off your clothes and throw yourself in front of me, saying something like, 'All right, big shot, show me what you've got.' "

She didn't know whether to laugh or scream. "Conar, you bastard—"

He caught her hand as it landed against his cheek. "Will you quit? Clark Gable did not have to endure such abuse."

"Clark Gable wasn't entertaining in his room previous to the great seduction."

"I'm glad you think it's going to be a great seduction."

"Conar Markham, you're out of your mind if you think I'm so desperate that I'm going to fall in your arms when you've just had a girl."

"Really? What if I didn't just have a girl?"

"How can you even do this?" she whispered heatedly. "That poor Molly is upstairs, having just left your room."

"She'd be so proud of me. Hey, be still, will you? This staircase scene with struggling cargo isn't at all easy. I wonder how many takes they did with Clark Gable and Vivien Leigh."

"Conar, really!" she said breathlessly. They

were in the hallway. "Look, Conar, you may find this amusing, I mean, you obviously do think I'm desperate, but I refuse—"

They'd gotten to his room. He closed the door with a shove, leaned against it panting, hair mussed, eyes silver with amusement as they stared down at hers. "Damn, that's a long hallway. Thank God we're here. I won't be much good with a hernia."

"Well, set me down, because I'm leaving. I won't follow in Molly's—"

"But what if you weren't following Molly?"

"Conar, I saw her in here with you."

"She's a friend. I love her very much.'"

"And that's—"

"She has a far different taste in sex, however."

"Excuse me?"

His eyes were truly alive with amusement then. "She's meeting a *girl*friend in San Francisco, Jennifer." She still stared at him blankly. "Jen, your friend Doug is surely one of the best-looking men ever to draw breath, but he's not your lover."

"Oh, really? Maybe he was at one time."

"No way, no how. And neither has Molly ever so much as been remotely interested in sharing a sexual experience with me."

He was still holding her. Smiling. Amused. And more. Her breath was barely making it in and out of her lungs. She didn't remember ever wanting anything more in her life than to touch him.

She touched his cheek. "I really don't want to be here."

213

"I know. It's okay, I understand. I'm just a bundle of sexual appeal, and you can't help yourself," he said, teasing her.

It was the pathetic truth.

"Maybe I'm just desperate," she said softly. Desperate seemed better than pathetic.

He curled his fingers around hers. "I'll live with desperate. It isn't casual lust anymore here, it's *insane* lust. I don't give a damn about your motives at this particular minute. So go ahead. Please, tell me there's nothing under the robe."

"There's nothing under the robe."

His mouth ground down on hers. His tongue seemed to reach to her womb. Her arms curled around his neck, and she met the kiss, trying to taste and feel and match his every movement. She was still in his arms, aware that he was walking again. Seconds later they fell to the bed, robes slipping, and his flesh was as hot as she had imagined, an inferno, so sensual against her own, sleek, hard, rippling with muscle, with fire and force. She felt his state of arousal against her thigh as he continued to kiss her, fascinated with her lips, hungry, kissing her with wet, passionate intimacy, breaking the kiss to meet her eyes, kissing her again. Her breath caught, her heartbeat was pounding. Her eyes met his each time his kiss broke, and he stared down at her with renewed interest. His body rose against hers, erotically rubbing against her own. She was deliciously aware of that subtle feel of muscle play, the flicker of flame, brush of flesh. Pressure was ecstasy, the world was alive.

His kisses ended, and her robe was pushed further aside. His fingers slid over her breast, the palm creating a vortex at the nipple, his fingers then tracing the peak, the aureole, the surrounding flesh, before his mouth fastened on. She could have screamed with the sudden pleasure, anticipated, but never such as this. Her fingers curled into his hair, kneaded his shoulders. Her nails scraped and stroked, her back arched, her body writhed. He moved lower. And lower. His tongue laved, touched, teased. His hand molded over her stomach and hip, slid between her thighs. Touching, stroking...the pressure of his thumb was within her...the wetness of his mouth invaded. Slowly, he increased the pressure, a faster pace, his body, his scent, oh, God, his touch, the things he was doing to her, where he was doing them...

When she would have shrieked in earnest, he rose above her, capturing her lips with a wet passion that swallowed sound and soul. He folded her into his arms and jacked himself into her with a sharp force that brought another gasp to her throat. Forever, it seemed, they lay there, entwined, and then his movement, just his first subtle shift, aroused her to a new fevered pitch, dear God, sweet agony, such ecstasy, she was sweetly drenched, straining, wanting, desperate, oh, Lord, yes! Desperate, arching, writhing, hungering for each stroke, deeper, richer, wetter...

She climaxed with a violent shudder that seemed to wrack the very world around her, and where she had been aware of nothing but the need for that sublime release, she was now aware again of him, his flesh, his heat, the dampness that pervaded them both, his weight, the thickness of his hair, texture of his face, thunder of his heart.

"*Gone With the Wind,* I knew it," he said softly, his fingers tracing a tiny bead of perspiration between her breasts. "The way they went up those stairs, and seeing Scarlet's face the next morning, hell, you just knew it was great."

"It was so great, Rhett left town," she reminded him.

He grinned. "Rhett was disturbed by what he considered to be his bad behavior, use of force, and excessive bad manners. I'm not disturbed in the least, except that...well..."

"You know I went to all-girls Catholic schools," she told him quickly. "Actors are notoriously bad at relationships. And...I came of age at a scary time. I was afraid that I'd die if I did," she explained.

He rose on an elbow, watching her. "So what happened tonight?" he asked.

"I was afraid I'd die if I didn't," she said simply.

He wrapped her in his arms again. "You know, I never did hate you," he whispered against her forehead.

"Um. I loathed you in all honesty," she admitted. "But I guess..."

"You were lusting for me all the while?"

"Maybe."

"I've admitted to some heavy-duty lust."

"Conar," she said after a moment. "You know...well, you're here to look after me. Because you love my mother."

"Thank God! You grant me honesty in that."

"Conar, I love her, too."

"Jennifer, I know that."

"But you have to understand. I mean to humor her—to let you 'guard' me. But I want you to realize as well that..."

"That?"

"I am a big girl. I mean, I wanted what happened now."

"Wanted. Hm. What I felt would give new meaning to the word."

She grinned. "Thanks. But tonight obliges you to nothing."

"Obliges?"

"I mean, I don't expect anything to be different. I—"

"Miss Connolly, this is an incredibly delightful way in which to look after you."

"But this will end. And you have to feel free to walk away. This was really just...something that I had to do."

"So I'm an experiment?" he inquired. "A damned obliging one. A teacher, at that."

"No, you're not an experiment...just...I've certainly had a lesson. I mean, I have to admit that you were wonderful."

"Thank God. A testimonial."

"Conar, I'm trying very hard to say that—"

"Don't worry. I'm not going to whip out a wedding ring tomorrow."

She stiffened.

"Is that what you meant?" he inquired.

"Yes. And...I should leave."

"I don't think so."

"But..."

"There's no reason for you to leave now."

"There is. We need to think about this—"

"No. We're not going to think about it. We're going to enjoy one another for whatever the reasons are. I like that you're here."

He rose over her again, catching her face with his fingers. His eyes pinned hers.

"Miss Connolly, you want a teacher? Lessons have only just begun."

"Conar, I didn't—"

"Jennifer, quit analyzing."

His lips ground down on hers. She felt the weight and pressure of his body. His hands...

Lessons had just begun, she discovered.

They could go on, and on.

She slept. It was wonderful at first, a deep, peaceful sleep. The mist that surrounded her was as puffy as clouds, as soft, as comforting.

Then it began to swirl, taking on a grayish hue. She was walking and she realized that she was on a path that surrounded Granger House. The mist began to dissolve, remaining around her feet as she took step after step, following the trail. She was dressed in soft, flowing

218

white, as if she had been costumed for the scene. Her hair was flowing, and the soft, luminous folds of the long white gown she wore trailed and billowed in the rising breeze as well.

She walked with purpose, following...

She could see that someone was running ahead of her. A woman. Dressed in white, as she was. The woman stopped and turned back to her. It was the film actress Celia Marston, the beautiful young starlet who had filmed her last movie in Granger House. The actress who had fallen to her death below, so near to where Brenda's body had been found. Her hair was blond and crimped in a long-ago style. Her dress was sleek, designed for a decade long gone. She was looking back, beckoning. "Hurry!"

"No, wait, please!" Jennifer moved faster and faster. She knew she had to catch Celia, to stop her from going over the cliffs. "Wait!" she cried out. "Don't go—"

"He's coming!" Celia called to her. "Run, run!"

Celia started running again. Jennifer felt a tremendous rush of fear, a strange terror. He was in back of her. *Look back!* She couldn't. If she did so, she'd see the face of the killer.

The beauty ahead of her started to turn back to her. It was no longer Celia Marston running ahead of her.

It was Brenda Lopez.

She wasn't clad in white; she was naked. Blood oozed from dozens of slashes that crisscrossed her body.

Jennifer came to a dead halt, watching, a scream caught in her throat. Brenda had reached the cliffs.

"Run, Jennifer, run! He's coming for you."

"Brenda, no!"

But Brenda was falling, falling...

Mist had risen again. Swirling, enveloping. There was the sound of the wind. No, it wasn't wind, he was *breathing*.

Brenda had warned her.

The house!

It was watching, she could feel the eyes.

It had been watching, a long time. It had watched her sleep, watched her dream. It had watched her before. And she could see herself, as she had been before. Making love. Touching. Being touched. Rising, falling, panting, gasping, stroking...

All along it had been watching.

Invading those incredible moments...

Wake up! she warned herself. He's still behind you. The mist swirled; Brenda was gone but the danger remained. The breathing...

Don't turn, don't turn, don't turn...

She had been fighting the dream, trying to awaken. At last she did. She bolted up, shaking. For a moment she was disoriented. Conar jerked up by her side. She gasped in terror, shrinking away from him.

"Jennifer?" The confused but deep sound of his voice touched her sanity even as his arms came around her.

She swallowed. Thank God he'd decided they should satisfy their mutual lust tonight.

"Jennifer, what?"

"I was dreaming, a nightmare, and still, when I awoke. I...This sounds so strange, but I still feel that someone...something...," she whispered.

"It's okay," he said. "Go on."

"I feel as if someone was watching us sleep."

"We'll check," he said softly.

He rose, walking away from her. She wanted to scream that he should come back. She managed not to do so—mainly because he hadn't gone very far. A moment later, the room was flooded with light. Conar was at the light switch, a baseball bat in his hands. He smiled at her, looking around the empty room.

"Closet?" he said.

"Please, if you don't mind. And the bathroom," she whispered.

A few minutes later, he was back beside her. "Nothing?" she asked.

He shook his head.

"Maybe my mother and I are both crazy," she said.

"You're fine."

"If I am crazy, you helped make me that way."

He grinned. "You're not crazy. I've..."

"You've what?"

"Nothing, I've just had dreams upon occasion, you know." He smiled. "We need some sleep. And don't worry, we'll keep the baseball bat right here."

"Leave a night-light on?"

"The bathroom light, is that okay?"

She nodded. He turned off the main light,

but the glow from the bathroom proved they were alone in the bedroom.

He slid in beside her. "You're staying in this room tonight, I take it?"

"I've been here, haven't I?"

"But you haven't suddenly gotten the urge to go back to your own room?"

"You're very amusing."

"Just checking. What was the dream?"

She shook her head. "It was..." She shook her head, falling silent. She didn't want to talk about it. It still seemed too real.

As if, had she just turned in her dream, she would have seen the killer.

"Dreams fade so quickly. I was just so very afraid."

Her eyes met his. She didn't go on. She curled against his chest.

"Conar?"

"Hm?"

"Are we all crazy?"

"No."

He felt so solid. And it was so good to be here. Bad dreams faded quickly in his arms.

His fingers settled over her hair. She felt the power and warmth of his heartbeat.

"What's going on, then?" she whispered.

"I don't know." His lips brushed the top of her head. "Maybe nothing. Maybe just a lot of fears we've created ourselves."

"I've always loved this house."

"It's a good house."

"So why does it suddenly..."

"Suddenly what?"

"Seem to watch us?"

"Houses don't watch people, Jennifer."

She shivered. His arms tightened.

"It's okay," he said softly. His fingers continued to stroke her. She slowly relaxed. A sense of sweet security swept over her.

Soon she was sleeping again.

Conar lay awake, thinking about what he hadn't said.

I've felt it, too. That rising-hackle sensation. The feeling of being watched. As if there are eyes everywhere...

He pulled the covers over her, drew her closer against him. He would protect her. Somehow, he would protect her.

Against what?

The eyes in the night.

No, houses didn't watch people.

People watched...

And still...

It felt as if the house had eyes...

Drew Parker wasn't sure what brought him driving up the path that wound just below the driveway to Granger House that night. He felt...*drawn*. That was it. He should have just gone on up to see them. No. It was well past midnight. They'd all be sleeping. And still...

He could just drive to the front door. Ring the bell. Wake Edgar. Good old Edgar, who would let him in, of course, because he was

223

Abby's dear old friend. Yes, he could go in by way of the front door anytime he desired.

He drove his old Silver Shadow Rolls Royce slowly along, watching the house now and then, and looking at his hands.

Age spots, too thin—he was getting a *gnarled* look about him. Hell, they said that he was good-looking. Strong, classic, debonair. He worked out, hell, he took Tae-Bo classes. He was strong as an ox, especially for a seventy-year-old. Seventy-year-*old*. Key word. He was old, and he hated old. He felt a lot like old Granger at times. David Granger had wanted to be many things. Drew knew the feeling. They'd both come close. Granger had known a little magic. A little talent, a little this, and a little that. Never quite enough.

That's me, on the fringes, Drew thought.

He was almost among the beautiful people but not quite. He'd acted a little, dabbled in magic, in land. He'd done some boxing, wrestling, and taken lessons in the martial arts—in order to take small roles in kung fu movies. He was a jack of all trades, and master of trivia. Yes, he was on plenty of party guest lists. He could entertain, tell tales of old Hollywood.

He had some purpose. There were so many things he knew. So many things he might have been.

He slowed the car and pulled onto the narrow embankment, looking up. Ah, yes, there stood Granger House. It looked alive in the night.

Shades of *The Haunting,* he thought with amusement.

Only *shades.* Abby kept up Granger House beautifully. She was a grand old dame. The house, that was. Abby...oh, yes. Abby was a grand old dame as well. And yet...

No matter what cosmetic repairs were made, human flesh could never survive as a house might. Abby tried so hard to hide her illness. She showed such strength, such character. She held on so well.

Because she had Jennifer. Her precious daughter. Yet if something were ever to happen to Jennifer, Abby would crumble, like wet sand. She'd just fall apart completely.

Jennifer. Beautiful, kind, gracious, charming, perfect...Jennifer.

If anything were to happen to her...

There were so many things Abby didn't know about the house.

In the night, it seemed that a cloud settled around the structure, high above. A shadow of evil. *Some houses are just born evil.* Shades of *The Haunting* again.

But houses weren't evil.

People were.

And yet...

Maybe there were some houses that helped people to be evil...

Chapter 11

Andy Larkin took his job as producer seriously. He loved acting as well—loved being a heartthrob, being adored by tens of thousands of women across the nation. He didn't read all of his fan mail—he couldn't. He'd never get anything done if he did. He had a secretary, and though she answered all his mail, she also made sure that he got the most effusive and complimentary pieces.

He was handsome, and he knew it. He played macho, and he loved it. And even if soaps hadn't quite turned him into a Tom Cruise, his face was known all over the country. He was constantly in magazines. He didn't just appear in *Soap Digest* and the other magazines aimed at the audience. He had been featured in *People* and *Time* and other important magazines. He and Joe Penny had seen to it that their show dealt with issues, real issues. They'd tackled drugs, gangs, violence, cancer, Alzheimer's and AIDS.

He arrived at Joe Penny's place about a half hour early on Tuesday morning. The two of them were due to meet with director Jim Novac to review the upcoming episode of *Valentine Valley,* written by Doug Henson.

He glanced at his watch as he rang the bell to Joe's Beverly Hills brick-adorned colonial manor a second time. He wasn't that early. Where the hell was Joe?

Joe at last answered the door in a bathrobe.

"You're early," he said, rubbing his face.

"Not that early. What, did you stay out late last night?"

"Yeah. Yeah, I stopped by to hear some music at House of Blues. Someone asked me to a party. I went. You're looking too chipper. What did you do—stay home and catch up on your beauty rest?"

"My good looks keep our soap on the air, buddy," Andy reminded him dryly.

"What, can't be happy with any other woman but Serena?" Joe asked, closing the door behind Andy and heading for the kitchen.

"There are lots of women out there," Andy replied defensively. The whole Serena thing really rankled him. She'd really wanted the divorce; she hadn't asked for anything—anything. She'd even been willing to give things up to get it. Yeah, he'd cheated. And yeah, he'd made a fool out of himself, asking for forgiveness.

It hadn't been just the cheating, she'd told him.

It had just been...

Well, frankly, it had just been him.

He was still angry every time he thought about that. It made him want to punch a wall, as a matter of fact.

In his high-tech kitchen, amazingly modern for the colonial look and feel of his manor, Joe poured coffee. "I thought that you really wanted to get back with Serena," he said.

"I think it would be good for the show."

Joe ran his fingers through his stylishly cut

227

hair, smiling slightly, shaking his head. "You know, I'm not known as a man regarded for his monumental tact, but even I know you don't tell a woman you want to remarry her for the benefit of a show. Or ratings."

Andy shrugged. "That's pure business sense. But I didn't say that to Serena. And it doesn't matter. I'm just teasing with her most of the time." He grimaced. "Just to get to follow her home."

"For a night in the sack, eh? I can see that."

"Yeah," Andy lied. That was another thing that rankled him. She acted as if she'd die rather than go back to bed with him again.

He was in good shape. He could work it like a rabbit.

Damn her. He hadn't had any complaints in that department before.

"Anyway, I met a girl at the party."

"Mystery girl?"

"That's right." Joe hesitated. "She's still here."

"Oh?" Andy arched a brow.

"Sleeping. I shouldn't have told you. Stay away from my bedroom door."

"All right, let's get down to business. I'm wondering, if under the circumstances, we should go ahead with the shower attack as we planned."

"We're going to let a little prima donna like Brenda Lopez ruin our show?" Joe demanded, aggravated.

"A dead prima donna," Andy said.

Joe sighed, running his fingers through his

hair again. "Hell, Andy, I'm not going to let anything change my plans. I think they're good plans. We've thought it over for a long time."

"What if we put the scene off?" Andy suggested. "It's not even written yet."

Joe poured more coffee. "I don't know."

The doorbell rang.

"Must be Jim," Joe said. "I'll get it."

"I've got to go to the can," Andy said.

"Not my room. Use the hallway bath."

"Of course," Andy said, frowning. When the hell had he ever gone into Joe's bedroom to use the bathroom? Sometimes, Joe did a screening in his elaborate room because of the immense state-of-the-art entertainment system in his bedroom, but...

Weird. Like the guy was hiding something. How the hell long had he known him?

He walked down the length of the hallway, watching Joe until he disappeared around the corner to get to the door.

Then, suddenly tempted, he found himself striding quickly down the length of the hall to reach Joe's bedroom. He pushed open the door.

The drapes were drawn, the room lay in shadow. There was a body on Joe's bed, completely enwrapped in the covers. She didn't stir. He closed the door quickly, wondering what the hell was the matter with him that he should decide to spy on Joe's choice of a bed mate. He walked quickly to the hall bath and pushed open the door, listening as Joe greeted Jim Novac.

He closed the door, walked to the john, picked up the seat, and froze.

Blood, or something red, was spattered in the white basin of the sink. He shriveled, forgetting the urge to urinate. He turned to the sink and touched the spots. Blood, yes, rinsed down the sink, but a few little spots remained...

He turned to the shower and drew back the curtain, expecting to see...

Spatters, pools of blood. A corpse, a...

"Hey!" he heard Joe call. "What the hell are you doing in there? Playing with your thing? Come on, Andy, get out here, we've got work to do."

There was nothing in the shower. Blood in the sink. Joe must have cut himself shaving. He let the shower curtain fall, feeling like a fool. He turned to leave.

Before he could put his hand around the doorknob, he noticed the wicker laundry hamper.

"Hey, Andy! Quit admiring that piece of equipment," Jim Novac called. "I've got things to do, places to go."

Andy lifted the little wicker top. Something lay in the basket. A flowered dress maybe, with a white collar. An old-fashioned, prim dress. And it was drenched in red.

Blood.

"Andy!"

He slammed the top back on the basket, his heart pounding.

He didn't know what to think. There was a banging on the bathroom door.

"Hey, man—!"

"Hell, I'm coming!"

"Not on my time," Jim growled. "Get out here."

He swung the door open. Jim had banged on the door; Joe stood just behind Jim.

Joe was staring at him. Coldly, he thought. Panic seized him.

What if his old friend was a murderer?

"Man, I'm...sick," he groaned, leaning heavily on the door as he exited the bathroom. Maybe he did have a green pallor to his face. But then again, he was a pretty good actor, not just another pretty face. "I think I ate something...," he apologized. "I gotta get outta here," he said, leaning on the wall of the hallway, edging along it.

"You can't go," Joe said incredulously. "We have to talk this out, make a decision. We have to meet with Doug Henson, to tell him what to write for Friday, to give him the step-by-step sequence for the rest of the week."

"We can't get rid of Jennifer," Andy said.

"We were never getting 'rid of' Jennifer," Joe said, eyes narrowed.

Andy lumbered down the hall, wanting to get out. Joe and Jim were following right along with him, staring at him.

"Come on, I'll get you an antacid," Joe said, shaking his head. "Andy, damn it, this is our show—"

"Gotta go," Andy said.

"And we've got to have a script tomorrow," Joe said.

231

He waved a hand in the air. "You make the decisions."

Thank God, the door. He inhaled air like a drowning man hitting the surface. Somehow, he made it to his car. Opened the door, slid into the driver's seat. He gunned his motor; winced.

Then he shot out of Joe's driveway.

He drove and drove. Finally he pulled in to park by a few of the hotels on Sunset. He leaned his head against the steering wheel. His stomach turned, then settled. He leaned back. The police. He should call the police.

Then his common sense kicked in. Joe Penny was a producer; he hired makeup men and women, costumers, and special effects people all the time. He often had people at his house. The dress might have been left over from a demonstration...

Might have, oh, come on!

What could he do? Pull it out of the hamper, let Joe know he'd been digging around in his bathroom.

A creepy feeling settled over Andy.

What about the covered lump in Joe's bed? He hadn't seen the woman's face, or her hair. Was there really a woman in his bed at all?

Or was the covered lump a corpse?

"And we're on in five...four...three..."

Jennifer, dressed to the nines as Natalie Valentine and poring through documents at the heavy oak table in the family dining room, looked up. Kelly, playing slightly older sister Marla, danced in, a smile on her face a mile wide. She started off humming, then began singing about being happy and in love.

Jennifer stared at her, just as they had rehearsed. That was the business of soaps. Quick scripts, rapid line memorization, and, if humanly possible, just one take before the camera. They worked hard, they knew their business, and they seldom made mistakes.

"Marla? What's up?"

Kelly spun around then, as if just seeing her and realizing that she wasn't alone. She quickly sobered and came up to stand by Jennifer. "I'm so sorry. I didn't know you were in here. And it's such a bad time for you. Dad said you spent the morning with lawyers. I know that you've just decided that your marriage is..."

"Over," Jennifer supplied. "Yes, it's over," she said tightly.

"It's so sad, and I am so sorry."

"He...he cheated."

Kelly was quiet a moment. "So did you," she whispered.

Jennifer brought large stage tears to her eyes. "He cheated on me. With Verona! And then he...he..." She let her voice trail off. They would insert footage of the fight the two had engaged in after he had caught her in the midst of her screen affair.

"I'm sure Verona never meant—"

"Oh, I think she meant it. She did it to destroy my marriage. She's miserable herself, and so she sets out to destroy everyone else. Well, she won't destroy me."

"But you were with—"

"No. We never really did anything. We wanted to get back at them." She set the papers aside on the table and rose, walking to a wine decanter at the dining room buffet. She poured out a glass of wine and sipped it. "Hey, sis. I'm sorry. You came in here happy as a little lark, and I've gone and thrown all my own misery on you. What's up?"

Kelly gave her a dazzling smile. "I'm in love."

"Oh?"

"He's come back."

Jennifer frowned. "Who has come back?"

"You can't say anything. You have to swear you won't say anything to anyone. If you don't promise me right now—"

"I promise. Who has come back?"

"Our neighbor. The most gorgeous man in the entire world."

"Our neighbor. The most gorgeous man...?"

"DeVille, the heir to the DeVille vineyards. Oh, you wouldn't believe how wonderful it was: He walked into the room and I felt like melting." She clutched her hands to her heart. "Our eyes met, and the way that he looked at me..."

"David DeVille?" Jennifer whispered.

Kelly nodded, still mesmerized. "David DeVille." She walked dreamily around the table, stretching out an arm in memory. "He kissed my hand. He said that I was one of the most beautiful women he'd ever seen. He was so distressed to discover that I was a Valentine...because there is such bad blood between the families."

"I'll bet," Jennifer murmured.

Kelly swung around, hugging her. "Talia, am I beautiful?"

"Of course you are."

"Could he really think so?"

"Of...of course."

"I'm supposed to meet him. Slip into the old horse master's quarters at the DeVille estate tomorrow at midnight. I'm so afraid that it can't be real."

"You are beautiful, you're bright, you're everything wonderful, but...Marla, should you trust him? He went to France, you know."

"He's back."

"Yes, but they've always wanted to take over our vineyards."

Kelly drew away. "But...it's me he wants! I know it!"

"Of course, of course..."

Jennifer drew Kelly into her arms.

"Cut!" Jim called. Striding onto the set, he hugged them both. "I have the best people in the entire world. One take every damn time."

Thorne McKay stepped forward to put powder on Jennifer's nose. "Are we moving right into the bed scene?"

"Ten minutes," Jim said. "Jennifer, that's you. Kelly, you're done for the day."

"Cool," Kelly said. She grinned at Jennifer. "Thank God. An early day. Except, sorry, not for you."

"One more scene. Then I'm out of here, too. We're out of here—both Conar and I. We've an appointment with my mom this afternoon."

"Best wishes with it," Kelly said sincerely. "You know that if there's anything I can do, anything at all..."

"I know that, Kelly. Thanks. Kelly...have you talked to Andy today?"

Kelly shook her head. "Andy wasn't on call today."

"Andy is a producer."

Kelly grinned. "Right. So when he isn't on call as an actor, he's a big shot and doesn't have to show up if he doesn't feel like it. And I'm going to get out of here before someone feels they need to give me rewrites or put me on a diet or dye my hair a new color or something else!" She gave Jennifer a kiss on the cheek. "Bye, Jen. Hope all goes well with your mom this afternoon."

Jim Novac was walking across the room, from the cameras toward the set. Kelly made a face in his direction and quickly fled.

"What's up with your mom this afternoon?" Jim asked, approaching Jennifer.

"Doctor's appointment," she said briefly. She smiled quickly at Jim. "Have to change for the flashback scene," she said quickly. "You said ten minutes, right?"

"Right. Have Thorne put some foundation on your shoulders—your tan line is too obvious."

"Yeah."

She hurried from the set to her dressing room. Once there, she went through her wardrobe for the flesh-colored strips of panties and pasty-like bra pieces used for their "nude" scenes. She had barely slipped her robe over her shoulders when she heard Thorne at her door.

"Jennifer."

"Come on in. I'm ready."

She sat in front of her mirror and waited while Thorne came in, armed with his makeup case. "You've been in the sun too much," he told her.

She shrugged. "My mother likes the pool area. I spend a lot of time in the sun."

"Well, this isn't easy to cover up."

"Well, I'm sure that Natalie Valentine goes to the beach."

"But she has the good sense to cover up," Thorne told her.

"Oh, but our Jennifer has such a lovely natural blush, don't you think?" Doug said, pushing open her door and entering without knocking or being invited. "You all right for this scene, sweetie?" he asked her, leaning on the dressing table.

She arched a brow, looking at him. "I seldom have problems with your scenes, Doug."

He grinned. "Look at her cheeks, will you, Thorne? I mean, you are a master of makeup, but don't you think our girl has a special glow today?"

"Yeah, yeah, she glows. Doug, you're blocking my light," Thorne complained.

Doug was nonplussed. He remained there, smiling at Jennifer.

"Did you make up with Wonder Boy?" he inquired innocently.

"Doug!" she said, and frowned at him severely. "We're too professional to have arguments, you know."

He laughed outright and bent to kiss her cheek. "I can't wait to watch this scene," he teased. Then he was out the door before she could say anything else.

"What was that all about?" Thorne asked.

"God knows."

Thorne inhaled sharply, spilling a pool of body makeup on her shoulder. His eyes met hers in the dressing table mirror. "Oh, my God! I've got it. You're already having a thing with Conar!"

Jennifer groaned, sinking into her chair. "Thorne, please, don't go weird on me. I was only given ten minutes between scenes."

In answer to her prayer, one of Jim's production assistants appeared at her door. "You're late on the set, Miss Connolly."

"I'm on my way."

"I'm not done," Thorne told her in dismay.

"Yes you are."

"You're not blended, Miss Connolly."

"I'll have to stay that way."

"Just give me one minute."

She was up, but he followed, spreading her body makeup as she reached for her robe.

"Hold still," he commanded.

"I don't have any more time."

"Give me thirty seconds!"

She bit her lower lip and stood still.

Thorne was good, and true to his word—within two minutes she was on the set. It was hastily—and cheaply—designed. It wasn't a standing set, such as the Valentine dining room, but designed for this one flashback scene only. The lighting kept most of the room in shadow, and the double bed with flowered sheets—supposedly French—was the focal point of the room. Naturally, there was an ice bucket, champagne glasses, and all the other paraphernalia of a little love nest.

As Jennifer walked through the cameras and crew and toward the set, Jim suddenly accosted her again, standing in front of her. "Are you going to be all right with this, Jennifer?"

She frowned. "Excuse me?"

"Everyone knows how you feel about Conar. Are you going to be all right with this?"

Apparently, everyone didn't know exactly how she felt about Conar. Yet.

She smiled. "Fine, Jim. Just fine. You know, we're all professionals here."

"Yes, of course, good. I just wanted to make sure. Think we can get this scene in with just one take?" he called out cheerfully. "We'll rehearse first, of course."

"We don't need a rehearsal," Jennifer said.

"Well, Jen, I don't just expect you to be able to do this."

"I'm fine."

"We can really rehearse."

"We don't need to rehearse," she insisted.

Jennifer kept walking toward the set, toward the bed, center stage.

Conar was already in it. Shoulders bare and bronzed. He was naked to the waist, and the flowery sheets covered his body below his upper torso.

"Conar, I suggest a rehearsal."

"We don't need a rehearsal."

"The two of you are pigheaded. All right, one take with the camera rolling. Now, remember, both of you. This has been a totally passionate affair. Jennifer, you're going to find out who he is. The burning question here is—has he or hasn't he been after you, seducing you, for the purpose of taking over the vineyard?"

The "burning" question...

"Jennifer, remember, passion, honey, please, lots of passion, no matter how hard..."

Smiling, Jennifer approached the bed, shedding the robe. She could see his smile, his amusement, and the encouragement in his silver-gray eyes. Jeez, but he was great-looking. She crawled atop the bed, slipped beneath the covers.

"Jen, remember, you're in love here, show some real emotion."

She crawled on top of him, kissed him. His body was rock hard, warm, and his arms quickly encompassed her. God, he could kiss. Lips formed over hers with confidence, purpose, determination. Mouth passionate, wet, forceful. Tongue between her lips, the smell of him, the taste of him, the movement, the feel of his hands on her...

"And we're on in five, four, three..."

Jennifer broke the kiss. This was, after all, a scene on a daytime soap.

"I've got to go."

"Why?" he demanded.

"My...my father is due in tonight."

She pulled away from him. Found the robe at the foot of the bed, subtly slipped into it, trusting the cameras to do the work of covering for her.

He sat up, watching her as she rose. "And you jump every time your father says you should?"

"No! But he's just arrived in Paris."

"And you're afraid to tell him that you've met a man, that you've become involved."

She shook her head, her back to him. "It's just that I don't know anything about you at all. This was all so sudden. We met at the cock-tail party. Then I started talking to you about California, my home, the vineyards...and all I know is that you've been a student in Paris."

"I have been a student in Paris. While you've been running away."

"I wasn't running away. I needed time. From my family."

"But now Daddy is here."

"Yes, and I love my family. They can just be so intense. And I don't have to tell you any-thing else. I know nothing about you."

He reached out for her, caught her hands, drew her back to him with passionate force. "You know me, you know what it is to be with me, and God help me, you want to be with me."

He kissed her again.

Lord.

What a kiss.

For a moment she forgot the scene. His lips broke from hers. She felt them slightly swollen and very damp.

"I...I...know nothing."

"Maybe it's better if we keep it that way," he said harshly.

"You act as if there are things I shouldn't know about you."

"Maybe there are."

"Like what?"

"Like my name."

She drew away from him. "What do you mean? What is your name? Do I know it?"

"Too well. Far, far too well."

There was dead silence in the room. The cameras kept rolling and rolling. Staring at Jennifer, Conar began to grin. She smiled in return, and at last turned to Jim.

"Aren't you supposed to call 'cut!'?"

"What? Oh! Cut, cut, yes, cut!"

"Did we get it right in one take?" she asked.

"Enough passion for you?" Conar asked.

"Wise-asses. Just what a director needs—a cast full of wise-asses."

Conar was all business then, reaching for his robe, rising. "Miss Connolly and I couldn't

242

possibly flub a scene today, Jim. We've an appointment this afternoon. Ten minutes enough time, Jen?"

"Absolutely," she agreed.

She was out of makeup and dressed in a mere eight minutes, but Conar was already dressed and ready and waiting outside her dressing room door.

He grinned at her. "Jim had no idea that you had decided I wasn't entirely repulsive. He thinks you're the best actress in the world."

"Maybe I am," she said.

He watched her for a moment. "Maybe you are," he agreed softly. "Shall we? We may be a little early, but that's better than late."

"I'm absolutely ready. But don't go thinking that because I've decided you're not entirely repulsive that I'm going to agree about surgery for my mother."

"We'll see what the doctor has to say."

"From every angle."

"From every angle."

He wasn't such a great actor, Andy thought ruefully. He really was sick. And he wasn't going to be able to hold it.

He crawled out of the car, glad to see that he was by a weed-infested vacant lot, being used illegally as a dump. There was a half-broken picket fence in front of some wire mesh. He leaned on it and was sick.

He held still for a few minutes, closing his eyes.

243

Amazing. He felt so much better. But what had caused it? He hadn't really had any kind of wild night, he sure as hell hadn't gotten lucky.

Nerves. Idiot nerves. He'd known Joe forever. Joe wasn't trying to conceal some awful crime.

He thought he was going to be sick again. Bile rose in his throat. He heaved and instinctively swallowed, heaved and swallowed again. Time to get the police.

And tell them what?

His best friend had apparently murdered a woman?

He was losing it.

From every angle! Jennifer thought.

She, Conar, and her mother sat in the office of Dr. Theobald Dessinger. He had a model of the human brain, and he took it apart. He explained neurons and what science knew about the function of the brain. He had shown them a tape. He had explained the progression of the disease—and he had talked about what surgery could accomplish. He was so thorough that, although Jennifer had always considered herself to be a reasonably intelligent human being, she had no idea of what he had actually said by the time he had finished. He talked about the changed lives of patients who had survived the surgery, and he admitted that not all patients survived. Conar pointed out that younger patients had a better chance with the surgery, and that in this instance

244

Abby was considered a younger patient. Jennifer pointed out the fact that her mother had a weak heart, and the doctor again admitted that certain patients weren't meant for surgery. In the end, he pointed out the fact that each human being saw life, and the quality of life, differently, and in the end, it was the patient who had to make the decision.

As they drove home Jennifer and Conar were still arguing. Abby at last interrupted them. "You've quite exhausted me. May I get home and to my own bed before you continue speaking about me as if I were not present?"

"Oh, Mom, I'm so sorry," Jennifer exclaimed. She and Conar were in the front, Abby in the back. She turned around, but Abby refused to look at her. She was staring out the window.

They returned to the house. Edgar was there ready to greet them, ready to help Abby to her room when she announced that she was exhausted. And that she wanted to be alone.

Conar went into the den. Jennifer couldn't help but follow him.

"Conar, she could *die*."

He swung around on her. "Jennifer, *she* doesn't feel that she's really living."

"Well, of course, her life is different."

"Different? It sucks! She was a brilliant actress."

"She's still a brilliant actress."

"Jennifer, she shakes. She can maintain a normal mode of behavior for about half an hour on a truckload of medication. She won't always be eligible for the surgery."

"It could take her life."

"It could give her a real life back."

Jennifer swung around and started out of the house. She knew that her mother was upset with her. She couldn't help but feel that it was partly Conar's fault. He was supporting Abby. Neither of them seemed to realize what a risk they would be taking.

She had used her clicker to open the lock on her car door when she realized that he was behind her. He reached around her to open the driver's side.

"I'll drive," he said.

"It's my car."

"But you're upset."

"Right. And I'm trying to get away from you."

"You're not going to get away from me. I'm here to look after you, remember?"

She didn't answer. But she knew him well enough to know that she wasn't leaving without him. Abby had brought him in as a guard dog. There was no way he would fail in his duty to Abby.

"Fine. Drive."

She strode around to the passenger's seat, jerked open the door, sat, slammed it. A second later, her car revved into gear.

"Where are we going?"

"Away from the house—and you."

"On the first I can oblige," he murmured. They were both silent. Jennifer rolled down her window. The air rushed in. He drove fast, taking the curves with an expertise born of long experience. After a while, she realized that they had come to Sunset Boulevard. He pulled down a side street and parked the car. They were in an area of hotels, bars, and clubs. She stared at him blankly.

"It's late. I thought we'd get something to eat."

"I'm not hungry."

"Then you can watch me eat."

He got out of the car and walked around to open her door. She stepped out and started ahead of him down the street.

The sun had almost set. Deep red shadows were forming over the landscape. She wasn't paying attention where she walked, as long as she was ahead of him. That's why she almost tripped over a whiskey-sodden bum lying in the street. He stirred himself enough to ask for a handout.

"Got a twenty, lady?"

"A twenty?" The request startled her so much that she stood still, staring at the man. He had all his limbs, and he didn't appear to be too thin. He grinned at her. He had all of his teeth. They were heavily tobacco-stained and contained little pieces of whatever his last meal had been as well.

"Aren't you supposed to be asking if I've got any spare change?"

"Inflation, lady. But I'll take change, too."

Conar was right behind her. He dropped a five on the guy. "Use it for food—no more booze, you hear?"

"Oh, yeah. Sure."

"Yeah, sure." He grabbed Jennifer's arm and

hurried her on past the bum. She wrenched her arm free.

"You are a fool. No wonder your mother called me out here."

"I was in no danger from the bum."

"How the hell do you know? There are lights and businesses to the left of us—dark empty lots to the right. Which way do you go? To the right!"

"Conar, I'm not really thinking about bums or directions, light or dark. What you're planning is insane."

"I'm not planning anything."

"You're agreeing to idiocy. And...you're going to kill my mother," she said, wrenching free from his touch and spinning on him.

"Are you thinking about your mother—or yourself?"

His eyes seemed very dark in the shadows, deep, riveting pits that seemed to fill his face. His jawbone was set and hard; he seemed almost a stranger.

"What do you mean by that? I'm thinking about my mother."

"Your mother, who is proud, dignified, talented, intelligent, able, compassionate, giving, and a million other things."

"Yes—which is why she should live a nice long life!"

"She has a chance at a nice long life with *quality*!"

"Who makes the decision on what gives life quality?" Jennifer demanded. "You?"

If possible, his jawbone clicked harder.

"No, not me. Each person individually. Abby sang like a nightingale, danced like Ginger Rogers, and was possibly one of the best actresses of her generation."

"She's a person first, my mother first—"

He gripped her by the shoulders. "Do you want her to live for her—or you?"

Jennifer wrenched free from him and started walking down the street again.

"Jennifer!"

"Leave me alone."

"The hell I will."

"I'm not running away from you, I just need some space."

"You want space, you got space!" he snapped angrily. "Just quit walking off blindly like an idiot."

She had gotten some distance from him. She turned back and lifted her arms. "I'm walking toward the lights and—"

She broke off. A car was going by them, beaming headlights into the slope of the empty lot at her side.

Despite the NO DUMPING signs on the property, it had been used as a trash heap. There was a discarded refrigerator halfway down the slope, clearly defined by the sudden glow of headlights. There were broken chairs tossed into the lot, and tons and tons of Coke bottles, beer cans, and candy wrappers. There was a discarded coat lying in a pile of overgrown grass, next to a torn bag that had once contained "the world's best rippled potato chips."

Something about the coat gave her pause.

"Conar?"

"I'm right behind you."

Another car drove by. Another set of headlights, another beam on the coat.

"Conar!"

"Jennifer, what the hell are you doing?"

She had already cut into the lot, not thinking of any personal danger. The headlights had revealed that the coat was not empty.

"Conar, hurry."

"Jennifer, what the hell are you doing? Where are you going?"

"Conar, there's someone..."

"Jennifer, damn it, stop!"

He came up behind her fast. But she reached the coat before he did.

"It's a woman," she called back, knowing that he had nearly reached her.

"She's probably wigged out, like the last bum you decided to befriend."

"Hey, she might need help."

"This isn't a good time to start making friendships with bums in vacant lots."

She reached down, thinking that the woman beneath the coat might indeed be wigged out, too messed up on something to help herself. She might be hurt, or she might have passed out.

She drew the coat back and screamed.

And screamed and screamed.

Chapter 12

The woman had been strangled to death with a necktie.

The necktie remained garrotted around her.

Her nude body had been hidden by the coat until the breeze, growing brisk at sunset, lifted the fabric, exposing enough flesh so that Jennifer had recognized that a body lay beneath.

Jennifer had never been in such a situation before: No role she had ever taken had prepared her for the reality of finding a murder victim. The ghastly color of the flesh. The way the lips had swollen, the way the tongue protruded.

The way that the eyes of the dead woman still seemed to stare at her.

She hadn't wanted to think, realize, or see.

For once in her life, she had been glad for Conar to take control. She was grateful, still in shock. She had let him lead her away, to the closest business establishment.

It was an upscale adult entertainment club. People clad in nothing but G-strings and nipple rings helped and consoled her, and she didn't even notice anything out of the ordinary. A woman with monstrous breasts, who later confided in her that she'd had a sex change, gave her a large snifter of brandy and wrapped a boa around her for warmth as Conar took the police to the victim. Then he sat by her, arm around her, as they questioned her and she gave all the answers she could. Not many. She'd seen a coat in a vacant lot, over a form. She'd just stepped over a bum. She'd assumed it was another. The police went to look for the first bum, hoping he might have seen someone. He hadn't. The night was filled with sirens. The medical examiner arrived. The cop who had arrived first continued to quiz her as to why she thought there would be a body in a vacant lot. She explained for what felt like the millionth time that she hadn't expected to find a body in a lot. She had just seen the form and thought that it was a woman who might need help. How had she known it was a woman? Something about the shape. When had she realized there was a body there? Why was she walking down the street?

Conar did not escape the same questioning. Why was he there, when did he realize there was a body in the lot, why had he decided to pull off the road right there?

She heard all the questions. At last she roused herself from her state of shivering shock to get up and scream. "You idiots! We're the ones who found the body, not the ones who put it there!"

Conar, about to answer a question, paused, a brow arched, a look of amusement in his eyes. A few minutes later, Liam arrived on the scene, and the pressure was eased off of both of them. A while later he came over.

"The behavioral guy is saying that these

killings are very different—a stabbing and a strangulation. There may be no association whatever."

Liam looked at Jennifer, frowning. "I'm sorry you were the one who found her, Jennifer. In any case, we don't need you two anymore. Conar, you might want to take Jennifer on home."

"Definitely," Conar said. Standing, he drew Jennifer up with him. He had started for the door when he muttered, "Shit!"

"What?"

"The press is here."

"Maybe there's a back way out."

"Maybe. Why don't you ask your friend, the bosomy blonde? You can return the boa while you're at it."

Jennifer and Conar made a neat turn, heading for the rear of the establishment. The blonde smiled at them both. "Lap dance, honey?" she asked Conar.

"You think you can sneak us out the back?" Conar asked her.

"Sure thing."

The blonde walked them around the stage, where an exotic dancer with a ball python around her neck was getting erotic with a pole. She led them through a dressing room filled with naked women sitting in front of mirrors.

"I can see why you don't want to meet the press!" the blonde said. "You two are going to be headlines tomorrow. This isn't a publicity stunt, is it?"

"God, no!" Jennifer said, horrified.

"This isn't the kind of publicity we want," Conar told her.

She looked him up and down. "You are a good-looking hunk. You're the kind of man I became a woman for. But I like soaps—watch 'em all the time." When Conar didn't react at all, she said, "Anyway, that dead girl out there is not one of ours."

"You're certain of that?" Conar asked.

"The owner went out with the cops—naturally. She was found naked and this is an adult club and strippers do have to be careful about what kind of freaks they get to know. But the girl wasn't a stripper. Not here, at least. Her face didn't look too good, but Arnie—he's the owner—he would have known if she was one of ours."

"I wonder who she was," Jennifer said.

"An actress."

"How do you know?" Conar asked sharply.

The blonde grinned. "Hell, honey, this is Hollywood. Everybody is an actress out here. Every waiter, waitress, bellhop, and cab-driver."

"Not everyone," Conar said. "There is a real world out here, too."

"Somewhere out here. Maybe," the blonde agreed with a vague shrug. "Well, there's the back door. Get going before those nosy newshounds figure it out, too."

Jennifer returned the boa with thanks, then they fled.

Edgar was stunned by the news. He'd been up, waiting for them, and brewed tea while he listened to them tell about finding the body and talking to the police. He kept shaking his head, assuring them that Abby was well when Jennifer paused to ask about her mother. "She heard nothing on the late news tonight, Miss Jen. I know that. She's been sound asleep now for several hours. I saw to it that she had some sleep medication this evening," he told them. "She had such a full and restless day herself. That long doctor's appointment. And then, after you left, Mr. Parker came by. He and Miss Abby talked for ages, even though she was shaking, and losing her breath. Then that big-shot director showed up."

"Do you mean Jim Novac from my set?" Jennifer asked, sipping the chamomile tea he had brewed.

"No, I mean that slasher big shot." Edgar made a face. His opinion of Hugh Tanenbaum's movies was quite obvious.

"What did he come here for?" Jennifer asked, tensing.

"I don't know. I wasn't in on the conversation."

"But, Edgar, you shouldn't have let him in."

"I work for Miss Abby," Edgar said.

"Yes, but you know that she isn't always in her right mind! Edgar, you have to look out for her when I'm not here."

"Jennifer! He's right. If your mother chooses to see people, there's little that Edgar can do."

"Yes! You know that her medication leaves her in a state that isn't...that isn't quite right!"

Edgar sighed, looking down. Jennifer clenched her teeth together, sorry to be so wretched to Edgar, but unable to believe that he had allowed Abby to be so vulnerable.

"Edgar, from now on, if I'm not here, don't even tell Mother when those underhanded rats show up, all right?"

"Mr. Parker is hardly an underhanded rat, Miss Jennifer," Edgar said indignantly.

She'd hurt his feelings. Injured him.

"Jennifer's just upset, Edgar," Conar said, apologizing for her.

She bit into her lip. "I'm sorry, Edgar," she said softly.

"I know, Miss Jennifer," he assured her.

"Let's go up to bed," Conar suggested.

"I'll never sleep. I'll just keep seeing that woman..."

"I can get you some brandy," Edgar said.

Jennifer smiled at him, reaching across the kitchen counter to squeeze his hand. "They gave me brandy at the club, but thanks, Edgar."

"What club?" Edgar asked.

"The strip club," Jennifer told him.

He looked at Conar like a protective bulldog. "You had Miss Jennifer out at a strip club, Mr. Markham? You didn't tell me about that part of the evening."

"That's where the police came to interview us—I had to use their telephone."

Edgar made a tsking sound. "Where is your cellular, Mr. Markham?"

"I need a new one. Broke the old guy in the airport on my way here."

"Miss Jennifer?"

"I never remember to carry mine," she admitted. It was rather idiotic. Cellular phones were certainly the rage. Everyone was always waiting for a call from his or her agent.

"Please, Miss Jen, you make sure to carry it from now on," Edgar said worriedly.

"I will." On impulse, she gave him a sound kiss on the cheek. "Good night, Edgar. And thanks for waiting up."

"I just checked on the dogs. You should see them. Snug as two bugs in a rug. That little one of yours is curled up on Lady's front paws, Mr. Markham. They're just as happy as can be together."

"That's wonderful. Well, thanks again, and good night," Jennifer said.

They left the kitchen together and walked up the stairs together.

They paused at Jennifer's door. "Well...," she murmured.

"You're not staying in my room?"

"You hadn't asked," she told him.

"All right. Will you stay in my room?"

"I'm afraid that I'm not feeling terribly amorous."

"No sex. That's okay."

"I need to get my toothbrush."

257

"Want me to wait?"

"Yes."

He grinned. "I'm right here in the doorway."

She went into her bathroom and grabbed her toothbrush. On second thought, she scooped up her facial soap and deodorant. He made no comment as she reappeared in the bedroom. "Don't worry, I'm not moving in for good or anything. I mean, I'm not presuming anything. In fact, the way that we were fighting this afternoon, I probably shouldn't be in there tonight. We're sure to fight again. I mean, maybe even tonight. I'd almost forgotten about my mother and the possibility of surgery and the fact that we absolutely disagree. I mean, really, if you stop to think about the whole thing—"

"Jennifer."

"What?"

"Stop fucking analyzing everything. Let's get some sleep."

"I didn't mean—"

"Jennifer."

"Let's go."

She preceded him out the door. He followed her down the hall. They entered his room, and he closed the door behind him.

"Did you lock it?" she whispered.

"Yeah, I will," he assured her, doing so.

"Eyes, you know," she told him gravely.

"I know. You want first shower?"

"Please."

She showered for a very long time. She felt as if she were wearing all the dirt in the vacant lot. Worse, she felt as if she were wearing traces of death. When she emerged later, he was in his briefs on the bed, face hard as a rock as he watched the television.

"We're on the late breaking news," he told her curtly, then walked on into the bathroom.

She curled up on the bed. The anchor was talking about the discovery of a body off Sunset, cause of death: strangulation. The victim's identity was as yet unknown. The coat that had covered her had apparently been discarded previously in the lot. According to the medical examiner, she had lain there most of the day. She had died some time between two and five the previous morning.

The next thing Jennifer knew, there were shots of her and Conar.

The police saw no reason to suspect that this murder and that of Brenda Lopez were related, but they had not ruled out the prospect that there might be a serial killer in the area, preying upon young, beautiful women in L.A.

The news ended. A late-night talk show began. Jennifer shivered.

Conar came out of the bathroom naked. He crawled into the bed without a word, slipping an arm around her shoulders, pulling her close. He was tense but remained silent, and did nothing but hold her, staring at the television.

There was a singing dog contest on.

Then a farmer brought on the biggest pig Jennifer had ever seen.

A rock group performed their latest number.

"Want to try to sleep?" Conar suggested, aiming the remote control at the television.

"Sure."

The television went off. Conar had left on the bathroom light, giving the room just enough illumination.

She closed her eyes. She had thought that she'd never sleep because the vision of a dead woman's eyes would haunt her. But the fear and horror faded. She began drifting off, thinking that the mind must have some self-protective mechanism.

Conar suddenly jerked up.

"What?" she gasped, sitting up beside him.

She saw his face in the shadows. His features were tight and drawn. For a moment she was afraid.

"Nothing. I'm sorry. I didn't mean to startle you."

"Well, you did."

"Go back to sleep."

"The hell I can just go back to sleep. Conar, tell me what. Did you hear something?"

"No, no, nothing like that." He threaded his fingers through his hair, then gave himself a little shake.

"Conar!"

He looked at her. "All right. Liam is wrong. There is a connection between the killings."

"What?"

"*Frenzy.*"

"I beg your pardon?"

"The movie *Frenzy*. One of the last pictures Hitchcock directed. Filmed in England, early seventies, I believe. The killer strangled his victims with his neckties." He turned to look at her in the shadows. "Brenda was stabbed, like the victim in *Psycho*. This girl was strangled with a necktie, like the victims in *Frenzy*."

"Someone is out there imitating the killings in Hitchcock movies?" she whispered.

"Could be," he said, then staring at her, he added quickly, "And I could be dead wrong."

"Don't use that word."

"It could all be...coincidence."

She hugged her arms and the covers over her chest.

Suddenly, outside, from the kennel by the patio, Lady began to howl.

"Oh, Jesus," Jennifer breathed.

"She's a hound, Jennifer. She's just baying at the moon. But if you're worried, we can go downstairs and—"

"No!"

"Are you all right? Now I feel like a real fool, waking you up and making you scared."

"No..."

"I'm supposed to make you feel safe and secure."

She smiled. "You do. Honest."

"Want to get back to sleep?"

"Sure."

She snuggled back into the sheets. He started to come down beside her.

"Conar?"

"Yes?"

"Let's check out the house. Please. Let's just check on my mother."

He hesitated a moment, and she held very still, realizing that he was thinking she was being a silly woman.

"All right," he said. "Let me grab a pair of robes—and a baseball bat."

A few minutes later, they started out in the hallway. He could move very quietly; she did the same. They were both barefoot. "You think I'm being ridiculous," she whispered.

"No, I don't."

"Lady does howl sometimes."

"She's a hound."

"You don't seem worried."

He hesitated as they reached the staircase. He paused, turning to her. "Lady was howling, but I didn't hear Ripper barking."

He went down the stairs. At the ground level, he checked the front door. It remained locked. The alarm was on.

They went on down the hallway to her mother's room. She opened the door, and they both entered. Abby was sleeping peacefully.

In fact, Jennifer thought ruefully, she looked far more peaceful and happy than she had when she had last been with Conar and her.

Conar gave the arm of her robe a tug. She accompanied him out of the room. "Happy?" he asked in the hallway.

"Yes. Thanks."

Lady let out another loud howl.

"Edgar," Jennifer murmured. "Do you think we should check on Edgar?"

"Sure, why not? We'll just tell him we're checking on a grown man in a locked house with an alarm because we're a couple of nervous nellies. No problem."

She ignored his sarcasm. "Thanks."

She took the lead, starting up the stairs to the second floor, and then to the third, the attic which had been totally refurbished for Edgar.

At Edgar's door, Jennifer lifted a hand to knock.

As she did so, she suddenly heard Lady baying again—and something more. A deep barking interspersed with the howls.

Edgar's door flew open so quickly that Jennifer jumped back.

"Do you hear that, sir?" Edgar, in pajama trousers and smoking jacket, demanded of Conar. "There's something going on down there."

"There sure as hell is," Conar said.

He turned to start back down the stairs. Jennifer followed, her hands on his back, and Edgar followed along behind her.

They took the stairs quickly to the second floor, then hurried down the hallway to the grand staircase that led down to the first.

Just as they reached the landing, there came a pounding on the door.

"Hello, hello? Is anybody there?" It was a male voice. A muffled, familiar voice.

Lady howled from the rear of the house. Ripper barked ferociously.

"Please, is anybody there?"

"Oh, Lord, it's—" Jennifer began.

Conar stepped forward and opened the door.

"Andy Larkin," Edgar said, stunned.

It was Andy. He stumbled in, clothing mussed and torn—and bloody.

Chapter 13

"Andy!" Jennifer exclaimed. "What in God's name happened to you? Are you all right? Edgar, dial 911!"

"No, no!" Andy protested, putting up a hand. "No, please—"

"But you're hurt," Jennifer said.

"What the hell happened?" Conar demanded.

"I'll get you a scotch, Mr. Larkin," Edgar said.

"Oh, bless you, my man! God bless you!" Andy said.

"What happened?" Conar persisted, not moving out of his way in the foyer.

"Please...may I come in?"

Conar looked at Jennifer, then lifted a hand. "Hell, sure, you're our producer, you should just arrive after midnight and come bursting in all bloody."

Andy shook his head, leading the way to the den, where Edgar was waiting with his scotch. He took the drink and drained it in two seconds flat.

"I'll fix you another," Edgar said.

"Just hand me the bottle, if you will," Andy told him, taking the bottle from Edgar's hands.

"Andy," Jennifer said quietly. He was acting so strangely. "All right, Andy, what's going on? It's late."

Andy nodded, taking a long swig on the bottle. He pulled it from his mouth, then sank to the couch. "Accident," he said.

"What?" Conar said sharply.

"I was half a mile away. Just driving. I was upset. I'd heard the news. You know. You two found her. The body."

"Andy, why were you so upset?" Jennifer asked, feeling strange little pricks of fear along her spine as she watched him. His usually impeccable hair looked as if it had been coiffured with a mixer. "Andy, no one knows who the woman is as yet."

"She's dead, isn't she?" he asked.

"Of course, but..."

"Why were you so upset about it?" Conar asked more bluntly. "You didn't find her. You didn't kill her—or put her in that lot, did you?"

"No! Hell, no!" Andy protested.

"And you don't know who did?" Conar continued, staring at him.

Andy glanced at Jennifer and Edgar. "Hell, no," he said.

And yet he didn't sound as certain.

"Andy—"

"I was just upset, damn you, can't you understand? Another murder—when Brenda was just killed. Bad things upset people, right?"

"Of course."

Edgar was the one to nudge him next. "So, Mr. Larkin, what happened to you?"

"I was just driving, thinking...about how horrible it was. And the next thing I know, I'm being sideswiped. Headlights, brights, glaring, coming at me...in my lane! I tried to veer off, and the next thing I know, I'm in a ditch."

"So you are hurt. We should call an ambulance," Jennifer said.

"No," Andy protested. "No, no, I don't want an emergency room, paramedics—*media* people coming at me. I'm not really hurt."

"But if you hit your head, you might have a concussion."

"I didn't hit my head."

"There's blood on your cheek," Jennifer informed him.

"I didn't hit my head," he protested again. He exhaled on a long sigh. "I drove into a ditch. I sat there shaking. I realized that I was okay, or at least I thought I was okay. I started to get out of my car. But the other driver was there."

"Someone you knew?" Edgar suggested.

"I don't know. As I turned, he belted me!"

"Another person forced you off the road, stopped to see if you were okay, then slugged you?" Conar asked incredulously.

"Yes," Andy said.

"That's got to be the biggest pile of bull—" Conar began.

266

"I swear," Andy protested.

"Andy, you should call the police," Jennifer told him.

He shook his head. "For what? My car is just half a mile down the road. There's nothing wrong with it, except that it's in a ditch. There's no way to prove another driver was involved. And I've—well, I've been drinking."

"Really?" Conar murmured sarcastically.

Andy didn't recognize the tone. "Yes, really. My alcohol level would be sky—well, it wouldn't be good. I can't call the police. Please...could I just stay here for the night? I know it's late, I don't mean to be a bother, but..."

"You are not just one hot babe, but one of my producers," Jennifer said with a sigh.

Andy actually grinned. "Something like that."

"The room where Mr. Henson stayed the weekend is ready for company," Edgar offered politely.

"Bless you again, my man," Andy said. "That is...if..."

"Well, of course you can stay, Andy. We can't throw you out on the street," Jennifer told him.

"We could call him a cab," Conar commented.

"Conar," Jennifer murmured.

"Please," Andy said. "I'd just as soon not be...alone."

He was still deeply disturbed, Jennifer thought.

"Fine. Edgar, thanks. I'll see that the front

door is locked up and the alarm back on," Conar said. "Andy, you'll forgive us if we go back to bed?"

"Sure," Andy, happy now, waved the bottle of scotch at them. "I'll be just fine. Edgar will see to me."

Conar left the den, heading for the front door. As Edgar remained, Jennifer looked at Andy.

"Really, Andy, what's wrong? What's going on?"

For a moment she thought that he was going to speak. Then he shook his head.

She realized that Conar was behind her, that he'd finished locking up. "Well, good night, then," she said.

"Night, Jen. Conar."

They left him. Conar was silent as they walked up the stairs. When they reached his room, he gently prodded her inside, then locked the door. She shed her robe, yawning. "This must be one of the longest days and nights of my life."

He hadn't shed his robe. He had dragged a chair to his wardrobe. As he stood on it, she saw that he was taking something from a case.

A gun.

He was loading it.

"Conar?" she whispered.

He looked at her. "Sorry. Just being safe."

"You know how to use that?"

"Jennifer, I spent time in the military. Yes, I know how to use it."

"But..."

"Hey. You didn't think the baseball bat was enough."

"You're not going to go shoot Andy, are you?"

He stared at her.

She crawled into the bed, pulling the covers to her chin. He opened the drawer to the bedside table, set the gun in it, and crawled in beside her. His arms came around her.

"Let's get some sleep."

"Yes."

She closed her eyes. But a few seconds later she sat up. "Conar, why the gun now? Now that Andy has arrived?"

He sighed and sat up.

"He never really explained himself, did he?"

"Sure. He was upset, and driving around."

"Um. But why was he driving around a half a mile from your mother's house?"

Hugh Tanenbaum often had insomnia.

It didn't matter. He could function on very little sleep. When he did lie awake—and alone—at night, he watched old movies.

Some of them were musicals. Mainly, he followed certain directors. He liked Stanley Kubrick films. Elia Kazan. Old classics like *Spartacus* and *Ben-Hur*. And he loved Hitchcock. He had every one of the fifty-three movies Hitchcock had directed. He didn't care if they had been critically well received or box office hits—he simply loved Hitchcock. He had studied the man. A weird, fat fellow, schooled by Jesuits, Hitchcock had fallen in love with his wife, Alma, in England, where they'd both worked for a film company. Some people had considered him to be a little bit psychotic—obsessed with sex and death. But most of the time he had put on film stories written by someone else. So if he had been psychotic, others had certainly been psychotic as well.

He had worked with such beautiful women. Ingrid Bergman, Janet Leigh, Tippi Hedren, and Grace Kelly, to name just a few. His career had spanned decades. He had been fabulous with his twist endings. Hugh sincerely believed that any would-be director was worth his salt only if he studied the films of Hitchcock.

That night he had been watching *Notorious*. When the film ended, he channel-changed over to regular television. He caught the late-night news. And there it was. Another murder.

Watching the story about the discovery of the murdered woman made him shake. He got himself a drink.

He sat alone in the dark in his bedroom with the television channel changer in his hands. He flicked from channel to channel, hoping that one of the newscasters would identify the victim. They never said that her identity was unknown—they said that it would not be divulged until her next of kin had been notified.

He watched, and watched, and watched.

A prickling fear swept through him. *She had been strangled to death with a tie.*

He thought about his missing ties.

And about Brenda Lopez.

And he was sick.

Andy was unbelievably sober and poised the next day, his behavior calm and reasonable through all the talk that flowed on the set. He still seemed careful, though, talking normally, but always watching, as if he were afraid someone might be threatening his back at any moment.

Joe Penny, too, seemed disturbed.

But then, Abby was disturbed that morning as well, upset about the dead woman and about the fact that Jennifer and Conar had found her. She saw the story first thing in the morning. She hadn't been hysterical or panic-stricken, but she had warned Jennifer to be careful, and to stay with Conar.

Perhaps it was only natural that everyone should be distressed. The poor murdered woman Jennifer had discovered was the only topic of conversation as people first filed into work. Newspapers were spread all over the studio—everyone had read them.

"Have they given out her name yet?" Andy asked, coming up behind Jennifer as she sat near the cast's breakfast buffet, sipping coffee.

"Not that I know of," she said.

"Did you recognize her, Jen?" Joe Penny

asked. He sounded anxious, she thought. He looked tired and worn. His immaculate white hair was tousled.

She eyed him uneasily. "No."

"Conar, did you recognize her?" Jim Novac, grabbing a half bagel, asked.

He shook his head. "But if I didn't...I might have."

"What?" Joe demanded.

"She wouldn't have looked the same," Serena said.

"What do you mean?" Joe persisted.

"It's not a nice way to die," Conar said impatiently. "Her face was mottled, her eyes were bulging..."

"That's enough," Kelly whispered.

"Yes, I think so," Conar agreed.

Andy rustled a newspaper, shaking his head. "It's so terrible that you two found her."

"Maybe not," Joe Penny said. They all stared at him. He shrugged. "Well, we are getting lots of free publicity out of it."

"Joe, that's awful," Jennifer told him.

"Hey, it's our livelihood," he said. He sounded so completely dispassionate that she felt a chill sweep through her. "Don't go looking at me like that. I've had my plot lines determined for a long time now."

"Maybe we should change them," Doug said.

Joe stared at him, shaking his head. "We've changed it all enough. I don't care how many bodies they find."

"Joe Penny, you should be jailed for that comment!" Serena told him.

He seemed defensive and irritated. He hadn't shaved, Jennifer thought. Strange. He was always such a man about town. Older but dignified, and usually so immaculate in every aspect of his appearance.

"Sorry. I'm just a little unnerved."

"I'm feeling a little unnerved myself," Jennifer murmured.

"It's awful, what's happening," Vera Houseman said with a shudder.

"Awful for the world at large. Worse than awful for Jennifer," Doug said. "And Conar, of course."

"Yeah. Hey, Conar," Joe said seriously.

"What?"

"You know what you should do the next time you find a body?"

"Jennifer actually found the body, Joe. And I'm really hoping that I never find another."

Joe waved a hand in the air. "Well, if either of you ever comes across a dead body again, here's what you do. Walk on by. Just walk on by. That way total strangers won't bother you about it."

"Joe!" Jennifer exclaimed.

Conar was watching him, gray eyes narrowed. "Didn't you say that you were enjoying the publicity?"

"Yeah, sure. Publicity, of any kind, is good. I was just thinking about the two of you. Hey, what is this, by the way, a gab fest? We're on a tight schedule here. Let's get to work."

Self-consciously, they all began to move.

Despite the way that the morning began,

rehearsals and shooting went well. In the first scene, Andy's character accosted Jennifer's before she could beat her sister to a meeting with the newly arrived David DeVille. She managed to escape him and plunge into a party scene at the family manor. She wasn't in the second scene filmed that day, in which her soap parents discussed her impending divorce—and the arrival of David DeVille. The police arrived at the Valentine manor house to warn the Valentines that there had been a murder in a nearby vineyard—the daughter of one of the town's most renowned vintners. In the third scene, she accosted Conar's character, warning him to let her sister alone—and to stay away from the Valentine cellars. He wanted their vineyard, nothing more. Naturally, he dragged her into his arms, reminding her that there had been Paris, that Paris had come before her ridiculous marriage or her desperate attempts to seduce her oldest sister's husband. She slapped him and ran.

She wasn't scheduled in the rest of the scenes for that day. She retired to her dressing room, figuring she'd wait for Conar to finish up, even though he was scheduled straight through the next several hours. They had only brought one car. It was hers, but she didn't want to leave him.

Nor did she want to go home alone.

The phone rang, and she picked up.

"Yes, it's Jennifer."

She expected someone in the cast, her

mother, or a friend—not many people had the number to her private extension on the set.

"Jennifer Connolly?"

It was a woman's voice.

"Yes?"

"I need to see you."

"I'm sorry. Who is this?"

"It's really important. I was a friend of Brenda's."

"Brenda Lopez?"

"Yes, of course, and I knew Trish Wildwood as well."

"You've lost me. Who is Trish Wildwood?"

"You haven't seen the news in the last few hours, Miss Connolly. Trish Wildwood is the woman you found last night."

Jennifer sat still and silent, suddenly finding it difficult to breathe. "Was Trish Wildwood an actress?"

"Up-and-coming, but she'd been surviving. Which is more than you can say for some folks in Hollywood."

"I'm so terribly sorry."

"I believe that you are. I'd really like to talk to you."

"We are talking."

"Not on the phone. And alone."

"You're more than welcome to come to—"

"Oh, no, I'm not coming to your home, Miss Connolly. That's the last place in the world I want to be seen. Meet me, please, meet me to talk."

"Frankly, you haven't told me yet who you are, and while you're telling me that my mother's home is the last place you want to be seen, meeting strangers alone doesn't seem to be high on my list of priorities at the moment."

The woman laughed with a pained note. "We are all getting paranoid, aren't we? Two murders, in a huge city—and everyone is frightened."

"Look—"

"My name is Lila Gonzalez."

"Lila Gonzalez. Your name is familiar."

"I'm flattered."

"You're an actress?"

"Yes, but not really one in your circle of acquaintances. Still, I'd really like to see you. And not somewhere dark or deserted—just not your house. If we meet somewhere, it could be a casual occurrence and nothing more. Will you just meet me for a cup of coffee? Anytime would be fine."

Jennifer gave her the name of a restaurant she knew right off Sunset. There were a number of outdoor tables at the place, and she decided she'd go home and pick up Lady, bring her big dog with her. She'd leave Conar a note telling him to grab a ride with one of the others.

"I can see you around six, I think. I may be a little late," Jennifer told Lila, trying to calculate traffic.

"Great."

Jennifer started to hang up, then hesitated. She thought she heard a clicking, as if someone else were hanging up. She looked back at her phone. It had twenty-one lines. Anyone in his or her own dressing room might have picked up on the call.

A tapping on her door made her jump.

"Jennifer?"

It was Doug. She felt like a fool.

"Doug, come in."

He entered, plopping down on the couch opposite her dressing table. "You look great with Wonder Boy. You're doing such a remarkable job of getting along with him."

He was teasing her, she could tell. She wondered how Doug had figured out that they were sleeping together.

"Why are you acting like the cat that ate the canary?" she inquired.

"I'm just glad that we're doing things the way we're doing them."

"Which is...?"

"You'll see on Friday."

"Great." She stood up. "Okay, Mystery Man, Conar drove in with me this morning, but I think I'm going to take off—he's going to be hours yet. If you're going to be hanging around here, will you give him a ride to the house for me?"

Doug frowned. "Well, I can, but I thought that we might go have coffee."

"I'm really tired, Doug. Would you mind just bringing him for me?"

He shrugged. "Sure."

"See you later, then," she said, and fled quickly.

When she reached the house, she found

that Drew Parker was visiting her mother. They were sitting by the pool. Abby seemed relaxed in Drew's company. Both dogs were running around the yard. It was a domestic, normal picture.

"Sweetheart!" Abby said, pleased to see her. Drew rose and squeezed her hands warmly, and kissed her cheek.

"Hi, to both of you."

"Where's Conar?" her mother asked with a frown.

"Still on the set. Doug will drive him home."

Abby was still frowning, but she seemed to accept this. "Have some tea and scones with us, dear."

"Scones?" Jennifer said.

Her mother smiled. "Mary has been cooking. Edgar has hardly taken more than a few hours off in weeks."

Mary McDougal was one of the two maids who came in on a part-time basis to help Edgar keep the house up. She was as Irish as a four-leaf clover, in the States barely a year, and very industrious.

"A scone sounds great. Quickly. I just came home for Lady. I'm—" She hesitated, not wanting to worry her mother. "I'm meeting a bunch of the girls for a bite at the Flamingo Café just off Sunset."

"Alone?" Abby said worriedly.

"Mom. I'm meeting a bunch of the girls. I'm taking Lady with me." She was only lying a little. She was going to a heavily populated section of town with a very big dog. She'd be okay.

"Jennifer, I don't know...," Abby said.

Drew gave her a sympathetic look. "Abby, Lady is one big dog."

"I'll be okay," Jennifer said firmly. She flashed Drew a smile of gratitude and took a scone. It was delicious, a raisin scone with cinnamon. She was glad she stopped to eat. Mary's tea was delicious as well, brewed with leaves to a perfect point, strained, and served in her mother's delicate little teacups. "Mary makes the best tea," she said.

"Don't let Edgar hear you say that," Drew warned.

"I won't, I promise you," she said, and laughed.

"Have another scone," her mother suggested.

"Mom, I'm meeting people at a café for something to eat," she reminded Abby.

"All right. But, Jennifer, when you get back, may I talk with you for a few minutes?"

"Of course, Mom. What is it?"

"When you get back."

Did Abby want to talk to her alone, without Drew present? She would have pushed it now, except for that fact. She didn't want to make waves. Abby looked good. Really good, better than she had looked in days. She wasn't shaking with any of her violent tremors.

"Of course, Mom."

"Don't be long, please."

"I promise. I won't be."

"Take your cellular phone."

"Yes, ma'am."

279

She kissed her mother and Drew and went to the coat tree in the den where the dog's leashes were hung. When she came back for Lady, Ripper was suddenly all over her, barking and distressed.

"I can't take you, too," she told the little Yorkie, scratching his ears and setting him down firmly. He jumped at her again, barking wildly.

"Ripper!"

"I'll get him," Drew offered.

"Thanks."

He came for the Yorkie, but when he picked him up, the dog tried to snap.

"Ripper!" Jennifer admonished. The little dog hung his head, but then started barking again.

"He'll be okay when you're gone," Drew assured her.

"I'll take him, Drew," Abby called. "He does well with me."

For once Jennifer was glad that Conar's dog liked her mother. She needed to get going.

With Lady on her leash and her cell phone thrown into the car, Jennifer started back down toward Sunset.

Traffic was terrible, and it took her far longer than she had expected. She had to park her car much farther from the restaurant than she wanted, but she left it on a side street and felt confident walking with Lady back toward the restaurant.

It was closer to seven than six. She hoped Lila Gonzalez had waited.

With Lady, she stood outside the café, watching anxiously for a young woman who might be Lila. Finally, a waiter approached her.

"Miss Connolly?"

"Yes?"

"Miss Gonzalez is waiting for you inside. I'm afraid the dog isn't allowed in."

"Can we have a table outside?"

The young man shrugged, then said, grinning, "Miss Connolly, believe it or not, I watch *Valentine Valley*. I'd love to get you a table out here. Quickly. But all these people just sat. And my boss is big on no favorites for television and film people, or we'd have pissed-off clientele all the time. Inside is all we've got. We barely have that. Miss Gonzalez has been sitting there for a while now as it is."

Jennifer hesitated, then felt like a paranoid fool. She wouldn't be staying long. "Please tell her I'll be right back. I've got to put the dog in the car."

"Sure thing. Make sure you roll your windows down, huh?"

"Of course."

"Sorry, Lady," she told her wolfhound.

She walked back to the car. It was slightly uphill. She realized that she had parked past another vacant lot, and then a condemned house.

"And they say property is so expensive down here," she muttered to the dog. "They need to make better use of it."

She slid back into her car and rolled the windows partially down. "You protect the home front, eh, Lady?"

The dog whimpered.

She locked Lady in the car with plenty of air in the cool night, and hurried the few blocks back to the restaurant. The young waiter had just delivered two glasses of wine to an outside table, and he quickly motioned to her, escorting her inside to a table at the rear of the restaurant.

The woman sitting at the table was very attractive. She had long, sleek ash blond hair, large brown eyes, and nearly perfect skin. As she stood up, Jennifer saw she was tall and slim and handsomely dressed in a business suit. "Hi," she said, flashing a quick smile of thanks to the waiter. "I'm Lila Gonzalez."

"Jennifer Connolly, and I'm so sorry for being so late. It took me longer to get here than I expected."

"It's all right. I'm glad I've been drinking decaf cappuccinos, but it's all right," Lila said, smiling again. "I really wanted to talk to you."

Jennifer sat down.

"What will you have?"

"The same," she said.

"How about an appetizer platter, too?" Lila said. Leaning forward, she added, "I've been taking this table a rather long time."

"An appetizer platter sounds great," Jennifer said.

The waiter left them.

"So you were friends with both Brenda and Trish...the girl I found last night," Jennifer said.

Lila nodded. "L.A., the whole scene out here is huge. But then again, it's very small. Brenda kind of crawled above the pack, but I met both her and Trish because we'd go to lots of the same auditions and parties, you know."

"It's a small world."

Lila grinned. "With a pecking order—films, TV, what have you, but still, lots of the players go round and round, and you get to meet them time and again."

"I'm so sorry that you lost two friends in such a horrible way. I knew Brenda, not well, but I knew her. Trish I had never met."

"They were both good people."

"I'm sure," Jennifer said, then hesitated. "I'm still not sure why you were so anxious to meet with me."

"You're moving in their world, Jennifer."

"What do you mean?"

Lila moved forward with a pained expression. "I read in one of the papers that Hugh Tanenbaum was trying to cast you in his movie."

"There's been some talk, that's all."

"Brenda was supposed to take a role as well. And Lila had told me that she was going to try to meet Tanenbaum. She thought appearing in one of his movies would be good for her career."

The irony of Lila's tone was not lost on Jennifer.

"You're suggesting that Hugh Tanenbaum—"

"No, I'm not saying that he's a psycho killer."

"Then—"

"I'm just saying it's a strange coincidence. But there are other coincidences you should know about—regarding the people in your world."

"Such as...?"

Lila didn't reply. She sat back as the waiter delivered Jennifer's cappuccino and an appetizer tray for the two of them.

He left.

"Brenda was a free spirit, you know."

Jennifer frowned, trying to follow the drift of what Lila was implying. Lila sighed. "She slept around."

"Oh, yes."

"She slept with lots of your friends and coworkers. She had quite a thing for a while with Joe Penny—and Andy Larkin. She caused a fight between them once, and thought it was incredibly amusing—and just. If they wanted to use a Hollywood casting couch, she told me once, they should pay a price for it as well."

"I knew she slept with a number of people. What about your friend Trish?"

"We'll get to Trish," Lila said, spearing a crab-stuffed mushroom cap with a pirate flag toothpick and moving it onto the small appetizer plate in front of her. "Brenda also slept with your director, Jim Novac, and even Jay Braden—just to finish it all out. She'd wanted a part on the show once, and apparently, Andy Larkin told her there was just no real way to write her in."

"I didn't know that."

"I didn't think that you did."

"But still—"

"Then...there's Conar Markham."

"I knew that Conar—"

"Brenda had been really good friends with his wife, Betty Lou. You know, they were both beautiful Hispanic girls making it in Hollywood—a really upward climb, I can tell you."

"I was aware of that friendship."

Lila nodded, looking at her. "Trish was in a movie he did a few years ago. So he was friends with her as well, did you know that?"

She felt cold; she didn't want to give the uneasiness away. *Last night he said he'd never seen the girl before.*

"Really?" she said smoothly. "Well, that was a few years ago."

It was true, and the poor woman looked so horrible, her own mother might not have recognized her.

"Yes, so your Mr. Markham knew Trish, just as he knew Brenda. Trish was also interviewed for that space movie being filmed now—the one they tried to get Conar for as the main star."

"That's interesting, but it's unlikely that they were interviewed together."

"Oh, yes," Lila said, sitting back again, watching Jennifer. "Trish told me that she saw him at a get-together the director had in New York. She liked him, you see. She liked him a lot."

"You're going to tell me that she slept with him?" Jennifer said.

Lila looked down at the table for a moment, then back at Jennifer. "I don't know. When Trish came back from New York, she talked about little else other than how kind and generous he had been during her audition. But she didn't get the part. And apparently, Conar chose not to take a part in the movie either, since he's here now. And Brenda is dead—and Trish is dead."

"If sleeping with people in Hollywood made people murderers, the majority of the town would be doing life," Jennifer reminded her.

"Hey, I'm not accusing anybody of anything. I just wanted you to be forewarned and forearmed about some of the things going on around you. When I saw the news about Trish this morning...and saw that *you* were the one who had found her, and *with* Conar Markham...well, I wanted a chance to talk to you. Hell, these murders may not have anything to do with one another. I just thought that I should warn you to look out for yourself."

Lila was sincere.

Jennifer nodded. "Thank you. Thank you very much."

Lila lifted her hand for the check. "I've got to get moving. I have a job as a singing waitress."

"I'd love to see you some time."

"I'd like that. I'm good, honestly. I have a pretty darned good voice. Let me know if you want to come, the place is right in downtown Hollywood. Angelo's. Give me a call, let me know. I'm listed."

The waiter brought the check.

Jennifer reached for it; Lila snagged it.

"Really, let me—" Jennifer began.

"Singing waitresses make good money, believe it or not," Lila told her. "I brought you down here, please, let me."

With little choice, Jennifer thanked her.

"You're gracious as well," Lila told her as they stepped out to the front. Ironically, most of the outside tables were now empty. "Keep care of yourself, huh?"

"You, too."

"Want a lift somewhere?"

"No, thanks. My car is right up the hill there."

Lila nodded and started down the block. She stepped into an old BMW, waving as she did so. Jennifer turned thoughtfully to start walking toward her car.

It wasn't far; she could see it right up the hill. But as she started walking, she realized that it was dark now.

There were plenty of streetlights in front of the restaurant, but it was dark up the hill.

It was okay. Lady was in the car.

The sounds of voices on the street faded behind her. She could hear her own footsteps on the sidewalk. The vacant lot loomed like a black void to her right. Just beyond it stood the condemned building. When she had parked and there had still been some daylight around her, the building had just seemed a sad reminder of the ravages of time. But the light was gone. In the darkness, the building appeared evil.

Goose! she chastised herself. Her imagination was getting out of control. She had insisted that she was going to have a life, be normal. And still, she couldn't help these fantasies.

Walk! she told herself. *More quickly, please!*

If she listened closely enough, she thought, she would hear the old, crumbling building breathing. It was alive with evil and malice. Any minute now, there would suddenly be an eerie glow from within, and the windows would turn to eyes...

"Idiot! Lady is in the car; I'm nearly there," she told herself.

Nearly.

"Oh, hell!"

She stared to run for her car.

Running was the wrong thing to do. Staring suspiciously at the condemned building, she missed a crack in the sidewalk. Her heel caught and she went tumbling down. Smacking the concrete hard, ripping a stocking and skinning a knee, she swore at herself. "Your mother told you, Conar told you, Lila told you, everyone told you to be careful," she muttered to herself. "They've turned you into a silly paranoid! Get up and act normal," she admonished herself.

She started to crawl to her feet, slipping her handbag over her shoulder.

As she did so, she heard footsteps.

She turned back. The restaurant and the street below seemed very far away. But she didn't see anything, or anyone. She turned and started walking briskly.

Footsteps, running now.

She spun around.

Nothing.

She looked toward the car again. A giant shadow seemed to be emerging from the empty yard.

She reached into her purse. Where the hell were her keys? She should have gotten them out before she left the restaurant. She did have a very loud car alarm, if she could just hit the PANIC button on her little square beeper thingy.

From her car, Lady suddenly began to bark madly.

She needed to clean out her purse. Where was the damned pepper spray? Was it still good?

"Shit!" she swore. She had to go back down to the restaurant...

She felt prickles at the nape of her neck.

She turned around and screamed.

The footsteps had reached her. A shadow now loomed large and real and lethal, right in front of her.

Chapter 14

From the minute he learned that Jennifer had gone on home without him, Conar had been uneasy.

He was scrubbing his face in his dressing room when Doug arrived to tell him he was giving him a ride; Jennifer was gone.

"What?" he demanded harshly, straightening, bumping his forehead on the faucets, and swearing as he reached for a towel. It was amazing how things changed. When he had come here, he had been convinced that Abby was overly alarmed, the victim of a prankster.

And now...

"Hey, don't jump down my throat!" Doug protested, handing him the elusive towel and stepping back.

Conar ignored him and dialed the house. Edgar answered. "Granger House."

"Edgar, it's Conar. Is Jennifer home?"

"I just returned myself, sir. Let me check."

Seconds passed like eons. Edgar came back on the phone. "She went out, sir."

"She went out!"

"Miss Abby says it's fine, sir. She took Lady with her."

"Edgar, where did she go? Please, ask Abby for me. Where did she go?"

Edgar came back a few minutes later. "Abby had a great day, sir, and forgot to take her medicine, and now, I fear, she's taken too many pills together. She isn't very lucid. But Jennifer went to the Flamingo Café to meet with the girls."

"The girls? What girls?"

"Well, her friends from the soap, I imagine," Edgar said. "Sir, if I had been here, I would have tried to stop her—"

"Edgar, don't worry, it's not your fault. Where is the Flamingo Café?"

"Not far from the music store and that bookstore she likes so much, do you know the one, Mr. Markham? Near House of Blues."

"Thanks, Edgar."

He hung up. "Doug, let's go."

He gave tense directions. Doug kept telling him he was certain that Jennifer was fine—she was with her dog, after all.

Yet they didn't find Jennifer's car in front of the café. "Shit, well, she's near here somewhere," Conar said.

"Look!" Doug breathed suddenly.

"What?"

"Up that side street. Oh, my God, in front of that building...is that a body?"

Conar looked where Doug was pointing. A piece of canvas was haphazardly pulled over something larger. Conar started to walk toward the old place.

Doug caught his arm. "Don't! Let's not look, all right?"

"Doug, damn it." Conar pulled his arm free, his heart in his throat. He hurried across the overgrown yard to the front of the decaying building. He jerked up the tarp, stepping back. He nearly stepped on Doug.

"It's a pile of rotten wood," he said.

"Oh, Jesus," Doug breathed. Then he said, "Thank God, look there, someone's coming."

Conar looked out from the building and down the hill. It was Jennifer, heading up the hill at a run. He saw her fall, and swear.

"Damn her," he muttered. He started from the building toward her.

As he did so, he saw a shape dart out from the empty lot.

"Look!" Doug warned him.

"I see."

But Jennifer had turned. And the shape had risen. And the shape was a man with something in his hand, ready to strike out.

"No!" Conar yelled. The sound was a rush of rage and fear in his own ears.

Jennifer was quick—she ducked into the overgrown grass of the vacant lot to avoid her attacker. Despite the noise Conar had made, the attacker still was unaware that Conar was coming after him. The man turned toward Jennifer, striking out. She rolled. Conar plunged at the man's legs.

He brought the man down hard, knocking the wind out of both of them.

The fellow fought him, struggling, jerking. Conar managed to hit the attacker hard in the jaw. The man tried to strike him with the weapon in his right hand.

It wasn't a knife. It was a broken wine bottle.

Conar got a good grip on the fellow's arm and slammed his wrist hard against the ground, forcing him to drop the jagged bottle.

As he stared down at the bearded, stinking bum who had assaulted Jennifer, Conar could hear the sound of sirens coming toward them. His heart was beating a million miles an hour.

"You hurt my hand."

"I should be breaking your neck."

"Hey, buddy, give me a break, I wouldn't have hurt her. I just wanted her handbag!" the guy cried to him. "I'm a Viet vet. I've got children. Can't work...bad lungs."

Conar stood up, dragging the fellow up with him, giving him a good look. He wasn't a psychologist, but this guy didn't look like the type to plan out a murder.

In his peripheral vision he saw that Doug had gone for Jennifer and was helping her up.

"I didn't intend to hurt her!" the bum cried desperately again. Conar wondered if he looked psychotic himself at the moment, the way the fellow was pleading.

"You didn't intend to hurt her, eh? What was the wine bottle for?"

"I had to have some kind of threat," the man pleaded. "Please, let me go, I can hear the cops coming, Jesus, buddy, I don't know how, but they're almost here. Come on."

"Cellular phone," Doug supplied politely.

"I can't let you go," Conar said.

"Hey," the man said suddenly. "I know who you are. You're a movie star. Hey, buddy, you let me go right now or I'll say that I was paid to do this as a publicity stunt."

"What?" Conar said incredulously.

"No!" Jennifer said, stepping forward.

Her face was dirty, and her beautiful hair was threaded through with grass and twigs. "You attacked me with a wine bottle," she told the man angrily. "You just go ahead and say whatever you want to say. I will press charges because you're not going to do this to anyone else."

Conar stared at Jennifer. She was shaky but defiant.

"What the hell do you think you were doing?" he heard himself demand. He hadn't meant to.

"I had Lady with me," she protested indignantly.

"The dog is locked in the car," he pointed out, his temper growing.

"I was about to get him with my pepper spray—"

"You were a bit too slow."

"I had dropped it."

"Yeah."

"Buddy, I wouldn't hurt her," the bum whined. Conar stared at him again. The sound of sirens was growing louder.

The first cops to show were two fellows in uniform in a patrol car. Seeing them, the bum tried to run. Conar held him fast. Then he started spewing out his story about it all being a publicity stunt. When the cops didn't seem to fall for that idea, he started to shout that he wasn't a killer. "I didn't go killing no blondes. I didn't slash anyone, and I didn't strangle anyone, I swear it. All I wanted was some money."

From Jennifer's car, Lady howled.

"So you want to bring charges against him?" the cop in uniform asked them, removing his cap and scratching his head.

"We should drop this whole thing," Doug advised wearily. "Here, Jennifer," he said, passing her something.

"What is that?" Conar asked sharply.

"Her key chain with her alarm," Doug said, flashing Jennifer a sorrowful look.

"So you dropped that too," he murmured.

"Yes, I dropped it. But I...I could have..."

"You could have what?" Conar demanded.

She smoothed back a tangled strand of her strawberry hair.

The cop cleared his throat. "Charges need to be filed...," he reminded them.

"We should just drop this," Doug said.

"No," Jennifer insisted. "Doug, we can't."

"Jennifer," Doug said slowly, "I really don't think that he is the guy who killed Brenda and the other woman."

"I don't think he is either," she said, staring at Conar as if to say, *See, I might have gotten my purse stolen, nothing worse.*

"Hey, you never know," the young cop said. "He did attack you, and if he had gotten you with a broken wine bottle..." He gave a shrug. "Take a look at your man. He's criss-crossed with a few scars himself. This is one tough customer."

"We're definitely bringing charges against him," Jennifer said.

"She's right," Conar agreed. "Let's go to the

station. I'll drive your car, Jennifer. And try to calm the dog down."

"It's my dog," she reminded him indignantly.

"Fine, I'll drive, you calm down the dog. Doug can follow in his car."

The night became very long. The paperwork seemed endless, so much so that Jennifer insisted her dog be allowed in with them. The man who had attacked Jennifer didn't look much better in the light. He was taken away to be questioned. He might not be a killer, but the cops weren't taking any chances.

After Lady was brought in and the attacker was taken away, Conar, Jennifer, and Doug were seated at the officer's desk again, giving out the same information one more time. There was a round of questions regarding the attack—and then a round of questions regarding the fact that Jennifer and Conar had just been in the same area the other night, finding the body of a murder victim in a different vacant lot.

They started with the officers who had come to their rescue, but then a lieutenant came out of his office and began asking questions as well.

"Do you make a habit of frequenting vacant lots, Miss Connolly?" he inquired.

"No," Jennifer snapped angrily. "I live here," she informed him. "I had been at a restaurant, meeting with a friend."

"What friend?"

It seemed to Conar that she hesitated. Then she angrily supplied, "What difference does that make? I have the right to park near a restaurant and walk safely to and from that restaurant. And when I've been assaulted, I don't have to answer a lot of foolish questions."

"All right, all right." The lieutenant fell silent. Conar saw that Liam had arrived, and was threading his way through the desks toward them.

"You again?" he said to Conar, just a trace of dry humor in his voce.

"Jennifer was attacked."

"So I heard. I've seen him; I'm on my way to talk to him a little more in depth."

"Think he might be the killer?" Conar asked skeptically.

"You never know. The psychologists tell us that a killer who fantasizes about a crime and thinks it out is usually a more ordinary-looking person. This guy doesn't look...normal enough, ironically. Hey, Lieutenant Eaton, these folks have not had a great last few days. Think they could go home now?"

Eaton didn't look happy, but he replied, "Yeah, sure, charges have been filed. We're booking the guy."

"Great. Then you're free to go."

"Thanks," Conar told him.

"Sure thing."

Conar set a hand on Jennifer's back. She stiffened, her fingers curling more tightly around Lady's leash. She was preparing for the argument they were sure to have, he thought. He still kept his hand on her and propelled her toward the exit.

"Conar?"

He paused, looking back as Liam called him. His friend remained leaning against the edge of the other cop's desk. "Have you got any time tomorrow?" Liam asked.

"I can make some. In fact, I'm not on call until twelve. But I've been driving in with Jennifer, and she has a nine o'clock."

"I'll meet you at the studio around ten."

"Good." He paused. "Hey, you all have been asking a lot of questions, so it's my turn. Any leads on the woman we found last night?"

"Not really," Liam said. Not really, or nothing he was going to share with them at the moment?

"See you in the morning, then."

They left the police station. Jennifer hurried ahead of him, walking toward the car.

"Well, I guess I'll just go on home," Doug said pointedly. "No, no, don't thank me for being there in the midst of a bunch of trouble, don't say good-bye, good night, or anything. I'll just be on my way."

Grinning a bit grimly, Conar turned back to Doug. Jennifer wasn't going anywhere. He had the keys.

"Thank you, Doug. Thanks for the ride to find Jen, and thanks for being so patient at the police station."

From up ahead, Jennifer said coolly, "Yes, thank you, Doug."

"Much better," Doug said. "See you tomorrow."

He got in his car and left. Jennifer, standing by her driver's door, had just remembered that Conar had her keys.

"I'll drive," he said.

"It's my car."

"I'll drive."

"Is that some kind of a macho thing?" she inquired.

"Yes. Move aside."

She was angry, but she walked around to the passenger's side. He opened the door. Lady obediently jumped into the rear seat—she seemed to take up most of it. Conar slid into the driver's seat.

"You were kind of curt with Doug. Strange, because he did come to your rescue."

"You bullied him into driving you to follow me," she said, not looking at him.

"Yes, well, you know, don't say thanks. Don't say anything like, *Gee, I really was an ass, thanks for kicking butt for me.*"

Her neck snapped around and she glared at him with frosty blue eyes. "No one asked you to follow me."

"Yes, actually, your mother did."

"I was about to be mugged, that's all."

"How do you know? How do you know that bum wasn't going to kill you?"

"He...he...just wasn't. You could tell," she insisted, but she didn't sound that certain.

He stared straight ahead at the road.

"So who did you meet?" he asked her.

She was silent.

"Jennifer—"

"I met a friend. For coffee."

"Why would you do that? Why would you just leave and not say anything to me?"

"Look, you're not my damned keeper."

"Why didn't you tell me?"

She swung on him. "Why didn't you tell me that you knew the girl we found last night?" she demanded.

"What?" he asked, startled.

"You knew her!"

Yeah, he knew her. But he hadn't known it.

"And you lied to me," Jennifer said.

"I didn't know I knew her last night. Her own mother wouldn't have recognized her last night."

"You auditioned with her."

"Yes, I did. But I didn't know who she was until the police let her name out late this morning. I had no idea it was Trish."

She was staring at the road again. "You probably slept with her, too, right? Accidentally, or just once because she was there, or some such thing."

Irritated, he didn't answer her.

"You were a fool," he said softly.

"I was not a fool because I met a friend for coffee."

"Two young dead actresses, and a mother who thinks you've had death threats. Maybe your mother isn't so crazy."

She looked at him sharply again. "I never said my mother was crazy."

At the house, she slammed her way out of the car. She started through the house with

Lady, intent on taking her out to the kennel, but Edgar met them in the foyer.

"Miss Jennifer!" he exclaimed, horrified by her dirtied and torn appearance.

Jennifer had forgotten how she looked. "It's okay, Edgar, I'm fine."

Edgar didn't believe her. He looked at Conar, who said, "She was mugged. She might have been killed."

"But Wonder Boy appeared just in time," she said sarcastically, then added in a rush, "I'm fine, Edgar. Conar stopped the man, the police came, and we've been at the station. Is Mother sleeping?"

"Like an angel."

"Don't tell her anything, please."

"Jennifer, she's going to have to know. It will appear in the papers, I'm certain."

Jennifer shrugged, smiling ruefully at Edgar. "The mugger threatened to sue us."

"How outrageous!" Edgar said indignantly. "Here, I'll take Lady. I'm certain you'll want to shower and change, Miss Jennifer. I'll get some supper for you."

"I'm not at all hungry, Edgar."

"I'm starving," Conar said.

"Thanks for taking Lady," Jennifer said, and started up the steps.

"Will a sandwich be all right, Mr. Conar?" Edgar asked.

"It will be manna from heaven," Conar told him.

Jennifer bolted up the stairs, but he caught her arm. She stared at his hand on her.

"Jennifer, why can't you admit that you made a mistake and that you shouldn't have run off without telling me?"

"I'm not welded to you, Conar."

"I thought that we'd—well, come to some kind of an agreement."

"An *agreement?*"

He inhaled deeply. "Look, I did save your ass. You don't know what might have happened."

"I might have had my purse stolen."

"You might been in the hospital now getting your face stitched. Or worse. We don't know."

"I'm going in my own room, and I'm going to lock the door. I was fine before you got here. In fact, you do realize, don't you, that nothing happened until you got here. Think about that, Conar. Everything was just fine before you got here!"

He didn't reply. His facial muscles were locked. "I'll be outside your door despite the fact that you're behaving like a fucking idiot."

"Good for you."

She entered her room and slammed the door in his face. He gritted his teeth, fists clenched at his side.

He was furious.

He'd been scared to death for her. He'd rescued her. And she was mad at him!

He was still standing at her door. At last he raised a hand. "Right. Okay. Fuck you, Miss Connolly."

Long, angry strides brought him to his own

room. A hot shower did nothing to ease his temper. A sandwich and a beer didn't help either.

Because beneath the anger was a strange, gnawing uneasiness.

They were home, they were safe. She was in a house with an alarm, sleeping behind a locked door.

It didn't matter. Too many strange things had happened lately. It was as if everything was coming to a head.

Jennifer showered for a long, long time. She kept remembering the look of the man who had attacked her. Ugly. Scarred. His eyes had been wild.

He would have slashed her with that wine bottle without blinking.

But was he the killer? Was there one killer? Had Brenda and Trish been victims of two different random killers?

Was it all associated with her in any way?

Why had she lashed out at Conar so furiously when he had saved her butt?

Because she was afraid, she realized. Really afraid.

At last she turned off the shower. She wrapped herself in a towel, stood before the mirror, and dried her hair. When she closed her eyes, she could see the bum's face again. She shivered. But if he was just a bum then it was merely bad luck that he'd come upon her on the street the way that he had.

Her hair dried; she walked back into her bedroom. She felt so restless. She thought about her meeting with Lila, and all of the things Lila had said.

Had Conar really recognized the body of Trish Wildwood last night and refused to admit that he had known her?

Conar.

She was disturbed to realize that she really wanted to go to him. She wanted him to comfort her. It was more disturbing still to realize she wanted something else. His naked body next to hers. Whispers in her ear. His hands on her, his lips touching her...

She jerked open one of her dresser drawers and pulled out her comfortable Tweetie Bird nightshirt. Determinedly she curled into bed, by herself.

She considered watching the news, but she decided she'd never sleep if she saw any more about the recent killings in L.A. County.

She wanted the light on, but the light bothered her. She lay awake staring at the ceiling. She rose, turned on the bathroom light, and turned off the main overhead lamp.

She lay on the bed again, thinking.

Conar. The Wild Child turned Wonder Boy. Tall, lean, extraordinary, with his sharp gray eyes and rugged features, a man who drew women with a twist of his head, a glance, a look, the slightest nuance...

She tossed in the bed, wanting him, and wondering if other women had wanted him that way.

And if they had died for it.

Hours went by. At last she rose and took some p.m. pain medication. She hated to do it. She'd be groggy in the morning. But she had to have some sleep.

Forty-five minutes later, it began to kick in. She closed her eyes and dozed. She wondered where sleep really began and ended. She started dreaming again, and knew that she was dreaming.

Celia Marston was in the dream, beckoning her toward the cliffs. She followed, aware that she was being stalked as well.

No, Celia, no, wait...

Celia turned to her—and became Brenda.

Run, Jennifer, run, he's behind you...don't turn, run...

But she had to turn. The bum with the wine bottle and scarred face was behind her. "Your purse, lady, I only want your purse!"

But he started laughing, and his face started changing, and she knew that killer was indeed standing behind her...

She woke up. Her eyes flew open.

She screamed. There was a dark figure standing above her.

She leapt up from the bed, blinking furiously. *Dear God, am I still sleeping?*

The figure was gone. Just like that. Disappeared.

There was a pounding at her door. Conar.

She ran to the door, then hesitated. Had he somehow gotten into her bedroom? Had he been trying to terrify her in the night?

"Jennifer!"

She threw open the door, shaking. He stood there in his long pajama bottoms, hair mussed, eyes wild, features tense.

"What the hell happened?"

Caution be damned. She threw herself into his arms. "I don't know...there was someone there..."

He set her aside, stepping into the room. He walked across it, checked the closet, checked the bath, looked under the bed.

"There's no one here," he told her.

"I could have sworn...," she murmured.

"Were you dreaming? A nightmare?" he asked softly.

"Maybe. But it was so real..."

He stood still, watching her. She moistened her lips. "Thanks for saving my butt tonight."

"My pleasure," he said after a moment. "I have a vested interest."

She walked over to him. "Stay with me," she invited softly.

He shook his head. Gentle fingers touched her hair. "I'm not sure that I should. Not the way that you mean. You're just frightened."

She smiled, shaking her head. "I don't want to analyze the situation. I just want you to stay."

With that, she pulled the nightshirt over her head and tossed it to the floor. He stared at her for a moment. She parted her lips and closed her eyes, anticipating.

His kiss never touched her lips.

He slid to his knees. The warm moisture of

306

his breath fanned her intimately at the silky V of her panties. His tongue touched her through the silk. Her knees trembled; she nearly fell.

She forgot all else except for the feel of him...

God help her, no.

She didn't want to analyze anymore.

She just wanted...

Sex.

Later, when they lay exhausted, half-dozing and entwined, she realized she wanted more.

Him.

Chapter 15

In the morning, Jennifer rolled, stretching, reaching out, certain by the way the sun was pouring in that it was still quite early. But Conar was up, and gone.

Her room was light, the walls a soft yellow in the areas where they were not covered with 1920s paneling. Her bed set and draperies were in a traditional flower pattern by Ralph Lauren, and a handsome Persian rug covered the polished hardwood beneath her bed, and she loved the room very much. With the sun shining in, she wondered how she could have dreamed any strange night visitors in this room.

She glanced at her watch. It was only six-thirty. She took a leisurely shower, dressed, and came downstairs. Coffee, tea, juice, muffins, bagels, and toast were on the buffet in the dining room. Jennifer poured herself coffee, wondering why the house seemed so quiet. Had Conar already left this morning?

She wandered into the den and saw her mother in the rear of the room. The doors were open out to the pool. Abby wasn't alone. She was seated in one of the large wing-back chairs, and Conar was kneeling on one knee before her. Both of them had their heads lowered.

"You see, I swore that I would do it. For myself, and for him."

"Hello," Jennifer said, walking into the den with her coffee. "May I join in on this conversation?" She eyed Conar determinedly. He had certainly swept into their lives; she had invited him right in. But she didn't like him having secrets with her mother.

Conar didn't speak. He rose, returning Jennifer's stare.

"Young lady, you lied to me yesterday," her mother said.

"What?"

"You told me you were going to have coffee with your friends."

"I did. Mother, it just happened to be the day that an opportunistic bum was lying in wait."

"An opportunistic bum who tried to kill you."

"I think he wanted my purse."

"And you took the dog and locked her in the car."

"I meant to eat at an outside table, but there weren't any."

"You were hurt; you could have been killed. And you lied to me."

"Mother! I—"

"You said that you were meeting the girls. Implying that you were going with Kelly and Serena. But you weren't meeting them."

"Mom, how could you think that—"

"Kelly and Serena were still on the set, filming even after Conar."

Jennifer stared at Conar again, anger and resentment taking firm root. "I don't remember telling you that I was meeting those two in particular."

"So who did you meet?" her mother inquired.

"A different friend."

She glanced at Conar, then wondered what difference it would make if she divulged the name. "A woman named Lila Gonzalez, Mother." That was the truth. "I hadn't seen her in a long time."

"So you decided to go off alone in the midst of all that is going on?"

"Mom, please! I'm careful, honestly, but I've got to live a normal life as well. Please, don't be upset about last night. I'm all right."

She stared at her mother anxiously, wanting Abby not to worry so much. Abby kept her eyes on her daughter's. "I'm going into the hospital for some tests later this afternoon," she said, changing the subject. "I'll be staying through the weekend. You don't need to worry about your schedule. Edgar will take me, and you can visit at your leisure."

"Tests?" Jennifer said, alarmed. "What's going on? Why didn't you tell me, Mother?"

"I told you yesterday, before you ran out so pigheadedly, that I needed to speak with you," Abby said. "You remember my friend Vic, don't you?"

"Yes, of course, Mother. Your friend from all the trips to the doctor's office."

"He died yesterday morning."

"Oh, Mother, I'm so sorry. He was such a fine man." She squeezed Abby's hands in sympathy, then frowned and asked softly, "How? Were his symptoms so severe? Did his heart give out? Was it respiratory?"

Abby looked at Conar, then answered Jennifer at last. "He died of complications due to surgery."

"Oh, Mother! I am so sorry, but see, I'm right. The operation is dangerous."

"I'm going for tests in relation to having the surgery, Jennifer," Abby said firmly.

Jennifer rocked back on her haunches. She held her mother's hands more tightly.

"Mom, you just told me that Vic died because of the surgery."

"Yes."

"Then, Mom, you must realize—"

"Jennifer, you must realize that I function at times, but that I shake more and more violently every day. I'm losing control of bladder function. I talk to people in the walls. This will

310

only get worse as I get older. There is hope in the surgery. I want to do this while I'm young enough. There is an opening with my doctor in a few weeks. I'm taking a chance, I'm having the tests done. I can still decide against the surgery, but I don't think that I will. You just told me that you have to live a normal life. So do I, Jennifer, do you understand?"

Jennifer stood up, feeling the prick of tears in her eyes. She did understand, and she didn't understand. She didn't want her mother to die.

But she couldn't talk. This was between the two of them, but Conar was there. Supporting Abby.

"I have to go to work," she said simply.

Jerkily, she started out of the room. Edgar was in the doorway, his silver tray of medications in his hand. He looked at her in silent sympathy.

"Conar!" she heard her mother say. And she knew that Conar would follow her.

She whirled around. "I don't want him with me, Mother. I have to live a normal life, understand?"

She strode out to the foyer and exited the house. Still, she wasn't surprised to find Conar coming up behind her when she reached her car.

"I mean it. I need to be alone, I don't want you with me," she said stiffly, her back to him at the driver's side of her door.

He caught her arm firmly, turning her around to face him. He reached for the keys in her hand. "You just upset her even more," he said, "and I don't give a fuck what you want. Give me the keys."

She tried to hold on to the keys, but she didn't have the strength to fight him. He forced her fingers, and she relinquished her hold. She walked around the car, opting for stony silence. She had no intention of speaking to him on the way to the studio.

He didn't speak to her either.

Doug was in her dressing room, waiting for her, anxious to see if she was all right. "Fine. Absolutely fine," she told him curtly.

"Don't bite my head off," he protested. "What's up?"

She sat in front of her mirror. "My mother is going to have the surgery."

"Great!" Doug said.

"Doug, my mother could die. Don't you know what that means? No good moments and bad moments—you get no moments at all."

"She's afraid of losing you, you know."

"Conar is supporting her."

"So you're angry at them both."

"I have a right to be."

"Sure."

"I have a right to be!"

"Sure. Let's see, he's trying to help Abby make you see what she's feeling, and he kept you from being assaulted by a filthy mugger with a wine bottle. I say we shoot him."

She spun around. "What if Conar is the killer, Doug?"

"What?" he said incredulously. "Brenda

was already dead before his plane touched the ground." He hesitated a moment. "You're upset, aren't you? Want me to come back to the house for a few days?"

"No, no…I'm just talking wildly. He did come to my defense, and I guess I'm angry that he had to, because I was taking an unnecessary risk."

"I love all of you, you know. I could come for the weekend again. Act as referee."

She hesitated. Her mother was going to be gone. Maybe she didn't want to be alone in the house with just Conar.

"Yes, that would be great. Plan on coming to the house for the weekend."

"Jennifer!" There was a tap at her door. "Makeup!"

Thorne McKay was right outside. "How on earth does he manage to make the one word 'makeup' sound so obnoxious?" Doug asked.

Jennifer grinned.

"See you later. I've got a few rewrites for the scene this afternoon when you find out you're pregnant."

"I'm pregnant?"

"I guess you haven't seen the original 'revised' scene as yet. It's great. Really, really, wickedly soap, if I do say so myself. I mean, you've been sleeping with your own almost ex-husband, your sister's almost ex-husband, and now, of course, the enemy vintner's son."

"I thought that was a flashback."

"No, you're sleeping with him currently as well."

"And I already know that I'm pregnant?"

"We're building in the time span. That way, lots of people hate you at the moment. Verona, because you might be having her husband's baby. Your husband, because you might not be having his baby. Your new lover, because he doesn't want to be saddled down by you, and reviled by his own family."

"For seducing me?"

"Hell, no, just for not being more careful. Then, of course, there's the fact that your family might want to kill him."

"Great. So why am I telling everyone that I'm pregnant?"

"You're not telling everyone. You're taking a home test, and when you're showering, Verona is going to try to talk to you. You don't hear her over the sound of the water, she comes in, sees the test...voilà."

"I'm taking a lot of showers."

"You'll be very clean, you sleaze bucket of a heartbreaker," he said cheerfully.

"Jennifer!"

Thorne McKay pounded on her door again.

Doug threw the door open. "You again," Thorne muttered. "You know, this is my job. This is not very professional. I'm going to tell Joe and Andy that I just can't do my job when the two of you are always making it so hard."

Doug glanced at Jennifer. "He's going to tell on us."

She grinned. "See ya later."

He closed the door. Thorne sighed. "So you got mugged last night. You're like a catalyst for evil, Jennifer, do you realize that?" he said dramatically.

"Thorne, I was in the wrong place at the wrong time."

"So were those dead girls," he said. "Things are happening around you, Jennifer."

"I'm not a catalyst for evil. I'm not," she said angrily. And suddenly, she didn't want to be alone with him. She didn't want to be alone with anyone anymore.

"Maybe it's the house."

"Trish Wildwood had nothing to do with Granger House," she said. "Thorne, I have to be on the set in two minutes."

"So now you're in a rush. You left me standing at the door while you and Doug had a tête-à-tête, and now you're in a rush."

She groaned. "Thorne, please hurry."

Liam didn't want to stay at the studio. He and Conar left, heading for a coffee shop down the street.

Conar had black coffee. Liam had a mocha with lots of whipped cream and chocolate shavings. The girl didn't seem to want to serve it to him.

"I don't understand the problem," Liam said, stirring his whipped cream into the drink at a small back table in the coffee shop.

Conar grinned. "It's a sissy drink."

"Hey!"

"You don't look like a sissy. That's why they have a problem serving it to you."

Liam nodded.

"So what's up? Our mugger last night was not the murderer?"

Liam licked whipped cream off his straw. "We got back the profile from the FBI."

"What does it say?"

"Organized murderer, intelligent, plans out his crimes very carefully. Something of a showman, he wants his bodies found in a certain way. He's probably killed before, and been so organized that no one ever suspected a serial killer. He uses a different M.O., as we've seen."

"So the guy does think it's one and the same killer?"

"Yes, and we've put out warnings in the paper to young women, especially actresses."

"So even if Abby wasn't so worried, it would be a good time for Jennifer to be very careful, and not go out meeting with people after dark."

"Yep." Liam sighed. "Yesterday, I got a call from a woman."

"Let me guess. Her name was Lila Gonzalez."

"Yes. How did you know?"

"Because this Lila Gonzalez called Jennifer yesterday and they met for coffee, right before she was mugged."

"Lila Gonzalez gave me a list of suspects."

"And I'm on it?"

"Number one."

"Do I have a motive for these murders?"

"No, you just had intimate relations with the victims."

Conar shook his head. "I knew Trish Wild-wood. I didn't sleep with her."

"Lila seems to think you did."

"I don't care what she thinks, it didn't happen."

"Hey, I think you're innocent."

"So what else? Have you matched up any more crimes in your cold-case files?"

Liam hesitated, forming his words care-fully. "We've established that someone might be imitating the murders in Hitchcock films."

"Brenda, the shower scene. Trish, *Frenzy*, the necktie murders."

"Well, a young college student was killed about two years ago, a young man with no record, good grades, good friends—no ene-mies. No drugs. He was discovered in a trunk in an abandoned apartment building."

"That's *Rope*. Jimmy Stewart."

"Maybe it's not connected," Liam said, frustrated. "After all, you can connect almost anything, if you want."

"So you're still nowhere," Conar mur-mured.

"The good—and the bad, according to our profiler—is this: At heart, the killer is a showman. He wants his work to be found, seen, appreciated—applauded as art, if you will. So at this point, it's possible that he doesn't think that he's received the accolades he deserves."

"And that means?"

"He might grow more careless."

"And therefore, more reckless?" Conar asked.

"You got it."

"Maybe I'd better get back to the set."

"Maybe. The second name on Lila's list was—"

"Joe Penny?"

"No. Hugh Tanenbaum. But Joe Penny was the third, and she named Andy Larkin as well—and Jim Novac. I think she felt she just might as well point a finger at everyone on that set. Was she turned down for a job there?"

"I don't know. Maybe. I'm the new guy in town."

"The very well-paid new guy in town. No wonder she has it in for you. Oh, guess who else she mentioned."

"Not me, I'm already at the top of the list."

"No, not you. Doug. Doug Henson."

"But Doug doesn't enjoy women."

"Who says this killer enjoys them?" Liam inquired.

Jennifer and Andy had rehearsed a confrontation scene several times. They stood on the set alone together while Jim was setting up with the cameramen.

Andy still looked like a man who had been through the ringer. He seemed to be trying to behave normally, but every time his name was mentioned, he jumped.

"Andy, what's the matter with you? Why are you acting so strangely?" Jennifer queried. He had changed. He'd always been so damned sure of himself.

"Maybe I should tell you, Jennifer. God knows, I need to talk with someone. Maybe I should go to the police. But this soap is everything to me..."

"Andy, I don't understand you."

"There was blood all over."

"Andy, blood all over where?"

"And there was a body in his bed. He had a girl over. And then he strangled her. But then again, these guys are always dreaming up things for the show..."

"Who? Andy, who are you talking about?"

He looked at her seriously. "Jennifer, we have to be careful. Really careful. It's dangerous to know too much, don't you think? But what would you say if I were to tell you that I think someone involved with our show murdered those two actresses?"

"Andy, I'd say that you need to tell me who, and that we need to tell the police, and you need to tell them why you suspect someone in particular."

"Quiet on the set!" Jim suddenly roared. "Andy...Jennifer? Ready? And we're on in five...four..."

They went through the scene. Despite the fact that Andy was so upset, he was the consummate professional—he didn't flub a line.

"Cut!" Jim called, pleased. "That's it, we're moving quickly here...Andy, you're off."

He started to exit the set. Jennifer was intent on following him, but Jim called her back.

"Jennifer, wait, not you. I still need you. Move on over to the bedroom set," he told her.

"The props are set, so you're doing the scene where you're by yourself, taking the home pregnancy test out of the drugstore bag, all right? Just like we rehearsed, it's just you, no lines. We're moving right along here."

"Jim, wait, just a minute," she said. "I need to speak with Andy."

"Catch him later. Come on, Jen, we've got to keep things moving along."

She moved obediently to her mark on the bedroom set, felt the lights, heard the cameras follow her, heard Jim call, "And in five..."

That afternoon, Conar and Jennifer filmed the argument and passionate bedroom scene between her character and Conar's. In real time, when it was shown in about two weeks, it would precede the earlier filmed sequences in which she feared she was pregnant. Not even in soaps could they change such a fact of nature. Children might grow up overnight, but the parents still had to have intimacy before they were born.

Jennifer was scripted to throw things at him until he reached for her and drew her into bed, a forceful seduction.

Jennifer was a good actress. That afternoon she was more. All the venom she was feeling toward him came out in her soap character's voice.

Bursting into the DeVille cottage, where he'd been prepared to meet another lover, Jennifer came into the scene with wine on the table, the bed lushly made. She immediately began to accuse him of attempting to seduce her sister for evil gain. He had no right to suddenly return to their lives, to come back to the valley, to twist and manipulate them all. He suggested that he might be falling in love with her sister, and she reminded him that he had once claimed to be falling in love with her, when all that he was really in love with was power. She threw a wineglass at him.

Damned close. Far closer than she'd been directed.

Then a book.

That one scored him right in the chest.

By the time he seized her—as directed—he was definitely forceful, and it was definitely in self-defense. When he threw her on the bed, she flew. When she was supposed to be breathless, fighting his kisses, she was. When he crawled over her and the scene was due to end, Jim forgot for several seconds to call cut. Then he did, and there was silence, and then there was suddenly a barrage of applause from the prop people, costumers, production assistants, and others on the set. Jim effused over them. "Damn, will we get the ratings! You two are hotter than July on the equator," he said happily. "I love it; I can't wait to see the dailies."

Hotter than July on the equator.

Conar stared down at Jennifer, his teeth gritted, muscles tensed. She was looking back at him with ice in her large blue eyes. She was such a strikingly beautiful young woman. So perfect in so many ways. Yes, he'd seen that before. Now he had come to enjoy the sound of her voice, the curve of her smile, her loyalty to Abby, her feet-on-the-ground attitude. Yes, of course, he cared for her, wanted her. Not even Abby could have glued him to her if he hadn't found himself so attracted. But it seemed that the more he cared, the more she repelled him...like now. He could see cold suspicion in her eyes again.

"Conar—"

"Don't worry. I'm getting my hands off you," he told her.

"And your chest! And your naked legs," she hissed, quiet but vehement. He was in a robe and briefs, the liaison outfit the script had called for. She was still more or less dressed. She was wearing a low-cut cocktail dress from which he had done no more than lower the strap. "God, have you had any scenes in clothing yet?" she demanded, irritated, palms against his torso.

"Yes, a tux," he told her. "Excuse me, lovely working with you, Miss Connolly. If you try to ditch me here on the set again today, I'll break your arm."

He rose quickly, leaving her on the set bed. Turning to exit, he realized they still had an audience.

He nodded curtly to Jim, then walked on off.

In his dressing room, he changed quickly to his street clothing, anxious to find Jennifer before she could leave the building without him.

Jennifer thought that the tap on the door would be Conar. She steeled herself. The ride home with him would be worse than the ride here.

"Jennifer?"

It was Liam, not Conar, who was at her door. He left it open as he entered.

"Liam, hi, how are you!" she said, greeting him with a hug and a kiss on the cheek. "Do you have any information?" she asked anxiously.

He shook his head. "I'm so sorry, I really have nothing. We don't think your mugger is the killer. The guy is a scuz—did time for manslaughter in a barroom brawl, went to jail for abusing his ex-wife—but he doesn't fit the personality type we're looking for in the recent murders."

"Liam, you need to talk to Andy Larkin." Andy had left the studio. She was disturbed because of his behavior. Andy had talked so wildly, and he scared her, and she still didn't know what—or who—Andy had been talking about. "He seems to think that someone on the set might be involved."

"Interesting. Your friend Lila Gonzalez seemed to think the same."

"Lila?" she asked slowly.

"She called the station yesterday before she called you."

"Do you think...?"

"I think she doesn't know anything," Liam said firmly.

"Yes, but she told me something Conar didn't," Jennifer said, staring down at her dressing table. "Conar claimed the night we found her that he didn't know Trish Wildwood. Lila suggested that he more than knew her."

"And what?"

Her eyes shot up. It wasn't Liam speaking, it was Conar. He stood just outside her dressing room, gray eyes sharp and hard as tacks, tall and lean and wickedly rugged-looking in a casual black suede jacket. Something seemed to lurch inside of her at the way he looked at her. He had closed off. He'd had it with her, she thought.

Conar said smoothly, "Let me assure you, in front of Miss Connolly, that the police are welcome to anything they like—hair, skin, blood, semen, DNA, what the hell, whatever they want, anytime they want. Serena just told me you're giving her and Kelly a lift to her house. Would you extend your civic duties, Liam, to seeing Miss Connolly home as well?"

He didn't wait for an answer. He turned and left.

Chapter 16

During the drive home, Jennifer began to wish that she, too, were staying at Serena's. Tonight, they were going to order pizza, drink a bunch of the promotional wine made by a local vineyard and labeled Valentine Valley, and watch old movies.

"You're more than welcome to stay," Serena told her.

"I would, but..."

"I thought that your mother was checking into the hospital tonight," Kelly said.

"She is, but I want to visit with her, and I guess I want to be at the house just in case anything happens."

"Edgar could call you," Serena pointed out.

"I know. I guess I just feel closer to her at Granger House."

Liam met her eyes in the mirror. There was pity in them.

Liam dropped Kelly and Serena off then drove to Granger House. He didn't speak to her, and she wondered if he was angry that she'd accused Conar.

"Hey, you've got company," Liam noted.

She looked at the wide curving driveway. Her own car was back—Conar had driven fast, she thought. Drew Parker's flashy vehicle was there as well. And there was another car, one she didn't recognize, a white Park Avenue.

A young man in jeans and a T-shirt got out of the car, approaching them.

Liam apparently knew the man. "Ricardo," he said pleasantly.

"Ricardo?" Jennifer whispered.

Liam was already getting out of his car. She did the same. He shook the young man's hand.

"Ricardo Carillo, Jennifer Connolly."

"I recognize you," the man said, grinning. "My wife is a huge fan."

"Thank you very much."

"So," Liam said, "let me guess. Conar is hiring off-duty guys to watch the house."

"Yep." Ricardo grinned at Jennifer. "I'm LAPD, Miss Connolly. Off duty. Hired to keep an eye on the place. I hope that's all right."

"Of course. It will be great to have the protection. Are you coming in?"

"No, I'm on the outside. I've met the dogs, and another guy will be coming on duty when I go off duty. His name is Herb Jenkins, in case you see a different car out here."

"That's great, thanks."

Liam got back into his car. "Well, I'm on my way, then."

After he drove off, Jennifer asked Ricardo, "Can I get you anything? Something to drink, some dinner? I need to go in myself; I'm trying to find out if my mother checked into the hospital all right today, and what's going on."

"I have coffee in my thermos that your butler made for me. I'm fine. I'm supposed to stay out of the way."

"Don't hesitate to ask if you need anything."

He grinned. "I won't."

She went on in, and Edgar greeted her in the foyer. "There you are, Miss Jennifer."

"Yes, Edgar. How's Mom?"

"She's in room 408. She was watching today's episode of *Valentine Valley* when I left her. I would have stayed awhile longer, but she wanted me home for you and Mr. Conar."

"Thank you, Edgar. I'd like to go see her."

"Of course. I made a light dinner, sandwiches and salad. Everything is out on the dining room buffet. Mr. Conar suggested that you might want to eat, freshen up, and then go on over."

"Together?"

"Yes, is that all right?"

She made a face. "Of course."

Drew Parker was with Conar in the dining room. They had both made plates. "Jennifer, Jennifer, Jennifer!" Drew exclaimed, coming to her, taking her hands. "You are one busy little lady. One thing after another! Are you all right, dear? Tell me about your awful experience last night."

"Why? I'm sure Conar has already told you the whole story," she said, then winced. It wasn't what she had meant to say. Conar, however, displayed no emotion whatsoever. He watched her with his steady gaze. She felt a trembling sensation in the pit of her stomach. She wanted to walk over to him, lay her head against his shoulder, and tell him she was sorry. His eyes seemed to tell her to stay the hell away from him.

"Well, of course, but...you are all right?"

Drew said, not seeming to realize that the room rippled with tension. His eyes were anxious on Jennifer as he studied her.

"I'm perfectly fine, just anxious about Mother."

"Of course. Well, she's asked me to stay here at the house while she's in the hospital. Do you mind?"

"Drew, it's Mom's house, she can ask whomever she wants to stay here."

"Yes, she can. But I want it to be all right with you."

"You're her oldest and dearest friend. Of course it's all right with me that you stay here."

"Have a sandwich, dear."

"I think I'll just run up and shower and change quickly," she said.

She lingered in her room, hoping that Conar would come up and talk to her. He didn't. When she went back downstairs, they were ready to drive to the hospital.

When they arrived, however, Abby was sleeping. She was in a pleasant private room, but though she, Conar, Drew, Edgar, and Abby's nurse had piled into the room, Abby didn't seem to hear a thing. The nurse told Jennifer that she had been given a pill, and would probably not awaken until the next morning.

"Why?" Jennifer asked. "What was done to her?"

The nurse smiled. "Nothing, honestly. We're just trying to see that she gets the best rest she can."

"Maybe I should stay with her."

The nurse, a pretty, compassionate brunette, smiled warmly. "She said that you'd probably try to do that, and she told me that I was to tell you in no uncertain terms to go home."

Jennifer flushed, hearing Drew's soft laughter right behind her.

The nurse told her, "Seriously, she's fine, she's sleeping well. Go home. Those chairs are wretched. And if she opts for surgery in the future, well, you'll probably wind up sleeping here a night or two then."

"All right. Thanks. Thanks so much. For her."

"She's a doll."

Jennifer walked over to Abby's side. Her mother was sleeping so peacefully. She barely trembled. She looked so beautiful at rest. Jennifer kissed her cheek. "I love you, Mom." Abby couldn't hear her, but Jennifer had to say it anyway. She rose, thanked the nurse again, and left the room.

In the car, Conar sat in front with Edgar. Jennifer sat in back with Drew.

When they reached the house, it was late. A new car was in the driveway. The second off-duty cop hired to watch the house, Jennifer thought. Conar left to greet the man.

She went on in with Edgar and Drew. "Shall I make tea?" Edgar asked.

"I would love some," Drew said.

Conar came back into the house. "I'm going up," he announced. "Early call, and late day tomorrow. You, too, Jennifer."

He left the hallway. "Well, I guess I'm going up, too," she said. "Good night, both of you."

She kissed Drew and Edgar on the cheek.

She walked upstairs and stood in the hallway for what seemed like forever. Conar's door didn't open. She walked down the hallway and hesitantly tapped on it. He opened it in a towel. He had just stepped from the shower; his hair was still wet.

"Look, I'm sorry," she said.

"Are you? Well, thanks for saying so."

"No, I mean, I'm really sorry—"

"And I'm really tired of you saying one thing one minute, then accusing me the next."

"But I don't—"

"You don't what? You don't believe I'm a heinous killer? You should hear the things you say. And worse. You should see your eyes."

"I really..." She paused, lowering her head. This was hard. "I feel safe with you," she told him.

"Um. Well, wouldn't want you to worry about being safe. That's why I hired the cops. But wait a minute," he said. He turned, walking into the room, to the bed. He picked something up and came back with it.

The fur ball. It was Ripper.

Ripper let out a happy little bark.

Conar shoved the dog into her hands. "He'll keep you safe," he said. "He'll bark his head off at the slightest whisper of sound anywhere near you."

She was so humiliated that she couldn't come up with a snappy retort.

He closed the door on her.

"Bastard," she whispered to the closed door, tears stinging her eyes.

She quickly went down the hall to her own room. She didn't want Drew Parker or Edgar to come up and find her crying in front of Conar Markham's closed door—a door closed specifically to her.

She closed her door and locked it, sniffing, furious with herself. She set Ripper down at the foot of her bed and went into the bathroom and washed the tears from her face with cold water. She could imagine what her soap character's analyst would be saying to her. "Are you hurt, Ms. Valentine, really hurt, or is your pride bruised, your ego wounded?"

"I'm hurt," she told the mirror. "Damn him!"

She walked back out to the bedroom. "I think it's a Tweetie Bird night again," she told Ripper.

Ripper gave her a little bark and thumped his tiny stub of a tail.

"It's you and me, bud," she told him.

She tried to sleep but no dice. She wondered if she could call in sick the next day and spend the time at the hospital with Abby. But if Abby had surgery, she'd be asking for major time off. She couldn't take the days now. And tomorrow was the "big" day. Joe Penny's plunge into suspense. What were they doing with her character?

At last she fell asleep.

For once, she didn't feel anyone watching her.

She awoke late, and she wouldn't have awakened even then if it weren't for the fact that
Ripper was at her door, barking.

She bolted up. Sun was streaming in.

"Shit!"

She opened her door, letting Ripper out. She
was surprised that Conar hadn't been up to
tell her how late she was running. She ran into
her bath, discarding Tweetie as she did so, hop-
ping into the shower. She didn't bother with
street makeup.

But when she dressed and tore downstairs,
she found that Conar had already gone in. "I
think he had a few things he wanted to discuss
with Joe Penny. At least that's the gist of
what I understood," Drew told her. "I'm
giving you a ride in, and of course, he's got
your car, so he'll give you a ride back."

"Gee, does he remember that it's my car?"
she murmured.

Drew smiled a little weakly. "Ready?" he
asked.

"Sure."

As they drove, Drew seemed preoccupied.
Jennifer, preoccupied herself, didn't try to draw
him out. But then he began to hem and haw
a bit.

"Jennifer, you know that I sold your mother
that house."

"Yes, of course, she loves the house."

"But...well, it's a weird house," Drew said.

Smoothing back his white hair, he glanced her way. "Maybe it does have bad...vibes."

"Why?"

"Well, for one, it was weird, what happened with Celia Marston."

"The house didn't kill her, Drew."

"But there is a killer out there now."

"It isn't the house, Drew."

He sighed, staring ahead of him. They had reached the studio. He pulled the car over.

"Thanks, Drew, for getting me here."

"My pleasure. But, Jennifer..."

"Yes?" She stopped in her movement to exit the car and looked at him, giving him her full attention. "Drew, what is it?"

"You remember the Granger Room? That I couldn't find that secret staircase?"

"Yes?" She felt the strange prickling sensation that had touched her now and again in the night.

"Well, it's just that I'm pretty sure there is a staircase."

"And that's why I feel I'm being watched."

He nodded uncomfortably. "Or maybe not. I don't want to scare you. I just want you to be careful."

"I will." She kissed him on the cheek, feeling a new sense of creeping fear. She needed to tell Conar. Except that he had all but thrown her out of his room.

She bit her lip, heading on into the studio. She had a feeling it was going to be a very long day.

It was all about to get worse. She was in the first scene they filmed. It was a scene at the fictional Prima Piatti in which she got into an argument with Jay Braden, or her husband, old Randy Rock, then walked by Conar, and out to the street—and nervously clutched a street lamp and her stomach. Jenny Sinclair and Hannah Jeeter, two of the writers on the show beneath Doug, had argued about the scene. They were both mothers—of three and four children respectively—and argued that she wouldn't be holding her stomach at such an early date. "Mightn't she be as sick as a dog, even very early on?" Doug had demanded, and they had looked at one another, and the scene had stayed as written.

After her exit, Conar was then to have a confrontation with Jay, then Andy, then Serena, Hank and Vera as her parents, and at last, Kelly—whom he would let down gently, telling her that a previous commitment had him tied up for the moment. He couldn't form another relationship until he finished with current business.

Despite the number of characters involved in the filming, it went without a hitch. Jennifer changed to "naked" strips of clothing and robe, and returned for the scene in which her sister was to find her home pregnancy test. It was finished quickly, and the others were released for the day.

"Call us," Serena told Jennifer. "We'll get together this weekend?"

"I hope. I need to spend some time at the hospital."

"Of course."

"But let's get together."

Serena smiled. "I have a date Saturday night. But it's loose—we could still get together."

"Oh? Who is this date with?"

"The cop."

"Liam?"

"Yep. Don't you approve?"

"Sure I do. He's gorgeous, nice, trustworthy. What's not to approve?"

Jennifer's hair was wet, and with most of the cast and crew leaving the set, the air-conditioning seemed cold. She shivered and drew her terry robe around her. "Well, I guess I have to go film this top-secret scene of mine."

Serena grinned. "See you over the weekend."

Jennifer nodded and headed back to the center of the studio floor, where the camera crew was setting up in her "bed/bath" room. With so many people gone, the set looked eerie. Both the left and right walls were set up as the Valentine house, the vineyard house, the restaurant, the stables, the caretaker's cottage—the "permanent" sets for the soap. There were two extra stages that could be changed quickly and easily to resemble almost any setting. There were network storehouses in the same building, and there was a neighboring "boneyard," an area that housed larger, often unique pieces, used for a show or movie at some point, that were no longer needed for their original purpose but were too expensive to simply discard. At the moment all the stages on the set were empty. It did resemble an empty house—very strangely laid out. Teacups remained on tables, not yet taken away by props. On the bar at Prima Piatti, speared olives continued to float in two martini glasses.

"Jennifer!" Joe called.

Doug Henson, Joe Penny, Jim Novac, Andy Larkin, Conar, and Roger Crypton, Jim's head and favorite cameraman, were gathered together in a series of director's chairs while props people began picking up from the earlier scenes.

"Hey, guys, it's kind of cold," she told them. "I don't know what the big secret scene is as yet, but maybe I could change?"

"No, no, sit, Jennifer. Let me set up the scene for you," Jim told her.

"It's brilliant, really brilliant," Joe told her. "You'll love the ending we've decided on."

"I still don't think it's necessary in any way," Conar told him.

"I've tried to explain. We leave the audience hanging. We're preempted for those special sports programs the Monday after the Friday when we'll roll this episode—trust me. By Tuesday, all our matrons will be dying to see what happens next."

Joe did seem incredibly pleased.

"What are we doing?" Jennifer asked. "I've still never seen a script."

"You don't need one."

"I'm the only one in the scene, and I don't need a script?"

"It's all takes place in the shower," Jim said.

"What?"

"It's the shower scene," Conar told her. "You know, Hitchcock's scene."

"It is not 'the' scene. We could get killed for 'the' scene."

"Wait a minute," Jennifer said, confused, looking at all of them, an uneasy sensation slipping along her spine. "I knew you might be writing the character out of the show, but—"

"Jennifer! Never!" Andy said. She stared at him. He didn't look any better. As a matter of fact, he was white. His palms were sweating.

"If this is 'the' shower scene—sorry, not *the* shower scene but a character imitating the shower scene in a way that we don't get sued, I'm not so certain I can find a way to see it as a happy ending. Doug, I'm just not ecstatic here."

He grinned and leaned toward her. "It's all a dream."

"What?" she said.

"There's a stalker in the Valley—we established that in previous episodes."

"And we've let it hang awhile."

"It's a soap," Doug said impatiently. "Things are supposed to hang."

"Come on, pay attention, we've got a busy afternoon here," Joe said.

"All right, Jennifer, here's the concept.

You're upset, you don't know who the father of your child is yourself."

"Which, of course, we're going to milk forever," Joe Penny told her.

"Am I having a two-year gestation period?" she inquired sweetly.

Doug snorted. "Maybe only a few short months," he told her cheerfully. He widened his eyes, teasing her. "Maybe we'll be going to the baby's graduation next year."

"I thought you were explaining the story line," Joe said impatiently.

Conar leaned forward impatiently. "You're worried about your situation. You're suddenly very religious, and not at all pro-choice. You think each man is going to be furious. There'll be cuts at first into scenes in which you are envisioning fights among all of us, and all of us ending up angry with you. As you're busy being so afraid, the Valentine Valley Stalker comes upon you, unaware, and begins stabbing you in the shower. Naturally, his face never shows. The scene ends with you slinking down in the tub."

"Grabbing the curtain and falling forward with my eyes open?" she said.

"Yeah, that's what is intended."

"And we're not going to get sued?"

"No, of course, our killer is imitating a piece of pop culture."

"It's a mistake—a big mistake. You're going to lose your audience, not have it panting, Joe," Conar said irritably.

"I am the producer here, and this is the way the 'bible' was written."

"I still don't understand how I wind up happy with this," Jennifer interrupted.

"It's all a dream," Doug told her. "You're imagining how much trouble you're in, how much everyone hates you, what everyone might want to do...and how it could all end quickly if the stalker did come after you."

"I don't like it," she said. "With what's happened here lately, Joe, how can you do this?"

"I've had this idea for a long time, ever since all the hoopla on Hitchcock's hundredth birthday. Hey, Hitch was a good fellow. His actresses thought the world of him. Imitation is the sincerest form of flattery, and I am making no bones about the fact that I admire him," Joe said.

"And no bones about the fact that Hugh Tanenbaum has made a fortune playing off of Hitchcock originals," Andy murmured.

"You guys, I feel really, really uncomfortable about this," Jennifer protested. "And, Conar, your new superstar, is on my side."

"Oh, I don't like it," Conar said. "But I think that you have to shoot the scene."

"What?" she said, startled. Whatever personal was going on between them, she had been certain that he was on her side.

"Jennifer, you know, you are just an actress on this set," Joe reminded her politely.

She stared at him. Conar stood suddenly, taking her by the shoulders. "Give me a minute," he said to the others. He propelled her some distance away.

"This is *sick*!" she whispered furiously. "Help me out here."

"Do the scene," he said.

"But—"

"Liam is here."

She started to look around his shoulder. "Where—"

"Don't look, and trust me when I tell you— Liam is here. Do the scene."

"It's a closed set."

"It's a big building, with lots of ways in, and lots of ways out," Conar told her. "Shoot the scene."

"But—"

"Please."

"Yeah. Sure. Why not? When this is shown, my mother will be frightened to death."

"No, she won't. She's an actress herself. She knows it's make-believe," Conar said, walking away from her. "Jen is okay now, Joe. She'll do it," Conar called to him.

"Good, good. Okay, let's take positions, set the cameras...we're going for a lot of angles, and lights! Get the lighting right, please. I'm afraid we're in for a lot of shots, Jennifer."

"Really?" she murmured sarcastically. "The original with Janet Leigh took seven days to film, as I remember. We got that kind of time, Joe?"

"Funny, Jennifer."

"Show her the script," Jim directed. "Roger," he told his head cameraman, "check all your angles while we're here...Niall, get on those breakaway walls. Everyone, places. Jennifer, we're starting with just the thoughts in your head. I've watched interviews with both Hitch and Janet Leigh. You're washing away your guilt as well as dirt. The shower is good, it's cleansing, it will make you feel clean again, clean and innocent, except that no amount of water can make you clean. You've cheated on your husband, you've slept with your own brother-in-law—not to mention half the town in previous episodes. But that doesn't matter now. You're having a baby, and you don't know whose baby it is. Your father is going to string you up. Your mother will make you pay the rest of your life. Your conniving oldest sister, Verona, will see to it that your inheritance is stripped away..."

The water ran, she showered. They changed some of the walls, the point of view of the camera, and she showered again. Once more they changed the walls and the POV. And again, and again...

"Great. Andy, you're doing the killer, right?" Jim inquired. "I need you now. The black face netting is there; the robe is there, and the rubber knife."

"I'll do the killer," Conar interrupted. He stood, approaching the set. His eyes met Jennifer's. "You all right with this?"

"I'm only an actress on the set," she told him.

"Are you all right with this?" he repeated.

Of course she was all right with it! If she did suspect him of anything, she'd still be an idiot to think that he'd harm her here and now. And yet...

Jesus! She hadn't wanted Andy doing it!

"I'm all right with it; please, let's just get it done."

The first time was horrible. The curtain was ripped open. She couldn't help feeling a terrible pain at the pit of her stomach, a roil of fear as she saw the huge man before her— faceless. The netting Conar wore blacked out his features completely. It would keep the camera from betraying anything about him, anything at all.

The knife began to fall.

And she began to scream...and scream.

And she screamed, throughout the afternoon.

In all, they spent five hours on the scene. The rubber knife came at her again, and again, and in the end, she fell, clutching the shower curtain.

Just like in the original, they used chocolate for blood. The knife never really touched her flesh, and no slashes would be shown on her body.

She went down.

The cameras homed in on her face.

Once...

And again.

And at last Jim called, "Cut!" And this word was followed by "And that's it! It's a wrap!"

Conar reached out to help her up. He hadn't ripped off the netting yet.

She recoiled from his arm, stumbling up on

her own. Niall Myers came up swiftly with her robe. She quickly slipped into it, shivering.

The majority of the stage floor seemed dark. Yes, Jim had wanted perfect light, and so she was in a pool of it, and everything around her seemed dark. Liam was out there somewhere. That's what Conar had said. *Why?* Had Andy convinced him that the murderer was among them?

"Good girl, Jen, that was terrific," Jim congratulated her. He started to hug her. She was too unnerved.

"I need to change," she told him. "I'm freezing."

"Of course," he said.

"We'll go right home," Conar said, only he didn't look like Conar. He was a faceless, huge enemy; he was the man who had wielded the knife. She shook her head.

"Doug is coming for the weekend. He'll drive me."

She forgot her slippers, stepping barefoot onto the cold cement of the main floor. All the other sets were in darkness. The Valentine dining room, Prima Piatti...empty, and dark. And yet...someone might be lurking there. Someone might be watching from there...

She didn't know why, but she suddenly felt certain that she was being watched.

The killer was watching. He was out there. He had watched her in the shower, watched the lights, the sets, the camera, the action. He had watched the knife, slashing down on her...

Yes, oh, God! The killer was out there!
Out there...
Or nearer here.

She was surrounded, and yet she was alone.

She ran then, anxious to be away from all of them. Nearly desperate to reach her dressing room.

And still she felt that he was out there.

She could almost feel him breathe.

Chapter 17

Jennifer hurried into her dressing room and locked her door behind her.

At last, she thought, a safe haven. She sat in the chair before her mirror, shivering for long seconds. Then she looked up. She was white. *Get a grip!* she warned herself. Her shivering slowly eased, and with it the strange sensation of panic that had seized her. No one was going to hurt her on this set.

She quickly stood, dried, and ran a towel through her hair. She put on her street clothes, then hesitated. She was still really white, and come hell or high water, she was going to see her mother tonight. But she needed a little makeup if she was going to go see Abby.

She blended base onto her cheeks and dialed Granger House. Mary answered; Edgar was out, maybe visiting Abby—Mr. Drew Parker was out as well, maybe seeing Abby, too. Mary had talked to her mother a while ago, and Abby was doing well. Jennifer could just call the hospital and talk with her mother now if she wanted—it was probably right around dinnertime, and they wouldn't be giving Abby her sedatives for a few hours.

Jennifer called the hospital, using the extension Mary had given her. Her mother answered cheerfully.

She didn't know why, but the sound of Abby's voice brought tears to her eyes. Perhaps because she was so disturbed by the scene they had just shot. It was television, make believe. She was an actress, that was all.

"Mom? You're okay?"

"I'm fine, darling, feeling just a shade like a pincushion, but then, that feeling has been growing over the years with this sickness. But it's been fine, dear. Drew has come by, Edgar, and even your friends! The girls stopped by—"

"Kelly and Serena?"

"Yes, with that Randy Rock—what's his real name?"

"Jay Braden."

"Yes, yes, of course. Everyone has been so nice. And I'm only here for tests."

"I'm glad, Mom. They should be nice," she added, half teasing, "they're in the presence of a true legend when they're with you."

"Thanks, sweetheart. Maybe my legendary days aren't quite done," Abby told her. "We'll see. No rush here, or anything."

"Um, no rush, eh? Well, I'm going to hang

up and get out of here so that I can see you soon, okay?"

"Don't come alone, Jennifer. I know you think I'm crazy, but—"

"Mom, Doug is coming for the weekend again. And Drew is there, and Edgar and Conar—and Conar went and hired cops to watch the house. I'm going to be fine. You worry about you."

"But no going out alone, sweetheart, please. Even with the dog."

"Even with the dog," Jennifer promised. She hung up. Within a few minutes, she was dressed, her makeup set, her hair dried and brushed.

She unlocked her dressing room door and returned to the main stage floor. Walking along it, she heard her own footsteps, clapping against the cement.

"Doug?" she called. No answer. "Conar, Joe, anybody?"

She heard something...a rustling? Clinking? Ticking? *Something.* It came from the now darkened area of her character's bed/bathroom.

"Damn," she swore softly. "Doug! Damn it, where are you? Let's go."

Suddenly, even the few lights in the main section of the floor went out. The room was plunged into total darkness.

Then something—some*one*—was hurtling toward her. A person. She could hear footsteps. Coming toward her, faster and faster. She could see nothing in the darkness.

Neither, surely, could he!

346

Her heart was racing; her breath seemed caught in her throat. She slipped out of her shoes and silently ran across the room. She heard a whooshing sound.

What was it?

A knife striking out! she thought in panic. Striking nothing but air...

Then she felt it. Movement so close to her it barely missed her. She held her breath. Prayed that the pounding of her heart would not give her away...

She closed her eyes; gritted her teeth. The sound was to her left then, farther, farther...

She waited. It seemed like an eternity.

"Jennifer?"

It was Doug calling her.

"Hey, why are all these lights out?" someone else demanded. Conar. His voice was deep, angry—and anxious.

Once again, the main floor of the stage was illuminated. At the end of the length of the floor, near the exit doors, were Conar and Doug.

They stared at her.

"Someone—" she began, but she had no voice. "Someone was just in here," she whispered.

They both looked at her.

"Lots of people were just here," Doug said, not having a clue to the fact that she was standing there in terror. "Joe Penny and Andy were both very firm when they ordered a closed set. But you know, even with a closed set, for that kind of shot, you need people. So we had the cameramen, a lighting man, Niall from props, the two producers, the director, a writer, as in me—and Conar. Because he's...well, because he's Conar. I guess that sounds like a lot of people, even though it was a minimum of people. But most of them are still here...somewhere."

Conar was studying her. He walked toward her. She forced herself to move, walking back toward her shoes.

He stared at her hard. She slipped back into her shoes. "Someone was just in this room with me. And I think he had a knife."

"Jen, we just did a shower scene, for heaven's sake," Doug said.

Conar ducked down to the ground, where her shoes had been. "Here's your knife," he said. Rising, he produced the rubber knife he had used for the scene.

"Someone was playing a cruel joke on you," Doug said.

"Were they?" she murmured. Her knees were rubber. She didn't think that it had been a joke.

"Want me to look around?" Conar inquired.

Where's Liam? she wanted to ask him. But did Doug know that Liam had supposedly been there, watching the filming, watching the people involved. Why hadn't he seen who it was?

Conar hadn't waited for her answer. He didn't seem to mind the dark. He walked onto every set, moving things, looking around.

"Conar!" she called.

"What? I can't find anything."

"And you won't. Whoever was here left before the lights came on. Let's get out of here. I want to see my mother."

"I'll tell Liam about this. I invited him to come over later."

As she had said she would, she drove with Doug. Conar followed behind them. When they reached Abby's hospital room, she was awake and looking radiant. Drew Parker was at her side. They had been talking. Drew looked gravely at Jennifer, and then thoughtfully at Conar.

Watch out for the missing staircase, he had warned her.

He rose. "I'll let you three talk with Abby for a few minutes," he said. "I'm afraid they're coming soon with her sedative."

Abby smiled at Jennifer's tight look of concern. "I've had some really great rest in here."

"Well, maybe we could change medications at home," Jennifer suggested.

"Jennifer, I don't want to spend my life medicated and in bed," Abby said softly.

Jennifer fell silent, looking at her hands.

"So how was the day's work?" Abby asked cheerfully.

By some kind of tacit agreement, not one of them mentioned the shower scene. Doug took the lead, talking about the terribly promiscuous way Natalie Valentine was leading her life. Poor dear was preggers, without a clue as to the father. "We've a million miles to go with this one, of course," he told Abby, his eyes widening and eyebrows wiggling Groucho Marx style.

Abby laughed, enjoying the conversation. "Is she going to be pregnant forever—or only a few weeks."

"Well, for the next month, at least. We're actually changing the 'bible' around a bit, changing our main story line for the season, so I'm not sure. But I'm sure it's going to be fun."

"And outrageous," Abby supplied.

"Of course. Only on *Valentine Valley*," Jennifer told her.

Abby's nurse arrived; the same sweet girl who had been there the night before. Reluctantly Jennifer rose to leave. She hugged Abby tightly. "I love you so much!" she told her mother.

"You, too. Jennifer. You won't go out—"

"Jennifer will be as snug as a bug in a rug, Abby," Conar assured her. "She has me and Doug, Drew and Edgar—and a cop in the front yard at all times. Not to mention Lady in the back."

"And Ripper in my room," Jennifer said sweetly.

"He barks like a son of a gun," Conar said.

"All right. All of you. Behave and take care."

"We will," Doug promised.

They left her. She took her pill obediently, and the nurse shooed them out of the room.

Again, Jennifer opted to ride with Doug—Conar was right behind them in her car, and Drew Parker was right behind him.

When they reached the house, Mary was

gone, but Edgar was back on duty. He'd made them a Crock-Pot stew, and it was ready in the dining room, and very delicious. Throughout the meal, they talked about the shower scene, having sworn Drew Parker to secrecy. Doug defended their producers, while Jennifer continued to say that they shouldn't do it.

"Do you think that Hollywood is going to give up the horror film?" Doug demanded. "The mystery film, the suspense? Never. Nor are we going to stop making roller coasters. People want thrills in their lives."

"I think I've been thrilled enough," Jennifer said.

"That's why your set was closed and so carefully guarded," Drew said thoughtfully. Jennifer stared at him. He shrugged. "I came back to see you this afternoon. The guy downstairs—the building guard—was like an old bulldog."

"You were at the set?" Jennifer inquired.

He nodded. "I was afraid I had upset you this morning. I hadn't meant to, if I did do so."

Had he upset her? The whole damned day had upset her.

Just then Liam arrived. He was full of questions about what had happened that afternoon at the studio. After she finished, he excused himself to go make a phone call. "I'll have some men go over and look around," he told her.

She had finished eating. Ripper, she saw, was sitting calmly and obediently at Conar's feet. She felt a twinge of guilt. "I wasn't upset, Drew," she lied. "Excuse me, will you?" she asked them. "I'm going outside to see my dog."

She had forgotten the cop out front. She had barely stepped out to rub Lady's head before she jumped—alarmed by the sudden appearance of Ricardo Carillo.

"I'm sorry!" he said quickly.

"No, I'm sorry. I should have come and told you I'd be outside," she said, scratching Lady's head. Ricardo was looking behind her. She rose to see that the guys had all followed her—all of them—Conar, Liam, Drew, Doug, and Edgar.

And Ripper.

"I guess I'm going back in. Pet Lady for me now and then, will you?" she asked Ricardo.

He smiled at her. "Sure. Good night." He raised his voice. "Good night, Mr. Markham, and all."

Sheepishly, the guys staring at her from just outside the den called good night in return. Jennifer went on in.

Drew suggested Monopoly. Even Edgar agreed to play.

At midnight, Doug held both Park Place and Boardwalk and was ruthlessly running everyone out of money. Jennifer realized she was exhausted. She yawned. "I concede."

"You can't concede. You have to let me make mincemeat out of you," Doug protested.

"I have to concede. I can't move anymore. I'm going up."

Neither Conar, Liam, Drew, nor Edgar seemed ready to give in. Conar didn't even look up from the board. "Take Ripper with you," he said.

She hesitated. Had she hoped that he'd follow her?

She picked up the little Yorkie. He licked her fingers and gave her an adoring look. "Good night," she called, heading from the den and up the stairs. "You know, you're not so bad," she told Ripper. "I just feel bad that I have Lady locked outside. Of course, she has a beautiful kennel. Her doghouse is even air-conditioned, my mother loves her, but...Oh, never mind. I'm rambling on and on to a big pile of fur with huge brown eyes and a sloppy little tongue."

She brought Ripper into her room and locked the door behind her. She instantly checked out her closet and her bath, then set Ripper down.

"We're going to watch television. Maybe that will help us sleep."

Ripper barked his agreement.

Jennifer decided not to take a shower that night. She'd had enough showering for one day.

With her makeup off and a Taz cotton gown on, she turned on the news. An anchorwoman was talking about the new fashions being shown in Paris. Jennifer flicked to another channel and found the weather forecast. She flicked again, to the History Channel.

The program was about the use of forensic entomology and how the life span of flies and maggots in a corpse could help solve mysteries.

She flicked off it immediately. She wasn't

sure what channel she hit next, but she was pleased. Humphrey Bogart was saying to Ingrid Bergman, "Here's looking at you, kid." *Casablanca.* Yes, she could sleep to that.

She cuddled Ripper to her chest, and closed her eyes.

She awoke sometime later. She didn't know why at first. She had turned the television very low, but she could hear screaming. She squinted, looking at the screen. Great. No wonder she heard screaming. The movie playing was the teen horror flick *Scream.*

"Great," she muttered to herself. "I couldn't have left it on Nickelodeon and awakened to *The Brady Bunch.*"

She pointed and flicked the channel changer. She came upon *Bewitched.*

"That will do," she said softly.

Ripper, standing like a little pointer and staring at her closet, growled.

"What is it, boy?"

The dog's growling made her very uneasy.

"It's okay, Ripper. You're growling at my leopard coat. Don't worry—it's faux fur. I wouldn't own a real leopard, honestly."

The dog jumped off the bed, barking. "What is it?" she said. She sighed. It wasn't that big a closet. She had checked it out when she and the dog had come into the room.

"All right, Ripper, get over here. I'm going to show you the coat." She went into the closet and started to take down the coat. The hanger was snagged on an old wood pole and she leaned into the closet, trying to free it. She had too many clothes. She had to clean it out—this was only her room at her mother's house.

Leaning to reach the pole, she suddenly slipped and went plunging forward into her own clothing.

She should have been stopped by the back wall.

But she wasn't.

There was nothing there.

"Damn!" she swore, trying to catch herself, trying to understand what had happened. Clothing gave; she heard it rip from the pole, fall from hangers. And, tangled into it, head first, she was suddenly plummeting downward from her rear closet wall and into stygian oblivian.

Before going to bed, Conar had gone out to talk with Ricardo Carillo. He was a good cop. With a wife, a four-year-old, and a new baby on the way, Ricardo needed the time-and-a-half pay Conar was giving him to keep a sharp eye on the house.

"Everything all right?" Conar asked.

"Yep. Got a thermos of hot coffee, and I'm real good friends now with a real big dog," he said cheerfully. "Don't worry, I won't sleep on the job."

"I know you won't." Conar assured him. And, just for good measure, Liam was also around.

The Monopoly game had run so late, Conar invited him to stay the night.

Back in the house, he double-checked all the doors anyway. Then he went up to his room. He paused in front of Jennifer's. He could hear her television. He was tempted to knock on the door. No. He had turned her away last night. It was best.

Hell, no, it wasn't best. Not for him. But he couldn't stand the look he had seen in her eyes. She did suspect him. Maybe just a little. Maybe she wasn't quite certain. She had to trust him completely. If she didn't...

We could sleep together anyway.

That was coming from his lower anatomy.

No. It isn't right.

That, from his mind.

Who the hell needed right?

Swearing softly aloud, he went on into his own room. He changed into pajama bottoms, then started reading his book on Hollywood murders.

After some time, he rubbed his eyes and looked at the clock on the desk. After two a.m. He should get some sleep.

He lay down on the bed, noting that he had gotten into the habit of sleeping with the bathroom light on. It made for shadows in the room.

But shadows he could see. Fingers laced behind his head, he wondered about the way Jennifer had awakened from her dreams, convinced someone was watching her. Was the danger close, really close to them? What was

356

happening? Was there a killer who had been at it a long time, a killer growing frustrated that his work hadn't been discovered and applauded?

He frowned, thinking he should talk Jennifer into screwing the job—and coming away with him. Andy Larkin had told Liam that afternoon that he'd seen bloody garments at Joe Penny's house, and maybe even a body in Joe's bed. Liam had talked to Joe at some point, and to Jim Novac. And he had asked Conar to slip him onto the closed set so that he could observe what went on during the filming.

Suddenly Conar sat up in bed. He had heard a long, bloodcurdling, high-pitched scream—and it seemed to come from directly beneath his window.

She landed hard. Very hard, and covered in clothing. In a panic, she straightened herself in some tiny little space and pulled the clothing from on top of her. There was more light here. She gasped for breath, looking around. And then she realized that she was in the laundry room. The door to her right led to the house; the door ahead of her led outside.

It was open.

She swallowed hard. Lady was out there somewhere. What had happened to her hadn't been an attack—she had, after all these years, stumbled upon a secret laundry chute. She'd banged her head, but she was okay. She started to smile.

Then she heard something. Footsteps on the grass just outside…

She reached out, trying to find a way to stand. Her palm hit the washing machine. She clutched a water hose and staggered to her feet. Someone was coming.

The cop, she tried to tell herself. *Carillo.*

But it wasn't the cop. The footsteps weren't certain, assured. They were slow…stealthy.

Furtive.

She looked around wildly in the shadowy darkness.

Her eyes fell on a bottle of bleach. Her fingers curled around the handle.

A figure stepped into the doorway. Dark, tall, a man, wielding something, a weapon…

He stepped out of the shadows…

"Look who's here," he said, and stepped toward her, raising his hand. "You. Just the girl I've been looking for."

Chapter 18

"Jennifer!"

He stepped toward her, and no longer afraid of alerting a killer to her presence, Jennifer screamed for all that she was worth.

That brought Hugh Tanenbaum rushing in on her. She couldn't see what he held in his right hand. It had to be a knife, she thought, trying not to panic.

"Jennifer, stop, don't scream!" He grinned drunkenly. "I should have used the front door, huh? Is it late? Are you surprised to see me here?"

His words were slurred. He was truly insane, she thought.

"Hugh, get out of here."

"Jennifer—"

"Go—"

"You're the best. The brightest and best. I have to have you."

"No!"

He reached out for her. The weapon he'd held in his hand fell to the floor. She had a chance. She screamed again, bashing him as hard as she could in the head with the Clorox bottle.

He staggered back, holding his head. She hit him again in sheer panic. He crumpled to his knees.

She jumped over him, dropping the Clorox bottle in her haste, and tearing for the exit to the patio and yard. She screamed again as she turned back. He was up.

"Jennifer, please—"

She saw a mop and grabbed it, striking out at him. He reeked of alcohol, but he was still strong, reaching out to fight her for the mop handle. He looked at her with dazed, chilling eyes. "No, no, Jennifer. Let the mop go. I can make you famous. I can make you really famous. Forever." He smiled. A half-lip, strangely curled smile.

She let the mop go—and picked up a gallon

jug of Downy fabric softener. She wrenched off the cover and threw the Downy into his face. He cried out, throwing up his hands, but when she turned to run again, he was after her. She reached the grass on the right side of the patio. He flew at her, tackling her to the ground. She tried to scream again, but he was all over her.

"Jennifer, Jennifer, please, you don't understand." His hands were big. They were fumbling over her face, covering her throat. "I just need—"

Another cry of terror ripped from her lips. Suddenly, Hugh's blue-covered face rose above hers in surprise. She heard a growling sound, and then a cry of pain. The director was violently wrenched away from her. She staggered up, hands on her throat. Feet away from her, Hugh was on the ground, and Conar was over him—bashing him in the face.

"All right, Conar, stop!"

Liam raced across the patio to catch Conar's shoulder and pull him off of Hugh Tanenbaum, who lay in the grass, curled into a fetal position. Conar landed a few feet away on his knees in the grass.

Edgar, Drew, and Doug had come out of the house. Drew had brought a silver letter opener, Doug carried a hockey stick, and Edgar had brought out a frying pan.

Ripper, who had latched onto Tanenbaum even before Liam, was still growling. Lady, in her fenced kennel, was howling.

Conar eyed the prone Tanenbaum, who

moaned with a low, keening sound. It might have stirred pity in Jennifer's heart if she hadn't been shaking so badly. Conar's jaw remained locked, but he stared at the man with lethal fury in his eyes.

Over her, Jennifer realized.

Sirens blared. Liam came to Jennifer. "Are you all right?"

Edgar was hurrying over. "Miss Jennifer, Miss Jennifer!"

She threw herself into Edgar's arms. He held her. She kissed his cheek. She wrapped her arms around Liam, pressing her head to his chest. Then she pushed away, going to Conar. She fell down in the grass by his side. His fingers plunged through her hair on either side of her head, his eyes met hers with a blaze of silver fire. "My God, Jennifer." He pulled her against him, then he pushed her away. "What in hell were you doing out here?"

"I came down the laundry chute."

"What?" he said incredulously.

His hold on her hurt. She smiled anyway, ready to laugh and cry. "I came down the laundry chute. I didn't know there was one. Ripper started barking. He must have heard Hugh on the property. Ripper was barking at the closet. I tried to show him that there was nothing in the closet. I found out I was wrong. The back wall must have some kind of a secret panel. It gave...and I wound up by the washing machine."

The wailing of sirens seemed to be right on top of them. Uniformed men streamed into the yard. Someone was reading Hugh his rights. Hugh was still crying.

An officer lifted him to his feet. He couldn't seem to stand. He tried to jerk free in front of Jennifer, and was powerful enough to hold the officers there as he tried to talk.

"I didn't do anything. I came to see Jennifer, to get her to be in this movie...I'm losing my mind—"

"Losing it?" Liam said harshly, coming up to stand in front of him. "You fool, don't you understand? You're accused of the murder of two women. You'll go to jail for the rest of your life if I have anything to do with it!"

"Murder?" Hugh said, shaking his head. "No...no...I didn't murder anyone. I wanted to see Jennifer."

"Yeah!" Doug said, stepping forward—still holding tightly to his hockey stick. "You wanted to see Jennifer—at three in the morning?"

"I was...drinking," he muttered. He looked like hell, blinking against the still dripping blue pool of fabric softener that contorted his features.

He looked at Jennifer. His eyes were suddenly clear and expressive against his still handsome features. "No, no, they want it to look as if I'd killed someone. Because I like Hitchcock. I'm being framed. You know that I wouldn't kill anyone. Did Hitchcock kill anyone? No. I'm a director. I drink too much. I like women, yeah, so sue me. I didn't kill anyone, I swear, Jennifer—"

She rose. Conar protectively pulled her back. "What were you doing in my mother's yard at this time of night? Why were you trying to break in?"

"I told you, I was drinking. I wanted to see you."

"You attacked me!" Jennifer cried.

"I didn't mean to," Hugh said. "I wanted you to stop screaming. I wanted you to listen."

"Jennifer, Conar…you'll have to give a report, answer a few questions. But, Conar, you can take her on in for now. My guys will be out here for a while. Doug, Drew, Edgar, you can go on in, too. Edgar, maybe you wouldn't mind making some coffee for the men. And for you…time to go," Liam said quietly, nodding to the officers who held Hugh between them. They started to drag him away.

Conar's hand moved soothingly through her hair, then halted. "Where's Ricardo?" he asked.

No one answered. He tried to press Jennifer toward Doug, but she clung to him. He started around the yard, after the cops leading Hugh away.

In their rush to reach the backyard, the cops hadn't noticed the door to Ricardo's car standing slightly ajar. Jennifer was left behind as Conar rushed forward, wrenching the door the rest of the way open.

Ricardo flopped out in an unconscious heap.

Conar swore, lifting the man, instantly checking his pulse. He sat back, exhaling.

"He's alive," he quickly informed Liam. "His pulse is strong, his breathing regular."

"Drugged?" Liam said.

"I assume."

Paramedics were already there; they had accompanied the rush of police cars.

What Jennifer thought that she would remember the most about that night was not her terror, but the constant blue and red flash of the police lights, going around and around.

And Lady howling...

Ricardo was taken to an ambulance. The police stayed around awhile longer, taking all evidence from this crime scene.

It had been a long day.

It became a longer night.

Edgar did make coffee. Liam came in with his notebook and another officer. They all talked and he took notes.

"It's all so sad," Doug said.

They all looked at him. "Well, what he did is horrible, and I've actually always been a proponent of the death penalty, but..." He broke off and shrugged. "He did look crazy as a loon. As if he doesn't believe he did all this himself!"

"I'm sure his defense will be a plea of insanity," Liam said.

"I believe it will be true in his case," Drew said, shaking his head. "I mean, who would have known?"

"And Andy thought it was Joe," Jennifer murmured, touching her throat.

Liam was studying her. "I was ready to

believe him, too," he said. "Well, Andy will be happy. He told me he'd been terrified to say anything about his suspicions. He was afraid for his life—and his livelihood." He rose. "I think I'm going to have a late-night talk with Mr. Tanenbaum."

Conar smiled, an arm tightening around Jennifer. "Can you check on Ricardo for us? He's expecting a baby soon."

Liam nodded. "I have no idea of how Tanenbaum managed to pull that off, but I'll find out. Well, good night. Or good morning. It is the morning, isn't it? Light out, even. Well, try to get some sleep. I'll get back with you."

With Liam gone, the four of them left in the house sat in the den and stared at one another.

Conar shook his head suddenly. "Jesus, Jennifer, how you managed to find that stinking laundry chute tonight..."

"Ripper must have known Hugh was down there," Edgar said. "He was barking to protect Miss Jennifer."

"Yeah, great protection," Conar said.

"He meant to protect me."

"And using Downy, Miss Jennifer! What ho, you are a fighter, my fair girl!" Edgar told her proudly.

"Well, you were most impressive with your frying pan," she told him, smiling. "And you..."

She touched Conar's chin. He had a five o'clock shadow, double-time. His cheek was smudged from the dirt. "You have a gun," she reminded him. "But you came after him with nothing but your bare hands."

365

"I heard you scream," he said sheepishly.

"Don't worry," she said. "But next time, bring your gun."

"Let's pray there will be no next time," Doug said, rising suddenly. "Excuse me, I'm going to bed."

Drew rose quickly. "Me, too."

"I'll lock up," Edgar said.

Conar stood, drawing Jennifer with him, and she followed Conar up the stairs. He started for his room, but she shook her head. "My room."

He frowned. "But you just went down your back closet wall—"

"A laundry chute. Your room has hidden compartments."

"So you'll take your room, and I'll take mine."

She said, "Please, don't leave me again. I told you I'm sorry. Stay with me. Please."

He walked toward her slowly. He lifted her chin. "You do intend to apologize really nicely?"

She smiled. "Of course."

He slipped an arm around her shoulders and walked with her toward her room. They entered together; he closed and locked the door automatically. He leaned against it and touched her cheek. "You've been rolling in the dirt. Did you want to take a shower?"

"No!" she said emphatically.

"Oh, right, of course," he murmured ruefully. "Shall I draw you a bath?"

"Will you join me?"

"With the greatest pleasure."

"I may never take a shower again," she told him seriously. "Do you think you could live with that?"

"We'll just thank God for the bathtub," he told her.

She was smudged and scraped. They were both grass-stained and dirty. With water drawn and lots of bubbles, they started out with heads opposite, feet entangled. Flirting with toes became arousal, and they emerged wet and dripping and desperately in need. They trailed water across the bathroom and bedroom, wound up entangled on the bed, hot wet kisses falling over steaming flesh, bodies pulsating. They made love quickly, rising, soaring, climaxing, and still entwined, gasping for breath. As she lay beside him, spent, Jennifer knew that she should be exhausted, but as she curled against him, her mind was far too alive.

His arm was warm and secure around her. She rested on his chest, her fingers curled on the mat of dark hair there. His fingers moved in her hair. "You're really all right."

"I'm fine." She leaned up against him. "I can't stop thinking. I mean, I suppose that Hugh being the killer makes sense. He had easy access to starlets, that's for certain. And he had been involved with Brenda. There are just so many questions left open..."

"Like what?" he inquired.

"Andy. His behavior has been so bizarre."

"He told Liam he found blood all over a

hamper in Joe Penny's bathroom. We should make him explain."

"How?"

He crooked an elbow behind his head, looking up at her. "We'll have a pool party and clear the air. How does that sound?"

"You mean just..."

"*Party* isn't a good word for now. We'll invite the folks over for lunch on the patio, and naturally the discussion will be about the way Hugh nearly killed you and how the police nabbed him, and we'll all admit how easy it is to be suspicious of one another and we'll get Andy to tell Joe point-blank what he saw, and ask him what was going on."

She stared at him for a moment and nodded slowly. "Sounds good."

"We'll see Abby first, assure her everything is all right. Then we'll have an evening get-together. Think I should give the girls a call to come in and help Edgar?"

"We'll let him decide himself. He likes to make decisions, and he enjoys company in the house, so he won't mind, I'm certain." She leaned against him again. "I'm very lucky. That's what I've been thinking since...since you pulled Hugh off me. You saved my life. And then we came up here, and the bath felt so good and then..." Her voice softened to a whisper. "Then there was you."

He rolled her beneath him, staring into her eyes. He smiled. "Well, I knew I was in lust with you. But I've got to admit, you've become pretty damned important to me. You know we're going to fight again. Fighting shouldn't mean locking someone out."

"I was scared, for me and my mother. And you point-blank turned me down the other night."

"All you wanted was my body," he said gravely.

She had to smile. But he was still serious.

"Life is precious, Jennifer, always. But like you said, yours is rich with quality. You move without thought, breathe naturally. You can make love, feel bliss because of the way something touches your life...Abby needs quality. Can't you understand that?"

She trembled. "I'm afraid for her. I'm afraid for me, for life without her."

"I'm afraid, too. But we have to let her take a chance on the quality she craves."

His eyes studied her anxiously. "I'm not going to have a choice anyway," she said softly. "My mother has made her decision. She's only hoping for my blessing."

"Give it to her. She loves you more than anything on earth."

"I know."

"More than me," he teased.

"I know. But she does love you very much."

"She needs your support."

She nodded. He kissed her. It was meant to be a gentle kiss, caring, compassionate, tender. It was all that. It was more...

It was quality of life.

She reached for him, intensely feeling every nuance of his flesh, muscle, movement. The pulse of his sex, rough texture of his legs. He touched her back. Slowly. Fingers, lips, tongue, taste—she had never felt such a sensual and leisurely progress, never anticipated how it could bring on a thunder at the very end, a climax as shattering as any she might have dreamed, stretched out and out and out until she thought she would die, having touched such a pinnacle of pleasure.

They lay in silence for a long time.

Then there was a scratching sound at the door that made Jennifer jump. They both sat up tensely. Conar eased. "Ripper," he said softly. "Shall I let him in?"

She laughed. "Of course."

Conar rose and opened the door. Ripper raced in jubilantly, came to Jennifer's side of the bed, and ran in circles. She picked him up, kissed his cold nose, and set him at the foot of the bed. He curled up happily, as if he had belonged to the two of them forever.

"He's no problem."

"Hm," Jennifer murmured. "But you wait."

"For what?"

"Well, at my apartment, Lady sleeps in the bed as well."

"I guess we'll need a king," Conar said.

She didn't argue. There would be time to discuss the future later.

Chapter 19

Jennifer awoke late, close to noon. She was alone. She started to take a quick shower, changed her mind, and took a very quick bath. In jeans and a tank top she left her room, ready for coffee.

When Jennifer got downstairs the next morning, she found that Edgar had already called people for the party that night. "I've yet to contact Mr. Penny," he told her. "And the senior Mr. Valentine, Mr. Newton," he added.

"Edgar, you've called everyone already?" Jennifer said. "And you don't mind a houseful here tonight after all the excitement?"

"I think it will be lovely. A great relief," Edgar said.

"Thanks," Jennifer said, smiling at him. "You can call the caterers and bring in whatever extra help you want."

"Mr. Conar will barbecue, we'll have plenty of chips and salads, and Mary and I will serve, if that will suffice, Miss Jennifer."

"Lovely," she said. Then she glanced down at the newspaper on the table, and her stomach pitched slightly.

"It's not in there," Doug informed her, looking up from his seat. "It happened too late to make the paper. It did make the morning news, though."

"What does it matter?" Drew said, seated across from him. "The police have their man."

"This is America," Doug reminded him. "You're innocent until proven guilty. Then we blame it all on your childhood, put you into prison with cable television and conjugal rights—and let you go so you can kill someone else."

"Doug, it's not all that bad," Jennifer protested.

"Well, our friend Hugh is denying everything, and he has his lawyers working to get him out on bail," Doug said.

"Hugh is denying everything?" Jennifer asked.

"Well, of course he is. Who would admit to such awful crimes?" Drew said with a shudder. "Can you imagine? We all sat with that man, broke bread with him..."

"Hm," Conar put in, "and Abby has heard all about it. She's already had me on the phone. Jen, we need to get down to see your mom."

"Right. I'm ready whenever you are."

Only she and Conar went. Doug was going to get groceries for Edgar, and Drew was going to man the front, fend off phone calls from reporters, and be the general all-around person at the house.

When they reached the hospital, Conar urged Jennifer on in ahead of him. "She's going to want to see you're safe and sound," he said. "I'll get some coffee."

"You don't need to leave us alone."

"I'll be back."

Abby looked great. She'd put on lipstick,

brushed out her hair, and was propped up on her pillow. She saw Jennifer, reached out her arms—and started to cry. Jennifer settled into her mother's embrace. "Thank God you're safe, baby. That horrible, horrible man. To think I had befriended him..."

"To think I doubted you," Jennifer told her mother.

They clung together. "It's all right now. He's behind bars. If only we had known, if we had guessed..."

"God knows how many people he did kill, Mother. They're going to have to look into it. He hasn't talked at all yet...What's important, Mom, is that it's over."

"Yes, it's over," Abby said softly.

Jennifer looked at her mother's hands clutching her own, trying not to break down. "I'm still afraid. Very afraid. But if the doctors think it's safe enough for you to go for it, I'll support you in the surgery."

Abby stared at her a long time and then smiled, tears stinging her eyes. "You mean it, baby?"

"I do."

From the doorway, Conar cleared his throat. He walked into the room. Abby bit her lower lip and looked at Jennifer. "I did make him come, of course. And take the job with *Valentine Valley*."

"Of course. No one was ever fooled, Mother."

"And I guess, if you wanted to move on, Conar, I would have to thank you with all my heart and give my blessing," Abby said.

Conar shrugged. "I've taken the job. I have to stick with it. I don't want a reputation in the business for being flighty."

"Oh, well, good," Abby said softly. Her eyes filled with tears again. "You two have made me very, very happy."

"Hey," Conar said. He took a seat on the opposite side of the bed from Jennifer. "Frankly, it's good to be home," he said. Then he told Abby about having a barbecue that night to clear the air with everyone on the set. Abby thought it was a great idea.

Finally, they decided to leave. Jennifer kissed Abby and started out. Conar followed her. When they were at the door, Abby called them back.

"You know, he is denying it," she said.

Frowning at Conar, Jennifer paused. "What, Mom?" Abby had seemed so good in the hospital. She hadn't talked to the people in the walls at all.

"Committing the murders. He does have a drinking problem, you know."

Jennifer walked back and kissed her again. "Mom—"

"I'm all right. Don't go looking all worried on me again. I'm just telling you not to relax just yet."

"According to the news, he did get his lawyer, and he's being arraigned, and he will go to trial for murder. It's all over, Mom."

Ten minutes later, driving back to the house, Jennifer looked at Conar. "What did you think about what my mother said?"

His eyes were steady on the road. "If she says so, I think we might still want to be cautious."

"Conar—what if Hugh isn't guilty?"

He answered slowly and carefully. "Jennifer, I feel badly that Hugh has proven to be...what he is. He was a good director, and seemed to be a decent man—he gave a lot of people a start in the business, he's been at it a long time. But God knows what else he's been at."

"Yes, I guess...," she murmured. Then she turned on Conar. "I think my mother's right. I'm not sure that I believe it. It just feels as if...some pieces don't fit together."

He glanced at her, briefly taking his eyes from the road. "Don't you go trying to pin down Joe Penny or Jim...not on your own, anyway, do you understand?"

"You said that we would clear the air," she protested.

"Yes, we! With everyone around you, all right?"

"All right!"

"I mean it."

"So do I!"

"Hm," he murmured, casting her a doubtful glance.

"If Hugh is guilty, which he must be, then there are rational explanations for everything else, right?"

He didn't answer. They had reached the house, and he turned into the driveway. "I hope that Edgar remembered to call Liam," he said.

"I'm sure he did."

"I'll just double-check," Conar said, exiting the car. Jennifer did the same. When she stepped into the foyer, Drew came up to her. He had just shaved, and his steel gray hair was combed back. He was handsomely but casually dressed in tan Dockers and a sports jacket. "Hey, you two. Hurry it up. We invited our company for five—they'll be arriving soon."

Jennifer let out a quick expletive and hurried for the stairs. Conar followed behind her. In the hall, she paused.

"I..."

"What?"

"I still don't think I can take a shower."

He grinned. "We'll shower together."

"That could make us even later."

"Ah, but at least it will be for a good cause."

She did manage to get into a shower with him.

He did make them later, but it didn't matter much. When they came downstairs, Doug was manning the bar, Mary had come in, and with her, Kelly and Serena were busy bringing food out to the den and patio. The doors were open wide to the beautiful night.

"Jennifer!" Serena exclaimed, the first to see that she and Conar had arrived downstairs. She kissed and hugged her friend warmly. "Thank God you're all right."

She found herself surrounded by the cast and crew, all her friends, people who had heard the story of last night's events and who seemed greatly relieved that she had survived it.

Conar, too, was congratulated, and as questions and answers flew back and forth, Drew, Doug, and Edgar were all applauded as well.

"Naturally, *naturally,* it was really Conar who saved the day," Kelly said. "I did tell you from the beginning that he was an absolutely studly hunk."

"Thanks, Kelly. Hey, we guys try, you know."

"Oh, yeah," Andy said softly.

It seemed like the right opening. Everyone had a drink. They all seemed relieved, eager to move on.

"Speaking of studly hunks," Jennifer said lightly. "Joe Penny, a little bird told me that there's a new woman in your life."

Joe stared at her, startled. "I...I..."

"Oh, come on, Joe. The bird told me that she was sleeping in your bed when you were supposed to meet to discuss the suspense twist in the plot line."

Joe stared at Andy, frowning. "You told everyone?"

"Actually," Conar said lightly, "I think poor Andy was afraid that there was a body in your bed—that you might be doing away with Hollywood starlets."

"Andy!" Joe gasped, spinning around. "Andy, how could you?"

Andy stared at Jennifer and Conar, appalled. "How could I?" he whispered. "Well, I..." He spun around to look at Joe. "There were bloody sheet things in your laundry. And I went into your room—"

"I told you that I had a girl with me, sleeping," Joe exclaimed. He was shaking. He set his drink down. "You thought that I— Oh, God! You thought that I could have been the killer."

"Who the hell could have ever thought that Hugh could be the killer?" Jim Novac said miserably. He tossed back his head, draining half a martini with a shiver.

"Well, what the hell was going on?" Andy demanded defensively.

"I was testing some new type of stage blood for the shoot, you idiot," Joe said.

"But the girl in your bed—"

Joe sighed, looking down, shaking his head, looking up again. "It was the waitress," he told Conar.

"The waitress?" Andy said.

"The waitress from the afternoon when we had lunch," Conar said softly.

"Yes," Joe said, turning to Andy. "And she's alive and well and working tonight—if you want to go see. Damn it, Andy! How long have we been partners? You freaked out and thought that I was a killer?"

Andy looked at him sheepishly.

"But it's good to know that you were just practicing with stage blood," Jennifer said. "Hey, guys, come on. We work together. It's important not to be afraid."

"You were afraid of me?" Joe said to Andy.

"I am so sorry."

Liam Murphy chose that moment to arrive.

"Is it me?" he asked, stepping into the dead silence of the den.

"We were just clearing the air," Conar said.

"Wow. Clear, huh? Feels thick with tension to me, but then, I'm a cop. You people are theater. You'd know."

"Hugh is...really locked up, right?" Serena said softly, moving to Liam's side.

"Yes, he's really locked up."

"I still don't believe it," Jim Novac said. "He was a horror director, but a good guy."

"Well, he did meet Trish Wildwood at a bar—the bartender saw them together. And—" Liam began, but broke off abruptly.

"What?"

"We found a sheet with Brenda's blood on it tied up in a knot in his storeroom," Liam said softly.

"Damn," Jim murmured.

"But it's over. We don't have to be afraid," Kelly said.

There was silence.

"How's Ricardo Carillo?" Conar asked suddenly. "He was really knocked out last night."

"Yeah. You know what it was? His coffee was drugged."

"Poor fellow," Jennifer murmured.

"Lucky fellow," Liam commented. "If Hugh hadn't been able to knock him out, he probably would have killed him."

"Yeah, but...it's amazing that he was able to sneak around Ricardo to drug his coffee," Jennifer said.

Liam shrugged. "He could have waited until Ricardo went to check something out. Who knows?"

"I think we're in danger again," Kelly said.

"Oh?" Jennifer murmured.

"Doug just walked out to the barbecue. If he's cooking, we're all in serious danger."

"I'll refresh your drinks," Edgar, who had been standing by, said stoically.

His remark brought laughter, which seemed to lighten the mood again. Conar went on out to rescue the meat and vegetables on the grill. Edgar did refill drinks, while Drew told him the secret of the perfect martini.

Abby Sawyer lay in her hospital bed, half-asleep. They'd given her a sedative. They'd managed to get her into a nice routine. Long nights, lots of rest. One of the most awful parts of the disease worsening had been when she tried to hide it during the day, and she had been awakened by the wild tremors that had so treacherously seized her body in the middle of the night. Rest helped.

But the pills...

Well, the pills did strange things.

They made her see the people in the walls.

Tonight, she saw Hugh Tanenbaum. Over and over again, he pleaded with her.

"Abby, I didn't do it. I didn't do it..."

"Please, Hugh! Go away," she whispered.

"Abby, think!"

"Go away! Go away!"

She didn't realize that she had shouted aloud until the nurse came rushing in, a syringe in her hand at the ready.

By midnight, Conar had cooked the last of the beef, chicken, fish, and vegetables. The fire was out. Their company was fading.

He saw Jennifer lying back in one of the lounge chairs, smiling, at ease. Andy Larkin looked normal again. He and Jim Novac and Joe Penny were talking, laughing—laying out their new bible for the next week. Liam and Serena were together, their heads close as they talked.

Free from his duties as chief chef, Conar walked over to where Jennifer was stretched out. She was wearing a casual white cocktail gown that was snug around her breasts and waist and flared at her hips. It looked great against the honey tan of her flesh and the golden red of her hair. Sitting, he found himself thinking about the sleek feel of her flesh, the smell of her hair, the taste of her...Then he reined his thoughts in, managing to note objectively that she had staggeringly great blue eyes and a killer smile. Which she offered him. His heart thudded at that smile. Thud, thud, thud. He'd thought he'd go crazy last night, hearing her scream. He had been half-crazy, tearing downstairs to reach her.

Next time, bring the gun, she'd told him.

He'd been in lust...and now, he knew, he loved her. They needed time, but they would have time.

"Think that one's going to make it?" Conar asked Jennifer, taking a seat beside her.

"I can hear her biological clock ticking from here," she said with a grin. "Yeah, I hope so. I love Serena, she's a great friend, and Liam seems terrific as well."

"Well, we'll see, hm?"

"Yeah." She met his eyes, smiling. "We'll see."

He reached out, and she curled her fingers around his. He really did love that smile she gave him. He couldn't even imagine the days when he had thought of her as a spoiled brat.

He frowned suddenly, noting that Edgar was motioning to him from the other side of the pool. "Be right back," he told Jennifer.

Her smile deepened. She squeezed his fingers. "Mm."

He rose and walked around to Edgar, who seemed distressed. "Miss Abby has called from the hospital."

"Has something happened? Is she all right?"

"She's all right, she's just anxious to see you. But she knew about the party and she said that you weren't to come until all the guests were gone, and that you weren't to tell Miss Jennifer, you weren't to alarm her."

"Great," Conar muttered, staring at Edgar. What the hell was he going to tell Jennifer? How could he keep from alarming her?

As he stood there, Joe Penny gave him a sound slap on the back. "Conar, you are worth your weight in gold. But then, that's what you're taking from us, isn't it? Hell, boy, your weight in gold. But thanks. Thanks for tonight. It was good for us all."

"Yeah, sure, thanks. You're leaving?"

"Yeah," Joe said, and grinned ruefully. "I've got to go pick up a waitress."

"Good for you. And be good to her."

"Yeah."

After Joe said good night, Conar saw that Serena and Liam were behind him, ready to say their good-byes. Then Vera Houseman, who was leaving with her soap husband, Hank Newton. Jennifer was suddenly beside him, and they were saying good night to the rest of the cast and crew. And then they were alone, except for Drew and Doug and Edgar and Mary, and they had all started picking up. Frustrated, Conar at last took Jennifer's arm and pulled her aside into the den. "I've got to go out for about an hour."

"Oh?"

"Your mom called, and she wants to see me."

"You, not me?"

"I think it might be about what happened. And maybe it's because it's night, and she's on pills."

"Maybe," Jennifer said. She tried to smile. There was uncertainty in her eyes.

"I'll be right back, as fast as I can."

"Sure. I'll be fine."

He started away from her, then turned back. "Lock yourself in."

She smiled. "Your room is the one with the secret compartments, not mine."

"Yeah, but yours has a weird laundry chute.

Go up with Drew and Doug, lock yourself in, just to be on the safe side."

"How will you get in?"

"I'll dramatically break down the door with my shoulder."

"Rather loud," she said.

"How about if I knock?"

"That should do it."

"All right, then. I'm going. I'll try to be back before you're even in for the night."

She rose on her toes and kissed his lips. She whispered, teasing his ear, "Mom always liked you better."

"Jen—"

"I'm teasing, just teasing. Go. And hurry back. You've got me worried."

Mary was in the hall, ready to leave as he was going. "Mr. Conar, can you drop me off home?"

"Sure, Mary. Come on along."

He could hear Jennifer laughing at something Doug said as he stepped from the house with Mary. As he pulled out on the road, he thought, *Saturday night in L.A. Hell, this could be a long trip.* He looked anxiously at his watch, wondering why it mattered.

Because he didn't like being away from her.

Because lust had turned to love?

Something more...

Instinct. Intuition.

He just didn't like being away.

Crazy? Yeah, completely nuts. He pressed harder on the gas pedal anyway. He was going to get back as quickly as possible.

The house was quiet as Drew Parker returned to his guest room. It had been a satisfying night. He hung up his trousers and folded the silk knit shirt he had been wearing—aging might-have-beens needed to take care of their clothing. In a pair of cotton pajamas, he started to crawl into bed, but changed his mind. He walked over to the dresser where he had set up his brush and cologne, belt, extra watch, and books. He loved to read and had a voracious appetite for books, scripts, plays, even manuals. He had brought a Tom Clancy military thriller, a well-worn copy of *Captain Blood*, and a dogeared copy of an old book called *Hollywood Underside*. It was a possession he was quite fond of. There were few copies in print, since some of the material had been so scandalous that threatened lawsuits had caused the publisher to pull them off the shelves. There had been libelous suggestions regarding unprovable "facts" about the Kennedy brothers and Marilyn, the Mob and a number of Italian heart-throbs, and more. There had been a few crazy suggestions, such as aliens causing the strange deaths of some Hollywood personalities.

Drew didn't believe in aliens, but it was still a fun read. He'd frequently shown Abby pages from the book, and they'd laughed together over them. He'd even shown her the section about David Granger and the house, and they had speculated together.

Now he took the book to bed with him and flipped to that section. He had read it over and over again. Granger himself had died about thirty years ago, in his own bed, in his own room.

"Might have gotten a fright from those masks of his," Drew muttered.

He'd been hale and hearty, but his death had been deemed natural. The house had been left to his wife and daughters, though, and after he had been cremated, suspicions arose that his wife had poisoned him at the end. Despite the fact that he had gone out and bought her a beautiful stained-glass Tiffany window, she had never quite forgiven him for the scandal regarding Genevieve Borthny and the birth of her illegitimate child. Near the end of Katherine Granger's life, she had turned the house over to a trust for her daughters. At their mother's death, the daughters had been anxious to sell the house. "Though Granger had passionately disclaimed the existence of any illegitimate children during his lifetime," the book reported, "the girls apparently remained concerned that a bastard branch of Granger's family, the issue he was purported to have produced with Genevieve Borthny, would crawl from the woodwork to make a claim to the property."

No DNA checks back then. Granger had bought his wife the Tiffany window, and the Borthny woman had been paid off and packed off. Years later, it was rumored, she had reemerged in California, broken and destitute, and died on the street near Sunset Boulevard.

Drew set the book down, feeling a funny little surge in his stomach. He looked at the page again. The words were scrambling in front of him. Strange feeling, strange...as if he had been drugged.

As if he had been drugged.

He looked at the book again, still not quite certain what was nagging him, what it was he had needed to know. Words scrambled, unscrambled.

Suddenly, visions of *Rosemary's Baby* spun before him.

"The name is an anagram, Hutch!"

The name...

His thoughts were unclear. He envisioned Mia Farrow frantically playing with a Scrabble board.

He knew one thing. He had to get to Jennifer—warn her.

It was the greatest effort in the world to rise. Somehow...somehow...he must do so.

He staggered to his feet. The house. This wretched house. No, not the house. Houses weren't bad, no matter what they said in *The Haunting*.

Only people, jealous, cruel, bitter, cunning...

And patient.

He made it to his feet, staggered, fell to the ground. He couldn't rise again. He crawled, inch by inch, fighting the waves of darkness that threatened to sweep over him. Her door.

Just a few feet away. It seemed so very, very far...

Keep crawling, keep crawling! he implored himself. *Keep crawling...*

Chapter 20

Jennifer opted for sexy.

She didn't have that many great negligees, thanks to her Tweetie Bird habit. She hated the feel of scratchy lace against her skin. But she had one great little navy blue baby-doll silk nightie, and she slipped into it, brushed her hair, crawled into bed, and reached for the television clicker. She was concerned about the fact that Abby wanted to see only Conar, but not overly. Nor did it disturb her that her mother relied on him. She was never, never going to analyze what her feelings *had* been. She was just going to trust in the way she felt now, the way she knew he felt...and they would see. For the moment, though...damn, but she was in love with him!

She flicked on the television and started changing channels. There was an old movie on TBS—good, she'd switch back to it if she didn't find something else. She changed over to a network where a late-night talk show was on. A comedian had just begun his routine when a late-breaking news flash projected across the screen.

The terse newscaster was standing by the roadway south along the canyon; Jennifer recognized the spot. "Despite the fact that director Hugh Tanenbaum remains in custody for the murders of actresses Brenda Lopez and Trish Wildwood, another body has been found."

Staring at the television, Jennifer stiffened. As he spoke, the newsman was pressing his ear, receiving further information from someone at the other end of the headset he was wearing. "This just in—with her next of kin notified, we're able to tell you that the woman is indeed another actress, Ms. Lila Gonzalez."

Jennifer gasped, leaping from the bed. Panic swept through her—and guilt. Had Lila been killed for seeing for her? Were they wrong, was the murderer still at large? Had Andy been right—was Joe Penny the best liar in the world? Or had Hugh killed her before he had been arrested? Yes, that had to be it...

The newscaster was still talking. She couldn't make head nor tail of his words.

Then, suddenly, she heard a scraping at her door.

Her eyes darted from the television to the door. She heard the scraping sound again and then her name. "Jennifer...Jennifer..."

The call was so faint that it might have come from the grave. Old David Granger himself might have been calling out to her.

"Help...me..."

Drew. It was Drew Parker. *There was another body*. What if...

The newsman was still talking. Preliminary reports at the scene of the crime suggested that the young actress might have lain on the canyon floor for a few days.

Drew. He was old. Maybe he'd had a heart attack.

She hurried to the door. "Drew?"

"Jennifer, please..."

She opened the door. He was on his knees. He was ghastly white. "Drew! Drew, oh, God, I'm going to get you help. I'm going to call 911!"

She tried to drag him into her room, but she couldn't manage his weight. His mouth was open; his eyes were on hers. He was trying to form words. He couldn't seem to do so.

"Anagram," he mouthed, or something like it.

"What? Drew, you just try to breathe."

She left him, rushing to the phone. She picked up the receiver.

Dead. Dead as a doornail. How could the lines be dead?

Her cell phone was in her purse. She ran across the room for it. She dumped the contents of her purse on the bed.

No cellular.

From downstairs, she heard a door open and close. And then the sound of stealthy footsteps on the stairs.

He reached the hospital very late. "After midnight, please use emergency room door," a sign advised. Hospital personnel barely acknowledged him as he strode quickly through Emergency and to the elevators leading to the fourth floor and Abby's wing of the facility.

He entered her room only to find her dead asleep. He came by her bed. "Abby, Abby, it's Conar, you wanted to see me."

Abby didn't move. He touched her cheek, a feeling of panic surging through him for a moment: She wasn't dead asleep—she was dead. But no, there was warmth to her flesh. He felt for her pulse. Strong and sure.

Her nurse entered the room.

"Mr. Markham?" she whispered.

"Yes."

"What are you doing here?" The young woman seemed perplexed.

"She called me; she asked me to come over."

"Well, she's been asleep for some time now. And the sedative she's on...she has morphine in her medications. You won't have much luck waking her."

"You're right; I'll come back in the morning," he said.

He left hurriedly, nearly knocking the young nurse over. He had his cell phone out of his pocket as he raced down the hallway. He dialed Granger House.

The line rang. And rang.

And rang...

Maybe Conar had made it back.

Jennifer stepped over Drew and rushed to

the top of the stairway, looking down. She saw a shadow heading up the stairs. Shrouded in black. A hat, a cloak...what? He looked like the character from *Masque of the Red Death*.

He wasn't Conar. She knew that.

She raced down the hall to the Blue Room, where Doug was sleeping.

What if it was Doug? What if Doug was the killer?

No, no, someone had come in from somewhere downstairs. The danger was on the staircase now. Lady wasn't howling; Ripper wasn't barking. What had he done to the dogs? How had he turned off the alarm system?

She burst into Doug's room; the door was unlocked. He was there, in his bed. She ran to his side, frantically grabbing his arm. He didn't move. "Doug!" She smacked him good in the face. He still didn't move. He was dead.

No.

He wasn't dead. Drugged. As the cop had been drugged the night before.

She burst back out into the hallway. The man was almost up the stairs. She ran for the stairway to the attic, but then paused.

Conar's gun.

Standing by the Granger Room, she went to swing open the door.

Locked.

She tried again. Locked *tight*.

And the footsteps were coming closer and closer.

Edgar! Maybe he hadn't gotten to Edgar yet.

She flew for the stairs to the attic, reaching the door to his private suite. "Edgar! Edgar!" she cried, banging loudly. "It's me, Jennifer." The door was ajar. She pushed it open.

Near the garret window and television was a rocking chair. He was there. She could see the white cap of his hair. There was an old movie on. *The Birds.*

"Edgar!" she cried. He didn't answer; he didn't hear her. She rushed over to the chair, circling it, falling to her knees before it.

A scream caught in her throat; she couldn't breathe. She gasped for breath, so stunned and horrified that the world began to spin. It wasn't Edgar in the chair. It was a corpse. Not a stage corpse. A real corpse. Petrified, down to little more than bone and hair and patches of dried-out flesh, all dressed in a velvet smoking jacket...

"*Psycho,*" she heard pleasantly from the doorway. "It always was my favorite. But meet Daddy, not Mommy."

She stared at the man standing in the doorway, and the scream in her throat tore from her at last.

Conar dialed the police, telling them it was an emergency. But they wanted to know who he was and where he was, and then why he was so convinced that there was an emergency at an address when he wasn't even there. Then they wanted to know the nature of his emergency.

Roaring down the streets and then into winding turns, he started to swear at the emergency operator on duty. "Please, for the love of God! Get someone out there!" He clicked off the line and dialed Liam's number. Liam was probably in bed with Serena—things seemed to be going in that direction.

Liam didn't pick up. Swearing, Conar was about to slam his cellular against the steering wheel, when the phone was answered by a male voice. *Not* Liam's.

"Where's Liam?" Conar demanded.

"Detective Murphy is occupied," the man said flatly. "In case you haven't heard, mister, there's another body in Laurel Canyon."

Conar swore, dropping the phone, then gripping the steering wheel—he'd almost gone off into the canyon below him.

His tires screeched on the roadside. He had to get back to Granger House.

Edgar Thornby's proper British accent was entirely gone. He stood at the door to his attic quarters with a gun in his hand.

Conar's gun, probably.

He was wearing one of Abby's hats—a piece she had brought home from the costumes after doing a turn-of-the-century movie years before. He was wearing a long black cloak that looked as if it might have been worn in the early Hitchcock movie *The Lodger*.

Jennifer stood, staring at him. She swallowed down the horror from the sight of the petrified body. Edgar. She couldn't believe it. She didn't understand it. He had knocked out Drew and Doug—to kill them later, she wondered, or were they to take the fall for this?

"Edgar Thornby," she said quietly. She lifted her hands. "Maybe I should have known. I don't get it. Who is this?"

Edgar smiled. He had a far different look to his lean face. Cunning, sharp. "Edgar Borthny is the real name—Miss Jennifer."

"Granger's...illegitimate son?" she asked. Her fingers were so cold. Her feet were ice. She needed to be able to move. Great waves of darkness seemed to be cascading over her. She was going to pass out. But she couldn't. She had to fight for her life. She had to keep him talking, and she had to know...

"Anagram," she said. Rearrange the letters in Thornby and you get..."Drew knew who you were."

"I'm surprised the daft old idiot didn't figure it out long ago," Edgar said.

"But...you've worked for us for years. And years. And—"

"This house should have been my inheritance. I was the only male issue. Still, my father paid my mother off—gave her lots of money to move to England. But she came back here when I was still a boy. My mother—well, thanks to my old man, she had acquired quite a drinking habit. I think that Granger killed her, that he found her back in L.A. and had her killed. Doesn't matter. She was half-dead anyway." He frowned at the memory, then went on. "I wanted to get into the movies. Somehow, he had me blacklisted. The old bastard refused to acknowledge me, and he made certain I couldn't work. But I got him. He was trying to have a thing with that Celia Marston, that pretty little actress. I laughed so hard the other night. You and your uppity friends. *Did she fall, or was she pushed?* You and your stupid séance! Hell, she was pushed. I managed to keep my father from getting something he wanted. Ah, yes, and I did have to change things around a little bit. That's Dad in the chair, not Mom. I could have been a great director, but he didn't allow it. So I started directing my own scenes."

"You worked for my mother for years! Day after day. You tended her, gave her the medications—"

"Too many sometimes," he said cheerfully. "Oh, how I loved tormenting her. No one could have directed the story better. They say a director is a puppet master. I wrote her the note, warning that you were going to be murdered. Then I stole the note. It was so easy."

Jennifer shook her head. "But they found Brenda's blood on Hugh Tanenbaum's sheets."

"Now that was some work," he said. "I had to clean up that bathroom after I killed her and then dispose of the body—and keep some of the blood. The man has an alcohol problem. Wish I could have been there when he woke up to find a sticky pile of blood beside him! And what does he do? Naturally, he tries to hide the sheet. He thinks he is crazy. Does he call the police? Hell, no! He doesn't know what he might have done."

"But Hugh's arrival here—"

"He got in my way. Who do you think drugged the cop?" He paused to let this sink in, then chuckled, leering at her. There's more to your laundry shaft—and far more to the Granger Room. You fools never found the really interesting aspects of the architecture. There's a secret stairway to the Granger Room, and a passageway to your closet."

"So you have...watched."

"Yes. Great love scenes, Miss Jennifer. You're amazingly wicked!"

"You're a psychopath."

"Yes, probably, but so organized! And we're out of time. Let's go."

"Let's go?"

"Yes, my favorite scene is the shower scene."

"You think that I'm going with you so that you can hack me to death in a shower?"

"Of course, it's only fitting. You've already done the scene. We're going to do it better. You'll know exactly how you should have acted."

"I'm not going with you."

"Yes, you are. Because here are the alternatives. There's some excitement here, some real excitement. You'll do what I say, because you're playing for time. Conar has realized by now that Abby didn't call him. He's on his way, maybe suspicious, maybe not. Maybe he'll walk right into a trap. Maybe he'll find you on the floor...but maybe you'll live. If you don't come with me, I'll shoot you here and now through the heart."

She stood still. "Where did you get the gun? It's probably a prop piece, not even loaded."

He aimed above her head and shot. She heard the sound of the bullet, and its impact as it smashed into an attic beam.

"All right," she said, standing still.

"Move!" he directed. This time he shot near her feet. So close that wood splinters sprayed her flesh. "Get in front of me."

Could she walk? She had to. Her knees were trembling, about to give out, but she had to move.

Conar was coming back. And maybe he would know...

She moved too slowly on the staircase on her way from the attic to the second floor. She felt the gun press into her back, and his fingers curled into her hair at her nape.

"Keep moving."

He was shockingly powerful. His entire voice had changed as well as his accent. She cried out in pain as he held on tight. He kept his grip on her hair as he shoved her down the stairs and along the hall.

"I really am a great puppet master, Jen. I may call you that, I hope."

She cried out again, staggering, as they both tripped over Drew's prone body in her bedroom doorway and went down. The air was slammed out of her as she fell. Gasping, she saw the white-heeled sandals she had worn that night, discarded at the foot of the bed. She reached out for one of them. Edgar crawled to his knees, attempting to reestablish his hold on her hair. She grabbed her shoe, turned, and slammed it against him with all her might.

He let out a howl of pain, grabbing his face. She had caught him in the eye. He rose to his feet, staggering. She jumped up, about to run.

A bullet exploded into her bedroom door. She went dead still and turned. His left eye was blackened and swollen; blood streamed down his cheek. But he was standing steadily, and his gun was aimed at her.

"The shower, Miss Jennifer."

Where the hell was Conar? Her heart was beginning to sink. She longed to cry out, but she'd heard no car in the driveway.

"Let's go."

She walked slowly through the bathroom doorway. He followed, the gun on her. Never shifting his remaining good eye from her, he turned on the water.

"Warm, you like it warm, right?"

What was in the shower? Shampoo, conditioner, soap. A razor? What harm could she do with a plastic razor?

"Warm..."

She heard the water run and run...a mist of steam rose.

"Slip out of that nightie, Miss Jennifer. Don't worry, we haven't time for a rape scene, and this is *Psycho,* not *Frenzy.* Out of the gown and into the water. You step into the shower, and I'll get rid of the gun."

She slipped the gown over her shoulders, more quickly than she had intended. But she wanted to keep her eye on him.

She dropped the gown to her feet.

"In, Jennifer."

"The gun, Edgar."

"You first! Now! I'm the director here!"

She stepped hesitantly over the rim of the tub, clutching the shower curtain. She thought of the scene she had filmed, the terror she had felt even when she had known that it was Conar coming after her and that the knife he had wielded was rubber.

Edgar smiled, his face a grotesque mask, lean—cadaverous almost, half his face a bloody pulp from her assault.

She felt the spray.

He tossed the gun aside.

Conar jerked to a halt beyond the driveway, terrified of what could be happening, of what might have already happened.

But he didn't want Edgar hearing him drive up.

Edgar. *Why?*

No time to analyze—hell, who cared what was in the man's sick mind? He had to get to Jennifer.

He left the door open and ran to the house. He had his key out, but the front door was unlocked. He burst into the foyer. He heard nothing, nothing at all.

And then...

Faintly, from upstairs, he heard the sound of running water.

The shower...

Edgar got rid of the gun. "Soap, Miss Jennifer. Remember, she was a thief in the movie, a once good girl gone bad. She's washing off a mountain of sin. Come on, don't be shy...You want every last second of life, don't you? Then I'll close the curtain over..."

She soaped herself. Looked up to the spray.

"You are a fine little actress, Miss Jennifer. I know how well you do this scene. I watched you the other day."

"Gee. Thanks." She was amazed she spoke, she was so terrified. But talking was good. It took time. "So you were there. In the studio the day we filmed. You were on the closed set."

"Everyone knows I'm your mother's butler. They didn't stop me. I was hiding behind the Prima Piatti bar," he told her.

"I knew you were there."

"Of course you knew I was there. I meant you to know I was there. You would have been better if I had directed you. But we're fixing all that now, aren't we?"

"You really are totally psychotic."

"Turn around. Slowly. And don't look so petrified. You don't know you're in danger. Not yet."

"Like this?"

She was playing to his sick mind! No...

But yes, she wanted every second of life. She

wanted to live, to survive. She wanted to find out if she did really love Conar, if he loved her. She wanted the children her mother had suggested. She wanted to be there for Abby, understanding that she had to take a chance and live life to the fullest...

Edgar grinned at her. "Good girl, good girl. Yes, lift the hair...good."

He dropped the curtain. Through it she could see him reach into the cloak for his knife.

She reached for a large plastic container of creme rinse. It was all she had.

The shower curtain ripped open.

And there he stood. Right hand raised, injured face a repulsive mask of pure madness. He stood poised, head thrown back, body arched, knife gripped in his hand.

Jennifer let out a cry of fury, slamming the conditioner bottle against his face.

His knife slashed against air.

He raised it again. She screamed as he lunged toward her.

There was the sound of an explosion. She screamed again. Edgar was poised over her, the knife still raised. Yet there was something odd about his remaining eye.

Then she saw blood, spilling into the water as it raced toward the drain.

Blood gurgled from his lips.

Then he fell forward, crashing into her. She screamed again and again, but the knife didn't strike. Edgar crumpled to her feet. She looked past him.

Conar was in the doorway. He had the weapon Edgar had discarded.

He was staring at her, his face as white as her own. "You did tell me to bring a gun next time, didn't you? I forgot, but thankfully...Edgar left his." He stared at her. The water continued to run. The blood pooled in the tub.

"Jesus, sweet Jesus!" Conar whispered, his voice tremulous, his body shaking. He set the gun down. She crawled over Edgar's fallen body and into his outstretched arms.

Hugh Tanenbaum was released from jail that same night.

Despite the hour, he came to Granger House. Conar and Jennifer were alone; Drew and Doug had both been taken to the hospital by paramedics to make certain that there were no ill effects from the drugs they'd been given.

Hugh wasn't angry. He was amazingly humble and quick to forgive.

He was joining Alcoholics Anonymous in the morning.

He loved Abby, he told them. He loved the both of them, he hoped to work with them in the future. For the moment, he was shelving all his projects and taking a long vacation in Tahiti.

Conar insisted that they take a room in a hotel near Abby's hospital. The police would have Jennifer's bathroom cordoned off for some time, and she didn't think she could ever sleep there again anyway.

The next day Conar talked to Joe Penny, Andy, and Jim Novac as well. He and Jennifer needed time off. A week. They could work around them or sue him for breach of contract.

They were given the week.

Doug came to see them, hugging them both.

"The whole thing was very, very Hollywood," he said.

"How so?" Jennifer asked him.

"It's pure Agatha Christie. I mean, how many times do you get to say, 'The butler did it'!"

Abby was released on Sunday with all her tests complete; she was eligible for surgery. The three of them went for the week to Montana. It was cold there already. Very different. Drew accompanied them, anxious to help keep an eye on Abby. He felt guilty, as if he should have known more about the old place.

Abby frankly told him, *Bosh!* He was still her very dear friend.

They stayed at a private ranch belonging to some of Conar's friends. He and Jennifer looked after Abby, and then left her on the porch with Drew and went riding every afternoon.

"Next time we come, I'll be joining you on those horses," Abby told them.

"Damned right, Mom."

Liam called one evening to tell them that apparently Edgar had been killing people in a controlled manner for a long time. He had killed Celia Marston, pushing her over the cliff. His next murder had been ten years later—he'd strangled a woman he'd married and cut her body up to dispose of it. *Rear Window*. They weren't sure of what else yet. Maybe they would never have all the answers.

"But here's the interesting thing—we've been through lots of old court documents. The reason old Granger wouldn't acknowledge the boy is he really didn't believe that Edgar was his son. Seems Genevieve slept around long before she became a prostitute. There were many possible fathers. Likely as not, Edgar wanted to be Granger's son but wasn't. Since he'd dug up the body, we took some samples from the hair follicles. We'll know one way or another in about three weeks."

To Conar and Jennifer, it didn't matter. He'd been sick, he'd cost many people their lives, and he was dead.

They had the future.

She headed out one afternoon a few hours before Conar, riding Snowy, an even-tempered Appaloosa. She'd brought a book down to a stream, and was just watching the way the sun played on the water, grateful to be alive.

Conar came riding up. He rode very well, and he was big and tall in the saddle. When he dismounted, she smiled.

"What?"

"You should do a western."

He grinned. "Maybe one day. I still want to own a dive shop."

"Oh, yeah?"

"And I was thinking of a different type of movie at the moment. Actually."

"What?"

"*Splendor in the Grass,*" he told her.

And she started to laugh. Montana was very big, with soft grass and wide spaces. It was chilly, but...

They made love in the grass. And he warmed her up.

As they lay together after, he told her, "You know I love you—sis."

"Ah, well," she murmured, "anything can happen. 'Only on *Valentine Valley,*' of course." She rolled into his arms and told him very seriously, "I love you, too."

"Well, I thought so, I hoped so. I was just waiting for you to say it. What should we do about it?"

"Fool around some more. Spend lots of time together. Make sure that it really is the ride-off-into-the-sunset kind of forever type love."

"I like that," he said. "I like it a lot. Although..."

"Yeah?"

"I think I can already tell you, I'm into the sunset thing."

She smiled.

"The fool-around part. Now, that sounds good to me. I think the sunset is even coming. The smell of the grass is great."

"It is a bit chilly."

"Hey! I'll heat things up, I promise."

He did. He rolled with her again, and once again they made love in the grass. *Splendor,* he told her, was one of his all-time favorite movies.

Epilogue

The day of Abby's surgery, Jennifer was a nervous wreck. Conar had expected it. She moved constantly, prowling the waiting room. She ordered lunch with him but didn't take a bite. She jumped at him, then apologized. She cried, and he held her.

It was a long operation, but Abby pulled through with flying colors. It was because she had such wonderful strength of will, the doctor told them.

The first night, Conar stayed at a motel. Jennifer was sleeping in a chair in her mother's room. She stayed for several days, until Abby chased her out. They'd gone back to work again, and Abby wanted her to go home.

Despite what had happened, Abby was determined that the house wasn't evil. Conar agreed. Maybe the term evil wasn't even right, but it had been Edgar who had made a point of telling him that houses weren't evil—people were. Granger House was beautiful. Abby was going to keep it. Conar and Jennifer would stay awhile, letting go of her apartment while they looked for a place of their own.

Even so, Jennifer's bath was being demolished and rebuilt. They found all the old plans to the place, and had serious work done on the secret entries, and Jennifer and Conar remained together in the Granger Room while they stayed at the house. Abby intended to open the house one day a week to tourists and donate the proceeds to medical research. Jennifer liked the idea; so did Conar.

Three months after the surgery, Conar and Jennifer drove home from work together. Abby was out by the pool, resting, reading some of the scripts that had been sent to her.

She looked up as Jennifer came out to the patio, taking a seat beside her.

"Guess what, Mom? Conar and I are getting married."

Abby slowly lifted an eyebrow. "On the show?"

Jennifer smiled. "No. In real life."

"Wow!" Abby told her after a moment. Then she rose and cupped her face and kissed her, and when Conar arrived, she kissed him, too.

"Both my children!" she said. "Oh, dear, that sounds so..."

"Incestuous," Conar teased.

They were married one month later. Drew gave Jennifer away. Serena and Kelly were bridesmaids, Liam was best man, and Doug acted as Kelly's escort.

Abby fussed and said she was going to have to try to sit on both sides of the church, and she joked so to the press representatives who showed up. She wasn't really sitting in a traditional place at all. She had decided that her first return to performing would be at their wedding. She sat by the organ. During the mass that followed the vows, she sang "Ave Maria." Her voice was beautiful and rich, and Jennifer couldn't help the tears that poured down her cheeks at her own wedding.

They'd tried to keep the wedding quiet, but Abby had suggested they not be rude. "A wedding is a really big photo op," she told them.

And so it was. It was a beautiful wedding, a fairy-tale wedding.

On a day two months later, Conar and Jennifer drove home from work together and found Abby out on the patio, reading scripts. She had accepted a role in a local theatrical production of *Cats*. "I've always felt a bit like Grizabella, the old glamour cat," she told them.

Her glasses were on, and she was deep in thought. Jennifer cleared her throat as she sat down beside her. "Mom, guess what?"

Abby set her glasses down. "What, dear?"

"We're going to have a baby."

"On the show? You've already been pregnant forever, dear, remember?"

"No, Mom, in real life."

"Wow!" Abby said softly after a moment. "Wow!"

She hugged Jennifer. "And I'll be able to hold my granddaughter, dangle her on my knee," she said with awe.

Conar, who had reached the patio, cleared his throat.

"Abby, we just might have a boy."

Abby looked him up and down proudly.

"That will be fine," she said. "That will be just fine."